DONUTS

Are Meant to Be

EATEN

Book 1

ALEX COOK

CONTENTS

In her thirties, when Elizabeth was still struggling against her circumstance, the fact that God hadn't gifted her a girl was a sore spot. She had tolerated years of nonstop rough-and-tumble and felt due a reprieve…a small acknowledgment that life didn't always have to be loud and in your face—all black eyes and hard-ons. She wondered if there would be a time when her boys could let show even a glimpse of vulnerability or sentiment; a time when they could stop the posturing and not consider themselves lesser as a result. A time when soft would be permissible.

Later, with the indifferent marching of the years, she supposed if it had been the other way, three girls, she probably would have yearned still for the greener grass.

Finally, when they were all grown-up and dying, she realized the wanting didn't matter—Fortuna dealt the cards. All that remained was for her to play.

1979
Florida

CHAPTER 1—

He Introduced Me to Melissa

Keno lifted the sweating beer can to his lips and took a long pull. The crisp, sweet bubbles danced first across his tongue then down his gullet—eventually arriving in his stomach where osmosis slowly pulled the alcohol into his bloodstream. The rich and complicated history of ethanol and humans was lost on him. He just wanted to feel good. His two brothers were also drifting away, seduced by the beer's proposition of temporary well-being. As the worn Chevy sped them through the subtropical heat, Keno closed his eyes and opened his face to the oncoming night. The lush Florida air tumbled through the passenger window, caressing and encouraging like a fluffer before the big event. Nodding in time to the beat, Keno gradually raised his eyelids and looked left, catching a glimpse of his older brother, Clay, who was casually tapping his meaty hands rhythmically on the steering wheel. Like slouching giraffes, the two young men reclined on the vinyl bench seat, though Keno's lean had noticeably less ambition. His gangly, nineteen-year-old legs were crossed, right over left, extending up and away from his pelvis like a giant Levi's-covered erection that was crowned at the top with white canvas basketball shoes. The dust-covered dashboard supported the whole elongation.

Idle thoughts drifted through his head like wayward jellyfish on a lethargic sea. *Floating,* he decided. *That's what it mostly feels like....* A gradual drifting away from his travails as the alcohol worked its magic of diminution. A flash of lightning pierced the sky, and Keno gazed ahead, through the windshield, taking in the early evening cloud formations. Clusters of majestic Queen Palms raced by on both sides, their swollen, juvenile coconuts dangling thirty feet in the air. Around the base of the trees lay the decaying husks of matured fruit,

3

suffering through the indignations of irrelevance and old age. As the velvet torrent of salty air rushed through the vehicle, Keno inhaled the moment, unconsciously hoping that the youthful elixir of freedom was something that could be enjoyed forever.

As his mountains became molehills, Keno marveled at the therapeutic benefit of beer. Like most teens his age, he preferred to ignore the adult-sized responsibilities that loomed on the horizon and the alcohol allowed him that courtesy. He had no idea how he would support himself, let alone a wife (in theory, at least) and children. He knew he would eventually have to move out of his mom's house, but for now he was shamelessly ensconced in the warm embrace of his childhood cocoon. Happy to keep pedaling his bike in the general direction of unfettered females, he periodically tested his balance by releasing his grip on the handlebars, knowing that if things got difficult the training wheels of family would catch him.

Alternating his focus between the road and the gas gauge, Clay wondered how much fuel remained now that the needle was in the red. Two years older than Keno, he felt responsible for guiding the crew safely through their night-time maneuvers. The plans for that evening required a trip to the big city, across the manmade strip of pavement that separated the brackish bathtub called Tampa Bay. They were mimicking the perpetual migration of young people from rural to urban in the restless search for opportunities, especially reproductive. In their wake, to the west, lay the incorporated village of Clearwater, an optimistically named sleepy beach town the boys considered home.

Despite his relaxed veneer, Clay had an intensity that came through unfiltered. On leave from the Navy, he missed the time spent carousing with his brothers and had been looking forward to a return to his old stomping grounds. His inability to sit still was amplified by a longtime affliction of jock itch, a condition made worse by his recent time near the equator. His macho side would have trouble believing that his *tinea cruris* came from the same microscopic creatures responsible for vaginal yeast infections, but his inner comedian would have enjoyed the irony. Silently cursing the pinching of tight Levi's on his sexual organs, he fought off the squirming urge to scratch the fungus, and instead focused on emptying his beer. The nightly, systemic feeding of the dermatophytes with the fermented brew wasn't curing the malady, but it did provide temporary relief in the form of distraction. As Clay worked his way towards the bottom of the beer can, he slid *Eat a Peach* into the 8-track and turned up the volume. Twilight poured in as the Allman Brothers poured out, and the sweaty breath of August baptized their skin.

Relegated to the back seat was the youngest brother, Paul, who had decided to crank open the rear windows to match those up front. As the wind clambered in, a startled covey of yellow McDonald's wrappers burst from their resting place on the floor of the Chevy. Despite Paul's half-hearted attempts to arrest their getaway, they were soon spinning, tornado-like, up and out of the vehicle—a careless flight of liberation. A twinge of guilt pierced his adolescent indifference as he watched the trash fly from the confines of the car then quickly disappear behind them. It would be years before his conscience would become powerful enough to nag him into action for such a small trespass. Despite this instance of passive littering, Paul came closest among the three brothers to understanding the pernicious nature of their species. At seventeen, he was not only the youngest but also the most thoughtful and had lately been pondering the age-old questions of self-discovery. He knew he was unique when compared to his half brothers, and not just because he had come from a different uterus.

Feeling the late afternoon heat, Paul moved closer to the open window on his right. Like most of their blue collar friends, he had grown up without the indulgence of air-conditioning and knew how to take advantage of some shade and a breeze. This week was the first time Clay and Keenan had included Paul on their nighttime adventures, and his brain was buzzing with the sense of possibility that accompanied the unknown. Paul had been out to bars with friends before, but this evening was different—he was no longer swimming with the tadpoles. Going on night maneuvers with his brothers was a rite of passage that granted admittance into the adult world, an explicit acceptance by the people who knew him best. The promotion exposed the baby to a vivid rawness that seemed almost magical given his relative state of innocence. And then there was the comfort that came with the freedom of not having to make choices; like tagging along on your first bank robbery with Butch and Sundance.

Clay removed his right hand from the steering wheel and punched a few buttons on the stereo. Soon the soothing strumming of an acoustic guitar began lifting the boys to a shared place just south of heaven. Years before, in the timeless tradition of old passing to young, Clay had introduced his brothers to "Melissa." They were still in love. The nuance of the lyrics was neglected as the song warmly enveloped them.

Crossroads, seem to come and go . . .

The theme of nomadic disconnection wouldn't resonate until later; for now the three just liked the way the sounds made them feel. All around them, the swamp was pushing through the asphalt and concrete, reaching up with its warm embrace. From his place next to his older brother, Keenan joined the singing:

The gypsy flies from coast to coast . . .

Keno's focus soon started drifting from the music; he had the attention span of a six-year-old who had been banished to right field. He absentmindedly rubbed at his sparse beard, unconsciously aware that Clay was passing most of the other vehicles on the causeway. The Chevy's speed wasn't particularly dramatic, just enough to make a competitive sort feel as though they were winning. Like a pack of dogs, the brothers' hormones compelled a perpetual battle for dominance; and when the rare car passed them, all three felt a twinge of irritation. The cause and effect embedded in this pattern was lost on them— they weren't curious about its internal source. Donuts were meant to be eaten.

The boys' usual pattern of communication was a form of verbal jousting.

"Hey Clay, that douchebag just passed you," Paul needled from the back seat.

Clay was up for the challenge, quick to quell any insurrection.

"I'm driving a barely functioning fifteen-year-old station wagon and *Monsieur* Bag is driving a fuckin' new Trans-Am . . . idiot."

Paul was not intimidated.

"Or maybe he's just a smaller vagina?"

Keenan took pleasure in translating the insult that the brothers already understood.

"I think he just called you a 'big pussy,' Army man."

Wasting his breath trying to educate his younger brethren on the differences between the Army and the Navy was an effort Clay chose not to engage in; to him, all of his brothers' insults were nails, and he was comfortable introducing the hammer.

"That's mighty bold talk from the closet pail-jammer hidin' in the back."

The brothers' insults were born more from ignorance than experience. In their local Tampa Bay monoculture, respected men were strong and silent; being emotional, sentimental, or sensitive was considered a sign of fragility. The pecking order their friends understood put weak men on par with those humans who possessed vaginas—and those with vaginas ranked only slightly above the untouchable homosexuals. This was the South, in the 1970s. The pressure on young men to prove their virility was constant. In fact, if a high school boy didn't regularly try to "get some," he could find himself eating lunch alone in the school cafeteria, the victim of speculation about his sexuality. Of course "good girls" were expected to say "no", and so the ensuing hand fighting at the drive-in could be quite extended. (For further insight, see Meat Loaf's "Paradise By the Dashboard Light".) The brothers had no idea how much social perspectives would change over the next few decades, nor how their experiences would allow them to escape from the cultural back eddies of intolerance and misogyny. Driving this change for many was a steady stream of cable programming exposing the young masses to "alternative" lifestyles. MTV led the charge.

Before Paul could respond to Clay's homophobic insult, a huge flying insect smashed into the windshield, effectuating a loud noise and a nine-inch reddish green smear. The impact of exoskeleton on safety glass at sixty-five miles per hour clearly grabbed their attention.

"What the fuck was that?" Keenan gasped.

Paul couldn't resist.

"Your chances of getting laid tonight?"

Paul had been hurling bombs from the safety of the back seat ever since they left home. He now had a timely riddle he wanted to share, but to compete with the wind and the Allmans he had to shout.

"What's the last thing that goes through a bug's mind when it hits your windshield?"

Respect and airtime were things Paul had not been allowed, but with wit and persistence he had lately been able to establish a modest beachhead.

"I don't know, what?" Clay reluctantly played along.

"Holy shit?" repeated Keenan.

Paul delivered the indelicate punch line triumphantly:

"It's ass."

A brief silence. Then some respectful chuckling.

Clay ceded some ground, but not without the requisite qualifier.

" 'It's ass.' Hadn't heard that one. Not bad for a pigmy who takes it in the bucket."

They sipped their beers in silence while considering the intricacies of insect impact.

Soon Clay felt the need to regain the dominant conversational position. "Okay, boys, here's an easy one," he yelled to his brothers. "Who gives the best hummers in Rock 'n' Roll?"

Any conversation about sex, music, or sports was immediately of interest to the young men.

"Donna Summer!"

"Stevie Nicks!"

"Chaka Khan!"

"Linda Ronstadt!"

"Freddie Mercury!"

They were laughing now, enjoying the freedom of an uncensored, sophomoric conversation between brothers. The 8-track fed its contents into the stereo, which in turn pushed music out of the speakers.

Clay waited for it…

…with sweet Melissa…hmmm mmmm…

And then delivered:

"Nope…Gregg Allman…just listen to him hum!"

Clay grinned at his wordplay, but his brothers weren't as pleased, as their visions of Stevie Nicks engaged fellationally were displaced by a bearded Gregg Allman similarly occupied.

"Ahhhhh…man…so weak!"

"That's supposed to be funny? Ah, tight-man, those Army dudes must've gone AWOL with your sense of humor."

The criticisms washed over Clay like water off a frog's back. He felt like he had left Clearwater as a disappointment and was returning ascendant. By completing one of the most challenging training programs in the world, he had pushed himself back onto a positive trajectory. Keenan and Paul had not yet lost their belief in the eldest brother's judgment, still accepting Clay's seniority, despite his near twenty-four-month absence. The younger two actually found some comfort in relinquishing their decision-making to the alpha male. Small skirmishes were to be expected, but the pack hierarchy was pretty well grooved.

Having been abandoned by their father years ago, the boys' upbringing was left to their overburdened yet well-intentioned mother. They didn't think of the limited paternal contribution as a handicap. In fact, the modest indignities of poverty frequently had the effect of bringing the family closer, despite regular internal bickering. Their mother worried that the absence of a strong male figure fostered a state of perpetual recklessness among her three sons, calling into question the location of the brothers' good judgment. Of course, the socially accepted coping mechanism of drinking injected an even greater level of risk into their decision-making. In summary they were normal, healthy boys, given the context, careening wildly down the road to becoming (hopefully) responsible adults.

Their mom had been reticent to release the family's car to her children, but Clay had a charisma that was difficult to resist. When to dig in her heels and when to hand things over to God was a wisdom Elizabeth Barton had gained after long years of unsuccessfully trying to control her ex-husband. Besides, tonight she was hosting her book club discussion of Erica Jong's *How to Save Your Own Life*, and so she was happy to have the boys gone. A little wine and conversation, and then early to bed with a good book, would hopefully allow her to sleep right through the boys' reentry.

Keenan's eyes gazed languidly through the Chevy's windshield, watching a formation of pelicans skim the surface of the water. His hair, still damp from a recent shower, was secured by a backward-facing ball cap that kept his unruly blond curls locked down even in the wind and humidity. He had a late-summer tan that masked his lingering acne.

As if rehearsed, all three brothers tipped their cans of Old Milwaukee against their mouths until the icy cold contents swam past their lips and down their throats, continuing the casual journey prescribed by gravity. It was 1979. The restrictions of seat belts and MADD were yet to be imposed.

Keenan enjoyed the playful energy coming from his brother as Clay continued to lecture.

"The two greatest songs ever recorded by the Allman Brothers," he yelled over the wind, " 'Jessica' and 'Melissa.' "

Clay took a long pull from his perspiring can of beer.

"Nothing against 'Ramblin' Man' or 'Midnight Rider'...I just prefer chicks over loneliness, I guess."

The younger brothers let the assertion roll around in their minds for a bit. A rebuttal was necessary. In the Barton family such definitives, regardless of perceived truth, needed to be challenged.

Paul didn't yet rank enough to offer legitimate resistance, so it was up to Keenan to counter. He didn't have anything solid, but he thought he could at least scratch the surface and hope.

"I'm not sure Dickey Betts would agree with that assessment."

It was conversational in tone, but Clay was quick to keep order. He simultaneously leaned in his brother's direction, opened a broad grin, winked disarmingly, and deftly flipped off his brother's cap, all while remaining perfectly between the broken white lines of the road.

"Keno, *mi hermano*...if Dickey Betts spent more time with his guitar an' less time with the syringe, there's no tellin' how far those boys could go. Plus, Dickey loved 'Jessica,' he named it after his daughter."

Clay had an ability to manufacture details (and hence an aura of knowledge) that made it hard to distinguish fact from bullshit (especially in their preGoogle world). Challenging him on topics (especially those he introduced) was a game most of the brothers' friends had learned to avoid. It didn't matter that "Melissa" ached with a theme of loneliness as well; Keno wasn't on the debate team.

" 'Blue Sky!' " hollered Paul from the back, taking advantage of the brief pause and trying to get some attention, even if he suspected it would bring him ridicule.

The older boys laughed, happy to join forces against the baby.

" 'Blue Sky'? Hmm…wasn't that Olivia Newton-John?" Clay joked.

"Oh no, Clay," Keenan deadpanned, "I'm pretty sure that was Bread."

"Oh…that's right…the B-side of 'Baby I'm-A Want You.' "

Paul kept watch over the beer and ice-filled cooler in the back, happy to be acknowledged and not yet willing to fold.

" 'Elizabeth Reed'!"

Keenan and Clay simultaneously flipped empty beer cans in the direction of Paul's brown Afro.

A few moments later, Clay threw what he thought was a bone to his café-colored, baby brother.

"Don't worry, Pablo, I got some Ohio Players in here somewhere. Earth, Wind, and Fire…on deck, amigo. We *will* be bringing the funk, just waitin' for the right time, little brother."

Paul responded quietly, almost as if he had something that needed to be said out of principal, but he wasn't sure about the timing or his audience.

"I really don't appreciate your racial stereotypes."

Some of Paul's syllables got caught in the turbulent current of music and wind, arriving at the front seat a bit jumbled. Clay leaned slightly to his right and asked Keno for clarification.

"What'd he say about the stereo?"

Not wanting to veer off into a whole new direction, Keno offered an alternative.

"I think he said he appreciates your Specials and Skatalites…you know, the bands…the new 8-tracks you were playing the other day."

"Nothin' new about the Skatalites…wait…really? I didn't know he was into the two-tone, Rocksteady stuff?"

Keno just shrugged.

Unlike a lot of their redneck brethren, the Barton boys enjoyed all types of music, including "black" music, aka R&B and Funk. And, of course, they loved Reggae, including all the derivations. Their parents had raised them to be color-blind, but their broad musical appreciation was born more from a self-ish—rather than sympathetic—perspective. The music was good—deep and sensual in a soulful, primal way that fed into the "yearning"—the biological imperative to get it on. The boys were of an age that mandated a heightened level of sexual arousal, pretty much all of the time. Certain records fed their concupiscent tendencies. Back in the day when censorship still had teeth, album covers alone could attract broad attention for their smoldering graphics. For example, when forced to take matters in to their own hands, all three boys had squeezed off a few rounds in salute to the graphic cover art of the Ohio Players' album *Honey*. As if in acknowledgment of his hormonal shackles, Clay used to hypothesize that if he stepped on a land mine and lost his junk, he would just as soon end it. All of his young male friends would nod in agreement whenever he voiced this thought aloud. The boys' compulsion to mate drove much of their behavior, with the civilizing, overlapping constraints of conscience, reli-gion, mores, and laws serving as feeble governors. The Barton brothers' desires didn't result in frequent sex—at least, not with a partner—as they were each as unsuccessful as most of the other boys in their peer group; but, predictably, the infrequency only increased the demand. Like dogs to the scent, they were constantly on the hunt.

This maniacal need for physical intimacy gave the brothers the courage to push through some uncomfortable situations. For example, it had taken time, and had required overcoming some early trepidation and awkwardness, but the young men had warmed up to the benefits of dance. They eventually (and somewhat reluctantly) realized that one of the best ways to meet girls was by stepping out onto the floor, as young women who liked to move tended to be comfortable with their bodies, increasing the odds for some action. Also, danc-ing could be carnal—releasing certain libido-enhancing chemicals—especially when moving to a well-defined beat; and, not to be taken mildly, the messages inherent in the lyrics of songs like *Push, Push, in the Bush* and *You Shook Me*

All Night Long were far from subliminal; they established a randy subtext. One could get a sense for the physical talents of, and the level of inhibition likely to be encountered in, a prospective mate by observing her moving rhythmically. Perhaps most importantly for the self-conscious brothers, dancing precluded conversation, allowing them to perform physically, displaying their athletic bodies, as they tried to persuade the girls to share their goodies.

With the big city lights flooding the horizon, Clay pulled into a Pick Kwik parking lot on the Tampa side of the causeway. They had polished off the six-pack they had "borrowed" from the home fridge. A local hot spot named Bone Daddy's was on the agenda, but they needed to fine-tune their buzz a bit first—add a little duration without giving up too much *dinero*. Clay had sixty dollars in his pockets, which put him about fifty-seven clams ahead of his brothers' collective bank.

First turning down the stereo then pivoting in his seat, Clay looked at his brothers in mock disapproval.

"Any of you *ne'er-do-wells* got a job?"

The thin-walleted youngsters went silent while examining their Chuck Taylor canvas high-tops.

"I didn't think so…fuckin' commie pansy students still wallowing in your self-righteous beliefs, happy to ignore the real world while yer mama slaves away as a security guard and yer daddy rolls over in his gin-sodden grave."

Clay was on a rhetorical roll, channeling both his recent SEAL instructors and not-yet-expired father, while barely pausing to inhale. His vernacular revealed a combination of their parents' elite upbringing and the family's single-generation slide from upper crust to redneck. Nature and nurture combined seamlessly.

"Well, *hermanos*, tonight the US government, in a display of magnanimity not deserved, is bankrolling your slippery slide south. That's right, boys, not only am I here to escort and protect your worthless carcasses, but I will be covering your consumption—WITHIN REASON. You're welcome! Homos."

Then Clay turned up the stereo, got out of the car, half tucked in his shirt, and headed into the convenience store.

Paul smiled and mumbled at Clay's receding backside: "That's mighty nice of you," he waited until Clay was out of earshot, "and EXTREMELY UNCHARACTERISTIC."

Keno laughed.

The last great act of defiance. Paul was starting to become his own man. Generally the quieter and more withdrawn third wheel, lately he seemed more comfortable unleashing his sardonic wit; Keno was happy to see this development. Paul was supersmart, but he had had some trouble fitting in, given his mixed ethnicity.

The fluorescent glare and buzz of the lights pushed through the night, trying to mask the reality of the parking lot's swampish setting. Flying bugs clustered around the bulbs, while the more reclusive insects began exploring the darker perimeters of their surroundings…which included the car's interior. Some displayed a seemingly random flight pattern, frequently colliding with Keno and Paul, while those that were parasites followed a more intentional path to the boys's exposed skin. Infrequently a mosquito would overstay her welcome and quickly find herself flattened between palm and skin—a bloody micro-pancake. Mostly, however, the boys ignored the insect frenzy, revealing their local credentials. One couldn't spend years outdoors in Florida without ceding some territory to the bug kingdom.

Theirs was the only car in the crushed-shell lot, and inside the open vehicle a thick humidity prompted a light, oily, epidermal film which swathed their skin—a gloss that the brothers detested in their adolescence but would miss in their middle age. This greasy layer caused the skin on their backs to adhere to the car's vinyl seats; the permeable fabric of their shirts only facilitated the connection.

A noticeable change in tone came over the car with Clay's absence. Keenan began pushing stereo buttons, which started an FM exploration that interrupted the Allmans. He stopped when he found Lynyrd Skynyrd.

In Birmingham they love the Governor (Boo, boo, boo)
Now we all did what we could do…

Paul was nursing his second beer in the back, listening to his older brother sing "Sweet Home Alabama." Something had always bothered him about the Southern Rock anthem. Yelling over the speakers, he wanted to get the attention of his brother.

"Hey, Keno, should I be offended by this song?"

Keenan reached for the volume knob and turned down Ronnie Van Zant. He realized he needed to be thoughtful on this topic.

"You mean, are they saying, 'George Wallace is good'?"

"Yeah…I mean…Wallace is a racist…right?"

"I think so. I know he didn't want black and white kids to go to school together."

"So this song is kinda bad, right? It says the South and segregation is good?"

"Maybe, but I think it's more complicated than that. I mean, he says, 'In Birmingham they love the governor' but then he says 'Boo, boo, boo,' like they don't agree with the views of the people who like Wallace in Birmingham."

They both thought about it for a bit. Lately, Paul had been spending time studying the American civil rights movement, and was becoming more knowledgeable when it came to black history in general. He thought about the use of Birmingham in the song, rather than the Alabama state capital, Montgomery.

"Yeah, and in Birmingham the white police attacked Martin Luther King and the peaceful marchers…including women and children…with water cannons and police dogs."

"Good point…And then they say, 'Now Watergate does not bother me, does your conscience bother you?' I'm not sure if that means they like Nixon or not, or if it even has anything to do with Birmingham."

They both considered the lyrics a few moments longer. Paul was the first to break the silence.

"Could they be saying the racists in Birmingham like Wallace, but we don't, and don't judge us all in Alabama by our asshole governor?"

Keenan understood Paul's point.

"That makes sense. 'We all did what we could do' to stop him from winning—but he still won."

"Exactly. And then he compares Wallace and Alabama to Nixon and the US."

"Yeah, man, I get it. He's saying every US citizen isn't a criminal just because Nixon broke the law with Watergate, just like everyone in Alabama isn't a racist because Wallace is their elected representative."

They both thought about the lyrics for a few moments longer. In the background the song wound down.

"I like that meaning much better than the other way."

"Me too, Pablo, me too."

Keenan turned the volume back up as Stevie Nicks started singing "Sara."

Drowning—
—in a sea of love
Where everyone—
—would love to drown…

The boys allowed the haunting Fleetwood Mac song to overtake them as they listened without talking.

As the dying orange sunset painted the sky behind them, Keno and Paul wallowed in the moment, their good feelings heightened by the mysteries awaiting them in the night. The search for girls; the traveling; the beer-drinking; the music; the accompanying, give-and-take posturing of young men. Though Keno wasn't born in Florida, he felt a deep affinity for the peninsula. He recognized the juxtaposition of pavement layered over swamp surrounded by ocean, and could feel Florida's soul pounding up past the human edifices, surrounding him with the fertile smells and sounds of generations of rotting detritus.

When you build your house—
—then call me
—home.

Keno breathed a full, lush breath, and the fecund air caressed his lungs and skin. As he sipped the last of his second can of beer, he embraced the hyperbolic late summer of life and death. A Palmetto bug flew drunkenly through the window and landed on his wrist, attaching its legs hooklike to skin and hair. Keno watched it. He didn't need to act. He just wanted to be—to wallow with his brothers in the deep sensuality of a warm Florida night—an experience he intuitively realized was heading towards extinction.

CHAPTER 2

In Bloom

As Clay exited the Pick Kwik, Keenan took a mental snapshot of his older brother. Like a human tank, Clay's thick upper body effortlessly supported a case of Miller Genuine Draft in cans, a liter of Jose Cuervo, and a closely shorn blond head that featured a wide-eyed, hypnotic grin. He was wearing the uniform of his high school years: a faded, untucked, pastel Ralph Lauren shirt, the ironic Polo insignia stretched tight across his forty-four-inch chest (ironic because the Barton boys wouldn't be caught dead playing the "country club" sports of golf or tennis, let alone polo); beltless Levi's 501 jeans with a rear leather tag that revealed a thirty-inch waist; no socks or skivvies (he was, in fact, a commando); and rose-tinted skin that revealed a fundamental misunderstanding of the relationship between sun exposure, blue eyes, and melanoma. His size 10 feet were swaddled in an old pair of leather Adidas Roms. At six foot one and 190 pounds, his bearing wasn't particularly overwhelming, but his body and movement belied an animalistic energy that, when present, demanded notice. It had been eighteen months since Clay had successfully completed BUD/S school, and his physique and swagger, although always impressive, had taken on a new level of overdevelopment. An evening with the complicated, oldest Barton brother was always an event, and after nearly two years apart, the siblings were swimming in an intoxicating current of youthful overconfidence and anticipation. They were at that optimistic age that often confuses one's physical beauty with virtue and righteousness.

Clay had wrestled and played water polo in high school, claiming that both sports were essentially "scrappin' in yer underwear"—just in different settings. Eventually, he chose water polo. He liked wrestlers, as he felt they were old school tough and had no patience for vanity or conceit, but he hated cutting weight. He decided wearing a Speedo was a small price to pay to avoid starving himself. Clay also preferred the smell of chlorine to that of sweaty armpits—a truly "better of two evils" decision. In his senior year he captained the Clearwater team to the state finals, losing to a juggernaut Miami team by just one goal.

His prowess in the pool had been significant enough to catch the eye of a Yale recruiter. He accepted the venerable institution's offer of admission and a generous financial aid package. This development surprised his parents and kindled in them a nascent fantasy of familial redemption. The Bartons didn't realize he was a bit of a university-quota filler. At the time, not many blue collar, public school athletes from Florida considered matriculating at an Ivy League school. Much of the southern populace considered the region north of the Mason-Dixon Line to be a strange, frozen, foreign land; moving there was akin to falling off the edge of the world. After a long conversation with his Cornell-educated wrestling coach, Clay was able to overcome this backward notion. Comfortable in his future at Yale, he partied all spring with his fellow seniors, furthering his taste for *cerveza* and *pakalolo*. Unfortunately his already mediocre academic skills continued to suffer from a lack of prioritization.

In Clearwater he was well known—first for his athletic prowess, but also for appetites that aligned with his fitness and testosterone levels. Though he clearly had a narcissistic streak, he wasn't known to bully; in fact there were several incidences that added to his reputation as just and courageous.

Locals still talked about the time Clay crossed paths with a Clearwater delinquent named Denny Britton. Denny was conflict oriented, especially at night when he was drinking with his sycophantic friends. Those who knew him steered a wide berth, and those who didn't respected his size and demeanor. This lack of social pushback reinforced his entitled, offensive behavior. Britton had been cut from the high school football team for "corrosive behavior and general problems with authority." At least, so said Coach Smith's handwritten report. Denny dropped out and worked for the next five years changing tires at

Firestone. During this time he perfected his ability to creatively dodge responsibility and arrest, while regularly crossing over the line of civilized behavior.

A few months before the fight, Denny had become a prime suspect in a fire that destroyed the building housing the business and residence of an ex-girlfriend and her family. She had just recently broken off their relationship; Britton had sworn retaliation. It could've been a multiple homicide, but on the night of the fire, the girl and her parents had been visiting relatives up the coast in Tarpon Springs. Despite their willingness to creatively manipulate evidence, the local authorities couldn't tie Denny to the crime. What had kept Britton unjailed up to this point was a jurisdiction short on resources. The population of Pinellas County was growing faster than was the threat of his menace; and the frequency and significance of the crimes Denny was accused of lay just below the threshold necessary to be prioritized by a stretched criminal justice infrastructure.

In those days fights were common on the blue collar bar circuit the boys frequented…but weapons weren't. The skirmishes were more akin to a pack of dogs establishing a pecking order amongst themselves—a lot of snarling but limited amounts of blood. The etiquette inherent in the southern bar mating ritual was something the boys had been forced to learn through experience. For many single men, if closing time revealed limited romantic options, their frustration and need for stimulation led them to the next best thing: physical confrontation. Knowing when to stand and when to fold were necessary survival skills, and understanding the bouncers and the limits of what they would tolerate was also important. Denny didn't fold, and he had a mean streak that made him the kind of patron whom experienced bouncers always kept an eye on.

The fight occurred late in the summer after Clay's senior year. He and a friend were on their way home after sharing a few beers at a local dive when they stopped to get gas on the dark side of town. It was a little past midnight when they pulled into the self-serve lane, and Clay climbed out of the car to pump. Before he could reach the handle, a Pontiac with three contemporaries screeched in on the other side, and the large driver hopped out. The beast proceeded to simultaneously get in Clay's face; display a possessive attitude about the pump Clay intended to use; and, finally, use the rhetorical question that working men of that era and region commonly used to establish dominance.

"What? You want me to kick yer ass?"

Clay's olfactory senses registered that the man's breath *smelled* like ass. Taking an internal inventory, Clay also observed that he must've been pretty buzzed, because he was noticing (with humor) the linguistic irony embedded in all the ass that this asshole had just injected into his consciousness.

Then he started doing all the micro-calculations—wondering if he should back down, given the man's size, conviction, and his own degree of inebriation. He tried to recall the number of beers he had downed that night, and over how long a period of time. He wondered if the other men in the car would do the honorable thing and stay out of it, or would they jump in if things got difficult for their boy? He considered the last time he had worked out, tried to get a sense of the offender's fitness level, and wondered about his technical fighting skills. Was the loudmouth armed? While he calculated the probabilities, his survival instinct was pushing the fight-or-flight chemicals into his system—the shot of adrenaline, the hard hit of norepinephrine—and the bully's body language became more offensive.

Clay took a step back before calmly responding to an agitated Denny Britton.

"If you think you can."

The story goes that Britton started it and Clay finished it. At one point, Clay felt he had sufficiently proved his dominance and decided to show some compassion. He left the thug breathing heavily on one knee, turned, and walked confidently back to his car. A few seconds later, the late-night, predominantly black crowd that had gathered to watch the two white boys scuffle let out an audible warning. Clay turned just in time to dodge a screwdriver grasped firmly in Denny's hand. It was intended for his ear. The weapon sharpened Clay's focus. He was pissed.

Clay pivoted toward his opponent. Denny lunged awkwardly, and Clay ducked under the charging bear, catching the attacker's momentum then using it to lift him, arching his back as they fell to the ground. As they descended parallel to the earth, the tip of the ogre's screwdriver pierced Clay's torso—his thick latissimus dorsi muscle, to be precise. At the last second Clay managed to spin the snarling entanglement in mid-air, landing on top as Britton's head struck the pavement. The screwdriver rolled away harmlessly.

Dazed, running out of options, the big coward tried to kick his younger foe from his supine position. Clay secured Denny's outthrust leg in the crook of his arm, tugged off the man's cowboy boot, and then proceeded to beat Britton in the head with his own footwear. One particularly well-aimed blow dug the boot heel deep into the tissue of the bully's ear, eliciting a noticeable flow of blood…and crowd appreciation.

"Damn. That boy's kickin' the big fella's ass with his own shoe!"

As the two boys fought, Clay's friend (nicknamed "Crab," due to his adept lateral movement) had been holding Britton's two weasely friends at bay with the flathead. The two sidekicks didn't seem to need much dissuasion, given how badly their alpha was getting whooped.

Looking back, Clay still remembered the experience with surprising clarity, as if it had occurred in slow motion. He marveled at the effects of adrenaline: He didn't recall feeling particularly scared; more of a calm focus, like being "in the zone" or "in the flow." He remembered tiny details like the red plastic screwdriver handle sliding past his face in conjunction with Denny's fist, the whole conglomeration missing his nose by only a few inches. Those inches felt like two feet, so certain was he of the logistics and his own safety. He clearly recalled a shapely black woman cringing in the background about twenty feet beyond Britton's left shoulder. It felt like he could reach out and touch her. Her hair was hanging low, in yellow curlers. She had on a white, wife-beater tank top, a pink bra, dark athletic shorts, and sliders. He knew it was crazy given the context, but she registered in his consciousness as being brick house hot with an impressive rack.

When the police showed up several minutes later, they had to pull Clay off of Britton's deteriorating assemblage. The fight had continued for longer than expected. Clay's back—and one of his car's rear tires—exhibited punctures, courtesy of Britton's screwdriver. The larger man's face was a bloody mess. Towards the end of the fight, Clay had been brutally creative—and lacking in mercy. He had used his clunky but jagged metal watchband to rake Britton's face to great effect. Denny had spent much of the fight face down, or on all fours, trying to simultaneously get to his feet and cover his face. Attacking from above, Clay's fists delivered glancing blows to Britton's face on the downstroke, followed by ripping Seiko upstrokes. This technique proved quite efficient.

With an indifference that came with the job, the cops corralled the five of them, took the names and testimonies of eyewitnesses, then hauled the two combatants down to the station. They were both set free in the early morning.

Three months later in local court, a judge sent Clay home and Britton up the river. The local authorities had been tiring of Denny's psychopathic tendencies, and used this fight as a chance to hang an assault-with-a-deadly-weapon charge on him. Clay was celebrated as the wrong victim at the right time, delivering justice in a violent but legally acceptable way, given the interpretation of self-defense regulations and the consistent testimony of the noncombatants. Clay was compared favorably to cinematic vigilantes Charlie Bronson and Dirty Harry during his local fifteen minutes of fame. Unfortunately he couldn't fully enjoy the attention. He had to race up to New Haven to start his Ivy League career.

CHAPTER 3—

Down to the Waterline

For all of Clay's charisma and talents in high school, he no longer was considered a big fish once he moved to the larger collegiate pond. Academically, his public school education put him well behind the Exeter and Andover kids, leaving him struggling in the classroom. In the pool, he was only one of many studs, but he had never learned how to work hard, always coasting on his talents against weaker competition. Now, against a better-prepared crew, he needed all of his biological and anatomical gifts, and a discipline he hadn't developed. He floundered.

He had also continued his habit of exposing his brain to alcohol and weed with considerable frequency. The college environment granted him easy access to those twin insidious parasites; they soon began probing his biology for weaknesses that would allow them to take control of their host. It wasn't difficult for their allure to successfully seduce Clay: his neural composition came pre-provisioned for addiction. None of these developments tempered his large appetites for companionship, and he kept busy chasing the fresh herd at Yale.

A confluence of misguided events involving drugs, an underaged girl, and a car found Clay back in court for the second time in two months. This time he met an unsympathetic Connecticut judge who saw few redeeming qualities in Clay's back seat predations. He offered the defendant jail or enlistment, and Clay left Yale in humiliation, entering the Navy as a lowly Seaman recruit. His parents were once again left to wonder about their former lives' trespasses, and his status as hometown golden boy was tarnished.

Clay promptly shipped out to North Chicago for basic training at the Great Lakes Naval Station. He once again found himself swimming in a big pond, though with mostly small fish this time around. He consistently ranked in the top percentile while exerting little effort, and he coasted through various training rotations. The system soon deposited him at the top of the pyramid, staring at the metaphorical front door of the elite fighting team known as SEALS. He was invited to compete for a spot, and given his strong background as a waterman and his mandated separation from frequent alcohol and drug use, he was able to survive the BUD/S training intact. The team welcomed him.

Soon Clay found himself in Central America, using his limited Spanish language skills to train small brown men in the art of quelling the threat of communism in the Western Hemisphere. He didn't think of his trainees as allies of right wing death squads who would eventually be accused of murdering nuns and *campesinos*. He was told convincingly that he was fighting the "Soviet threat at our back door." Just another proxy war to keep the dominoes from falling in favor of the USSR. "Noble work enforcing the Monroe Doctrine," and such. After nearly a year of mucking around in the jungles of Panama, El Salvador, and Nicaragua, he began having trouble compartmentalizing his activities on the ground. The moral high ground he initially felt comfortable occupying was beginning to shift beneath his feet. During his infrequent leaves, he was medicating heavily with old and new friends: alcohol, Panama Red, and the local working girls.

Clay opened the Chevy's back door and slid the case of beer and bottle of tequila next to the ice-filled cooler over which Paul sat guard.

"Would you please ice these up my good man?"

"Certainly, Your Lordship."

Climbing into the front, Clay started the car and Y-turned out of the crushed-shell lot. He ejected the Allmans and inserted Dire Straits' first compendium. Immediately, Mark Knopfler introduced himself and his bandmates: the Sultans of Swing.

"These guys are so good."

"The whole album is awesome."

"Where are they from?"

"Australia or London or something."

Strumming his fingers to the melody, Clay started to enter his happy place. The boys had followed a time-tested schedule that maximized the cost effectiveness and duration of their buzz. The trio had started with a late afternoon weight-lifting routine focusing on the upper body. This got the blood flowing to some prominent areas, and signaled the pituitary gland and central nervous system to start producing endorphins. In addition, their high-intensity, heavy-load approach encouraged the production of testosterone and human growth hormone. Looking good, feeling good. Endorphin, a contraction of the words *endogenous* and *morphine*, was the body's natural pharmacological response to pain, stress, and fear. Besides allowing them to forget all the anxieties embedded in the transition from adolescence to adulthood, the endorphins took things a step further, bringing feelings of euphoria that allowed them to unleash their inner extroverts. Simplistically, it made them feel good about themselves. Without it the young men would be tongue-tied around young women. Their game would be limited.

Clay turned toward the back seat and sang out in falsetto, *"Oh bartender, a shot and a chaser if you would...."* He shifted to an Oxford accent, *"I could use some cooooorrrrrecting."* He drew out the *r* as if he were impersonating Lloyd, Jack Nicholson's confidant and barkeep in the iconic film *The Shining*.

Paul extended his long arms into the front seat and sequentially handed his brother the bottle of tequila and an ice-cold can of beer. Clay secured both can and bottle between his thighs and then unscrewed the tequila top with his free hand. With one hand on the wheel and one hand raising the tequila bottle in the general direction of his brothers, he offered what he thought was a clever toast.

"*Señorita* Caution, I'd like to introduce *Señor Viento*. Prepare to be tossed."

Clay sucked in a mouthful of the tequila, grimaced against the burn on his lips and in his mouth, then allowed the downward evacuation past his uvula, and eventually into his stomach. He followed the tequila quickly with a swig from his can of beer. Then he passed the bottle with a nod to Keenan. With an air of solemnity, Keenan raised the bottle to his lips and filled his mouth with the agave sacrament.

The alcohol was now ramping up its partnership with the endogenous morphine, which was already pegged at an ambitious level. After the weight lifting, the brothers had gone for a three-mile run in the deep sand, away from the water, at Clearwater Beach. The aerobic workout further stimulated endorphin production. As they showered and got dressed, their opioid receptors were dining on an organic, homemade dose of a chemical that was equivalent to morphine in its effect and potency. They had successfully started the evening by simulating the feelings of heroin without the cost, injection, legal risk, or potential for overdose. Rehydrating with a pint of whole milk was the final component of the strategy. The beverage coated their stomachs and moderated the absorption rate of the alcohol they would consume to a pace that would allow them to enjoy the fruits of their buzz for several hours.

"Hey Clay, how does it feel to be a professional killer?"

Keno was curious, and after they had all toasted each other with a shot of Jose and a chaser of Miller, he felt comfortable being direct. No contempt or taunting lay buried in the question. The three brothers had spent years marinating in a culture that respected the military, and they found the Special Forces to be particularly badass..

"So far, my kill skills haven't been much tested, brother."

"What do you mean?"

"You guys know I can't talk about this stuff."

There was an awkward silence. Clay decided to offer a tidbit meant to downplay his role and reduce the questions that his friends and family often had.

"I've only had to fire my Sig once at potential hostiles. It was pretty uneventful. A Panamanian civilian and I tried to finesse our way past a rebel roadblock. I was hiding under some blankets in the back of his little Toyota, letting the driver do the talking. It became apparent that the teenagers holding machetes and AKs weren't gonna let us pass unsearched. I let my driver know that wouldn't be acceptable by blindly firing a few rounds from my pistol through the back door, in the general direction of the voices, while simultaneously yelling an unnecessary '*Vamos!*' I guess the AKs were just for show, because we busted through the small wooden barrier without further gunfire."

Envisioning the scene, Paul asked about the guards.

"Do you think you hit anybody?"

"Not sure."

"How did you get back?"

"Took a different route."

"What else were you doing down there?"

"Mostly just training government soldiers in counter-insurgency tactics. Basic search-and-capture strategies. Interrogation techniques."

"Did you like it down there?"

"The people are superfriendly."

"What is our country doing there?"

"Just trying to keep the commies at bay."

"Did you like the fighting stuff?"

Clay shifted in his seat. "Let's talk about something else."

A few minutes earlier, during their conversation, Clay had parked them in the massive lot at Bone Daddy's. An awkward silence followed Clay's last comment and now the brothers were nursing their beers and feeding the bugs; watching the movement of the groups around them. Still in the back seat, Paul's concerns about peaking too early compelled him to interrupt the silence.

"We need to head in soon."

Ignoring Paul, a random thought struck Keenan.

"Do you think if I shotgun a beer while riding shotgun I'll go back in time?"

"Let's find out *mon petite frere…tete de bone…sur le pont.*"

Clay liked to throw around his *Frenglish* gibberish.

Paul passed out three more beers and the brothers prepared to first puncture the bottom of their cans and then quickly suck the contents from that hole. To optimize the laws of fluid mechanics they would also have to pop the tops during the process. The youngest went first. Paul pulled out a cheap Bic pen and placed the ball point against the bottom edge of the cylinder.

"The hair of the dog that bit me, Lloyd," he said, following the brothers' tradition of quoting a favorite movie line before chugging. As Keenan turned in his seat and watched Paul's head and neck tilt back, he clearly saw their father's contribution to his brother's facial structure.

Keenan's turn.

"Shakin' the bush, boss!"

He punctured the aluminum sheath of the can and sucked the contents without spilling a drop.

Hot on his heels was Clay.

"You fucked up," he quoted. "You trusted us."

CHAPTER 4

Paul

Keenan had been born in Paris, as had his older sibling. But unlike Keenan, Clay understood at least some French, the result of his nearly three-year exposure during his infant years.

At the time, their father, Aloysius "Al" Clancy Barton, was proselytizing the European Continent about the wonders of IBM mainframe computers. Aloysius came from a disciplined military family, and, as the youngest of four (and the only male), he felt the burden of primogeniture. A creative sort, his army obligations left him uninspired, and as a result he suffered often. Eventually he so willfully fumbled his military matriculation that his parents, fully exasperated, emancipated him from the burden of their expectations.

He became educated in the liberal arts, and, after graduation, landed in a sales role that granted him broad access and rewarded his charisma, looks, manners, and pedigree. From his father he inherited a strong taste for alcohol, which, in conjunction with his oratory skills, often proved useful when initiating relationships. His career path seemed promising at casual glance. Established lineage. Princeton education. IBM training program. Beautiful young family. A sales territory that included some of the most glamorous and civilized regions on the planet. Lurking under the surface however was a serious genetic predilection towards self-destruction. In his free time, Al was practicing to become a derelict. As a ripening reprobate, his employment opportunities would soon erode at a rate commensurate to the increasing frequency of his unpredictable behavior. Paris would soon be in the rearview mirror, and several brief stops would follow before the family landed in Houston. Paul was born there, to a different mom, during a volatile stint. Al was engaged by another large computer company to sell hardware to NASA, and his bride, Elizabeth, was undergoing a slow-motion nervous breakdown.

Al met Elizabeth Phinney Sutton at a mixer on campus his senior year. Attractive, smart, and flirtatious, she soon had him mesmerized. It didn't hurt the relationship that she found his drinking persona to be "wickedly fun." Several months before graduation, after securing the position with IBM, he asked the nineteen-year-old Elizabeth to marry him. She said yes and promptly got pregnant. Within one year Elizabeth had dropped out of school, gotten married, moved to Paris, and had her first child. They both spoke French, so the geographic transition was more romantic than strenuous. However, the daily tedium, combined with an absentee husband, soon outweighed any sense of romance for the new bride. The burden of responsibility was revealing itself to be a significant challenge for the young mother. Her husband shrugged.

In 1957, Sputnik 1's successful ninety-eight-minute orbit of earth had granted the Soviets the pole position in the space race. Alarmed at losing the high ground, the Americans began throwing money at NASA to be the first country to reach the moon; another kind of gold rush occurred in Houston over the course of the next fifteen years. Salespeople with technical capabilities were in demand, and if you could also drink copious amounts of beer, endure country music, and survive the inane banter of government engineers you could name your price.

The shoe fit Aloysius well. He soon had his family settled in Houston and was selling computer equipment at a rate that kept his annual commissions in the high five figures, a huge sum for the times. Given the amount of business being conducted, his bosses were willing to overlook his periodic aberrant behavior. Things were on a positive trajectory for the Bartons, but Easy Street was not a place where the paterfamilias took comfort.

Like a moth to the flame, Al was drawn to the physical charms of his young, university-educated secretary, who happened to be black. Earning dual degrees in Economics and Art History from Stanford, Cheryl Prudeaux enjoyed the discursive process and had quickly grown frustrated and bored with her limited career options. Given her university experience, she had been allowed to believe that her thoughts had value, so she was alarmed to learn that potential employers didn't agree. She had taken a series of entry level positions, none of which had moved her forward. The men she dated were mostly not conversant in the topics she enjoyed. Eventually, her usually benign sleep patterns were invaded by dreams of drowning. The combination of inexperience, impatience, and a very low glass ceiling made her vulnerable to Aloysius' advances. She also had no immediate remaining family to help offer perspective, and her few friends were all back home in Baton Rouge. Lonely and losing her confidence, she found Al's attentions flattering, even though she had initially rebuffed them. Eventually his urbane charisma preyed on her need for love and understanding and, after a particularly provocative conversation at a rambunctious office party, she capitulated. What had been smoldering office gossip burst into full conflagration when she decided to keep their love child.

In Houston in the early 1960s, the improbability of this scenario pushed everyone off balance. Family and friends were in shock, but Al kept calm and carried on as if nothing untoward was happening. Cheryl left her job during her second trimester, and the gossip lost momentum—out of sight, out of mind.

Things soon got tight for Al Barton. After his mortgage, taxes, unreimbursed "client entertainment" expenses, and support for a now unemployed and pregnant Cheryl, Al's take-home pay put the family below the poverty level. After months of forbearance (and broken promises) the Bartons' weekly pool and landscape maintenance services finally stopped showing up, and the lawn and shrubs started their steady return to a wild state. Al wasn't much for home improvement or DIY projects; the only exception being the keg of beer he had installed behind the bar in the family room. Luckily their algae-infested backyard pool was hidden from public view. The monkeylike boys weren't repelled at all by the green water or hovering mosquito larvae and would embellish their cannonballs by integrating a launch from the overhanging roof of their house whenever Elizabeth was distracted.

Of course her boys also discovered the Texas religion of American football and became obsessed with its violence. They would play one-on-one tackle football in the front yard, with seven-year old Clay kicking off, running downfield, and briefly chasing a football-laden Keno before planting the five-year old firmly in the thick St. Augustine grass, preferably on top of an anthill. Then Keno would kick off to Clay, and the bigger boy would tuck the ball under his arm, lower his head, and run full speed at his baby brother. This passed as fun for one of them, and an unbiased observer could wonder what purpose served the ball. Their adopted mutts liked to participate, and when not chasing cars, the dogs would add to the carnage with an overly enthusiastic bite. Ignoring the screaming and yelling became a daily discipline for their mother.

Elizabeth was a stay-at-home professional, putting in long hours of overtime while trying to keep her boys from destroying each other—and everything in their path. She once developed an inspired strategy to mitigate their energy: decrease their rations. The plan backfired when they started fighting betwixt themselves over portion size, bringing a new level of violence into the kitchen, which was alarming given the proximity of sharp, pointed culinary utensils.

Praying her spouse would outgrow his addiction to alcohol and carnal dalliances, she patiently chaperoned the boys. Not finding any charm in the suburbs of Houston, and having no friends to confide in, she would periodically levitate above the chaos of fighting boys, omnipresent fleas, canine excrement, unpaid bills, and a devolving husband; recognize her current predicament with clarity and horror; and lock herself, crying, into the darkness of the coat closet, surrounded by books of S&H Green Stamps that only served as reminders of her financial limitations. Without her Valium prescription she wouldn't have made it.

Elizabeth's debutante training had not prepared her for this fate. Not any of it. The polyamorous behavior of her husband; the dusty, flat landscapes of southeast Texas; the moist heat; the oil money of the crass nouveau riche; the architecturally numb suburban sprawl with inadequate planning and the accompanying horrendous traffic; the omnipresent Pearl and Lonestar beer;

the regional dialect that embraced an economy of language as evidenced by the dropping of syllables; the grammatical contractions that pushed forth illiterate spawn like *"No ma'am, as I was fixin' to say, this ain't what 'Lizbeth 'spected 'tall."*

At first, when Al had proposed, she actually thought the marriage would be a coup, given the declining remnants of the Sutton family fortune and her early mental health issues. During the courting process she developed a sense of his drinking proclivities, but she was comfortable overlooking those tendencies given the commonality amongst her socially registered WASP friends. She focused on Al's potential to bring economic stability, given his solid family and education, which was made easier by her finding him sexy in a clever, smoldering way. As she stood at the altar staring into his intoxicated green eyes, she never intuited the struggles and indignation that would accompany the oncoming moral collapse of Aloysius Barton.

Circumstances went from complicated to bizarre when a tragic automobile accident claimed Cheryl's young life. She had been rushing to pick up her boyfriend, who had been working nights as a rodeo clown at the Astrodome. In Houston, in 1965, a single black Mom with educated convictions meant the pickings in the husband orchard were slim. From Cheryl's perspective, Aloysius's disorderly attention was in extreme deficit, as his presence and money had gone MIA nearly two years earlier, during her baby's first year. She worked two menial jobs to make ends meet, and her earlier boredom and impatience as a single woman had transitioned to a growing mixture of resignation and nihilism. Her idealism and principled stances were losing their relevance in the face of life's indifferent onslaught, which included the responsibilities of raising a child.

It was late and raining. Visibility was poor. She badly needed glasses for her myopia but couldn't afford to visit the optometrist. The clown's car housed several tools of the trade: red noses, colorful wigs, and a bushel of inflated balloons that had been used that morning for a kid's birthday party. The situation conspired to render invisible a large tanker truck merging onto the freeway. Making matters worse, Cheryl was driving a 1960 Chevy Corvair, and the tires were inflated evenly (and incorrectly), leading to a poorly understood oversteering problem common to that make and model year. As the trucker blasted his horn, Cheryl swerved to avoid the collision, losing control at high speed and fishtailing into the center guardrail. Having neglected to buckle her seatbelt—an act she fervently believed inhibited her freedom—she was catapulted into the disintegrating windshield and died at the scene from massive cerebral and cervical trauma. Her soul—and the balloons—were simultaneously released to the heavens.

The silver lining for her son, Paul, was his rare absence, that evening, from his mother's side. A neighbor was safely babysitting the boy at the time of the tragedy; thus Paul avoided also being catapulted. With no immediate relative available to claim the boy, Aloysius displayed his weird, selective sense of obligation and honor and effected the integration of the three-year-old Paul into his family. Naturally, for Elizabeth, this reopened old wounds that had barely stopped festering. Not in her worst nightmare had she considered she would suffer such shame when she agreed to marry Aloysius Barton. The daily visual and public reminder of her husband's infidelity was something she would never overcome. Conversely, Clay and Keenan welcomed their new playmate.

They all cried when the family left for Florida, with Paul, the bastard son, in tow. Elizabeth's were tears of joy: she believed that anything had to be an improvement over Houston. It was 1972. Boca Raton's small- and medium-sized enterprises had already begun to feel the inconsistency of Al's sales effort, as he had led an expeditionary force (several weeks ahead of his family) on behalf of Xerox and their high-speed printers. At the box office *Billy Jack* was kicking tail, and Terry Jacks was getting ready to record one of the biggest global singles of all time. There was still hope for seasons in the sun.

The family started off enthusiastically in the southeast corner of what some call the "limp dick" state. Their hope began to grow flaccid towards the end of year one. Aloysius's decline was accelerating, and their feast-and-famine lifestyle was becoming mostly famine. In hindsight, Elizabeth wondered why she stayed with Al through such a dramatic socioeconomic slide. The deterioration had been somewhat incremental and episodic, and so she had never gotten in front of it. Initially, he was a functional alcoholic, and she didn't really understand the symptoms. Over time, the disease became more pronounced and the job changes grew more frequent. Aloysius would regroup from his most recent crash and burn, dust himself off, and move on to a new job with a promise of normalcy. After much reflection Elizabeth attributed her tolerance to a number of things: the gradual nature of Al's disease; insecurity; loyalty; perseverance; her love for the boys; her hope that things would work out; her shame when they didn't; and, eventually, the limited options available to an undereducated, middle-aged mother of three.

The last stop for the family had been the Tampa Bay Area, where the kids all went to public high school in Clearwater. Al struggled through several jobs, finally taking a shady position that required selling underwater cameras that didn't work. Their family started to crumble under the forces of entropy. During high school, economic limitations and hormones started pushing the boys towards self-sufficiency. The family members resigned themselves to a disappointing detente, as teenage rebelliousness, parental fatigue on Elizabeth's part, and general indifference on Aloysius's part led to a slow-motion unraveling. Pops Barton eventually eschewed his family responsibilities permanently, wandering off with a series of increasingly tolerant women. With the exception of his paycheck, he wasn't missed. Elizabeth did what abandoned women have done for generations—shouldered the burden. Having limited credentials and needing money, she took a variety of low-end jobs in the security and landscape industries to pay the mortgage. Life continued with apparent disinterest.

CHAPTER 5

Bone Daddy's

Sipping beer from containers poorly engineered to resist the subtropical heat, the three boys left the parked car and happily floated through the crushed-shell lot of Bone Daddy's. There wasn't much order to the queue at the entrance, it was more a milling herd of the usual nightclub sediment. "Disco Inferno" drifted out of the front doors as the DJ released The Trammps from their vinyl incarceration. This was one of the few clubs that played both Rock and Disco, and somehow the bouncers kept the two tribes from violent interaction. Mostly.

Paul noticed an even mix of late-twenties polyester Travoltas, and a younger cohort of Gap-clad denim and corduroy. The latter bubbled with an ignorant exuberance kindled by unreasonably high expectations. As usual, most of the faces sported a summer tan, but Paul stood out as uniquely pigmented. He had grown comfortable with his six-inch natural-Afro hairstyle at Clearwater High School, but he couldn't help but attract attention when he traveled to unknown turf. At seventeen, Paul couldn't legally enter Florida bars, but there were a variety of strategies and back-up plans he used to circumvent this inconvenience. To that end, Clay led his brothers to a dark exterior corner of the old wooden warehouse, about fifty feet from the well-lit entry.

"It looks like they're charging a cover tonight. You guys wait here and I'll go see what's up. I'll be back in five minutes."

"Roger that, Captain Barton," Paul replied.

Clay was back thirteen minutes after paying the three-dollar cover. On his way out, he had been stamped on the back of his hand so he could enjoy "in and out" privileges. He nonchalantly hustled over to his brothers.

"Give me your hands, before the ink gets too dry."

Keno and Paul each licked the back of their own hands before extending them. The ritual was familiar. Clay pressed the back of his hand in quick succession to his brothers's: first Keno, then Paul. The stamp now appeared with reasonable clarity on all three hands.

"This should work. They got a chick at the door checkin' the stamps with a black light. She seems pretty cool."

"She'll remember that she hasn't seen me yet," worried Paul.

Through experience the three brothers knew there were two kinds of doormen: those who were sympathetic to people who looked like Paul…and those who weren't. Whichever category a doorman belonged to, he would always remember Paul for the same reason—he was unusual—and those who were sympathetic would act like he wasn't, and let him in with his stamp. Those who were not sympathetic would claim "bullshit" on his stamp and either deny him access or, best case, force him through the normal entry protocol. Paul knew from experience that this outcome was difficult to handicap. The fact that the boys were willing to engage in this degree of legerdemain to save six bucks highlighted their pecuniary limitations.

"Panties a bit tight there, Paulina?" Clay extended his hand and put it on Paul's shoulder. "C'mon man, relax, we got this…first Keno, then me, then you glide in tight…right after me. We all go in casual with our hands out… piece of cake."

Keno sensed his little brother's tension.

"If you get stopped we'll wait for you. You got your fake ID?"

"Yeah."

"Okay. Here's three bucks if you end up needing it."

Keno gave his little brother all his money.

Paul nodded, took the money, and whispered his response: "Thanks, that's mighty black of you."

Clay and Keno smiled.

"Kill 'em and let's *vamos*," said Clay as he picked up the unfinished can of Miller he had secreted in some weeds. After taking a furtive look around, all three chugged the remnants of their cans.

Clay then bent over, placed the empty, upright can on the ground under his left sneaker, and, by applying pressure to the opposite sides of the cylinder with his two pointer fingers, allowed the can to evenly collapse on itself.

"*Listo.*"

Clay and Keno walked side by side, with Paul following closely behind. At five foot ten and 160 pounds, Paul was the slightest, but his hair brought him up to Keno and Clay's level.

A couple of people called out to Clay, and like a practiced politician he nodded to them and, never breaking stride, returned, "What's up, brother-man?" The trio got in the quickly moving "hand stamp line" behind several high-waisted, polyestered disco dudes; they kept their formation tight. Clay's reconnaissance had been good—the girl at the door wasn't particularly detail oriented—and all three passed the lazy, black-light muster.

Just as Paul started to exhale, a bouncer who had been positioned next to the girl stepped out assertively and stopped all three. He wore his hair in cornrows, had particularly clear eyes, and was not showing his teeth. All three boys' senses went on red alert.

"Where you boys from?" asked the beast in the suit and tie. He was bigger than Clay and put off a serious vibe.

"All over, but lately Clearwater," said Clay, as casually as possible.

If he kept his cool this wouldn't become physical, but there was something about this guy that made Clay's hair stand on end. He also didn't want to ruin a great buzz.

"What about him?" The dark-skinned bouncer nodded at Paul.

"He's with us," Keno said protectively, not as sure about his personal safety as his older brother.

"No hats inside," said the doorman, pointing at Keno's head.

A creeping realization dawned on Keno. He knew this man, but he couldn't remember how.

The next moment the big man glowered at him. "Your name Keno Barton?"

Clay frowned—this was heading in a potentially bad direction. Paul curled his hands into fists, while Keno's brain was racing. Finally it hit him. It had been a while…Keno wasn't sure where he stood and tried to defuse the tension.

"Trick Bowman? Damn you got big. Or should I say bigger?"

He tried to sound friendly in light of the glaring behemoth standing before him.

"What are you now, two-fifteen, two-twenty? Shit, brother, you gotta be at least six-two?"

The bouncer couldn't continue the act any longer. It was as if his teeth required oxygen. His eyes softened and his lips separated to reveal a blinding smile, a metamorphosis that changed the tone immediately.

The tension flowed out of the three brothers.

"It's been awhile, Keen-O." Patrick laughed at the change in the brothers' body language. Nonetheless, he stayed in character—the rival, black athlete. "What you Clearwater crackers doin' at an upscale place like this? Shouldn't y'all be out recruiting some young brothers to help you improve your mediocre football program?"

Patrick Bowman was only eighteen years old, though he looked and behaved every bit the fully grown man. Two years ago, as a precocious junior, he was playing varsity football for rival Largo High School when he met Keenan for the first time. At the young age of sixteen he had already developed his punishing running style: shifty yet powerful when necessary. At the time, Keno was a starting senior linebacker for Clearwater. They both weighed about the same then, but Bowman had added forty pounds and three inches, whereas Keno topped out ten pounds and one inch later at one-eighty-five and six feet even.

Both Largo and Clearwater had been undefeated and ranked among the Florida top ten heading into the final game of the season. The local sports writers had been anticipating this matchup for weeks, and the two small communities were licking their collective chops. At the kickoff, Trick and Keno knew each other only from newspaper reports that enthusiastically touted their feats.

The packed stadium was an amalgam of high school football in the Florida swamp: older men with gnarled, sunburned mitts, chewing Redman and bemoaning generational loss; short-skirted cheerleaders performing routines choreographed carefully to achieve a balance between tasteful and suggestive; adolescents cruising to see and be seen; teachers encouraging students to keep a lid on public romance and intoxication; band members stretching the limits of faculty tolerance.

It had been a hard-fought battle, with Clearwater leading 23–20 going into the final minute. Bowman had slashed Clearwater for over one hundred yards on the ground, and Keno, playing weak side linebacker, had racked up fifteen tackles and one fumble recovery. Keno and Trick had developed an intimate relationship by this point of the game, with both athletes punishing each other ferociously. All those hours being pummeled by Clay had turned Keenan into a pretty tough competitor, but Trick was just as committed. Largo had the ball at midfield, it was third down, and they needed two yards for a first. Everyone in the stadium knew Largo was gonna pound Trick behind their behemoth right tackle, work their remaining three timeouts, and try to get within field goal range for a shot at overtime. As the quarterback took the snap and moved to his right, he pressed the ball into Trick's gut. The Clearwater defense surged to control the line of scrimmage. The Largo QB stealthily withdrew the pigskin. He took a three-step drop, revealing his true intentions: to pass. As the Clearwater defenders changed their focus from runner to receivers, the whole Clearwater secondary realized they had been sucked in too close to the line of scrimmage in an effort to stop what was now clearly a fake run.

Keno's brain struggled. He had been meeting Largo players helmet to helmet all evening, and as the game progressed, he had developed a growing disregard for pain. His mentality and hormones kept him in a perpetual state of rage, as the battle had devolved into a series of brain-jarring collisions necessary to control his turf. He was currently out of position, as he had bitten hard on the run fake, shrugging off first an offensive lineman then shucking Largo's fullback while moving laterally to try and stop Trick before he could gain a first down. Multiple thoughts ran through his mind, including the realization that the offensive lineman had been too easy to avoid and was now retreating, the telltale sign of a pass. When he finally realized the Largo runner didn't have the ball, he hesitated a split second, trying to remember what his pass coverage responsibilities were.

The three Largo receivers flooded the left side of the field, putting pressure on the Clearwater corners and safeties to sag to that side. As Keno tried to collect his wits, Trick slipped through the line of scrimmage, lightly colliding shoulders with Keno before angling to the right—away from the other three receivers and the defenders they had attracted. A split second later Keno realized, to his horror, he had man coverage on the running back. He spun towards the departing Trick, turning on the burners while unsuccessfully trying to grab a piece of his man's jersey. As Trick separated from Keno, heading to the right corner of the end zone about fifty yards away, the linebacker hoped his teammate with deep-coverage responsibilities was paying attention.

Trick caught the ball in full stride at the twenty-seven yard line with Keno a step behind. They maintained that formation all the way to the end zone, Bowman impervious to the burden of the pigskin.

The next morning the *Pinellas Times* sports page led with the banner: LARGO STUNS CLEARWATER 27–23!! The front page photo recorded a trailing defender, both hands raised to his helmet in anguish as the Largo ball carrier crossed the goal line with arm, hand, and a single pointer finger raised to the sky in exhilaration. In the background was a stadium packed with fans standing in shock and jubilation. It was a classic photo, worth more than a thousand words—the thrill of victory and the agony of defeat. To remove any confusion about Keno's role, the photographer had captured the number "50" and the name "Barton" clearly displayed on the defender's jersey. Not only would everyone in the stadium have the image of a flailing Barton forever burned into their memories, but now everyone exposed to the paper's reach would enjoy a similar visual treat. The Clearwater cornerback with deep-third responsibilities was literally out of the picture.

Keenan had seen Patrick Bowman without his helmet only briefly, after the game, during the obligatory team handshaking exercise. With tears in his eyes, he still remembered the respectful, cocoa-brown face with almond eyes and perfect white teeth. The generous lips offered some brief consoling words.

"Tough break, number fifty, you played a great game."

"Thanks, man," mumbled Keno, as he shook Bowman's hand and then turned and hustled to the locker room to hide his tears.

He turned in his pads for the last time that evening.

For the next few weeks Keno was inconsolable. As often happens in adolescence, the magnitude of his failure lost all reasonable proportion. He felt he would be forever haunted by his half-second hesitation in his final game. He was certain that Trick and he were to be entwined as hero and goat—two sides of the same coin.

Eventually, this too passed. Spring comes early in Florida, and distractions become priorities. In the fall, Keno moved on to college, and a world that had no knowledge of his humiliation. Focusing on his books, he tried to make time to meet girls, drank free beer at the frats, and played intramural basketball. He hadn't thought much about Patrick Bowman. Once or twice he heard how Trick was tearing up the Pinellas County league his senior year: a man amongst boys, setting conference records as he carried Largo High School (metaphorically) and opponents (literally) on his back throughout the season. The reports didn't surprise Keenan, as Bowman had become somewhat of a local celebrity. His more current heroics overshadowed the season-ending play from the previous year, and hence disentangled him and Keno.

Anyone interested in Tampa Bay Area sports knew Patrick had accepted a full ride to Florida State, but Keenan hadn't heard much about how he was handling the challenge of playing against other genetic freaks at the NCAA Division 1 level.

"I heard you took a full ride with the 'Noles?" Keenan said.

Patrick gave a barely perceptible nod. "Yeah."

"What are you doin' back here?"

"Bad luck, man. Blew out my knee returnin' a kick in spring training."

"Holy shit! No way."

Keenan was scolding himself for the wisps of *schadenfreude* that seeped in to his sincere feelings of loss for Bowman.

"What now?"

"Workin' here, tryin' to make enough money to pay tuition. Realizin' the harsh world of a civilian, I guess." He laughed at his plight, and continued with the color. "Livin' at home with my folks. The dream dies hard, man, the dream dies hard. Not a lot of sympathy for brothers who can't run."

"I smell that."

Keenan turned to his siblings and then back to the doorman.

"Hey, I know yer workin', but…Patrick Bowman, stud Largo tailback, these are my brothers, Clay and Paul."

He made the introduction hastily, as a line had formed behind them.

Trick focused for a second on Paul, smiled, and gripped each of the brother's hands in quick succession. "Pleased to meet ya. Call me 'Trick.' Your brother here made me famous by letting me slip by him a coupla years back in a big game. You may have heard about it?" He smiled some more.

Keno shrugged off the comment.

"Hey man, how hard do they hit in the SEC?"

Bowman quickly sized up his audience and considered the gracious way Keenan had taken his ribbing.

"Like a ton of bricks, Keen-O. But none as hard as you when you forced that fumble two years ago. My ears are still ringing," he lied with a grin.

"Y'all gotta move on now," he said, returning to his duties, "and, sorry, but I need to confiscate that hat."

"Can I grab it on my way out?"

"Sure." He nodded. "Stacy here can keep it under her desk…or take it out to your car, your choice. Also, if anyone gives you a hard time in there"—Patrick focused again on Paul—"you make sure to let me know…catch my drift?"

All three Bartons nodded appreciatively. It wasn't often you found two mixed-race kids randomly thrust together in their neck of the woods.

"Oh, last thing…tonight we're havin' an air guitar contest, and I'm one of the judges. Stick around, it's always fun, and…" He lowered his voice and whispered conspiratorially, with a wink. "You never know who might win…."

CHAPTER 6

TEN

Buoyed by their inside connection and the well-planned chemical cocktail moving through their bloodstreams, the brothers glided from the lobby over to the main room. The Trammps' earlier exhortations had been somewhat successful; though the building was not enflamed, there was a decent approximation. Cigarettes and a smoke machine worked together to pump a cool fog through the shimmering, crimson, disco lighting. The temperature inside was in the upper seventies and climbing. Half of the patrons were watching from the perimeter of the dance floor, either standing or sitting at the few scattered tables; the other half were in the middle of the cavern, dancing to the beat pulsing through the concussing sound system. The movements of the gyrating forms were periodically accentuated by the rotating red lights embedded in the ceiling, adding to the overall illusion of an inferno. The DJ was blaring "Miss You" by the Rolling Stones, and the crowd was young and lively.

An old wooden stage ran along the left side of the refurbished warehouse. Here the DJ spun his records while particularly confident dancers competed for space. On the right was a thirty-foot long bar behind which bikini- and board shorts-clad barkeeps served the crowd. Patrons standing two deep jockeyed for position behind those sitting on bar stools, hoping to be heard over the room's pumping speakers. Hovering over the dance floor were scantily clad, cage-bound, go-go girls, who were giving it their all, thrusting their arms and pumping their exorbitant chests, pretending to wallow wildly in their captivity.

Couples were in various stages of intimacy both on the dance floor and in the perimeter shadows. Paul spotted an arresting blonde, shakily perched on a bar stool, leaning her arched back against an elevated table, a disco dandy tight by her side. One of the spaghetti straps on her tight red dress had slipped down her shoulder; the other strap was working overtime to reign in her ample bosom. Her legs seemed to be on a drunken freedom march from the dress, fleeing the red lace fabric, which left only the top few inches off display. Her heavily made-up eyelids were pinned at half mast: she appeared to be seriously impaired. A small group of observers had gathered nearby, feigning disinterest but stealing long sideway peeks. The aforementioned dandy in attendance (Paul thought of him as a reptile) was less than gallant. Paul realized he was actually putting on a show…with the girl as the unwitting star. The duplicitous scumbag had slipped one hand under the protesting fabric of the dress while the other kept the girl from collapsing into a gravity-compelled, intoxicated heap. She would periodically emerge from her inebriated fog, realize the exhibition on display for the crowd, and make an ineffective effort to divert the all-too-public groping. Paul wondered how far the fondling would go before someone stepped in and ended it. He weighed the risks of taking a stand and decided to mind his own business. Chivalry once again unhorsed by impropriety in the numbing haze of alcohol. The predators were working the savannah, and the scene reminded Paul that he needed to watch his back. It was 10:30, and the club was moving from simmer to boil.

The brothers knew they were facing a key transition period—they could not become spectators. From experience, they had concluded that movement was crucial, and dancing with a girl, any girl, could jump-start the evening. If they got too choosy, too anxious, bogged down, or sedentary, it could mean a fast downward spiral in confidence. Bar purgatory housed the untouchable class in the club caste system. It was a self-imposed mental state, but it felt as tangible as steel bars and a cell. The boys felt strongly that dancing, even displaying just a feeble intercourse with a partner and the beat, was the best way to avoid this negative trajectory.

As nonspontaneous as it seemed, they had developed an incentive system to get them involved. A way to depersonalize and even encourage interaction. The game was Ten, and the rules were simple.

Clay turned to his brothers. "Ten?" he yelled as the Stones wound down.

Paul and Keno paused, hoping the next song would be helpful.

The DJ worked his magic, and Rudy Isley started the call-and-response anthem with his brothers:

W-e-e-e-e-e-l-l-l-l…You make me wanna (SHOUT)!

"Let's do it!" yelled Paul and Keno jointly.

The enthusiastic crowd joined the trio in taking it up a notch. The Barton Brothers went to work independently.

Clay's first target was a cluster of four ladies standing near the edge of the undulating mass of dancers. They were in office attire, a step up from his Levi's and sneakers, moving to the rhythm while nursing their drinks. He guessed they were in their early twenties…clerical workers looking for someone to provide a permanent rescue from the monotony of their long days shuffling paper. He quickly ranked them 1 to 4 on a hotness scale. He asked number 3 to dance.

"Oh, you're so sweet," she said, looking for approval from the others.

She was met with smirks and raised eyebrows.

"Maybe later?"

She thought he was handsome in a rugged way, but his wardrobe left a little to be desired in the money department. She wasn't a risk taker.

Clay was on a mission.

"Thanks," he responded, and immediately turned to the girl on her left, whom he had ranked as the least attractive. "Would you like to dance?"

A bit flustered, number 4 wasn't used to being asked ahead of her friends. Especially by a cute guy. She wasn't classically beautiful, but she had interesting features, was smart, and liked to have fun. Clay was just playing a numbers game, and the other girls weren't sure what to make of this guy who seemed to be indifferent to their responses. They had no idea that he was competing with his brothers; that the first to collect ten rejections earned free drinks from the others for the evening. They worked on the honor system. Clay didn't care that his brothers had no money. The fun was in the game and how it positioned them mentally, as it almost always got them onto the dance floor.

Number 4 didn't want to stand around watching and waiting, so her decision was easy. She turned to her closest friend, number 1, and initiated the role reversal.

"Suzanne, can you hold my drink and bag?"

Being a good sport, Suzanne filled her rarely occupied post with a smile. Number 4 turned back to Clay.

"Sure, I love this song!" she shouted over the Isley Brothers.

Clay smiled, grabbed her hand, and prepared to move well away from the clutches of purgatory. As he led her into the middle of the teeming masses, the crowd began raising their hands as directed by Rudy, singing along to his vocals.

Clay turned and faced her, leaning into her ear.

"What's your name?!"

He caught a whiff of her scent as his face grew familiar with her hair and neck.

"Carla!" she shouted into his ear.

He smiled, stepped back, offered a formal, brief bow, and then proceeded to lose himself in the song—smiling and singing and pantomiming along with Carla and all their fellow contortionists. The alcohol was doing its job. The music and crowd were carrying him along like a funambulist without a rope. More powerfully, there was a feeling of hope in the air.

He caught the eye of another girl moving beyond Carla's left shoulder. She had the widest, brightest, most utterly open smile, and her long black hair was parted in the middle then tucked behind her ears, hippie style. A few moist strands rebelled against the coiffure, running perpendicularly to her strong jaw line. She was a transcendent wild child, and her eyes laughed at Clay for an instant, before she pirouetted in time with the song, and was enveloped, along with her partner, by the crowd. Clay felt Carla's eyes on him and returned her smile. He wasn't a total lout. Filing the wild child away for the future, he returned his attention to his partner.

Now w-a-a-a-a-a-a--a-i-i-i-t a minute…!

Clay started slowing it down, preparing to get in his crouch. Carla was doing the same, which gave her big points in his book. Not unusually, his initial calculation, based purely on visual data, had been inaccurate. Carla's unfettered enthusiasm, song knowledge, and silky moves were rapidly moving her value up….

As the tempo quickened and Clay started rising in tandem with it, he felt someone bump him heavily from behind. He turned to see a familiar, bouncing Afro partnered with what seemed to be a lithe, pale, leather-dressed creature with pink hair, raccoon-painted eyes, and a studded choker. Clay (unlike Paul) wasn't familiar with the Punk movement and hence found himself, to some extent, mesmerized. As he continued appreciating the contrasting optics, Paul, winking at him, came in for another laughing collision then pogoed away.

Earlier, Paul had been rejected by five girls with varying shades of pigment lighter than his. They had all dressed like girls from his high school—denim below, polyester above—and he had hoped to gain some acceptance from the familiar. After the pattern became obvious, he decided to switch strategies. He had seen his pink-haired angel standing alone, frowning at the scene, and he moved in for rejection number six.

"Would you like to dance?"

She slowly turned and inspected him. Her name was Robyn, and she was from Dunedin, just up the coast. All night she had been waiting for the DJ to play "My Sharona," as something was happening in the music scene and it spoke to her strongly. The Knack had broken through the Disco barrier, exposing the Billboard masses to a new sound from London. She embraced this musical wave with conviction: she was one of the few, lonely, local punks. Her frown changed first to a smirk then to a smile as she recognized another misfit. She grabbed his hand and pulled him into the vortex.

You been so good to me…

Keno was struggling, or winning, depending on your perspective. The first few rejections had made him self-conscious, and he was starting to worry about how stupid his hair looked without his hat. This week had also brought an attack of the zits, and he had spent too long in front of the bathroom mirror counterattacking with his fingers and other, more barbaric tools. He was sure his face looked like a swollen red moonscape, and he blamed the whole self-inflicted mess on his unfair genetic inheritance. He was certain that adolescent skin afflictions violated the limit on universal pain and suffering. In short, he felt unattractive; hence he was losing his buzz. He worried about the slippery slope to purgatory, and his anxiety increased as the Isley Brothers progressed. *Everyone who wants to dance is already on the floor*, he thought, pitying himself. *What's the point of everyone watching all these women reject me? I'm a troll.*

Just then the large body of Patrick Bowman appeared behind him.

"Not dancing?" he yelled into Keenan's ear.

Keenan shrugged in response, trying to imply his current predicament was voluntary. Patrick read him like a book, noting the dejection.

"Air guitar coming up!" Patrick shouted. "I hope to see y'all up there!"

He smiled, nodding his head to the beat, and prepared to resume his patrol.

As Trick was about to be carried away by the current of people, an attractive Latina appeared in his path. She reached up with an open palm. Bowman gently slapped her hand and just as gently grabbed her wrist, redirecting her between he and Keno.

The brunette looked up at him with laughing eyes, "Oooooh Poppy, I love it when you're rough!"

She continued teasing the bouncer, pushing her hip into his.

Patrick rolled with her, placing his large hand on the small of her back. They were good friends.

"Gina, this here's my bud Keno. He's good people, but is kinda scared of drop-dead gorgeous women like you. Could you give a few minutes to charity and take him for a spin?"

She looked skeptically at Keno and then turned back to Trick. Keenan looked pathetic with little effort. She needed more encouragement.

"Give him a little taste of what it's like to roll with the beautiful people?"

She remained noncommittal. Bowman raised the stakes with a grin.

"It could prevent a suicide…?"

Gina opened her effervescent smile, grabbed Keno's hand, and pulled him to the floor.

"Come on, charity boy, let's prevent a tragedy," she yelled back at him, wondering about the number and severity of this cute boy's flaws.

"Thanks! I'm Keenan!" he shouted, his spirits elevating rapidly as he bounced after Gina like a puppy.

Gina looked back at him again. "Just don't fall in love, charity boy. I got enough problems."

Gina kept with her tough, working-girl persona, knowing from experience that she was really coaching herself. Keno couldn't hear her over the sound system, but smiled back knowingly as if he could.

A little bit louder now, A LITTLE BIT LOUDER NOW…

The Isleys were winding up for their final delivery, and the crowd was frothing in joyful communion. All three Barton brothers had oriented themselves towards the middle of the floor, carving out some breathing room to allow for freedom of interpretation to the iconic song. They acknowledged each other's presence without being obvious, and all three felt that their partners seemed to have potential as nonplatonic, later-night companions.

As the song wound down, the DJ asked for any air guitar competitors to report to the stage in the roped-off area behind his booth. One of the go-go dancers had been sprung from captivity, and she stood with her hand raised, behind the booth, indicating the gathering venue. As couples separated and left the floor, the Bartons were left looking at each other. Their partners, not wanting to appear overeager, offered hurried thanks—and then politely abandoned them.

Keenan looked at Paul. "Pablo, you gotta do the air guitar contest!"

Paul smiled, still glowing from the Isley Brothers and his Punk girlfriend, and now the attention from Keno.

"Did you see that chick's hair?!"

"What the fuck is an air guitar contest?"

Clay had been out of the cultural loop for eighteen months.

"I didn't know they actually had contests," said Paul.

He had taken guitar lessons in Houston when he was younger, but when they moved to Florida the lessons hadn't been a priority. He had a reputation among a small group of friends and family for imitating classic Rock guitar solos, including doing a wicked Hendrix.

"A hundred bucks prize money, bruddah. You'll crush it!"

"What the fuck are y'all talking about?" Clay was still uninformed.

Keno had been introduced to air guitar competitions during his freshman year at college.

"Air guitar, Clay. You go up on stage and act like you're playing lead guitar to a record they play."

"But you have no guitar?"

"Correct. You pantomime playing an absent guitar."

"And the crowd votes for the winner by cheering?" guessed Paul.

"Yep, or maybe they have judges…or both."

"Got it." Clay paused briefly for thought. "Uh, yeah, Paul's definitely doing that."

The brothers convinced Paul to climb on to the stage and enter the contest. Patrick Bowman was assisting Go-Go Girl in writing down names and taking money.

"Five bucks to enter. We'll start in thirty minutes. Be back here ready to go," Trick said sternly.

The group enthusiasm slowed significantly at the speed bump of the entry fee.

"Entry fee? That's bullshit," Keno said to his brothers.

"Total scam," said Paul, relieved to be off the hook.

Clay looked at Paul and considered his skills. He looked at Trick.

"How many judges?"

"Three."

He reached into his pocket and grabbed a wad of bills. He found a five and placed it on Bowman's clipboard.

"Paul Barton."

The bouncer wrote down the name, kept the money, and repeated the instructions.

"Back here in thirty minutes. Sharp."

Clay grabbed Paul and hustled him off the stage, hurrying him towards the entry. Keno followed closely behind. When they reached the lobby, Clay turned to Keno.

"Go out to the car, and bring back Jose. Haul ass. We'll get Pablo prepped."

From the lobby, Paul watched Keno rush out the front door. Clay started thinking about what they were going to do with all the prize money.

CHAPTER 7—

Air Guitar

Paul huddled with a small group around the DJ booth. This would be his third and final performance of the night and he was pulsating with adrenaline…and Jose Cuervo. Keno had smuggled in the bottle of tequila, and the brothers had found a secluded area away from the stage to augment the youngest's blood alcohol level. Paul figured he had ingested the equivalent of four shots over the last thirty minutes and was delicately balancing on the wall that separates *really lit* from *totally fucked up*. Standing still without swaying was hard, but once he started moving things generally came together.

Twenty-eight people had signed up for the contest—twenty-three guys and five girls. The first round had consisted of four groups of seven; one contestant from each group moved on to the semis. The DJ had made special two-minute edits of songs that emphasized lead guitar, and these were the recordings he played while the contestants competed. The three judges were Trick, the DJ, and Go-Go Girl. They had the final say—with considerable input from the crowd.

The first round song was Led Zeppelin: "(Been a Long Time Since I) Rock and Roll." Paul had easily won his heat. Two of the competitors in his group had never even heard of Jimmy Page. It was a little frenetic, with seven people battling for stage position; but for once, Paul's appearance allowed him to separate from the crowd in an advantageous way.

In the semis, each of the four remaining contestants performed in succession, with the order determined by random draw. The semifinal track was "Walk this Way." For years Paul had been mimicking Joe Perry performing Aerosmith's rollicking Rock poem—and, unsurprisingly, he nailed his performance and moved on to the finals. The white audience loved seeing a black kid playing

56

classic Rock and Roll. The irony of the situation wasn't lost on Paul—white people cheering a black kid who was imitating the moves of other white dudes who had co-opted the music of black Blues musicians. Life imitating art imitating…whatever. Whoever said life was fair?

Coincidentally, the other finalist was the raven-haired hippie chick who had caught Clay's eye earlier. Her name was Jessica, which brought about conflicting emotions in Clay. Not only was she beautiful, but she had a charisma that captivated the audience. Her fierce energy belied gender stereotypes. She had somehow smuggled a beat-up, felt, cowboy hat that had made her stand out even more. It also served to widen her appeal to include those with redneck tendencies. Her smile alone captured half the audience.

The two finalists got to pick the songs to which they would perform. Jessica got her first choice—"Barracuda" by Heart. Paul asked for "Foxy Lady" or "Purple Haze" by Hendrix…and the DJ came up empty.

The brothers were speechless. Keno directed his vitriol at the disc monkey.

"No Hendrix at an air guitar contest? What the fuck?"

The record honcho shrugged; this wasn't his first rodeo. As a younger man he had played a pretty good lead guitar in a regional band that had had some modest success, and now he was stuck spinning records and judging stupid contests to pay the bills. He felt the whole air guitar phenomenon was beneath him.

"What about 'Johnny B. Goode,' by Chuck Berry?" asked Paul.

Clay nodded vigorously at the choice. "Yeah, yeah, yeah…fuck yeah! If this guy doesn't have it…"

Clay's greed was starting to turn to fear as he worried about the Nazi DJ and his records.

"Ummm, I think…yep, here it is," said the DJ, pulling the disc from his collection.

He admired the black kid's taste.

"That'll work," encouraged Keno.

Their father, Aloysius, had been a huge Chuck Berry fan. The boys had grown up listening to his records and watching video clips of the guitar virtuoso.

"I'll do that," said Paul.

The DJ placed the record next to "Barracuda."

Jessica lost the toss. She went first. The finalists would both perform the full songs they had chosen. Paul realized that maintaining crowd interest for longer than two minutes would be tough. He would need more than what he had already shown in the first two rounds. He was hoping he could pack as much drama into his nearly three-minute window as possible; his brothers had decided props would be helpful, and had somehow wrangled a vest, a necktie, and some sunglasses from the crowd.

Trick ordered Paul and his brothers off of the stage. Then he grabbed the microphone and announced the final rules and format. He introduced "Jessica, from Tombstone, Arizona" as the first finalist then asked her to step to the front of the stage when she was ready to begin. About thirty seconds later, after some yogic breathing and a nod to the DJ, she burst into the spotlight; the DJ set free the galloping guitar riff of the Heart classic. For over four minutes Jessica entertained the crowd as the diamond needle of the turntable's stylus converted the Wilson sisters' studio-recorded vibrations into electric pulses: Heart's priceless soul poured forth from the vinyl. The lyrics were reputedly about record execs behaving like predatory fish, but no one cared about the words. Jessica might have overdone the high kicks, but it was such a classic Nancy Wilson move that she kept returning to it. It didn't hurt that her denim miniskirt barely covered her racy knickers. She could feel the energy from the crowd, and she was flying over the stage purely from the high of the moment. She ended with a classic leaping arch, her feet nearly kicking her head in an iconic profile that brought her raucous applause. Doffing her hat, she bowed and then looked up, revealing her 100-watt smile. A harsh critic would've noticed a few lulls, but all in all it was a passionate performance.

While Jessica began winding down, Paul was getting ready at the confluence of stage, dance floor, and rear wall. His brothers were in attendance. He had removed his shirt and replaced it with the red velvet vest and loose necktie. The sunglasses finished his makeover; they would provide his eyes a bit of relief from the bright lights. The older brothers were topping him off with liquid courage just as silky voiced Go-Go Girl announced:

"Our next finalist, Paul, from Clearwater!"

The youngest brother swallowed a final hit of the fiery liquid, filled his lungs with a deep breath, bounded up the stairs, and stepped into the stage lights. Remnants of tequila swam in his mouth, and his stomach was very close to turning rebellious. With a lucky synchronization, he caught the opening riffs of Chuck Berry's electric Gibson just right, dropping his strumming hand from above his head down—and onto—the imaginary strings. He let his unthinking brain take over as he channeled Chuck Berry and stepped into the warm embrace of the music. Over the next two minutes and forty-one seconds he preened, duck walked, did the splits….as he aced his transitions, his momentum began to build. His final move was spontaneous. He was in the zone, felt he could fly, and the crowd was with him. Mr. Berry was urging him on…

Go! Go Johnny Go, Go, Go!

Paul did an about-face, and, in time with the music, ran twenty feet to the back wall of the stage, took two steps up the vertical wall, and, as the spotlight barely caught up to him, performed a backflip and stuck the landing. Taking just a split second to reorient himself, he spun one hundred and eighty degrees and duckwalked back to stage center. His sunglasses hadn't budged. He ripped into the last chords in a standing soul arch, ending with a deep bow.

The crowd went bonkers.

As he looked out over the sea of upraised faces a rush of inborn chemicals joined the tequila in his bloodstream, pushing him to new levels of elation.

So this is what it feels like to be a rock star!

The judges were unanimous: Jessica was good…but Paul was sublime. The usual histrionics followed. Jessica was gracious in defeat, curtsying to the new champion as the two brothers bounced up the stairs just in time to watch Trick count out five twenties and place them into Paul's hand. As runner-up, Jessica was entitled to twenty-five bucks.

After a few minutes of congratulatory pomp, the DJ started to once again feed the crowd. It was 11:30—time to pander. He decided to play some of the new dreck that the record companies were flogging. He was convinced this stuff was just a fad, but he felt anything was better than more Bee Gees.

Robyn's ears perked up as she heard the sound system pouring forth the opening double-time drumbeat of the Knack's "My Sharonna." She saw Paul and his brothers pushing through the crowd about ten feet away; they were heading to the bar, but they didn't notice her. Too many people were closing in on Paul, congratulating him and basking in his brief celebrity. Robyn had enjoyed dancing with the new champion, but she wasn't the groupie type, and she definitely wasn't going to miss any more of the Knack. She joined the two other punks who were already bouncing on the floor. Go-Go Girl was hoisted back into her cage, and Patrick Bowman returned to his post in the front lobby. The DJ surveyed the scene with a smug look of amusement.

CHAPTER 8

The Spoils

Paul was faced with a conundrum. He needed to keep moving or the tequila would catch up with him, but everywhere he turned one of his new "friends" was offering him a free drink with the implicit understanding that the star-of-the-moment would favor them with his company..

"Hey, it's Hendrix!"

"Hey, Chuckie B., come join us!"

"It's the air guitar guy! Let me buy you a drink!"

The youngest Barton brother loved the attention, but he had to be careful: he didn't want to cross the threshold where his system could no longer tolerate the alcohol—a circumstance that would turn his world immediately dark and likely require a voluntary or involuntary commitment to regurgitation in order to prevent acute alcohol poisoning.

Attractive women were making themselves subtly—and not so subtly—available.

"You were great. Wanna dance?"

"I love the way you move. Can you do that between the sheets?"

Paul had never received such adulation. Like good bodyguards, Clay and Keno stayed close, while their charge just smiled and tried to stay on his feet. They were all enjoying their quarter hour of fame.

At around midnight, the trio found themselves dancing with three uptown babes from Clearwater Beach. Keno knew them each distantly, but Paul's recent fame had brought these heretofore out-of-reach hotties into their orbit. As if on queue, the DJ started caressing the crowd with 10cc's "I'm Not in Love," and all three girls accepted the intimacy of a slow dance. Towards the end of the song, Clay decided to make his move. His mild, exploratory grinding was not met with resistance.

"Do y'all wanna head back to the beach?"

His girl, Kim, smiled seductively, "What do you have in mind?"

"We've got a cooler full of ice and beer. I hear the grunion are running?"

Be quiet, big boys don't cry, big boys don't cry…

Kim didn't drink beer but didn't let that detail and the weak proposition derail the moment. The girls were slumming it with the Barton boys, and Kim was curious about seeing where this odd interaction would lead them. She knew about Clay Barton by his reputation: not lacking in confidence…or ability. At least the numbers worked, she noted: three a side—no one had to sit out for the team; and she was pretty sure he found her attractive—she just wasn't sure how far she wanted to take it. Clay wasn't known as the monogamous type, a detail that didn't align with her nascent, somewhat subconscious hunt for an appropriate husband. There wasn't a palpable sense of urgency…more like a whisper of an agenda in the far recesses of Kim's mind. Feminism wasn't a mental construct she yet felt comfortable with, but as her thoughts on gender stereotypes developed, she felt inclined to periodically notice and redirect her matrimonial biases. A combination of sexual equality, alcohol, and hormones started elbowing her prudish sensibilities into the background. She weighed whether or not she wanted to be a notch on someone's belt.

Fuck that! she suddenly thought. *If I want, he'll be a notch on my belt!*

To Clay's delight, Kim continued to offer limited resistance to his advances.

"We're all staying at Kat's house at the beach, and her parents are out of town. Maybe, if y'all can behave yourselves, we can all party over there. Let me ask Kat."

Kat was vacillating between satisfaction and amusement: she had captured the hero of the night. In fact, at this moment his mouth was nestled tightly against her neck; she also could feel his enthusiasm pressing against her lower stomach. She felt comfortably in the driver's seat. Unlike the boys at college, this one was remarkably sweet.

I'm not in love,
so don't forget it…

She and her longtime friends had split two bottles of her parents' 1974 Chalone on the drive out from the beach. She had planned on not drinking too much, as she had been fighting a persistent yeast infection, but the power of the moment and the quality of the California Chardonnay had weakened her resolve. Later, while she was flirting with the gorgeous bartender in green board shorts, he had comped her two Long Island Iced Teas. She was feeling fine, with good options abounding, and wondered what her sorority sisters up at Vanderbilt would think if they could see her now. All three of her sexual partners to date had been white. She had never even kissed a black guy, and this black guy—"Paul from Clearwater"—was just a baby. He was Keno Barton's YOUNGER brother.

How did that work? she asked herself.

She decided she didn't have to make up her mind about anything right now. Her parents were gone, her friends all seemed to be having fun, and school was hundreds of miles away. Thanks to Paul she was a tangential center of attention and, she had to admit, he could definitely move. She entertained an idea, just to see how it felt rolling inside her head.

Maybe time for a new experience?

Kim, Kat, and Michelle gathered as 10cc faded away. Emerging from the huddle, Kat was confident she had good news for the boys.

"Why don't y'all follow us in your car to my house? You guys provide the beer and we'll provide the attitude?"

Everyone nodded in affirmation, with the boys having a little more trouble masking their enthusiasm. The girls felt safe that if for some reason they changed their minds, they could lose the guys during the long drive home.

"We're driving my Scirocco. Burnt orange."

"What's your address in case we get lost?" Keno asked.

"If y'all get lost then we've badly misjudged you!" chided Kim.

"*Listo!*" said Clay, accepting the challenge and choosing not to reciprocate with a description of their wagon.

"What?"

"Let's go," he said, "we'll follow you."

As the three couples walked through the lobby in various amorous combinations, Patrick caught Paul's eye and mouthed "You're welcome" with a big smile. He simultaneously handed Keno his hat. "Have a great evening folks," he sang out, as his job prescribed. "Thanks for coming!"

He watched the six, young, hormone-saturated backsides as they exited the club. The buoyant brothers were on a roll, and the smell of anticipation was in the air.

CHAPTER 9—

Dante

Paul was the first of the group to exit into the warm, humid night. The parking lot was littered with groups committed to prolonging the evening's charade—anything to mask the soul-numbing reality of their daytime routines.

In his mind, Paul was the reigning conqueror of Bone Daddy's, but his mood had passed a zenith. He was still feeling good, but it was more of a mellow contentment than the pyrotechnics that had inhabited his conscience at the peak of his air guitar performance.

Floating down the steps, holding Kat's hand, was when he first sensed the menace. To his right, just a few feet away, stood an older, dark-haired guy, probably in his early thirties. Heavyset, with a mustache, not short, not tall, and apparently with a small group of three women and one other man. Both men were wearing sport coats over dress shirts, with a pair of pleated khakis below.

Could be brothers, thought Paul.

Mustache was delivering an intense, up-close monologue to a younger woman who seemed to be open for business. The guy had his two large paws on the woman's shoulders.

What is it with these scumbags? wondered Paul.

The newly crowned champ was in a different mental place than he had been when he earlier saw the abuse of the girl in the red dress. At that time he was hesitant, unsure of his judgment, and lacking in confidence. Now, after winning the air guitar contest, he was full of bravado and righteous tendencies; he was the king of the realm—and one of his subjects was being mistreated. He began to feel a nascent sense of *noblesse oblige*.

Perhaps a subtle intervention would remind the man to corral his more brutish tendencies? he speculated.

Just then Mustache raised the intensity of his lecture, took his rough paws off of the young woman's shoulders, and placed the left one on her throat. He started pointing his right paw at her face, intent on getting his message across.

"No, Gary, please…" The woman was mumbling, pleading, looking down at the man's feet.

With the right paw he delivered a short, open-handed slap.

"Fuckin' lyin' bitch."

"What the…?"

Paul's vision flashed red, filled with rage as he released the grip on his date's hand.

What happened next occurred so quickly that to this day Clay's recollection is a bit of a blur. As he exited the lobby with Kim, he was a few steps behind Paul; but he noticed an intense, stocky guy, a few feet from Paul, slapping some slutty-looking girl. Paul immediately exploded in a ball of fury, unloading a haymaker from right field that blindsided the mustachioed man, knocking him to the dirt. This action brought forth an immediate, violent change in tone as the proximate, high-heeled women released a bevy of screams. Clay's senses went on red alert.

The other sport coat jumped at Paul, knocking them both to their knees. Clay saw Mr. Mustache, bleeding from above his eye, reach his right hand inside his sport coat—towards what appeared to be a leather holster; the soldier's instincts took over. As the revolver began to be revealed, Clay was already diving. Just before he crashed into the prone man, he heard him try to enunciate.

"Pa-lease!"

As the crown of Clay's head came down on the gunman's temple, his forearm pinned his right wrist to the ground. He simultaneously heard his opponent groan, felt a slackening in the man's resistance, and saw a stiletto-bound foot kick the gun away.

In the background, Clay heard more screaming. He saw people scattering in all directions. Through the confused tumult he felt a trickle of blood run down from his scalp. Strong hands hauled him to his feet and whispered in his ear to run. In his peripheral vision, he thought he had seen Keno knock the other man down, pull Paul to his feet, and urge him to move.

"Let's Go! Go!"

Clay saw the other man reach inside his coat.

Running for their lives, Keno took off towards the car with Paul stumbling after him. Clay ran from the gun, ducking behind the warehouse where the old loading docks fronted a canal feeding into Tampa Bay. Not sure how many people he was facing, how heavily they were armed, or what their tactics were, he just knew that he and his brothers had assaulted two men who had guns. The pathway behind the docks was sparsely lit and dead-ended into a cyclone fence topped with aging razor wire. Clay searched the detritus for a place to hide, saw a stack of boxes and pallets near the back fence, and ran behind them. Knowing he was cornered, he prayed for a few more undetected moments while he quickly and quietly removed his shirt and shoes, and stuffed them under an old stack of crates. He took his wallet from his Levi's back pocket and lowered himself over the edge of the dock and into the warm, brackish water. Listening intently, he thought he heard people approaching from the parking lot, but no one materialized. He used his free hand to pull himself under the wooden dock, trying to avoid the barnacles and rusting hardware as he reached down with his feet. He half expected to feel a silty ooze, but the bottom stayed undisturbed. Finding some planking that had pulled away from a joist about a foot above the water, he jammed his wallet into a corner crevice under the dock. More warm blood trickled down his forehead as he took three deep breaths, pushed the thought of alligators and sharks from his head, and submerged himself. Working his way up current, parallel to the docks, he quickly circumvented the cyclone fence barrier while surfacing every sixty seconds or so to confirm his heading and reinflate his lungs. He was silent and invisible as he quickly worked his way around to the other end of the warehouse, avoiding any light that might reveal his presence.

Both gunmen—Gary Donovan and Dante (Dan) DaVito—were now on their feet. They were more angry than injured. Gary had a mild concussion—but he had experienced much worse during his infantry stint in Viet Nam.

DaVito was trying to piece together what had just happened, knowing he would be responsible for filing a report....

Working undercover on our first assignment, we're trying to gather intel on the exploding cocaine trade in our jurisdiction and had been in the process of interrogating some prostitutes when some black guy sucker punched Gary. When we tried to identify ourselves as police officers and make an arrest, some other perps jumped in.

Now they were pissed, and looking for revenge. They needed to set a tone on the streets that allowed them to do their jobs and keep the low-level riffraff respectful. Gary had learned this the hard way in the jungles overseas. Being nice to strangers had consistently gotten his friends killed; he had come to realize that a certain class of people only understood force. *Well, it's time for the local scum to meet the new Sheriff,* he thought.

They headed after Paul and Keno, knowing that the parking lot was enclosed on three sides by an old chain-link fence. As they moved past the entryway for Bone Daddy's, Dan showed his badge and yelled at the doorman to call 911 and ask for backup. Patrick Bowman had already moved back into the main room, losing himself in the crowd. *Just doin' my job patrolling the bar and dance floor,* he thought, practicing the line to himself. He was already mentally working through his story in the unlikely case that they questioned him about his involvement in the fight. He knew these cops by reputation, and they were to be avoided.

Lagging behind Keno, Paul felt like he was running in his sleep, as he couldn't make his legs move quickly enough. His heart was pounding in his chest when he heard a voice yell out from behind.

"Police! We know you're in here. We have dogs." Officer DaVito was bluffing. "You will be caught. Give yourselves up, and save us all a lot of time."

Keno was getting farther ahead of his little brother as he was out of his mind with fear, had no idea where his siblings were, and kept making random cuts between parked cars. Paul briefly lost sight of him and then spotted a denim-clad figure climbing over the fence at the rear of the lot. The tequila was really impacting the air guitar king as he finally reached the barrier Keno had just scaled. He placed hands and shoes onto the woven, diamond-shaped, galvanized wire and tried to join his emancipated brother, who was running into the tree line fifty yards beyond. The alcohol was now his enemy. His legs and arms refused to generate the necessary strength and coordination to pull him up. After several aborted efforts, he slumped, defeated, against the bottom of the fence. Listening to the cops, maybe a hundred feet away and closing, he forced himself to start moving along the fence line, ducking down into a crouch. He was suffocating from terror, mind racing as the wolves closed in. Up ahead he saw an old battered, pick-up truck; crawled over to the back of the vehicle; climbed into the bed; and hid under an old tarp covering a bunch of yard clippings. His heart felt like it would explode, and he thought he might vomit. Some voices made their way into his consciousness, and he tried to still his breathing. He didn't know it, but one of his white high-tops wasn't fully covered by the tarp.

By the time Clay made it to the other side of the warehouse, he felt comfortable no one was following him. He had stayed towards the middle of the canal in about six feet of water. Periodically he would kick an old wooden piling or piece of submerged, discarded, metal junk; but in general he was safe in the water. He found a dark spot in the weeds where he could slide up onto the bank and observe the back of the parking lot where they had left the Chevy Malibu.

What he saw next sickened him. About twenty-five yards away, the two men had Paul.

"Resisting arrest, huh, Sambo?"

Dante was dragging Paul by his collar through a pool of vomit, while Gary pointed his gun at his head. The kid's hands were cuffed behind his back.

The truth was starting to dawn on Clay. These were cops.

The peace officers had found Paul hiding, barely covered, in the back of the old pick-up, and had decided to teach him a lesson. It hadn't occurred to them that when Paul attacked he didn't know they were cops.

Clay had interacted with plenty of law enforcement professionals, and in his experience, most were pretty good guys—but these two were different. They had little empathy for their captive and were displaying a sadistic streak that chilled him.

Fucking bastards! he swore silently.

The oldest brother began weighing his options. As Dante pulled Paul to his feet, Clay immediately decided he had to try to stop the beating: his brother was in bad shape and could barely stand. As he started crawling through the grass, his peripheral vision caught movement to his left. He saw Keno moving out of the tree line in a stealthy crouch, about thirty yards away.

Finally a break, Clay thought.

If he could get Keno's attention, they might be able to come up with a strategy to rescue Paul. They would at least have numbers. Before Clay could think of his next move, flashing red and blue lights imposed themselves on the setting. A police car pulled into the parking lot. Keno immediately dropped to his belly.

"Lucky prick, saved by the bell," whispered Donovan into Paul's ruptured eardrum.

"Don't worry, we'll go a few more rounds at the station," said Dante on the other side, as they dragged him to the police car.

CHAPTER 10

Crumbling

Elizabeth Barton didn't understand what was happening. One moment she's happily drinking sangria with her book club friends, and the next she's being shaken awake by her boys at two a.m. The interruption was made that much more offensive because one or both of them stank of tidal marsh methane. Even though she was barely awake, and despite the smell, Liz realized immediately that Paul was missing. With a feeling somewhere between surprise and alarm, she wondered what could have happened to the seventeen-year-old. Paul was the sweet one, a boy she had grown to love as her own. He was respectful, never got into trouble, earned good reviews from his teachers, and hadn't crashed the car or impregnated anyone. She couldn't even recall him breaking a bone.

During those days, she had a standing, clearly communicated rule not to bail the boys out for at least twenty-four hours. This parenting wisdom, admittedly somewhat antiquated, had been passed down through generations of Suttons with the idea that some of the best learning experiences occurred within the four walls of a cell, where patient contemplation could be realized with few distractions. But tonight there was also an unusual vibe. In the past, the boys had tried to downplay the magnitude of their trouble, with phrases like, "no problem" and "no big deal" tossed around freely. Tonight they were serious and conveyed a sense of urgency. This was not the usual, small town shenanigans.

"I'll meet you in the kitchen in fifteen minutes," she said. "Oh my god, one of you absolutely reeks to high heaven."

The boys nodded, affirming the former statement and ignoring the latter.

"I'm sorry, Mom," said Clay in a moment of remorse.

"It's okay Clay. Get out of those wet, foul-smelling clothes," she said, biting her tongue.

What she really wanted was to scream, *What the fuck is wrong with you imbeciles! Thoughtless savages! I should have had you all castrated at birth!*

Initially, the police logs showed no record of Paul having been in police custody earlier that night. This lack of documentation was particularly troubling to the Barton threesome as they stood discussing the matter uncertainly in the precinct station. Elizabeth questioned the boys' sobriety while the boys questioned the cops' integrity. Paranoid visions of their baby brother being fed to the alligators, and the accompanying police conspiracy to hide the incident, were fanning a growing outrage. Of course these mental images did nothing to assuage the brothers' already guilty consciences. They finally started making headway when Keenan remembered that the only identification Paul had on him was a fake Wisconsin driver's license that bore the name John Carlos.

The precinct ledger revealed there had been a black male, eighteen years old, identified as Carlos, J. He had been brought in at 1:23 a.m. According to the police reports, he had assaulted an officer and resisted arrest. He had tripped while trying to escape custody at the police station, hit his head, and been transported to the hospital at 2:57 a.m.

"Nurse?" asked Elizabeth. "We're looking for room forty-seven?"

"Halfway down the hall, on your left."

"Thank you."

When they walked into the room, Elizabeth started to cry. They had finally found him at Tampa Community Hospital, in the indigents ward, sharing a small room with a woeful-looking derelict suffering through delirium tremens. The dignity provided by a dividing curtain was in absentia. Paul's beautiful facial features had been rearranged into an asymmetric, discolored, swollen mask; the two black eyes (one eye was swollen shut) were still positioned over a broken nose, but in a way that compelled one to look away. That misshapen nose crookedly occupied the space over a swollen, split lower lip. He was conscious, but not alert. He was handcuffed to the bed, but there was no need for restraints, as Paul was barely breathing.

The difficulty in locating him had resulted from Paul being driven to three different medical centers before finally being admitted at Tampa Community. The Sisters of Mercy (and Saint Mary's) had apparently hit their weekend limit for impoverished John Does of color. The ward policeman responsible for Paul's custody had three other captives in similar nonambulatory states. He was downstairs getting a refill of his coffee.

It took four hours before Elizabeth was able to get a diagnosis from a doctor.

The ER physician had developed an air of competent resignation, which he found useful in cases like this. He had already had two patients die on his watch that morning, one from a gunshot wound and one from a motorcycle accident. Notifying families of bad news was always hard, but at least this patient was still alive.

"I'm sorry to be the one to tell you this, Mrs. Barton, but it appears your son has spinal cord damage between cervical vertebrae six and seven."

The questions came pouring out from the Barton trio: What did the ER physician mean "spinal cord damage"? How did the damage happen? When would Paul get better? Is his brain okay?

"I think it's just a matter of time before we see improvement with his facial cuts and bruising," the physician explained. "We reset his nose, so that should be fine. His eardrum was ruptured; that should heal on its own after a few weeks if he keeps it dry. He has some bruised ribs, but nothing broken. We didn't see any evidence of cerebral bleeding in the images, so his brain should be fine. Perhaps just a small concussion."

The doctor paused to make sure the family was following along; he didn't want to repeat himself, as there were other pressing needs. It was early Sunday morning in a big urban trauma center and business was brisk. Looking quickly at each of them directly in their eyes, he continued when confident they were paying attention.

"As to cause, we were told he attacked two police officers in a rage, and they were forced to take repeated measures to restrain him. The reports indicate that at one point he tried to escape, tripped, and hit his head. The trauma that your boy sustained would be consistent with that report, but of course I'm not in a position to assess the validity."

As the doctor relayed the police report, Keno and Clay's emotions steadily morphed from inquisitive, to disbelief, and finally to outrage. Their mouths set and their heads began shaking back and forth with denial and indignation. The doctor briefly paused to again refer to his notes.

"There were concerns he may have been on some form of stimulant? We checked his blood for PCP, methamphetamine, and cocaine, but found no evidence of those drugs. However, his blood alcohol was quite elevated at .22. Can you tell us anything that might help us treat him?"

"Total fuckin' bullshit," burst out Clay, who couldn't take the lies anymore.

"Clay! Language!" Elizabeth did not want to be identified as part of the great unwashed.

The doctor had already made up his mind regarding with whom he was conferring, given the demographic jumble.

"They handcuffed and beat him in the parking lot. He couldn't even defend himself. We saw it!" added Keenan.

The doc realized he needed to tread carefully.

"I'm a doctor, not a lawyer, and I'm not qualified to substantiate the police report. I can say that I'm sorry, and we're doing our best to help your young man."

Clay and Keno remained incensed.

"They're lying Mom," pleaded Keno. "We have to do something."

Elizabeth shushed her boys; she was frustrated with their naivete. It was obvious to her that they were angry and hungry for a fight, but in her mind they had put Paul in this predicament, and now they wanted to use the same strategies to try to make things right. She asked the doctor for a moment, and then grabbed both of them by the arm and gently led them to a family huddle a few feet away. Reaching deep for a few remnants of patience and strength, she proceeded to lecture.

"Listen to me, both of you…I believe you, but this isn't about truth…this isn't a John Wayne movie…bad things can happen to good people. You think you have the truth on your side? In my experience, when power fights the truth, the truth ends up losing. You want justice? You want to go to war with the police? You'll end up next to your brother, or worse. You want revenge? By fighting the system? You'll be squished like bugs. This is what power does; we think of it as wrong, they think of it as expedient. We're just collateral damage. Clay, you thought this stuff only happens in Panama?" she asked rhetorically while staring at the boys.

She could see their outrage was losing some steam.

Women have been dealing with this forever, she wanted to add but decided better of it.

She paused for a breath. This whole evening was sapping what little energy she had left. She was hoping to just get everyone home and get some much-needed sleep; she was sure they could then nurse Paul back to normal.

Testosterone, she thought, *the bane of my existence…*

She pulled her two offspring closer.

"Right now Paul is in a bad way. He needs us. Let's focus on that."

She looked squarely at both temporarily obedient boys and turned her remaining family back towards the doctor. She was happy that she had had the strength to deliver her speech and perhaps keep her remaining offspring from doing something stupid.

"When can we take him home?" she asked the doctor.

The doctor paused again, ignoring the question and assessing his audience's ability to absorb what was to come next.

"Unfortunately, damage to the spinal cord is irreversible. He will likely be wheelchair-bound for life."

Elizabeth turned a terrible shade of pale as her face started to reveal a deep pain that emanated from a profound place within. Her life began to crumble around her.

The doctor was in a hurry and continued. He had to get through this.

"He will likely have limited to no use of his limbs. Fortunately, he seems to be able to breathe without a ventilator. We will know more over the next few weeks. Sometimes these symptoms are a result of bruising to the cord, and we may get some recovery of functionality. We just don't know for sure."

The doctor's words were the final straw. Elizabeth was having a breakdown, and suddenly her body's resistance to gravity vanished along with her will to fight. Before anyone could grab her, she crumpled to the floor. Although still conscious, she felt finally and fully defeated.

1984 (Five Years Later)

East Coast,
Left Coast

CHAPTER 11—

A Bag of Bricks

Lola Collins didn't know how much more of this she could take—the mood swings, verbal abuse, high-risk behavior—and the worst was that he didn't seem to be getting any better. In fact, she thought he might be getting worse. Bending over the incoherent, intoxicated man, she noted his usual position: back against the wall, feet thrust out, head lolling forward against his chest.

"Come on baby, I got ya, put your arms around my neck."

The too-often repeated ritual had quickly lost any romantic appeal and was now just a pathetic chore.

"Come on, Keno, you can do it…I need your help, baby."

He was still in his business casual work clothes: Oxford button-down, tasseled loafers, some nice grey slacks she had picked out; he had forgotten his jacket somewhere…again.

"Come on, baby. It's cold. Let's get you home."

The fog had rolled in earlier that evening, and the famed damp chill of San Francisco had invaded the night and his corpselike body.

"Really cold…" he mumbled.

This was the third night this week she had had to search for him. The previous month he had been doing so well. Functional at work, some exercise to get the ya-yas out, coming home at a reasonable hour for dinner and some TV—a little quality time with Bill Cosby and Don Johnson, and maybe Bruce and Cybill later. They were even enjoying some fulfilling sex a few times a week—not too acrobatic, but still interesting. It almost felt normal, and the stability had allowed her to start to entertain thoughts of a family.

"That's right, baby, you can do it…one foot in front of the other."

He often ended up across from the Bank of America Building in the Financial District, next to a heat vent on California Street between Kearney and Montgomery. It was where his maternal grandfather had spent his first night as a young, west-Texas migrant during the Great Depression. The Scot-Texan had grown up to become a successful San Francisco businessman before passing away a few years earlier. Despite her efforts to understand it, the symbolism evaded her.

Keno was heavy, like a six-foot bag of bricks, and she was barely able to keep him upright and moving. She didn't know how he did it—his amazing energy levels. When he wasn't medicating with alcohol, he was chasing his demons over the surrounding hills and in the chilly waters of San Francisco Bay. Running, riding his bike, swimming, hoopin' on the public courts with the brothers. His job was suffocating him and he needed to compete physically; he called the skyscraper where he worked "a multistory, air-conditioned, steel, glass, and concrete coffin."

Neither one of them understood fully what was going on. She had heard about the night, nearly five years earlier, when Paul had been paralyzed, and she knew both Keno and his older brother Clay felt responsible, but she didn't understand how self-sabotage helped anything.

Her mother regularly advised her to move on.

"He's an alcoholic, sweetie. All you're doing is enabling him."

"Mom, you don't understand," Lola patiently replied. "He's getting better… he really is trying…he needs me."

"You've been saying that for nearly a year now. He needs to hit rock bottom before he'll change. We went through this with Uncle Fred. He needs to get treatment. He has to want to do it…it doesn't matter how much you want it."

When Lola finally got Keno to the Trooper, she opened the back door and dumped him in. Their dog, Quinn, immediately started wagging and licking.

She got into the Isuzu, buckled up her seatbelt, and left Keno to roll around in the back with the dog.

Right now I'm valuing Quinn more than my boyfriend. Maybe I should strap the dog in?

As Lola turned the keys to start the car, the Fine Young Cannibals burst from the radio speakers, singing their hit, "Johnny Come Home."

What is wrong, in my life, that I must get drunk every night?

"Tell me about it, Roland," Lola said to the band's gifted lead singer.

She drove to their tiny apartment in Cow Hollow. When she finally tucked him in it was two a.m.; she had to get up at six-thirty for work. The poor judgment inherent in her agreement to cover a friend's early breakfast shift was now obvious. Going deeper, she reviewed with self-admonishment her junior year academic slump (which had derailed her med school plans). She questioned the following year's impulsive and immediate exodus to California following graduation. Exhaustion and disappointment overwhelmed her as she fell asleep reexamining her commitment to Keenan.

CHAPTER 12—

Bronxville

"**P**lease pass the asparagus, Dad."

Lola was back in New York for a week, trying to recharge her batteries in the sanctuary of her childhood home. A graceful and permanent disengagement from Keenan was also teed up for thorough consideration. She loved him, but it was just becoming too much of a sacrifice, and she was already working through the details: the intricacies of a shared lease; where she might move; how she would tell Keenan. Of course, her mother was pregnant with advice.

Joining Lola for dinner the first night home were her mom, Madeline, and her youngest sister, Donna, who was a junior at Bronxville High. Kelly, the middle of the three sisters, was off playing soccer at Colorado College, trying to get through her junior year. Their neighbors, Abel and Natasha Hagopian, were also present. After watching the three Collins girls grow up next door to them and their three boys, they had a soft spot for Lola. Aside from the rare game of tree-house doctor during their preadolescent days, there hadn't been much romantic interplay between the two groups of children. The boys gravitated towards the chess club and the girls favored athletics. Later, the girls would question their judgment as it pertained to this period, but they had been obstinate in the moment.

They were just starting on their beef stroganoff when Lola's mom decided to reveal her agenda. Natasha was a practicing psychiatrist, and Maddy liked to use the doctor's credentials to buttress her parenting.

"Tasha, do you have any patients who are addicts?"

Dr. Hagopian was used to a lively dinner conversation at the Collins house, and well understood her role.

"Maddy, you know I can't speak about patients specifically, but, generally, I try to avoid treating addicts."

Leading her on like a lawyer would her star witness, Maddy continued her line of questioning.

"Interesting...and why is that?"

"Well, I think addiction is just too difficult. The recovery rates are below ten percent. I can't even begin to get at the underlying mental health issues if the subject insists on obfuscating them with alcohol or narcotics."

Lola's dad, Michael, was unaware of his wife's agenda, but still jumped in.

"Why do you think the recovery rates are so low? Do you have an opinion on the best strategy for curing alcoholics?"

"Addicts have problems controlling their impulses. They don't exhibit the ability to delay gratification. I suspect there is a genetic component to these behaviors for some, but it can be very hard to parse the nature from the nurture."

Donna took advantage of Natasha's pause for breath.

"Aren't these just losers with no self-control? Selfish people who can't see all the pain they are inflicting on those around them?"

She had developed most of her opinions on addiction from the television.

Tasha responded gently.

"Addiction can definitely cause a lot of pain and frustration to the friends, family, and colleagues of the addict. Not to mention health-care providers. I think this is a very complicated problem. We don't know why the recidivism rates are so high. As far as best strategies, we generally direct people to twelve-step programs like Alcoholics Anonymous."

Lola couldn't restrain herself any longer. The combination of her academic background and current relationship had given her plenty of food for thought. She rushed forth with the urgency of a passionate young person who knew she could lose the floor (to a member of her older audience) at any moment.

"What if we're looking at it all backwards? Missing the forest for the trees? What if the real problem is a lack of connection in a post-industrial world? Maybe we need, at a very deep, even spiritual level, the ancient rituals that effect an intimacy with other humans and that also include physical movement in a natural setting?"

The table was both intrigued and slightly taken aback. They weren't sure where Lola was headed, but they knew this wasn't part of Maddy's well-choreographed dinner. They decided to gently probe the upstart before denying her admission.

"What rituals?" Natasha asked.

Having been rejected at the family dinner table before, Lola knew she would need to defend her thesis if she wanted to continue sitting with the big kids. Worried that her views would be rejected as too rudimentary, she tried to encapsulate into a cogent view what she had been mentally cultivating.

"I don't know…the basics…hunting and gathering…preparing and eating food. Grooming rituals and rites of passage. Unstructured play. Quantity time with loved ones instead of quality time. All the stuff we did for most of the last one hundred thousand years."

Abel was a high school calculus teacher, and though he would never admit it, he had his doubts about the abilities of most women when it came to logic. This despite his wife's impressive credentials. Trying hard to minimize a patronizing tone, he took Lola's pause as a chance to continue the prodding.

"Well, that was a mouthful…an interesting mouthful. How would one prove your theory?"

The table's focus turned first to Lola and then rested on the expert.

Dr. Hagopian had been distracted. The Collins' little, untrained Jack Russell, Archimedes, had just started sniffing her under the table. "Archie" had made previous public advances on Barton guests that had proven to be quite awkward, and Natasha did not approve of her hostess's indifference to the dog's predatory sexual tendencies. She felt Maddy was overly indulgent when it came to the dog. The therapist had tried to deflect the terrier's infatuation with her shin, but he was persistent. Ninety-nine percent of her was annoyed, but one percent was intrigued. As she drank, the one percent grew…along with other things. She looked contemptuously over at her husband.

At least I have one suitor in my life who is persistent.

Gathering her wits, she redirected her attention to the conversation.

"Abel, you know we can't 'prove' things in the social sciences like you and your colleagues do in mathematics. You are also aware of my firmly held belief that that doesn't make psychiatry any less important than calculus as a discipline."

"Yes, Natty, I am aware. But as a person of science, how do you live with the blatant squishiness of it all?"

"Hmm…"

Dr. Hagopian pondered, her husband's attempts at derogation ignored, as she turned to Lola.

"Are you suggesting that addiction may result from purely environmental circumstances?"

Lola quickly explored that path mentally. She avoided the dead end.

"Not completely. But I am suggesting that we are animals that have evolved with an intense communion with nature…and, like all animals, over the millennia our minds and bodies have developed an intense interdependence. I guess I'm suggesting that for many, the current environment neglects our species' need for movement in nature with friends. We move from bed to chair to car seat to chair to bed. All in climate-controlled indoor environments."

Lola was now thinking specifically about her experience over the last year with Keenan, which, in conjunction with her college psychology and anthropology classes, had been fermenting into a theory that she was now trying to more fully develop.

"Could it be possible that we lose touch with our bodies, nature, intimate social connections, the essence of who we are as humans? We develop strategies…coping mechanisms…masking agents to…um…inure us to this loss of soul?"

Maddy felt a need to regain control of the conversation.

"An interesting theory, Lola, but where does that leave us in terms of getting addicts rehabilitated to the point where they can be functional members of society? We can't turn back the clock, we live in a modern world."

"I don't know, Mom. Maybe more movement in nature with friends? I'm talking about hiking or biking in the woods with friends, or swimming in the ocean with your kids, or any of an infinite number of permutations."

Maddy responded with a muted eye roll, and a dismissive comment:

"Why not 'humility, gratitude, and compassion'? Or, 'meditation, sleep, and yoga'? Or 'cannabis, vegetables, and oysters'? Or any other armchair platitude that helps push this month's self-help pablum to the top of the best-seller list?"

Feeling chastened, Lola bit her lip while gathering her thoughts. Retreat seemed a viable option, and she realized she hadn't given her theories enough consideration. Before she could withdraw into her stroganoff, her father spoke up. Michael had been intrigued by Lola's theory, and his daughter's "loss of soul" comment had resonated with him.

"What do you mean 'masking agents'?" he said.

Lola's encroaching feeling of failure was temporarily eliminated as she focused on explaining the nuance to her dad.

"You know, Dad. Cloaking devices, coping mechanisms, mind-altering substances, whatever term you want to use…so we can get by in our artificial worlds. We use a variety of…strategies and chemicals…to keep us habitually distanced from the sense of elemental disconnection and loss. Strategies that might allow us to fulfill our daily responsibilities."

Again, she was thinking about Keenan and his cravings, which seemed to swing between a drive for escape and a subsequent deep need for connection. Having consumed much of her energy for the last year, she hadn't even considered that their relationship, and Keenan's condition, might be unique; for her, it was the only observation she had.

She tried to continue without revealing her personal biases.

"All these masking agents…or maybe a better term is *coping mechanisms*… their regular use implies a necessity that I don't agree with…over time their regular use changes us…eventually we lose touch with our unadulterated mind and body…our…I don't know…essence. It even changes our brain chemistry. We rationalize that it's okay because everyone is doing it. Caffeine to wake up, alcohol to celebrate, pot to chill out, other drugs, food…look how fat we're all getting."

Abel looked down at his forty-inch waist, sat up a little straighter, and reached into his lap to reposition his linen napkin.

Maddy was still feeling contentious. She offered a matronizing smile.

"Are you suggesting we are all medicated, Orwellian somnambulists in a technologically distorted parody?"

Lola stared back hard, regaining some confidence and not intimidated by the syllables.

"Maybe…after all, it is 1984."

Realizing that she might be losing the high ground, Maddy resorted to the low road; she got close to making her point personal.

"It sounds like you are excusing alcoholics for their character weaknesses."

Lola had recovered her footing. She parried with sarcasm.

"Maybe *all* alcoholics are noncontrite, selfish, laze-abouts. Browbeating hasn't shown much efficacy so far, but why quit on something that's been so unproductive? Of course, turning addicts into pariahs makes it so easy for these people to talk about their problems and seek treatment."

Michael intervened on behalf of his wife.

"Lola, that's not fair. "

Abel had regrouped. He had recently been coerced into joining his wife in a Jane Fonda aerobics class and was still suffering from feelings of betrayal and humiliation.

"What about exercise? Couldn't jumping up and down, indoors, in absurdly tight and colorful clothing while Cat Ballou insists everyone do 'one more' be considered an artificial masking agent?"

Only Natasha understood the nuances of what her husband was describing, but she feigned ignorance.

As a regular runner, Lola had already considered the exercise angle.

"I suppose exercise would qualify as a coping mechanism. Although a much healthier one in my view."

Lola wanted to further explore the anthropological point.

"Look, there may be a genetic predisposition for addiction in some people, and other specific life challenges may incentivize some to escape through drugs. But think of how a boy lives now compared to how he lived for most of the last twenty thousand years. Heck, for the last one hundred thousand years. In the past, he spent all day outside being mentored by adults who taught him how to hunt or farm or fish. Doing hard physical labor. He had nonstop contact with a community network that included other males of all ages. He was learning skills from role models and also learning how to lead. He was learning standard behavioral norms. His relationship with nature was intimate. We admired those with a tremendous capacity for physical productivity. The most celebrated were those who melded their physical and intellectual capabilities in this context."

Again, Abel's ego required it be noticed.

"Let's not forget about the omnipresent parasites and tooth decay."

Lola couldn't find a point to acknowledge.

Below the table, Natasha's clandestine suitor was becoming more insistent. She casually took a healthy sip from her wine glass before casting a furtive glance around the table.

Lola continued adding color to her thesis.

"Contrast that to today's boys. We celebrate academic success. Boys that can sit for hours on end, inside, at a desk, memorizing stuff. A thousand years ago that boy spending his entire day inside was a real concern for his parents, given his lack of usefulness. Today he's granted society's golden ticket: a seat at one of our trophy universities, where he'll do more of the same."

Donna simultaneously interrupted and encouraged her older sister.

"You go, girl! But why all this talk about boys? The world's a lot harder for us girls, too."

Donna had already overindulged in the wine department. She wasn't sure she agreed with Lola, but she was proud of the passion and sophistication of her sister's discourse.

Lola took a sip of Perrier and felt the bubbles descend, massaging her throat on the way. The floor was still hers, so she put down her glass and continued.

"What about the average boy—or *GIRL*—from a thousand years ago? The physical ones who were celebrated for being strong and energetic? Who wanted to be moving outside? Who were curious about their natural surroundings? Who, along with their family and two mules, cleared forty acres and built a house, all by hand? How are they doing today?"

She let the rhetorical question rest for a brief moment before continuing.

"They fidget and chafe at being inside for hours at a time, sitting quietly in a chair, being instructed in a unilateral, abstract, non-physical way. We shame and criticize them for not having self-control. In some instances we even medicate them."

This last sentence was new information for Maddy. She turned to Dr. Hagopian.

"Tasha, this can *not* be true? We don't prescribe drugs for children who are active?"

The doctor was struggling. Her miniature Casanova was now trying to start a fire with her shin, while her colleagues' prescription practices were under siege. She was professionally alarmed by the growing bestiality fantasy that was occupying a part of her consciousness; the more she tried to dismiss it the stronger became its grasp. She tried to dislodge the pooch with a shake, while simultaneously responding to her hostess.

"OVERLY active," she clarified, "and only in very rare circumstances. Let me be clear. No one wants to unnecessarily prescribe drugs for children. But we are seeing a small cohort of parents who are feeling incapacitated by their children's inability to absorb information at the rate necessary to advance academically with their age group in a normal institutional setting. They could be considered 'learning impaired.' These children—mostly boys—can be disruptive and act out in the classroom. They seem to have attention issues. This can be tremendously frustrating for both teachers and parents."

To Lola, the boys sounded a lot like Keenan. She wanted to know more.

"How large is this problem?"

"This is a very small percentage of the overall demographic. Anomalous. Many of my colleagues think this is a phenomena that is already in decline."

"I know a boy like that in my school…Jimmy Foster," offered Donna.

"And—?" Maddy asked.

"And what?"

"And how is Jimmy Foster doing?"

"Well, I'm one of his oldest and closest friends…and maybe the only one he's told about the pills…but, well…anyway, he's very sporty, probably one of the best athletes. All the girls have a crush on him, and he can take apart and fix anything mechanical. Before the pills he was really struggling and frustrated by school, but now he's doing really good in class. Oh, and he seems to be a lot less stressed out."

Dr. Hagopian was relieved by, and grateful for, the positive data point, regardless of its anecdotal nature; but she wanted to remain balanced in her description of the problem.

"It's quite a dilemma. The parents see their children failing relative to their peers. The children feel like failures. The teachers feel unable to fulfill their responsibilities to all their constituents. The parents come to us for solutions. They are anxious, frantic even, for some hope. No one wants their kids to take drugs, but the alternative, in many parents' eyes, is a life of underperformance for their kids…or worse."

The Jack Russell was nothing if not focused. Penetration was not compulsory. He loved Dr. Hagopian for her mind.

…knockin' me out with those Armenian thighs.

Lola reinserted herself.

"Because in the current world, there is a growing emphasis on brain power and a lessening need for physical, human strength."

Abel was unaware of the surreptitious cuckolding unfolding next to him. He was focused on Lola, and as a teacher he had something to add.

"But isn't this the way it's always been? A growing population with increasingly sophisticated technology requires standardized and higher level educational programs?"

Michael's years as a corporate lawyer likewise compelled him to participate.

"To prepare them for specialized, institutionalized jobs…and to be useful members in a functioning democracy."

Lola wasn't ready to give up.

"All with little physical movement and little interaction with nature."

Natasha realized the illicit tryst was getting out of hand. She was concerned about a mess and the lack of protection. She effected *coitus interruptus* by excusing herself from the table. She felt like a tease.

Archimedes came bounding out from under the tablecloth. Maddy leapt on the opportunity for interaction.

"Oh, there you are, Archie! Where have you been my liddle, widdle, wuvvy, bunny, baby?"

She reached down and pulled him into her lap. A pronounced component of his anatomy was already receding.

Archie's current position reminded him of the many fish in the sea. He accepted the attention from his new love interest with impenitence. He was, after all, just a dog.

Donna, feeling a bit overwhelmed by the broadness of the topic, turned to the grown-ups for some clarity.

"Do we have any solutions?"

Natasha shrugged as she headed towards the powder room, not sure there was a well-defined problem. She kept a conflicted eye on the dog.

Abel offered his views.

"You'd be asking us to collectively stop the advancement of technology and knowledge. We all enjoy the benefits of productivity enhancement, just some more than others. These challenges are some of the collateral damage that accompanies economic growth."

"Who decides when the collateral damage overwhelms the productivity benefits?"

"In democratic societies, I suppose we all do."

"What about redistribution?"

"You mean central planning, socialism?"

Everyone around the table looked a bit uncomfortable. Ronald Reagan had brought a new optimism to much of the country. Stocks were up and interest rates were down, and the Evil Empire to the east was in decline. In Bronxville there wasn't a lot of sympathy for the collectivist philosophies of Marx and Engels.

Michael was still pondering an earlier point.

"Wait a minute, what about professional sports? We seem to celebrate the physical quite a bit, both through attention and financial reward."

Lola hadn't considered her dad's point and so took a second to gather her thoughts; before she could respond, her mom, whose brother, Fred, had been a minor league baseball player, weighed in.

"I don't think many young people have a realistic chance of making a living as a professional athlete. Maybe one in a million? Maybe we celebrate our athletes to some degree because we envy their freedom to explore and develop their physical sides? A freedom that we've lost?"

Lola hadn't expected that sort of buy-in from her mom, and looked down at her plate as she stifled a grin.

A thought popped into Donna's mind.

"What about eyeglasses?"

Everyone looked at her quizzically. Maddy finally asked the obvious.

"What *about* eyeglasses?"

Donna pushed her fright aside and verbally stepped to center stage.

"Well, corrective lenses are a broadly used artificial tool for improving human performance in the modern world. Why aren't they further distancing us from our cavemen essence as a 'masking agent'?"

There was a pregnant pause. Donna didn't know if her question was so good that it stumped the grown-ups, or so bad that it was obviously silly.

Michael finally spoke up. "I think Lola is talking about mental health issues such as anxiety, not physical deficiencies such as hearing or vision deterioration."

Lola turned to her sister, making an effort to support her while adding some more color.

"It's an interesting point, Donna. You could argue that technology, for example, the invention of the printing press, has brought about a much higher rate of reading, which in turn stresses our eyes in a way that is long-term damaging. One could argue that reading is an artificial construct that takes us away from nature."

Donna was relieved to have received at least partial credit. She took another gulp of wine and used her newfound confidence (and increasing intoxication) to make things interesting.

"What about masturbation? Could that be a 'coping mechanism'?"

The question was obviously provocative and effected another awkward moment as the group's demographics made everyone a little uncertain about what was appropriate dinner table conversation.

Given her regular observations of Keno's seemingly overactive libido, Lola had considered sex as an escape; but she felt uncomfortable sharing her thoughts. Trying to keep it clinical and nonjudgmental, Michael finally broke the brief silence.

"I think that when overdone, masturbation, or sex in general, could be considered a coping mechanism. Like so many healthy things, when overdone it can become toxic."

His comments were met with nods of agreement and a collective sense of relief that the topic had been navigated without too much discomfort.

Lola played back the recent conversation in her mind and realized the dialogue had put her in a place she hadn't intended.

"Hey…I'm sorry…I…my goal wasn't to judge certain behaviors as right or wrong…I was just thinking out loud about addiction and other mental health issues…and wondering why so many people can't deal…with…um…their daily existence…without some sort of coping mechanism. I'm not against technology. I don't have some romantic vision of Voltaire's noble savage or prehistoric man… it just seems like for most of our evolutionary history we spent a lot more of our time having to move in nature to survive…and now we don't do that much."

Every one was trying to digest the ramifications of Lola's ideas. After a lap around the living room, Natasha returned to her chair with a clear head. She had come in on the tail end of the masturbation question, and was intrigued, but decided it was not the time or place to delve. She had a broader perspective she wanted to float, and as she took her seat she turned to address Lola.

"I believe your theory is that our society is evolving at a rate faster than our species?"

Lola was grateful for the appearance of a finish line and, hopefully, an ally.

"I'm not even sure I have a theory. These are just thoughts that've been rolling around in my brain. But…I think…I think that could be a good summary. Maybe I would say that certain segments of society are effecting technological changes that are stressing other parts of society."

The fairer Hagopian accepted Lola's words as validation and an invitation to continue.

"And that this disparity in societal change, or evolution rates, this tectonic pressure, if you will, is affecting many people's ability to cope, as seen in increasing mental health issues: depression, bipolar disorder, schizophrenia, varying degrees of social anxiety?"

"I think that's fair."

"And that as a society we are self-medicating, dealing with this friction, with a variety of 'masking agents'?"

Lola's thoughts crystallized in time to Natasha's words.

"I think so…yes…you've really helped me…thanks, Dr. Hagopian. My theory is that for our health…mental and physical…we need connection. Connection to nature, connection to our bodies, and connection to each other. We need…"

"Love?"

Just then the doorbell rang.

Donna pushed her chair from the table in such a disjointed rush that she almost tripped in a collective heap.

"Excuse me…despite the scintillating conversation…that's my date!"

Michael asked after his youngest daughter with more curiosity than authority:

"Where are you off to?"

Before answering the door, Donna made a brief, out-of-sight inspection in the hallway mirror. She quickly freshened her lipstick and unbuttoned an extra blouse button, allowing the goodies to surface, while hoping this would help keep Eric focused. She called back over her shoulder as she opened the door.

"Eric got Prince tickets! Mom has details. Bye!"

Michael turned quizzically to his wife.

"Wha-a—?"

Maddy smiled back at her husband.

"This is what it sounds like when doves cry?"

Then she turned to her guests.

"Well, SHE seems to be far from sleepwalking."

Everyone gifted the hostess with a courtesy laugh, after which Maddy got up and asked Lola to help her with dessert.

Grabbing her plate, Lola followed her mom with a bit of trepidation. Weary of her mom's counsel when it came to Keenan, she suspected she would soon be the recipient of more nagging.

Once they got into the kitchen, Lola's fears were realized.

"Honey, I'm worried that you are stubbornly rationalizing behavior that is long-term destructive for both you and your young man."

Lola didn't want to address the concern her mother had raised, so she diverted the conversation by raising a side issue.

"My 'young man'? Really, Mom? It's been a year and you can't even say his name?"

"Well, you've never even brought him home."

"My home is three thousand miles away," she countered angrily. "Which I share with a man named Keenan."

The conversation was getting redundant.

"Keenan comes from a family without much money. He is trying hard to carve out a life for himself, and us."

"I hate myself for saying this, but things would be a lot easier if you found someone with some money…who wasn't damaged goods."

Lola took a deep breath.

"Mom, I know your advice is well-thought out and comes from a place of caring, but every time you tell me what to do it makes me want to do the opposite."

Wow! There it was, Maddy thought. *Her daughter actually said it; years of suspicions confirmed.*

She could try to make Lola see the stubborn idiocy of such behavior, but she knew it had been inherited. At that moment she realized she was pushing her children away with her good intentions and unsolicited advice. She took a deep breath and allowed a moment of silence.

She opened the refrigerator and pulled out the dark-chocolate cake she had made that day. It was Lola's favorite.

"That may be the most honest thing you've ever said to me."

"More honest than, 'Mom, I'm pregnant'?"

Maddy almost dropped the cake.

"Kidding, Mom."

A deep inhalation, smile of relief, and an under breath mutter:

"Asshole."

"Excuse me?"

Maddy smiled and nodded to a ceramic bowl on the counter just behind Lola.

"Would you mind rinsing and slicing those strawberries? There's freshly made whipped cream in the fridge door…not too sweet…just the way you like it."

"Oh my god, Mom, this looks awesome."

"Tell me more about your theory on evolution and modern humans, I'm interested."

They both smiled knowingly at the other, before Maddy added one last thought:

"But can we neglect the part about food as a coping mechanism? Just for tonight?"

CHAPTER 13—

Strange but Not a Stranger

Lola was awakened at dawn by the morning doves outside her window. Filtered by faded yellow curtains, the early sun gave everything in her childhood room a gilded tint.

She liked to sleep in the nude. Usually in the mornings, as she escaped the protection of her bed sheets, modesty required prompt cover-up. The mildly vulnerable feeling of moving naked through space could be more pronounced in unfamiliar locations. An additional level of sacrilege accompanied the intrusion of fully developed Lola into the historic sanctuary of pre-adolescent Lola. She hurried into a T-shirt and pair of Keenan's boxers, so as not to offend the ghosts, and headed out the bedroom door. At the top of the stairs she paused and watched her dad, strapped in to his suit, hustling out the front door with his briefcase and newspaper. Her mom was giving him a peck on the cheek and a thermos of coffee.

God it's reassuring to see the continuation of certain routines, she thought.

For as long as she could remember, at least twenty years, they'd been doing that. She wanted to inject herself into the comfort of the Norman Rockwell scene.

"Bye, Dad!" She rooted him on, waving from the banister.

She was able to return, for a brief moment, to a time when life was simple and all felt secure. With a greater appreciation for the accomplishment, she wanted to give a shout of encouragement to her parents, and, perhaps, motivate them for the next twenty years.

"Bye, Fancy Pants!" her father responded with his enthusiastic smile and a wave.

Her mom looked up at Lola, beaming from ear to ear. She had on her low-cut, black, sheer, piece of sultry provocation that caught her at midthigh. Still having a body that could make the lingerie sing, she called that particular negligee her "racy-lacy"; or, when feeling really naughty after a few drinks, her "nookie jar." Lola fought the urge to cringe at the memories; she successfully reversed field.

Good for them, she admired silently.

After Maddy closed the door on her commuter husband, she turned to Lola.

"Good morning, Lolie-baby! Would you mind feeding and walking Archimedes?"

The little Jack Russell was spinning around Maddy's feet at that moment. Her mom felt compelled to explain her tardiness.

"I'm sorry, but I'm a little behind in my routine. Dad was a teensy slow getting up for work, and I still need to finish last night's dishes. I would really appreciate it."

"Of course, Mom, no problem. How cold is it outside?"

"Not too cold. Jeans and long sleeves. It's gonna be a lovely day."

"I'm on it. Archie, up. Give me ten minutes?"

"Of course, baby. How's your young ma…ahem, Keenan…how's Keenan?"

"He's doing good, Mom, thanks for asking," she lied.

Not unusually, Lola's thoughts had further coalesced during the night. There was something about her relationship with her mom—specifically, their conversation in the kitchen last night—that was important to her developing strategy for Keenan, but she couldn't quite put her finger on it.

Lola walked out of the house with a series of doggie-poop bags attached to the handle of the retractable leash. Attached to the other end was Archimedes. His ferocity so overmatched his size that she was constantly caught off guard when his frequent sprints extended the leash fully. For the first one hundred yards she suffered through a series of shoulder-jarring yanks until she finally figured out when to brace herself. Lucky it wasn't icy out, she told herself. Archimedes had been a post-Lola addition to the family. Michael was indifferent, but Maddy was possessed; another baby over which to dote. At this point Archie was three years old, but Maddy still loved him unconditionally. He had the heart of a lion, and the body of a barrel-chested armadillo.

Aaron Hagopian caught up with the two from behind.

"*Hola,* Lola! *Como estás?*"

Lola was happy to see him.

"*Muy bien, gracias,* Aaron. *Y tú?*"

"I'm supergroovy, thanks. Is that your new pet rodent?"

"*No, mi perro.*" She faux pouted. She had just about exhausted her high school Spanish.

"Remember Lola, it's not the size of the dog in the fight, but the size of the fight in the dog."

"A variant on the old adage concerning boat size and ocean motion perhaps?"

"Perhaps." He pondered dramatically, pointer finger on chin.

Aaron and Lola had been friends forever. They had grown up as neighbors, played together, studied together, and shared dreams. Lola enjoyed a certain comfort in his presence. Being in the same grade, and both wanting to be doctors, they had shared a lot of advanced-level classes in high school. Currently, Aaron was following in his mom's footsteps at Harvard Medical School, while Lola worked in the food service industry in San Francisco. Whenever she was around him now she kicked herself for her academic divergence. There had been a temporary lapse in judgment; an event that she casually referred to as "that stupid Wolfgang thing."

The same old story, she lectured herself. *Girl throws away ambitions for boy.*

As always her neighbor was nothing but gracious. Lola wondered why he wasn't at school.

"Why aren't you up in Boston?"

"I'm home on a one-week break. What are you doing back here?"

"Struggling to get some traction with my life. Home for some perspective."

"Can I help?"

"Have you started your psychiatry rotations yet?"

"Uh oh, sounds bad. I'm sure we can operate."

She didn't smile.

"Oh no! I'm sorry. You were serious. Let me start again. Yes. I've done a lot of work with psych patients. What do you want to know?"

"Well, what's the hardest thing about moving through adolescence and joining society as a functioning adult?"

"Wow." Aaron pursed his lips and whistled through his teeth. "That's a big, open-ended question. How much time do you have?"

"Cliff Notes?"

"Hmm…statistically, automobile accidents involving other adolescents and intoxicants kill the most adolescents, hence preventing them from becoming functional adults. I believe unintentional overdoses and suicides are also big challenges for that demographic."

"Okay," Lola replied, "but why do adolescents have higher rates of those outcomes than other cohorts?"

"I think the most credible theory is brain development. The underdeveloped prefrontal cortex limits judgment. The limbic system is also adjusting the amount of neurotransmitters like dopamine and serotonin, which can lead to some volatile mood swings. Risk tolerance increases."

"Is it all about brain chemistry?"

"It depends on who you talk to. I think everyone's challenges could be somewhat unique."

"So if we categorize brain development as nature, can we assume that the changes we see today in adolescent brains are similar in process to what we've seen for the last two hundred years? In other words, would you say that we haven't seen much change in the cognitive hardware of humans as a result of evolution in the last few centuries?"

"I think that's a fair assumption."

"Okay," Lola said again. "Now tell me about environmental effects, or the changes in nurturing practices over the last two hundred years."

"Hmm…interesting approach. You're trying to segregate nature from nurture. Okay, I'll bite. I think today's world is much more complex than the world humans experienced two hundred years ago. I would be comfortable saying that on average we are a much more complicated society today than we were even fifty years ago. I believe the pace of technological change, perhaps a reasonable proxy for complexity, is increasing every decade. Moore's Law and all that. Two hundred years ago we were mostly farmers, fisherman, tradesmen, and homemakers. We learned a skill from a family member or a guild. Girls learned from their moms. The learning of a trade began at a young age because we grew up in proximity to it. Today we require much greater mental functionality, including abstract thinking, and much less non-mental or physical functionality. That is, if we want to be useful as an economic unit, and obtain a greater-than-minimum-wage-paying job. There are exceptions of course; but on average, yes, much more complex. More brain, less brawn."

"So in this more complex world, would you grant that individual humans, on average, have to learn much more information to become employable today than we did even fifty years ago?"

"Seems reasonable."

"And that when born, our brains are similar in functionality today to what they were fifty years ago."

Aaron nodded. "Agreed."

"So if we still expect people to have employable skills by the age of, let's say, twenty-one, but the volume of learning they need to be employable is much greater, then by definition we have to increase the rate of absorption of information? Cram more details into brains in the same period of time?"

"I got it. Let's simplify this by using basic math. The bricks in the example I'm about to give you will be metaphors for education—learning and skill retention. Fifty years ago, on average, we each had to move five hundred bricks from point A to point B by the time we were twenty-one years old to be considered 'qualified' for a decent paying job. Today we have to move, let's say, fifteen hundred bricks, or three times as many, over the same distance, A to B, to reach a level which is useful to employers."

"Exactly. Which explains why more and more education is necessary for higher-wage, non menial jobs. So why are standardized test scores not increasing dramatically?"

"Hmm…not sure. Either our theory is wrong; the education system is failing to provide qualified employees; we're testing for the wrong things; the mean test score is a poor representative of the population; or some combination of those four."

"Let's assume our theory is right."

"Feels better, doesn't it?"

"I'd call that peer review."

They both giggled. Archimedes stopped to sniff a hydrant.

"Good boy, Archie," Lola praised.

Aaron casually examined the overhead tree branches as the dog lifted his leg.

"You know, I think Archie is usually short for Archibald, not Archimedes."

"No feces, Holmes," she deadpanned.

She waited for the dog to finish.

"Where were we, *Señor* Smarty Pants?"

"Cramming more knowledge into static grey matter, I believe."

"Right, carry on, Doctor."

"So, can we conclude that the societal demand for increasingly complicated and changing skills is placing tremendous stress on our population? Metaphorically, we all have to move a lot more bricks in the same amount of time to get paid. Those that can't increase the volume and rapidity of learning are left behind in the ongoing search for more-capable employees."

"Exactly. And, this demand for greater mental function is forcing many to cut back on their physical activity. There's only so much time and energy per day. We lose connection with nature, our bodies, and our friends. This shift in prioritization is placing tremendous stress on us as individual biological ecosystems."

"Hence all the mental health and addiction problems. The widespread use of 'masking agents' is the theme you presented last night, I believe."

"Your mom told you?"

"Yes, and I think you're on to something. What are you doing waiting tables in San Fran?"

She shrugged.

"Drinking for free, while I wait for my hormones to stop handicapping me?"

"Another interesting theory. When does it stop?"

She ignored the question.

"I've been reconsidering my masking-agent assumptions. I'm guessing it holds true for much of the last one hundred thousand years, but there is probably some pretty good anecdotal evidence that a lot of worker bees in a lot of professions were drunk a lot of the time over the last millennia. For example, British sailors for much of the last three centuries."

"Yes, but they were drinking because the physical conditions were so brutal, not because they were missing a primal need for connection. Plus there was no confidence in the potability of the water. I hate to instruct you on your thesis, but your point isn't that masking agents are present only during circumstances of disconnection."

By this point they had reached a favorite neighbor's lawn, a place where Archie preferred to squat and unburden himself. Lola ripped off one of the plastic squares, placed her hand inside the small bag, scooped up the warm specimen with the covered hand, and, holding on to the poop, flipped the small sack outside in. Archimedes eyed her with a look of triumph. Lola took it as taunting. Tying a knot at the top of the bag, she firmly enclosed the caca in plastic and commenced a visual search for a garbage can. But another idea popped into her head. Mightn't her gallant companion succumb to it…?

Channeling Julie Andrews, with horizontally extended arm holding the plastic wrapped turd as far from her nose as possible, she made her play.

"Oh Aaron…or is it Erin? I have an errand for you…"

Aaron responded good-naturedly, moving away from the offensive gift.

"Uh, let's see…your choice: A. Fuck-off, Eliza. Or, B. I'm not relieving you of that awful offal?"

"Eliza!?!" Lola replied in mock horror. "Not *My Fair Lady*, you dolt. *Mary Poppins!* Now you've ruined my day."

Another *faux* pout.

"You're offended because I mistook you for Audrey Hepburn? Pleeeease."

She tried to regain the upper hand by pointing out his misuse of the word "offal."

"I wasn't offering you entrails, it was poop."

"Technically, I agree, but the near-homonym was too good to pass up."

Lola smiled. It was fun to spend time with a med student who also had a linguistic sense of humor. After a few moments of silent walking, her problem with Keno reinvigorated itself.

"Can I poach your brain on a few more topics?"

"Sure."

"I've been thinking about the trade-offs between liberty and responsibility."

"Meaning?"

"I believe that we all start in infancy with zero liberty and zero responsibility. Our parents control nearly everything. We have no freedom, but we also

106

have no duties. As adults we have huge amounts of freedom but also massive amounts of responsibility."

"Not always."

"Humor me. On average."

"Go on."

"The question is how do we go from zero to a lot in a healthy way? In adolescence we want all of the freedom and none of the responsibility. My dad says that's at the root of every intergenerational fight. Our parents try to ladle out equal amounts depending on performance, and we, as adolescents, keep demanding more freedom but refuse to accept more responsibility."

"Interesting. One could argue that the whole sixties hippie movement was an example of that phenomena."

"Have you read *The Electric Kool-Aid Acid Test*?"

"No. Should I?"

"I think so…to get a quick glimpse of American twentieth-century culture, I think you need to at least read *A Moveable Feast, On the Road*, and *Electric Kool-Aid*…."

"I've read the other two."

"Good for you. Let's move on; we were talking hippies."

"Right. I believe the catalyst for the hippie movement was the Viet Nam war. A small group of rebellious students taking a principled stand against a stupid invasion. But it quickly morphed into this infantile fantasy. A utopian lifestyle that embraced unlimited freedom and rejected any of the accompanying responsibilities. Free love, free drugs, communal everything. Rejection of the institutions that require personal responsibility—like marriage, religion, corporations, private property rights…"

"Wasn't it all worth it just for the music and hash brownies?"

"Let me think. Um…no?"

"I knew we should've invited you to our tie-dye orgies!"

"I'm still bitter."

Archie took off after another phantom menace. Lola was ready and braced herself. As the dog reached the end of the leash in midstride, she gave a firm tug and watched with great satisfaction as his feet left the ground and his body reversed direction, forcing a dorsal landing, tail positioned where his head had been. He scrambled to his feet undeterred.

Lola wondered if she would need to defend her harshness to Aaron.

"He deserved it."

"Definitely."

They walked for a minute in silence.

"So, let's put it all together. First, we agree that becoming a functioning adult in a post-industrial world means absorbing more information than our brains are evolutionarily prepared for…"

"Yep. While those same brains are going through biological changes that impair judgment and enhance mood swings…"

"Agreed. And our bodies, in this post-industrial world, are not receiving important connections with friends, nature, and physical movement…"

"And we naturally look for ways to increase freedom while shirking responsibility…"

"Holy tomole! All that could lead to a lot of fucked-up, anti-social behavior during the early adult years."

"Right? To be fair, I think the second and fourth points have been around for a while. It's the first and third points that are new and interesting. The post-industrial stuff. Also, the increase in mental health issues could just as easily be caused by another factor or factors, like environmental degradation, a compromised food chain, or by something else that we can't even measure."

Lola considered Aaron's points. She lost some of her enthusiasm.

"I guess that's fair. It's so hard to disentangle all these potential catalysts."

"Welcome to science and the scientific method. Anyone can pull stuff out of their trousers, but science requires you prove your theory with a lot of testing."

"Thanks for the lecture, Einst—"

Not really interested in the stupid human conversation, Archie unexpectedly took off after a taunting squirrel. The reel let out so quickly that Lola didn't have time to brace herself and was pulled sideways into Aaron. The doctor-in-training caught her deftly around the waist, and kept them both on their feet. Their faces were inches apart and Aaron locked his eyes on hers. He could smell her toothpaste as he closed his eyes and reached down with his lips to kiss her mouth. Lola turned her head, and his lips grazed her cheek. An awkward second later, Lola popped up with some uncomfortable laughing, trying to distance them from the somewhat-romantic moment.

"Whoa…sorry…thanks Aaron! Talk about fight in the dog! That crazy rodent nearly buried me!"

Aaron weakly laughed off the rejection, looking away as if nothing had happened. Lola turned her attention to scolding Archie, then turned an about-face and suggested they head back home. Aaron wanted to disappear.

After an uncomfortable silence, Aaron tried to return things to normal.

"Hey, um, was there anything else you wanted to talk about?"

"Hmm…yeah, there was one more thing."

He was grateful for the opportunity to move on.

"Okay?"

"I've noticed a reluctance in people I know, including myself—although it's debatable as to whether or not I know myself—to follow instruction or advice, no matter how appropriate, when it comes from certain familiar sources."

Lola walked over to a neighbor's curbside garbage can and deposited the poop bag.

"In fact, just last night, I noticed that when my Mom gave me perfectly reasonable and well-intentioned advice, I became immediately annoyed, and had an unthinking and contentious impulse. I also had an equally strong impulse to do the opposite of what she suggested. Regardless of the risks. Any thoughts on this?"

"Hmm." Aaron took the opportunity to dramatically bring pointer finger to chin yet again. "Not sure. I think there is a diagnosis called Oppositional Defiant Disorder, or some such; but I think that disease is more extreme and consistently problematic than what you are describing. It is also generally limited to children."

He looked over at Lola.

"Can I assume you've experienced your first menses?"

Unfazed, Lola raised the ante.

"I'm not sure. Can you describe this menses phenomena?"

Aaron smiled, and let the hot spud fall. It felt good to be back hangin' with Lola.

"I don't recall your disease in the textbooks; but, now that you mention it, I've noticed similar tendencies in myself."

"Cool."

"Babies."

"Strange but not a stranger."

They both smiled at the inside joke.

"At least I'm not the only one with these crazy feelings. I've noticed I can actually get more entrenched in my positions, stubborn even over time, as the advice builds in frequency. Especially if I perceive it as nagging. It can become self-destructive."

"Hmm…yes…I see."

Aaron stroked his chin and wrinkled his brow in comedic fashion. He was getting his mojo back.

"Thoughts?"

"You need to get laid more in Frisco?"

"Not funny…I get laid plenty…and don't call it Frisco!"

He looked at her like she was insane.

"For some reason that pisses off the locals."

"I can help with the getting laid part," he offered.

"Aaron. Remember? I. Live. With. Another. Man? Stupee."

"So do I! He's my roommate. And we don't have much sex either!"

"Much?"

Now it was Aaron's turn to pout in a dramatized way.

"Go ahead…it's okay, pour salt in the wounds…emasculate me. I'm used to it. I don't have any feelings."

"*Pobrecito.*"

They walked another half block in silence.

Aaron cleared his throat. He had gotten over the other guy.

"Okay, without giving it a lot of thought, here's my theory. It's all about power, control, and ego. I believe we are all involved in ongoing, subtle dynamic struggles with those around us. For lack of a better term, let's call this context 'the dominance hierarchy.' We are constantly competing for a position in the pecking order. For most of us, these tensions are subconscious. Beneath the surface we are not only aware of our place in the hierarchy, but most of us are always struggling to improve our positions. Again, this is occurring almost intuitively, without much conscious thought. Daily, subtle evaluations are occurring when we interact with spouses, siblings, colleagues, friends, parents, and children. Even with people we don't know. Everybody. For example, in line at the bank, or in the elevator, we are constantly comparing ourselves to others, wondering where we fit in."

"I'm not one to look a gift horse, but I'm not sure that's particularly insightful?"

"What do you mean? Thanks for the support, by the way."

"Sorry, just fulfilling my peer review responsibilities; so my problem is this: I think we already have a variety of social manifestations that define hierarchical positions. For example, in Spanish, you address someone above you in the 'Usted' form of the verb, and someone beneath you in 'Tú' form. There is some subjectivity on the speaker's part, so they have to evaluate their relative social position regularly. It is very explicit."

"Okay, I see your point, but I think the key word here is 'manifestation.' This is a bit chicken-and-egg, and involves subtlety."

"Oh, *subtlety*! No wonder I'm not getting it." She smiled.

Aaron recognized the sarcasm, but didn't mind. Most of his friends at Harvard were very self-important. He had forgotten how much fun it was to talk to Lola. Plenty smart, but irreverent and funny in a self-deprecating way. She was also willing to dish and take it.

"What I'm talking about might be considered the precursor to the explicit hierarchies. It's implicit, a very nuanced, intuitive, omnipresent part of our subconscious. We are always comparing, evaluating. Just watch, next time you're with a group of people. Your mind does it automatically."

"That could partially explain some of our demand for status symbols like fancy cars and designer clothes."

"Yep…and all the questions to try and evaluate position and dominance. 'Where do you live?' 'North or south of Eighty-Second Street?' 'Where do you go to school?' 'Where do your kids go to school?' 'What was your time in that race?' 'How much can you bench?' 'What do you do?' 'What were your SAT scores?' 'Where do you work?' 'You must know so-and-so from your neighborhood?'"

"That's right. Most people aren't really interested in the answer, it's more about establishing dominance. No one asks about something they suck at. You don't bring up jobs if you're unemployed."

"Or neighborhoods if your homeless."

"The status symbol thing…that's a really interesting point. Remember, for a lot of us it's not cool to admit you notice these things or attach importance to them. For most, vanity is not considered a virtue. But clearly we are conflicted on this point, or marketers wouldn't sell so many Porsches and Rolexes. We aren't supposed to care about the dominance hierarchy, but most of us compare most of the time. We just don't want to admit it. We suppress because we were taught it's crass, but it's always there, lurking below the surface. My dad likes to say that when it comes to status symbols, 'the people who care don't matter, and the people that matter don't care.' Many of us understand this intellectually, yet we're still caught up in the competition…after all, we are herd animals. It's hard to ignore something that's so deeply seated in our collective consciousness."

"Your belief is that most of us understand this competition only on some sort of alternative-consciousness level?"

"That's my belief. Maybe it's a limbic-versus-cortex brain thing? Of course, I can only see things through my own eyes. Perhaps I'm the only one who isn't blatantly aware of these interactions?"

"I can't speak for everyone, but I don't think you're alone in your lack of awareness. I wouldn't call you ridiculously unaware, maybe just significantly."

"Funny."

He looked at her sideways.

"I'm sorry. All of a sudden I've become significantly unaware. Refresh my memory. Who's helping whom here?"

"*Touché, mon amie.* More, *s'il vous plait.*"

"Okay, where were we? Oh yeah, dominance hierarchies and irritation with unsolicited advice. Now, here's the rub: By definition, when someone offers us unsolicited advice, they are implying they have greater knowledge than us in an area in which we specialize: the maintenance of OURSELVES! They are implying something is wrong with us. They are telling us they are more aware than us. That alone is annoying to our ego, but it also makes us feel subtly but palpably vulnerable to a descent in the pecking order. If we agree with them, then we are admitting on a very deep and intuitive level that we are vulnerable AND they are superior. Again, this acknowledgment will cause us to lose turf in the dominance hierarchy, hence the immediate feeling of irritation and defensiveness. The unsolicited advisor is metaphorically elbowing onto our turf, which is why we get annoyed, contrarian even, because we don't want to cede power or position to the threatening interloper. We have to defend our turf against invaders. We cannot admit that their unsolicited observation may be accurate."

"I gotta think about that. If this has any validity, this stuff could have far-reaching, daily implications."

Aaron stopped and turned to face Lola.

"Whoa…slow down, Sigmund Freud, we're just thinking out loud here. This is all really touchy-feely stuff. I'm not sure even my mom would call it science, and I know my dad wouldn't even sleep in the same room."

"Yeah, but I like where you're going."

He turned and started walking again.

"It beats talking about the weather and who's sleeping with Lisa Bonet."

"Lenny Kravitz? I know, I'm pathetic."

"On that we agree."

"Sphincter."

"Accepted and deserved."

Lola was warming up. She took off her cashmere sweater and threw it over her shoulders, loosely tying it around her neck.

"A lot of this dominance hierarchy stuff is about communication and trust, right?"

"Well, I think it's all about communication. And I think effective communication starts with trust, so I guess I would agree."

"And maybe anger and frustration? If someone's behavior is pissing you off, you vent or even punish them by nagging? And if you're being nagged you punish the nagger by not changing? You could get into a real chicken-and-egg thing."

"Could be…makes sense to me at first blush. This stuff can be really subtle, but once it gets entrenched it could destroy relationships. I think it could be quite insidious. For example, some people would rather blow themselves up than admit they were wrong. They feel their turf is so small that it must be defended at all costs."

"My dad says that when he was younger he had nothing but his pride, so he would fight furiously to defend it. But now, as an older man, he has so much more than just his pride that he's okay with a little leakage."

"Yes, insecure people can be very sensitive if they feel others are encroaching."

Archimedes started rolling in a pile of leaves. Something in there smelled good to him, and it was important he do his best to share that stink with everyone back home.

"How do we test your thesis?"

"If my theory is right, I would guess advice from a source that doesn't know your identity, a book for example, would not be threatening. Or maybe advice not directed at you specifically, possibly someone mentioning, in a group setting, a revelation they had?"

Lola was nodding as she worked her way through the examples.

"That's why teaching by parable can be so effective. It depersonalizes the lesson."

"Exactly. It's not usually the content that's threatening, it's the messenger."

"Got it. How about advice from someone who is well above or below you in the hierarchy? Someone who isn't perceived as threatening? I would guess that unsolicited counsel from those people would not be irritating?"

"Maybe."

It took Lola a while to digest it all. Her mind was working feverishly.

"Holy feces, Batman, this is all super interesting! Definitely makes a lot of sense. So when we are young children, we mostly worship and respect our parents and follow their advice because we accept their dominant position. But as we approach adolescence, and from that time on, we start to become more willfully oppositional as we try to work our way up the pecking order."

"Correct. We see this in the animal world, with dogs for example, all the time."

"So how do I stop feeling irritated when people do this to me? Like with my Mom? And how will I know if my unsolicited advice is welcome?"

"I would suggest that now that you're aware of this phenomenon, you acknowledge and observe this behavior when it arises. Identification is the first step."

"How do I do that?"

"Have you tried meditation?"

"No, I don't think I'm flexible enough."

Aaron gave her a look of consternation but decided not to go down that path.

"I would suggest you try to recognize and understand the purpose of the subconscious, egoic impulse to defend hierarchical turf. When someone gives you unsolicited advice, you should search for value in the content of the message and not worry about the messenger. Try to let the oppositional impulses go, because the dominance hierarchy no longer has any practical value for humans. It's an irrelevant, archaic vestige of our evolutionary history."

"Focus on the message, not the messenger."

"Nice sound bite."

"I'm not sure the dominance hierarchy ever had any value for humans."

"Maybe long ago, when we lived in small packs and competed intra-pack for scarce resources?"

"You're just making shit up now."

"Pretty much…but in science we like to call it *developing an hypothesis*."

Lola smiled

"Well aren't you special?"

And then got back on point:

"How do we sort this stuff out in the modern world?"

"We have a variety of other, more transparent hierarchies that serve to identify positions in modern society. These hierarchies generally come with defined roles and responsibilities. Institutions like corporate or military chains of command, elected or appointed officials, the family unit. These groups have proscribed duties for specific roles, and come with labels like manager, admiral, mayor, policeman, and parent."

"Okay, so your advice is to identify and thoughtfully defuse these subconscious bombs as they arise. Recognize these oppositional feelings come from a vestigial system that no longer serves any societal function. Got it."

"Remember, I don't think this will be easy. I suspect these responses are deeply buried in the limbic systems in our brains."

"No kidding. What else?"

"I would try to accept guidance that you think is rational, regardless of the source, because it's in your best interest. Reject guidance that you think is not helpful. Don't be a pushover, but *do* be thoughtful about your battles."

"Got it." Lola nodded. "Boy, if I could get on top of this I could kiss a lot of anxiety good-bye."

"Right?"

"What about me giving unsolicited advice? I'm having some problems with Keenan right now. I'm worried I'm pushing him away, but he keeps doing obviously self-destructive stuff. It's very hard not to point this out to him."

"Ah, man, now I'm the gay sidekick giving boyfriend advice? New lows."

"You should be flattered. Gay men are smart, thoughtful, and have a wonderful fashion sense."

"Stereotype much? Besides, you don't even know any gay guys."

"Um, I live in San Francisco?"

"Can we get back on topic?"

"Please."

"I think when it comes to giving unsolicited advice, your default should be, 'Just say no.' Except in two situations I can think of off the top of my head: First, when you're in a defined position of authority and your job description requires it; and, second, when there is a clear and present danger."

"What if another person's behavior is affecting my relationship with them?"

"That's a tough one, sorta the spinach-between-the-teeth of this conversational meal. I think you need to say something if it's affecting your relationship. BUT, after you've clearly made your point, back off. Allow the other person to arrive at the appropriate conclusion without your browbeating. They can't own the solution if you're always sitting on it."

"God, that's so true. I'm never leaving Keenan if my mom keeps telling me to do it."

Aaron nodded.

"I'm willing to bet that Keenan knows what's best. Give him some room to get there on his own. Remember, in this theory, when you offer someone unsolicited advice you are threatening them. If they follow your advice with your knowledge, they are ceding power to you. This is very hard for most egos to do. Also, if you really want someone to consider your future counsel, never tell them 'I told you so.' You want the result, not the credit. Every time you say 'I told you so' you diminish trust. Very few people want to be reminded of their subordinate position or weaknesses. Taking credit is about alpha positioning. It's about competitive, adversarial power struggles within a relationship. It's about control."

Lola hesitated, deep in thought. Then she smiled broadly.

"Holy shit, Aaron, you're the brilliant one!"

He smiled, clearly pleased with himself.

"Co-author credit?"

"Of course! We'll call it 'Non-Oppositional Behavioral Therapy.' NOBT. Not a Robot. Think before you act."

"How about 'Pacifism'?"

"Nah, sounds too old-fashioned."

"Fuck, yeah…tear it all down…burn, baby, burn. You really do live in California, don't you?"

Lola ignored his teasing. She was focused on her Keenan strategy.

"One minor adjustment: Non-Oppositional Behavioral Therapy. Think before you *think*. Whadaya think? Has kind of a discordant ring to it, doesn't it?"

"Yeah it does."

Aaron wasn't sure he had added much value, but he had enjoyed the walk.

"I'm sure there's a million caveats we haven't considered, but hopefully we unearthed a few kernels of wisdom."

They were back in front of Lola's house. She turned to Aaron, put her arms around his neck, and startled him with a big kiss on the cheek. She had a plan for when she returned to San Francisco, and it gave her a sliver of hope. Accompanying that hope was the beginning of a manic jag that she knew from experience could energize her for a week or more, as long as she was moving forward with her mission. Backing off, she patted Aaron's chest with both hands, and looked into his eyes.

"It was awesome to see you, Aaron. I am *so* proud of you, staying the course and all; I really appreciate your help. Can we not wait two years for the next time?"

Aaron was glowing; he'd had a crush on Lola for as long as he could remember.

"I'm sorry if I offended you back there…I just got this nice vibe, and…"

His words drifted off.

Dropping her hands from his chest, she started her 180-degree turn towards the front door.

"No worries, *amigo*," she said over her shoulder, "You know I'll always love you."

Lola did a beauty queen wave and followed the terrier inside. The trip back East had served its purpose; San Francisco was calling her now. She had to pack and see if she could find an earlier flight.

Aaron stood on the sidewalk, dazed, watching Archie lead Lola's blue jean-covered bum back inside. He was humming his favorite Kinks song:

Lo-la...L-O-L-A...Lo-la...L-O-L-A . . .

CHAPTER 14

The One-Month Hail Mary

Lola returned from New York prematurely, unannounced, and with an unconventional plan. Her anger intentionally put aside, she allowed herself a modicum of hope.

Currently employed as a server at a high-end restaurant, she had talked to her boss and asked for a one-month leave of absence. Her boss told her to take as much unpaid leave as she needed, but he couldn't guarantee her hours when she returned. The tips were good, but the lifestyle was brutal, and she didn't see herself there in five years. She rationalized that it was worth investing a month and risking a dead-end job to see if Keenan was the man with whom she should spend the rest of her life. Understanding her strategy was a long shot, she embraced the approach anyway because she needed a conclusion.

She arrived at SFO from JFK on a Wednesday afternoon. The shuttle dropped her off in front of their tiny second-floor flat on Greenwich Street. Taking a deep breath, she slung her travel pack over her shoulder and went up to inventory the damage.

Back into the belly of the beast, she thought, steeling herself.

She pushed her key into the keyhole and turned. The dead bolt wasn't engaged, and the door rotated open as she started twisting the knob.

It was uglier than she had expected. His slide appeared to have been fast and hard. She spotted him sleeping on their futon couch, in the living room, with his work clothes on. The pizza boxes and beer bottles were expected, but not the smell—he must've neglected the dog. She quickly confirmed her olfactory suspicions, noting Quinn (who looked anxious and contrite) had emptied his canine bowels in the corner. She'd never seen Keenan miss work, or drink to the point of passing out during the day, or fail to attend to the dog, but witnessing the simultaneous execution of all three left her commitment teetering on the edge. Unshouldering her pack, she looked around while heading to the kitchen. No time for reflection, she reminded herself, the clock was ticking. She had a one-month agenda to do the Herculean, and was in a hurry to be patient and full of grace.

Is that even possible? she wondered.

She gathered some supplies and started cleaning.

Bienvenidos, hermana, she sighed sarcastically. *Listo!*

It was a sparkling San Francisco spring day.

He first felt a presence before he saw anything. Something moving over in the corner had woken him up.

What the fuck, Quinn? he thought angrily. *Mellow out, buddy, we'll go for a walk soon.*

Lately he'd been waking up in some strange places, so he wasn't really sure where he was. He did recall he had been having a killer dream, with a trouserful of morningwood as evidence. Slowly opening one eyelid, he scanned what he could of the room.

Damn it's bright!

His head hurt and his cotton mouth was excruciating, but the sensations weren't unusual. Usually when he came home with a good buzz he went to bed with a quart of Gatorade within reach, but lately he'd been forgetful. Planning ahead took too much effort.

As he stumbled further awake, he felt a pervasive sense of doom, like he had really fucked up recently, but he couldn't recall the details. Then he remembered: his job. He had missed one too many deadlines, and his charm had been overwhelmed by his incompetence. Security had escorted him from the building yesterday afternoon. After that he couldn't remember anything else about the day.

Hmm…is it really all that bad? he wondered. *That job sucked, anyway.*

He was basically a data entry monkey in a suit. Another week and he would've had to install a keg under his desk to keep from blowing his brains out.

In the corner of the room he saw Lola mopping something up.

Lola? He was having difficulty understanding what was happening. *What's she doing here?*

He looked at the apartment through her eyes.

Holy shit, this place is a total disaster!

His memory was a bit foggy, and he wasn't sure about her itinerary, so he decided to just act like he had expected her arrival. He knew that when she had left he was on shaky ground. Her mom, whom he had never even met, was lobbying hard for his dismissal.

How fucked up is that? he asked himself.

There was a good chance she would dump him at any moment now; she'd sit him down and let him know *it's not working.* Especially after she learned about his job. She'd say she needed to *take some time off,* that she needed *to work through a few things on her own;* that *it wasn't him, it was her.* He knew the drill, he'd been on both sides. If she took Quinn it would be a clean trifecta of loser-dom. Job, girlfriend, dog—and all in the same week! He felt like Bill Murray at the beginning of *Stripes.*

He started warming-up his defense mechanisms.

I knew from the start she wasn't a good fit; she grew up a rich kid, and that's just not who I am....

Feeling sorry for himself, he started silently singing a Marshall Tucker Band line that helped during these times.

Well it ain't gonna be the first time
this old cowboy
spent the night alone.

123

He missed his brothers. He wondered where Clay was. *Probably off killing people,* he thought. Why did that seem appealing relative to his current predicament?

It was still light outside, he had a galloping hangover, and he was already craving the hair of the dog. He roused himself and started helping Lola clean up the flat. There was no doubt she was focused. When she first saw that he was awake, she had just raised her eyebrows questioningly. It was a rhetorical inquiry into his activity during her absence. He knew he would be catching a ration of shit at any moment, and didn't want to have to explain himself. Barely able to maintain his balance, he did a good job of behaving in a polite and loving manner, all the while acting like his weekday afternoon presence in the apartment was normal. He kept his shields partially raised.

As the day moved on, they got most of the living space squared away, and he was getting hungry. The small feeling of accomplishment from cleaning the apartment was quickly offset by his screaming hangover. He really needed a beer, so he suggested they go grab a bite in celebration of her return to the West Coast. As they walked uphill the two blocks to Union Street, he couldn't believe how winded he became. He knew the lecture was coming and was already preparing his counter-strategy.

His brain was working overtime: *Lola always gets bent out of shape when I go on a bender, as if I've got a big problem. She calls me a "borderline alcoholic in denial."* He hated being labeled. *So what if I quit my job (involuntarily)? Lotsa people move around until they find their niche. She should have spent some time growing up with my family, then she'd really know what* irresponsible *was.*

He was starting to work up some hostility towards her anticipated judgmental bullshit.

Lola was silent.

They walked over a few blocks, to Perry's, where Lola could get a salad and Keenan could get a burger. At dinner he ordered a pitcher of beer. He realized more drinking would likely catalyze a confrontation, but he was feeling defiant, which led to more rationalizations.

We're not married. I don't have a problem. A lot of guys have a few beers every now and then.

He was already projecting himself as abandoned.

Who cares what I do around this short-timer? Fuck, I've paid more than my fair share of our expenses, I'm a grown man—I'll do whatever the fuck I want. I don't want to fight about it. If she's gonna leave, so be it. Besides, if I don't get a drink right now my fuckin' head is gonna explode!

Lola watched him closely. She had no idea if her strategy would work, but she felt like she had to make one more sincere effort before writing him off permanently. Reminding herself to think of him as a scared boy, not as a selfish addict, was difficult; his behavior was infuriating. He didn't even appear to be aware there might be a problem.

It's like he's not even thinking, she concluded sadly.

She was committed to not offering unsolicited advice…no angry reprisals. He had already heard everything she had to say—a thousand times or more. The grooves of their relationship were well worn.

She worked her way down the mental checklist: very few people want to be addicts, and very few adults want to be told what to do. Could she allow Keno the space to reach a conclusion about healthy behavior on his terms, without her constant attempts to control and cajole? Would his conclusions match hers, or would they at least share enough common ground to make him an acceptable lover and companion—a potential husband and father to her children? Right now he wasn't really close. She was convinced connection was the key, a potential portal to trust and communication. But which came first, and how could she get there? Her theory suggested he needed to somehow have enough hope for economic viability and future connections that he would forego the masking agent of alcohol. Hopefully one month of patience and love would make him strong enough to find it on his own.

Oh fuck, she concluded in a brief moment of clarity, *this whole thing is a ridiculous crapshoot.*

She knew demanding and shaming hadn't worked. Pedantic lecturing was useless, and ultimatums passed unfulfilled. All of these strategies only increased his stubborn, contrarian, isolationist resolve. She was committed to the one last idea she had developed while back home: Non-Oppositional Behavioral Therapy. NOBT. Non-judgmental listening, presence, observation, touch, love. This was her Hail Mary.

Reviewing his background for the umpteenth time, she tried to find some compassion. She knew Keenan's mother had never nursed him as an infant, so he had missed out on the early colostrum and some degree, ipso facto, of the maternal bonding. His family had moved regularly, and his father, though not abusive, was supposedly not around much. Another missed connection.

She shook her head and laughed at herself silently. *Jesus, Lola, just listen to yourself. A degree in psychology combined with a broken love interest—and suddenly you've become a left-coast fruitcake. Carl Jung's undereducated California nut job. Are you that hard up?*

She resisted the doubts, tried to focus on the positive.

This man has something inside that's special…something I think is worth trying to save. I owe it to us to try. One foot in front of the other. Crawl, walk, run. It's only a month. If he doesn't get better, I move on and leave him in an unemployed heap. No guilt and no regrets.

Keenan was on his third glass of Bud while Lola was still sipping her initial glass of iced tea. She was polite and present, but not gratuitous, and with no apparent agenda. Keenan was feeling pretty good and marveled at the diminishing properties of beer. As he took a huge bite of his pepper-bacon cheeseburger, all of the colossal anxieties that had weighed so heavily during the climb to Perry's were now receding from his consciousness. His mind started to wander. *The simple pleasures of bacon*, he thought, as he chewed through the meat, bun, and garnish, his mouth simultaneously pulverizing the food with his molars and injecting saliva into the salty aggregation. With the help of peristalsis, his esophagus gradually migrated the soft, wet, fatty mass to his stomach, successfully completing the first steps of digestion. He considered the future journey of the caloric bundle and wondered at which point it would officially change from nourishment to excrement. He supposed it was a matter of perspective, and suspected that Quinn was much more flexible as far as the issue of shelf life was concerned. His worries finally submerged to nothing as he took another long drink of the draft beer.

No wonder people like this stuff…it works! Like fucking magic!

He looked across the table.

God I love Lola, he thought. *She is so incredibly, fuckin' beautiful. And no nagging tonight.*

She was really starting to understand him. Finally.

The first week was ridiculously hard, and she almost walked out multiple times. Keenan had two sober nights; the rest were just depressing. There was no trust, and she had to treat him like a criminal, shadowing him everywhere. Not willing to make love when he was drunk frustrated him, but she stuck to her guns, telling him she loved him but wasn't willing to have sex with him in all circumstances. She didn't even mention alcohol; she knew he could figure it out.

He didn't like to drink alone, so at night he would go out and she would stay with him. Everywhere. She would even follow him into the men's room… which made for some awkward moments. The other men, almost all of whom behaved well in her presence, had mixed reactions as she stood in a corner and stared at her feet. Some thought it was hot, most were embarrassed, and a few were outright hostile. A few deviants would go out of their way to wave what they thought were noteworthy penises into her field of vision, but that sort of behavior was unusual. She considered writing a novel: *How the Other Half Pees.* Eventually she developed a speech that served to alleviate the tension. She would tell her fellow bathroom inhabitants that she was sorry, but her brother was a veteran with epilepsy and some other mental health issues, and his condition required a caretaker's presence at all times.

She never got a complaint after that.

At first Keno thought her presence in the head was funny, but after a few days he got tired of the joke and started to object. Soon thereafter he became resigned to her commitment, and accepted his epileptic role. When he asked her what she was doing, she always had the same answer:

"I just want to be with you."

When they got home he would often pass out. That was a happy ending for her. The hardest times were when he stayed up, as those nights were frequently occupied by intense ranting and invective. He was ruthless, his intuitions were strong, and he knew her weak spots. Especially when he was drinking. He would tell her to leave him; to go home to her "hoity-toity, rich parents." He would say she wasn't the right woman for him, that whatever she was doing, trailing him everywhere, was "unnatural" and "not healthy." He accused her of being "codependent." Other common themes were that she was "pathetic" and "evil" and needed to "get her own life." One time he told her she was "a fat toad" and "a lousy lay," to which she barely turned away in time to hide the tears.

She practiced an extreme form of empathy, telling herself it was the alcohol talking, not Keenan, and reminding herself of all the challenges he faced. *These are his insecurities talking*, she reminded herself. *He's full of self-loathing; he's never learned to fully trust and communicate.*

She went through her checklists: Movement. Nature. Friends. Personal growth. Service. Humility. Compassion. Gratitude. NOBT.

Fortunately, he never turned threatening or violent. *That* she would not have tolerated.

The mornings were the best. He would generally wake up remorseful and apologize for acting like a crazy person.

"It's okay baby," she would tell him, "we all have bad days."

She'd touch him gently and ask if he'd like some breakfast. He'd insist on first going for a run. He'd try to cleanse the demons by setting off at a punishing pace down to Crissy Field, stopping for pull-ups along the way.

One afternoon they went windsurfing together…chasing each other out to the Golden Gate Bridge and back…mowing the lawn until the sun dipped into the Pacific. Because the wind and tides were right, they raced over to Fort Baker in Sausalito, gybed, and then sailed back to Crissy, jumping the wakes of the massive oil tankers as they motored through the shipping channels.

Twice they went over to Mount Tamalpais to ride mountain bikes, starting together in Muir Woods. They climbed under the shady canopy, and she'd chase him up Deer Park Trail, both of them breathing hard as they wound their way through the giant redwoods and worked their way to the summit. As they gained elevation they burst out of the fog to be greeted by a panoramic view of the Bay Area, with the smells of manzanita and the Pacific Ocean enveloping them. They completed the loop by flying down to Muir Beach on the Coastal Fire Road, passing herds of elk along the way. She was continually amazed at Keenan's capacity for physical activity, especially given the amount of abuse he heaped on himself at night.

She kept his exercise clothes clean and in plain view, and was always there, gently touching him, patiently observing, listening, not judging, hoping her presence made it more difficult for him to rationalize his behavior. She made dates with their friends, trying to help him to a better place through example and connection. He couldn't fool himself any longer: she was an ever-present witness, her ambition to be a loving audience for his reconstruction. When he lashed out she always just asked if she could be with him, not ever presenting him an opponent to fight. She was hopeful that he could see their untroubled future through her eyes.

There were moments when she was sure she couldn't stand another minute playing her role. *I'm a feminist…this is crazy!* she constantly thought.

She often loathed what she had become, feeling stuck in some stand-by-your-man film on the Oxygen network. In college, she had hated all the self-help and relationship books her girlfriends were reading…and now she was living one. The only thing that allowed her to continue with the plan was creative pride—the fact that the plan was hers. And, sadly, the finality of it all: she knew she could put up with pretty much anything for just a month.

She didn't have to say anything about alcohol being the problem. He knew. The fact of it hung in the air of the one-bedroom apartment like a foul-smelling pile of ordure. It was up to him, he just had to walk over and clean it up, as he was responsible for the mess. Hoping he'd eventually tire of it, she never even acknowledged it was there.

Throughout all the insults and questions, she continually stuck with the same answer:

"Please, can I just be with you?"

During the tail end of Lola's second week back, Keenan put together three days of sobriety. He started talking about looking for a job and asked Lola for her opinion. Supportive in a general sort of way, she told him at some point they would run out of money, and rent and food weren't free, so looking for work made sense. Outwardly, she was neither snippy nor jubilant with this observation—but she did smile.

The third night, while he was thinking about jobs, he remembered that he had run into a friend from his high school days who was doing pretty well. They hadn't been particularly close, but they had recognized each other at a financial district happy hour event. The friend had told Keno to come talk to him about a job if he ever wanted a change, and that he was always looking to hire rabid competitors. Keno asked Lola what she thought? She said she felt he could do anything if he set his mind to it and then asked what the friend did. Keenan couldn't remember. He asked if she knew where they kept the business cards they had collected? She got up off of the couch, went into his desk, found the business cards, and brought the box to him without showing much emotion. Inside she was doing backflips.

He made it through his third night and into the fourth day without a drink. She didn't change her interaction with him in a significant way, as she was convinced he had to own this, but she noticed he seemed to have regained something, though she couldn't tell what. Focus? Ambition? Intention? Hope? The change was subtle but significant.

Midmorning Keenan asked for some privacy so he could make a business call. She listened in the hallway, out of sight, while he used the kitchen phone to call his friend.

"Hi, my name is Keenan Barton, is Patrick Bowman available?"

Lola found herself silently cheering Keenan's efforts. *Nice job, Keno!* she thought. *Only slight Southern drawl. Decent enunciation. No contractions.*

"I'm a personal friend...."

Fingers crossed!

"No problem, I'll hold...."

So far so good. Lola caught herself holding her breath.

"Hey Trick, man, how'r'ya? Thanks for taking my call...."

She began to lose some of her optimism. *What type of grown man goes by the name "Trick"? A pimp? A drug dealer?*

"I'm great thanks, howz biz...?"

Violent, I bet!

"Good to hear, man....Hey, I don't mean to bother you, but I was hoping we could maybe grab a beer or something?"

Lola's entire body stiffened. She wanted to scream. *No! Fuck! What an idiot! Two weeks of work down the drain!*

She could barely keep from running into the kitchen and clocking him with a rolling pin. She hated all of Keno's Florida friends! They were mostly criminals who lacked any sensitivity to violence.

"Uh huh...Okay, I understand, no problem. "

She had returned to concentrating on the conversation.

"Yeah, man, I know that area...of course I remember that. It torments me every night." He laughed. Lola's imagination was running rampant. She imagined Keno and his friends at some delinquent high school party where they got a poor uneducated swamp girl high on Quaaludes and alcohol, then coerced her into pulling a train. Lola had spent nearly two unnatural weeks preparing for the sainthood, and now things were starting to badly unravel.

"Thanks for asking, he's doing better…."

Again her ears perked up. *What's this about?*

"Yep, still in a wheelchair, but he can use his arms now."

She knew whomever Keno was talking to was probably complicit in the tragic events from long ago. But he couldn't be a total asshole if he was asking him about Paul.

"Okay, see you at six. Thanks a lot, man, really appreciate it."

Lola slipped silently out of the hallway and into their bedroom while Keenan replaced the receiver. It took everything she had to keep her mind from galloping from disappointment to devastation—and finally to anger.

Great, she thought. *A drinking reunion with one of Keenan's derelict, high school friends. So much for connection.*

Keenan walked into their bedroom with a sheepish look.

"I need to meet a friend tonight."

She was sitting on their bed, fighting hard to control her emotions.

Stick with the game plan…only two more weeks to go.

"Okay, baby. I'll come with."

"No, baby, this is for business."

"No problem, I won't interrupt. I'll be your chauffeur and bodyguard," she quipped with a forced smile.

"I'll be back early."

"Can't I just be with you?"

He raised his voice and hardened his tone.

"I'm trying to get a job, Lola. I'm a grown man. I don't want him to think I'm unemployed and need a babysitter."

She was losing it. Her patience had run out. Her resolve was crumbling. *Fuck it.* Her voice increased in volume and gained a tone of bitterness.

"But you are and you do."

He stared at her while the muscles in his jaw tightened.

She couldn't restrain it. It came pouring out in a flood of emotion.

"Keenan, I care about you. I don't want you to go out with an old high school drinking buddy. You're doing so well. We're doing so well. Don't throw it all away. Don't throw *us* away."

She started tearing up. *No, not this,* she thought. *This wasn't the type of woman she was. She didn't use tears to manipulate men; she negotiated from a position of strength and mutual respect.* She couldn't help what came next.

"I love you. Keno. Please don't do this."

She started sobbing uncontrollably, whispering through the tears.

"Oh god, I'm such an idiot…."

She thought about all the hope, all the time, all the stupid dreams….

I should've listened to Mom.

Later, Keenan would realize that it's often the revelation of our vulnerabilities that makes us most endearing. That there is an element of trust embedded in such intimate exposures. At first he was feeling frustrated and hostile for what he perceived to be Lola's lack of confidence in him. But as she broke down in tears, a wave of empathy overtook him. He subjugated his feelings in favor of hers. If he were more self-aware, Keenan would identify that moment as the inflection point in their relationship. It was as if something in his head clicked…he could see and feel her pain and wanted to make it go away. It wasn't an effort or an obligation. He *wanted* to do it.

For a moment he stood defiantly in the doorway, but then he walked over and sat next to Lola on the bed. He put his arms around her and kissed the side of her head through her hair.

"Patrick doesn't drink alcohol. We're meeting at a place in Japantown. His mother is Japanese and his father is Jamaican. He likes to drink tea."

Lola heard the words but they didn't register through her congestion and tears.

"What—?" She stuttered. "Who's…Patrick?"

"Patrick? Trick? My friend from Florida? I'm meeting him at six tonight. He doesn't drink."

"Really?"

"He says he may have a job for me."

Lola took in Keno's words. The next moment, a heavenly ray of light penetrated her gloom. She dried her tears on Keenan's shoulder, squeezed him hard, and offered a silent prayer.

1992
California

CHAPTER 15

The Tropicana

Sitting, partially clothed, on a cold, metal bench, Keno found himself being kept in what appeared to be an abandoned, low-ceilinged, second-floor locker room. The space was dark, like the interior of a damp, windowless, thirty-foot-wide box in considerable need of repair. Exposed wires and pipes ran across the ceiling. More than once Keno's peripheral vision had picked up the telltale glimpse of scurrying shadows; but when he focused on the darkness the phantom rodents disappeared. An open area to his right contained a handful of syphilitic shower heads dripping their contents onto a moldy tile floor. His business suit, tie, and dress shirt hung from a peg on the wall, while his leather shoes carefully kept his skivvies and socks from touching the floor.

It was chilly. Keno's fellow detainees were also in various stages of undress. As the alcohol began to wear off, their constitutions slowly deflated; previously, they had collectively regarded themselves as a group of five "winners" awaiting their respective turn to participate in that evening's show at the Hollywood Tropicana. The three Japanese businessmen were suffering through serious cases of nicotine withdrawal. The Guatemalan dishwasher, who was supporting twenty-two grandkids back home, had already dropped three days' wages on that evening's activities and was feeling his early enthusiasm change to guilt as he berated himself for succumbing to the pressure of his younger coworkers. The smaller men glanced around nervously as the bass from the sound system forced its way upstairs. Keno was by far the largest, youngest, and most pale of the men. He also appeared to be the only one who spoke fluent English.

All of them had come to the venue with groups of friends or colleagues to watch nearly naked American girls wrestle in a pit of mud. Each of the five had bought themselves a place in the show by successfully bidding to challenge one of five girls—or more accurately, their groups had won the bidding, and they had been selected by their friends to have the honor of getting in the mud. The slots had been auctioned at an average price of about one hundred dollars. Each of the girls had been dressed in costume; Keenan's opponent was a blond policewoman. He couldn't recall why his colleagues had deferred to him, but he was feeling more duped than chosen.

One of the club's bouncers, uniformed in a black-and-white striped referee's jersey, had led the group upstairs and given them brief instructions.

"Wait up here…I'll come get you when your girl's ready. Find a pair of shorts to wrestle in from that box over there. You can hang your duds on the wall. Relax, it'll be a few minutes." He nodded to them quickly. "Name's Telford, my job is to make sure you make it in to the ring on time. I haven't lost anyone yet."

Then the brawny zebra turned and left them alone. Apparently one of the Japanese guests had been to the Tropicana before, because he immediately grabbed the tall cardboard box and started working his way through the clothes inside. When the box finally made its way to Keenan, the only thing that came close to fitting him was a pair of red Speedos.

Fuck! Keenan thought. *This is gonna be really bad.*

He dug through the box again and this time spotted what appeared to be thin, cotton pajamas. He pulled out the boys' size XXL bottoms. They were pathetic; threadbare with sagging elastic, covered with blue race cars, and ending midcalf.

What the fuck?

He shed his street clothes and slipped into the PJs. The thin material brought his junk into obvious relief.

When life gives you lemons…

Two hours earlier, Keenan and two colleagues had been hosting a dinner for a client at the LA hotspot, Citrus. As a relatively small enterprise, the client didn't warrant such firepower, but Trick had decided to use the opportunity to spend some quality time with his new partner. Michael "Pee Wee" Jones had been a thrower at UCLA, focusing on the discus and hammer. A larger-than-life character, his six-foot, five-inch frame carried 280 charismatic pounds in blatant disregard of gravity. If it wasn't for his quick-release grin, some might consider him menacing. Pee Wee ran the LA office of Bowman Barton, the real estate merchant bank that Patrick and Keno had started four years earlier. Keno had hired Pee Wee, so it made sense that they got along well. Their comfort with each other likely came from a shared upbringing in the blue collar south; they both spoke the language of sports, beer, and family dysfunction, and had been smart (or lucky) enough to not let that spoil their ambitions. Currently in their early thirties, their experience had softened some of the rougher edges; but they could still access redneck when the job called for it. They also appreciated the dance of genteel seduction embedded in human interaction—the verbal and physical cues found in word selection, tone, inflection, and the well-placed touch. Like all good salespeople, they were skilled at *connecting*: they could find common ground with nearly anyone. They would then use that small foundation to build a skyscraper of trust.

After a lovely early dinner, Trick found himself ordering dessert—as well as the check. He picked one of everything off of the dessert cart, knowing that whatever the group didn't finish, their client would take home to his family. This was his version of corporate swag. Trick knew if they missed the 8:30 back to San Francisco, the next option didn't leave until 11:45. As the founder and managing partner of a small business, he couldn't afford to lose three hours waiting for a plane in LAX.

Eight years ago, in 1984, when Keenan had first called looking for a job, Patrick was a rising star in the SF commercial real estate world. The former football celebrity already had a capable mind and a strong work ethic; what was really propelling him was fortuitous timing. As a friend dryly noted years later, Trick had "fallen onto the up escalator." On the eastern rim of the Pacific, in the early 1980s, Japan was exploding in an economic frenzy of government-co-ordinated manufacturing and banking. As the island nation moved strongly to expand east into the United States, California absorbed the first wave of the invasion. People started to notice as armies of Japanese workingmen arrived with trillions of yen to invest. The price of assets ranging from iconic office buildings to Pebble Beach golf courses started trending up. All the Japanese businesses needed services—lawyers, accountants, dentists—and, of course, office space. At first, Trick wasn't even aware of the incoming tide.

After graduating in three years with a joint degree in economics and philosophy, Patrick moved out to Northern California. The loss of his football scholarship brought an awareness that the real world could be just as competitive as the football field, and he had seen enough of what Florida offered an under-educated man of color to know that path wasn't for him. A week after leaving Tallahassee and returning home to Largo, he packed all of his possessions into two bags, hopped on his ancient BMW motorcycle, and rode the Christopher Columbus Transcontinental Highway all the way to California. He pounded the San Francisco pavement relentlessly for two weeks and was finally able to catch on with a large commercial real estate outfit that was starting to feel some anecdotal pressure to diversify racially.

During his first few months he drank from the fire hose. He did everything—sorting the mail, picking up dry cleaning, all the while listening and asking questions. Sleeping on the couch of a distant cousin, he rode the bus to work every day, was the first one in and the last one out, and read everything about real estate he could get his hands on. His daily routine became a time-motion experiment in efficiency: he ate Top Ramen noodles, rice, beans, potatoes, raw broccoli, canned tuna, and hard boiled eggs. It allowed him to save nearly every penny of his meager salary. He cut out everything superfluous—no alcohol, no dating, no TV, no going out. Knowing that for his long-term health he needed exercise and sleep, he carved out time to make sure he was getting enough of both. Every morning he was summoned awake by Sly Stone singing "Underdog". It was his call to arms. He would immediately roll out of bed, do one hundred push-ups, one hundred sit-ups, and then go for a three-mile run. He had two dark suits, three white button-down Oxfords, and three ties; everything that needed washing or pressing he did by hand. Having long ago abandoned his dreams of becoming a professional running back, he had no doubts or conflicted internal conversations about whether or not he was following his passion. This wasn't about self-fulfillment. He didn't have that luxury. This was purely about making money and building a future. The bottom rung of the white corporate ladder allowed just enough space for two or three of his fingers—and the gators were snapping at his heels. Years later, Patrick discovered a Ray Wylie Hubbard song named "Rabbit" that reminded him of himself during those early make-or-break years:

> *I saw this ol' dog he was chasin' this rabbit*
> *I saw a dog a'chasin' this rabbit*
> *I saw this dog he was chasin' this rabbit*
> *It was on Sunday, about noon.*
> *I said to the rabbit, "Are ya gonna make it?"*
> *I said the rabbit, "Ya gonna make it?"*
> *I said to the rabbit, "Are ya gonna make it?"*
> *The rabbit said, "Well, I got to."*

In Trick's mind he was the rabbit and life was the dog.

He had been hustling hard for six months and was aching to close his first deal. Generating some revenue would allow him to feel like a contributing member of the team, and he was sure if he could just get some points on the board he would soon be hanging out with the guys and telling his own war stories. Unfortunately he had no connections on the West Coast—no listings, no clients who needed office space—and he was having trouble developing his own network. Management wouldn't carry a nonproducer forever, and he felt the dog nipping at his heels. He was still the youngest and least experienced broker, and so he was often stuck handling dead-end inquiries that came over the transom. Patrick's break came early one morning in spring, when he was sitting in the bullpen answering phones.

"Patrick Bowman, Strunk and Eden, how can I help you?"

He had worked hard to lose the "black" in his voice, but most could still pick up on it. He felt it wasn't as damaging here in progressive San Francisco as it would be in other more backward regions, but he still had his concerns.

"Harro? Ees Shtrunk Erden?"

The halting voice on the other end of the phone was clearly that of a nonnative speaker.

Probably Asian, thought Trick.

"Yes, this is *Strunk and Eden*, can I help you?"

"Mmmar…neem rees Kanji Hanasono. Arrr werdth Mitsui Trust."

Poor guy, thought Trick. *This is like pulling teeth for both of us.*

He considered just hanging up and moving on to something more constructive, but his conscience wouldn't allow it. Then Trick realized he could speed things along for both of them. He switched to Japanese.

"Hai, hai, Hanasono-san….How can I help you, most esteemed gentleman?"

Thanks to his mom, he was fluent in the language and nuanced culture of Japan. He hadn't spoken the language outside of his infrequent calls home for years, but he still had a basic grasp.

The voice on the other end of the phone was simultaneously astounded and grateful. He had been a top Tokyo University graduate but was finding it very difficult to communicate with the *gaijins* in their native environment, despite the high English marks he had received back home. There was always the threat of a shameful recall to Japan if he was unable to fulfill his responsibilities. Patrick's voice hit him like a breath of fresh air.

They continued in Japanese.

"Yes, my name is *Hanasono-san* and I am looking to rent office space for my company, Mitsui Trust."

"Well, sir, I am so glad you have called our well-respected firm. I am pleased to make your acquaintance. My name is Patrick Bowman, and we humbly are controlling more Class A commercial office space on the West Coast than any other local real estate business. May I gratefully host you for some tea at a time that is convenient for you, and we can discuss your needs?"

And so it began.

Patrick signed Mitsui Trust as a Strunk & Eden client after one meeting. It was unprecedented. The Japanese were notorious for their patience in executing business transactions. In eight months Trick went on to become the "go to" broker for prospective Japanese firms looking to purchase or lease real estate on the West Coast. By the time other firms figured out he was eating their lunch, it was too late. He had the early mover advantage and had developed his own network. *Bowman-San* controlled a big chunk of the Japanese demand, so the landlords started coming directly to him with their supply. Within eighteen months he was a huge player in the Class A market.

It all started with *Hanasono-san,* and all by word of mouth. At first the Japanese appreciated the similarities they shared with Patrick—the things that made their time in the United States easier—his facility with the language and cultural sensitivities, such as understanding the importance and ritual of tea. Over time, they grew to respect his honesty, business intelligence, and thoughtfulness. And, finally, it was his differences that brought him legendary status. The huge black man who went out with them, didn't smoke, drink, or chase geishas and yet always seemed to be having the best time.

Keenan's call had been serendipitous, and it was onto the rocket ship fueled by Japanese clients that Patrick invited his old friend. There weren't enough hours in the day to provide the level of competent service that Trick's clients expected. He wasn't getting enough sleep or exercise, and his health was suffering. The stress was getting to him. His morning routine had been whittled down to twenty push-ups and sit-ups and a run to (first) the coffee maker and then the bathroom. Trick recognized he needed help. He was being overwhelmed by his success and didn't really like any of his colleagues at Strunk enough to bring them behind the curtain. He needed a partner he could trust, whom he knew would go to war with him and never waver. Keno was as close to family as he could get. They had spent only about five hours together in total, yet the nature of those hours had allowed Trick to see into Keno's soul in a way that one hundred hours of interviews and barbecues could never match. After meeting Keno for tea, Trick decided to trust his gut and bring his Florida friend on board. He tasked him with being his shadow. Trick didn't have time to fuck around, he needed someone smart, someone whom he could trust, or he would lose new business. It was raining money all around him and he needed to put out a bigger bathtub.

The gamble paid off. Keno saw his opportunity and, like Trick before him, dedicated his immense energy to learning how to compete in a new arena. He did everything with Trick but sleep and bathe. First, he just helped support Patrick with his clients; but as he started to figure things out he developed his own network. Their flow of business became self-reinforcing…they operated as a complementary duo. In their second year together they started to diversify away from their Japanese base; when the Asians began their inevitable retreat, the pair's collective business hardly slowed at all.

After they had worked together for two intense years, they decided to expand beyond their role as agents, and they made their first syndicated investment as principals. They bought an underleased office building in the South of Market area that was never even listed. The exclusive opportunity to bid on the property materialized as a result of their networks and their reputations as ethical operators. In two years they successfully rehabbed the building then pushed rents to nearly double their previous level.

A year later they decided they no longer needed the ballast of Strunk & Eden. They formed a new partnership: Bowman Barton. Trick put up seventy-five percent of the capital and was the majority and controlling partner. After ten months they were in the black and never looked back. Three years later they decided to open an LA office. Keenan committed to commuting to SoCal for six months until they could find a new junior partner. Every Thursday night he flew home for the weekend and then took the first hop south early Monday. Lola became a full-time mom and raised their first boy in Mill Valley.

After three months in LA Keenan identified a competing broker, Michael ("Mickey") Jones, as his guy, and set out to convince him to join their start-up. When Keenan learned the titan's nickname was "Pee Wee," the tongue-in-cheek moniker only increased his resolve to bring him on board. Keno closed the Biloxi native a month later, after hosting Pee Wee for the third time at a hole-in-the-wall seafood shack on the Pacific Coast Highway ten miles north of Malibu. The two Gulf Coasters had split four dozen oysters and two pounds of peel-and-eat steamed shrimp, while regaling each other over pitchers of draft beer and tales of high school shenanigans. As the pair exited into a fog-enveloped parking lot, Pee Wee felt like he had known Keno forever. The next morning he accepted Keno's offer to join Bowman Barton as manager of the LA office; he was on a short track to becoming the third partner.

As Pee Wee drove them out of the Citrus parking lot in his Bronco, Trick took a call from his assistant. She had switched Trick and Keno to the later flight because the 8:30 had been cancelled due to mechanical problems. Pee Wee lived in Westwood.

"Well boys, we're pretty much toast," said Trick. "Three hours to burn in LA."

"Ahhh man, that sucks. Lola's not gonna be happy when I walk in at one-thirty."

In the passenger seat, Trick turned to Pee Wee.

"Well, Big Boy, any great ideas?"

Pee Wee ran through their options. A connoisseur of the nooks and crannies of SoCal nightlife, he also knew that his partners only rarely drank alcohol, and that changed everything. Then he remembered a recent conversation he had had with a workout buddy from UCLA. The place was right down the 101 on Western Avenue, just a few minutes away, in Hollywood.

"Hey guys..." he said. "There's a place on the way to LAX, just a few minutes away. I've never been...but I hear it's fun."

Knowing he was their tour guide, he didn't wait for confirmation. Accelerating into freeway traffic, he looked over his left shoulder then jumped two lanes. No more than six feet separated the Bronco's front and rear bumpers from those of the other cars, but none of the LA drivers complained. The giant looked over at his boss and gave him a big smile. Dinner had been great, but he had a big carnal hunger. The dessert cart had just whetted his appetite.

Time for an adventure, El Jefe!

In truth, Pee Wee thought that maybe the place was a bit sleazy for his partners—but he still thought it was worth taking the chance. They could burn a few hours then shoot to the airport on the 10. QED.

A short while later, as the three men got out of the vehicle and started walking to the club entrance, Keenan began feeling a bit of trepidation. He was silently questioning Pee Wee's judgment. Specifically, why the big man thought it might be okay to take his senior partners to what appeared to be a strip club. Tangentially, Keno was worried about how Trick might be perceiving the whole situation, but his poker-faced boss revealed nothing.

In a fortunate but not unusual coincidence, Pee Wee knew the Tropicana doorman and was able to save his team thirty bucks in entrance fees. Keno noted that there seemed to be a secret fraternity of unusually large and athletic human beings who all took care of each other. Everywhere he traveled with Pee Wee someone greeted him like a brother. Although he was certain that there was a secret handshake, Keno had yet to figure it out.

As they walked into the club, all three men were immediately surprised by the vibe. They had expected the usual, low-energy, catatonic riffraff. A sort of slow-motion, smoke-filled, circular panorama of losers preying on losers out of hormonal and economic necessity. But the Tropicana was different. The energy was more like that of a carnival. The paying crowd of mostly men buzzed with excitement. Large groups of Asians in suits and Latinos in clean ranchero kits were being served overpriced alcohol by young women. A DJ worked a killer sound system. But the most notable difference was the girls; they were gorgeous, enthusiastic... and everywhere. Serving drinks, selling kisses for a dollar, and just generally checking on the well-being of the customers. Most were dressed in tiny swimsuits, but Keno noted a sexy nurse and cheerleader in the mix.

Overseeing the whole circus was a loquacious Master of Ceremonies. A large man, he referred to himself as Big Daddy. Keno guessed (incorrectly) that he and Pee Wee were friends. Big Daddy was happily directing traffic, making sure the girls were being well-marketed but not overly pawed, and generally keeping the choreography on schedule. The club ran several auctions a night, where men bid on the right to wrestle with the girls in an artificial mud "ring," which was really more similar to a large, temporary, rectangular wading pool.

Like Pinocchio and friends heading into The Land of Toys, the three testosterone-soaked young men headed into the huge main room. After a brief scan they got lucky and snagged a table near the mud. Before starting the search for a server, they each settled in to their seats and wondered at their surroundings. Pee Wee caught the attention of a stunning, blue-eyed girl with auburn hair.

"What do you have on draft?" he yelled over the music.

The athletic beauty bent towards them at the waist, giving the boys an enticing view of her formidable assets. "Hi, my name is Joleen!" she yelled breezily into Pee Wee's ear. "We've got Bud and Miller Light!" She kept on smiling as the men's eyes responded to her generous exhibition. She was paid well not to care, so much so that she might even interpret the customers' attention as fun—as long as it came from the right source, and as long as the boys behaved themselves.

Pee Wee ordered a pitcher of Bud.

"Three glasses?"

She took a moment to look at all three men. She noted their suits, and Keenan's wedding ring. *Kinda cute,* she admired. *I wonder what they're doing here?*

Everyone looked at the boss. Keenan couldn't recall ever seeing him drink alcohol. Trick wound up and threw a wicked curve ball that caught his partners looking. He had to yell to be heard over the sound system.

"Yes, three glasses…and make it three pitchers…and three shots of your best tequila!"

Joleen smiled. *All right!* she thought. *This could be a pretty good table after all.*

Keenan looked hard at his pigmented friend, asking his question silently.

You sure you want to do this?

Trick returned the stare.

I didn't stutter.

Then Keenan looked at Pee Wee with raised eyebrows, again asking his question silently.

What do you think?

Pee Wee looked back, grinning and nodding his head. The B-52's *Love Shack* pumped out of the speakers. *Game on!*

Joleen smiled a last time, straightened her stance slowly so as to give the boys a last chance to admire her display, then went off to retrieve their drinks.

Keenan had grown tired of waiting in the dank holding pen upstairs. He suspected he would be the last contestant, and he was rapidly losing his buzz. He hadn't done much drinking over the last nine years, so he was a little concerned as to how his body might respond to the pitcher of beer he had just consumed.

Enough of this shit. What are they gonna do to me?

He grabbed his suit jacket off of the peg, put it on over his bare chest, and snuck back downstairs in the pajama bottoms, leaving his fellow cell mates behind and incredulous.

When Keenan reclaimed his chair between Pee Wee and Trick, the club was rocking. One of his Japanese cell mates had been sprung and was happily getting smeared by the nurse, who was now barely covered by a string bikini. A bewhistled referee roamed the perimeter walkway. He was supposed to be keeping the contestants safe but seemed mostly to be helping the nurse into more revealing positions, which the raucous crowd loudly appreciated. Adding to the whole bawdy feel was a running commentary of double *entendres* enthusiastically provided by Big Daddy.

Keenan settled in, first filling his empty beer glass, then topping off his colleagues' while he took a healthy swallow and explained to his curious table mates what was up. They applauded him for his ingenuity, and then proceeded to demolish their sixth pitcher of beer.

By the time the policewoman was up, Telford couldn't find her opponent. After searching every corner of the holding tank, he hustled back downstairs and shared his problem with Big Daddy. The MC figured it was just another shy guy from Tokyo, so he started urging the next contestant to "report to the ring." Then he continued priming the crowd, encouraging the missing opponent to reveal himself.

"Don't worry my friend," he insisted, "Veronica won't bite. Her guns aren't loaded…but her top sure is!"

Worried about the blemish on his otherwise spotless record, Telford was scouring the crowd for his missing charge, hoping to recover his own fumble. Seated at their table just a hop away from the ring, Keno was hiding in plain sight—pajama bottoms under the table and suit jacket open to expose his bare chest. He calmly drank his beer while his table mates laughed so hard that tears started falling.

After removing the last piece of her policewoman's costume, Veronica climbed over the railing and into the mud. She started taunting her unknown opponent by stretching provocatively and flexing her muscles. Noting that she was quite fit, Keno started formulating a strategy. Suspense was building as Big Daddy kept up his salacious commentary about Veronica's "gravity-defying assets." A spotlight searched the crowd. Pee Wee caught Telford's searching eye and pointed at Keno just as Joleen realized that Keno was the missing contestant. The DJ started playing the theme from *Rocky* as the spotlight, Telford, and Joleen all started to converge on Keno.

Keno chugged the rest of his beer then pushed back from the table. The volume of alcohol surging through his bloodstream was affecting his decision-making processes. Not sure about the stability of the ground beneath his feet, he nonetheless needed the liquid confidence to pull off the scene he was envisioning in his head. As a quick shot of tequila eroded the last of his inhibitions, he pushed himself to upright.

Now or never, pajama boy.

He straightened, making the most of his moment in the spotlight. He took off his jacket and handed it to Pee Wee. The *Rocky* theme was still blaring. Veronica was flexing and bending. Big Daddy was bantering. The crowd was waiting to see what came next. Telford and Joleen had arrived at their table.

Keno nodded to them. *Let's do this!*

He looked around at the crowd. Then he channeled his best Apollo Creed and ducked under the waist-high wooden railing separating the crowd from the square mud pit. All the time he stayed just out of the grasp of Telford and Joleen. He strutted with purpose to a more exposed position closer to Veronica. Stopping on his pre-chosen spot, he initiated a solemn stare down with the exiguously clad policewoman. Small parts of the crowd sensed the beginning of an uprising and began to choose sides; they had grown used to seeing compliant schmucks in diapers get mugged by near-naked girls. They had not expected a real confrontation. Maintaining rock-solid posture, Keno hiked up his drooping pajama bottoms and pointed slowly and intentionally, first at Big Daddy, then at Veronica; he finished by flexing both biceps. He now had the crowd's full attention. Pee Wee, who understood right away what was happening, hustled under the rail to join his buddy in the dramedy. Using Keno's jacket, he started fanning his partner as if the room were too hot and his man needed some cooling down. In an effort to build his momentum, Keno started jogging around the pit with arms upraised, slapping high fives with the wildly excited crowd. He would periodically backpedal, point at Veronica and yell:

"I want you, Ver-on-i-ca! I want you! I want you!"

The *Rocky* theme song continued to roar along with the spectators.

Pee Wee chased behind his pajama-clad friend, continuing to fan him with the jacket like a trainer between rounds. Much of the audience recognized the iconic scene from the first Stallone movie and started to join in the chanting and taunting, either for or against the Pajama Boy. The volume and the temperature were rising. Trick was laughing so hard he actually fell backwards out of his chair.

The scene had switched so quickly from one of coaxing a shy customer into the spotlight to that of an out-of-control pair of rogue players, that Big Daddy was momentarily at a loss. But Veronica, having some acting experience, started hissing and clawing at Pajama Boy and the human mountain that was Pee Wee. She had recognized how her role had changed and had immediately embraced it.

The crowd was frothing. Veronica and Pajama Boy worked their way around the pit. Big Daddy finally figured it out and went back to stretching word play and stereotypes in ways that barely made sense.

"Wow," he proclaimed, "it looks like we have one feisty pussy out there…at least she'll be able to rescue herself next time she's stuck in a tree!"

After one more lap, Keno slowed to a walk. But he continued pointing and taunting. Pee Wee continued his role as second until the referee stepped into their path. He blew his whistle, taming the house. But the audience still simmered as the ref announced the format: three one-minute rounds, the first starting in thirty seconds. He looked at his wristwatch for five seconds then looked up and barked "Twenty-five!"

Keno bid adieu to Pee Wee and waded into the concoction of water, cooking oil, and chocolate cake mix. In the opposite corner crouched a dramatically snarling Veronica, poised for attack. Stifling a smile at the thought of battling his petite opponent, Keno prepared for combat.

Halfway through the first round, with Veronica on her back trying to put Keno in a waist scissors, he acquiesced and found himself in a suggestive missionary-type position. He rolled on his back and she ended up on top, straddling him, her knees pinning his arms. As she tried to smear mud in his hair, he pulled her closer to restrict her movement.

"You're really fun!" she whispered in his ear, as if that wasn't usually the case.

"So are you!" His enthusiasm almost made up for his lack of conversational creativity.

They continued the faux confrontation, wallowing like porcine gladiators as the gooey chocolate mess infected everything within a six-foot radius of the action. The crowd fed loudly off of Veronica's villainous charisma and over-the-top acting; Big Daddy was egging the whole mess on, and Keno was hoping he wouldn't have a gastric rejection of all the alcohol he had ingested. Between each round, he hopped out of the mud and jogged around the ring, taunting and pointing, once again responding to the high fives of the crowd. Pee Wee hopped under the railing and followed him, trying to avoid mud spatterings while fanning his boy the whole way.

Big Daddy periodically tried to regain control of the program.

"Please, sir…you must stay in the ring!"

But Keno had the crowd on his side, and he continued to play to his strengths.

In the middle of the second round, the cheerleader from the previous bout ducked into the ring and joined her friend, double-teaming Keno.

Keno just laughed.

He let the girls do whatever they wanted until the end of the round; then his ego took over. He easily pinned both girls simultaneously. As the referee's whistle indicated the end of round two, Keno popped up, flexed his biceps one more time, and placed his foot on Veronica's mud-covered and inviting bum: the big game hunter lording over the carcass of his prey. Veronica took his gesture good-naturedly: she and her friend promptly reached up and pulled down Keno's pajama bottoms. When he realized what they had done, Keno reached down to rectify the situation…but then thought, *Who cares?* He returned to his trophy-hunter pose, with his mud-covered junk on display and his pajama waistband fighting to maintain its mid-thigh grasp. A burst of cheers pierced the noisy arena. The crowd appreciated Keno's indifference.

The referee blew his whistle and the final round began. Keno luxuriated in his role as a prop: he gave free license to the girls to give the audience a show. They slathered him head to toe in cake batter while he struggled to keep his pajamas in place. He spent the round's final thirty seconds monitoring his stomach to control any embarrassing bodily evacuations. By the end of the fight the women had recaptured the audience's loyalty. When the ref declared Veronica the winner, the entire house exploded in unrestrained agreement. Keno quietly shook Veronica's hand then hung his head in despair. The fickle reign of Pajama Boy had come to an end.

Keno rinsed off under the array of rusting shower heads in the upstairs holding cell. He got as much of the sticky mess off of his skin as possible, and then he headed back to his friends downstairs. His hair still secreted small deposits of oily mud, but he was mostly returned to his pre-wrestling state. Patrick wobbled to his feet and gave Keenan a standing ovation as he approached their table. Keno had never seen him like that.

"Well done, my brother. I haven't laughed that hard in years. Just. Fucking. Awesome."

Pee Wee gave him a massive hug and high five. "That was so much fun. Can we come back tomorrow, Dad? Pleeeeeaase?"

Keno thirstily poured a glass of water from the pitcher that Trick had recently switched to. He watched the circus that was continuing all around them. Before they could ask for the check and head to the airport, Joleen came up to the table, with a shining Veronica standing right beside her. The music was still deafening. From her standing position she leaned over and yelled into Pee Wee's ear:

"Veronica and I were wondering if you guys wanted to maybe party later? Casey? The cheerleader? She'd be up for joining too."

Pee Wee was stunned. In his experience, this NEVER happened. These girls were hit on so many times every night, he assumed spending more time with customers was the last thing on their minds. Most of them had real lives—real *relationships*—outside of the club and treated their jobs solely as a paycheck.

Considering the decision a no-brainer, Pee Wee didn't even ask his partners for their opinions. He could see the three of them in wheelchairs, fifty years from now, entertaining the guys in the nursing home with their story about the night the Tropicana girls invited them out. There was always another flight.

Smiling at Joleen and Veronica, he hurriedly accepted their invitation. Trick was quick to intervene.

"Excuse me, Michael, Joleen?" he interjected. "I hate to overrule my partner here, and we recognize and are flattered by the generosity of your invitation, but we have to get Pajama Boy here on a plane to SF in one hour. Please excuse our poor manners. Maybe a rain check?"

Pee Wee and Keno first looked incredulous, then crestfallen, as Pee Wee tried to plead their case with his boss. But Patrick held firm. They grabbed their things, paid the bill, and started weaving their way to the car. Miraculously, Pee Wee got them to the airport with a few minutes to spare, then drove home without injury.

After he had sobered up, and for years afterwards, Keno appreciated the sacrifice of Trick's intervention on his drunken behalf. Patrick had served as one of Keno's groomsmen; he knew the vows.

Later that night, while Keenan and Patrick were sharing a row on the flight home and laughing at a replay of the evening's events, things became more personal. They were both still pretty impaired, and after tonight Keno felt closer than ever to his business mentor.

"Hey man, how come you've never gotten married? I've never even heard of you even dating anyone. Don't you want kids?"

Trick had heard the questions before and was prepared.

"I guess I just haven't met the right person, brother. Besides, I'm married to my job."

"Lola has some hot single friends. I'm sure she'd be willing to hook you up?"

"Thanks Keno, but I'm good."

"Sorry, man just trying to help."

Trick looked at his partner for a second or two longer than usual. Keno could tell he wanted to say something. Then he looked away, and whispered something at the window.

"What, Trick? Sorry, say again?"

Trick looked away from the window, then turned partially back towards Keno with a sad smile, not meeting his eyes.

"We all want love and understanding, Keno, and nobody gets enough."

This was obviously a touchy subject for Patrick, Keenan tried to redirect with humor.

"Okay, boss man, I'sa sorry. Me'sa just tryin' to make massa be happy."

If anybody else had said this to Trick he'd likely be offended, but from Keno it always brought a smile. It worked again tonight. Keno changed the subject.

"How about Pee Wee tonight?"

"He's a good egg. I really like him. You did a good job finding him, Keno."

They started laughing again, picturing Pee Wee fanning his jacket as he chased his two-hundred-and-eighty-pound body behind his colleague's smaller frame. Keno running around the mud pen in skintight PJs, high-fiving the fully charged crowd, taunting and pointing at Veronica..

After a few minutes of silence, Patrick moved the topic north of the Tropicana.

"Hey Keno, have you ever heard of the Columbia River Gorge?"

"Isn't that a crazy good windsurfing spot up in Oregon?"

"Yeah, windsurfing, mountain biking, snowboarding. It's all there, everything we like to do within a half-hour's drive."

"Don't we already pretty much have that in San Fran?"

"Tahoe? A half hour?"

"You just need to drive faster."

Patrick smiled back at Keenan, but then he turned serious. He had a point to make.

"What do you want to do with your life?"

"Hmm, let's see…how about…and I know this sounds impossibly crazy… but remember—you asked….I start with dinner at Citrus, for free, with my best friends. After dinner I order everything off of the dessert cart; then I mud wrestle with two gorgeous bikini-clad chicks at the Tropicana who actually like me…while my friends and the crowd make me feel like a rock star. Then I go home and make love to my smokin' hot wife. How's that?"

"Smart-ass."

They both shook their heads in disbelief, grinning some more…but Patrick had something on his mind.

"Did you ever meet Mr. Strunk or Mr. Eden?"

"Not officially, but I've seen Eden in his office when he comes in on Fridays."

"They're both in their eighties now, and have more money than god."

"Sounds good so far," joked Keenan.

Patrick ignored him.

"I wasn't there but I heard parts of the story from several of the early partners over there, and I think it rings true. You wanna hear it?"

"I get the sense I don't have a choice."

"You're right." Patrick paused a moment then launched right in. "They started their business from scratch, just like us, and over five decades, sacrificed intensely to build the operation…the typical American entrepreneurial dream. They were incredibly successful, but at some point the business consumed them…like the plant in *Little Shop of Horrors*. They had relationships to maintain, employees and their families to feed, budgets to meet, people to manage and train. The world changed, the industry changed, commission structures changed, clients changed, it was a constant battle to maintain market share. A new challenge every day. Junior people spun out, stole their business model, stole their relationships, and chiseled away at their competitive advantage. They had to work hard to not become dinosaurs, to be current and competent."

"Sounds like a high-class problem."

Patrick pushed on.

"They had three things that each simultaneously required infinite energy and attention: their business, their family, and themselves; so they had to prioritize. They were always frustrating somebody as everybody needed more of them, and they essentially operated in a world where no one's expectations were being met, least of all their's. In short, everybody wanted love and understanding, and nobody was getting enough."

Keenan nodded. He could now see where Patrick was going.

"They started prioritizing the business—it was what they were good at—and the growing pile of money was an easy way to prove their value. It also went a long way towards solving their other problems. They were rightfully proud of what they were building; their successful business gave them power and prestige. They had both come from modest backgrounds, where money was always a challenge, and they tried to use the money as a surrogate for themselves; they bought things for their families: cars, jewelry, bigger houses and vacation homes, tennis and piano lessons, spa treatments; but underneath it all there was an inner decay. The replacement of quantity time with quality things wasn't working. Their families felt the implicit message that they were not as important as the business, and they resented it. Their wives were lonely and their kids were entitled. Disconnection and disillusionment followed."

Keenan was sure he would never get entangled in such an obvious morality tale.

"Success in the business world constantly reinforced their egos. They lost their senses of humility, compassion, and gratitude as the world clamored for their money and business, and lavished praise on them. Even their own employees constantly kissed their asses, as bonuses were subjective. They felt they were modern-day kings and rationalized bad behavior as being deserved given the burden of their lofty positions. They 'upgraded' their wives with newer models, but all they accomplished was replacing one set of problems with another."

The flight attendant passed by with the beverage cart.

"Something to drink?"

"Just water, and keep it coming, please." Patrick nodded wryly to the attendant. "I think we overdid it tonight."

The woman smiled knowingly.

"Been there, done that."

"Thanks."

After the interruption, Patrick looked back at Keenan.

"Am I boring you?"

"Not yet."

"So, Strunk and Eden both started having health problems as a result of too little exercise and too much stress. Hip replacements, TMJ, arthritis, gastroenteritis, inability to sleep, weight gain. With each new challenge they kept returning to what made them feel good. Their roles as businessmen. Those positions allowed them to temporarily forget their other problems. It was what they knew. As more time passed they started to disengage from their childhood dreams. They never got good at skiing or playing music. They never traveled the world on twenty dollars a day. They never danced to the Dead at the Pyramids in the shadow of the Sphinx. They had limited interaction with people who didn't acknowledge them as important. They got frustrated and impatient when trying to learn new things that didn't give them instant gratification. They looked down on people who had less money than them."

Patrick paused and looked at Keenan for some feedback.

"Can't we get rich and not become assholes?"

Patrick smiled at Keenan's ability to get to the core of it.

"I'm trying, buddy, but this 'get rich' stuff is a tricky business. No one hands it to you. You have to work your ass off for every penny. It's fuckin' hard to stay balanced."

"Preachin' to the choir on that one, Reverend. So what's your plan? I know you always have a plan."

Patrick took a deep breath and started laying it out.

"Becoming a commercial real estate broker was never my dream. In a perfect world I don't wear a suit and spend all day at the office; or spend my time hustling to show clients available space or a good time. My dream was to get enough money so I could do what I want, when I want, without worrying about the ramifications."

"Pure freedom, with limited responsibilities…pretty heady stuff. But what do you want to do?"

"Hang out with family and friends, learn new things, help the less fortunate."

Keno gave the answer some thought before responding.

"Not too specific and highly idealistic…where do you want to do this?"

"All over the world, but I want to make my home base in a small town, where the cost of living is low, the pace of living is slow, and people know their neighbors. Where being a good person is valued more than income, and the quality of life is valued more than material things. Where the recreation is world-class, and the environment is pristine."

Keenan was conflicted. He had grown to expect big dreams from Patrick, but this sounded like he had been listening to too much of the Staple Singers. He started singing both the call and response lyrics to "I'll Take You There":

I know a place (I'll take you there),
Ain't nobody cryin' (I'll take you there),
Ain't nobody worried (I'll take you there)…

Patrick was only slightly annoyed. A thought struck Keenan.

"Why can't you do this in San Francisco?"

"I could, and people do, but the ante is too rich for me. I'd have to work for twenty more years in the Bay Area. The cost of living is too high. And, I lose too much intimacy in an urban center. Time is our most precious resource, *amigo*. Sooner or later, for all of us, it runs out."

"That's why you asked me about the Gorge?"

Patrick nodded. "In another ten years I figure I'll have enough to pull the plug and never look back. There's two little towns I have my eye on. One in Oregon and one across the bridge in Washington. Hood River and White Salmon. Housing costs are about a fifth of San Francisco's, and the people are supercool. They're all crazed outdoor enthusiasts, like us. No one gives a shit about your Mercedes or gazillion square-foot monument to yourself. They all just want to move in nature with friends. We'd be normal there."

When Patrick first started talking about his plans, Keenan had been skeptical. He loved his life and what the three of them—he, Lola, and Patrick—had built; but he also knew the edifice they had constructed took long hours and a huge amount of energy to maintain. He couldn't keep running anaerobically forever. Already the stresses were revealing themselves at the edges of both his family life and his fitness level.

As Trick continued, Keno was hearing the proselytizing like a sinner who hadn't known he was lost. He had felt something was missing with his current life, but he couldn't put his finger on it. Sensing that something had also been gnawing at his partner, and knowing Patrick was capable of somewhat unique aspirations, he still hadn't been ready for a direction this dramatically different. As he thought about it further, Patrick's vision made more sense. *Besides*, he thought to himself, *even when his ideas seem crazy, Trick always does his research. He's gotten us this far hasn't he?*

Keenan was too smart to say or do something important without sleeping on it, especially with two pitchers of beer clouding his brain. He knew the vagaries of perception as it relates to time, and the power of words. However, his mind was already working excitedly on this new adventure, thinking about how long it might take to become a bona fide snowboarding and windsurfing virtuoso. He wondered how Lola would feel about it.

Maybe some horses to sweeten the deal…?

A Three Dog Night song from his childhood glided into his consciousness.

> *Everyone is lucky / Everyone is so kind*
> *On the road to Shambala.*

1996
Still Out West

CHAPTER 16—

Aloysius

It was an early Friday morning and Aloysius Barton was hurtling across the desert in his silver 1973 Mercedes-Benz 300D turbo diesel. He was headed south, from Las Vegas to San Diego, on a warming strip of pavement known as Interstate 15. The vehicle was twenty-three years old and hence "dated" in technological terms, but he loved it just the same; maybe even because of its aging dignity. Though he hadn't given the conveyance a name, he did consider that he and the Mercedes shared several overlapping traits, perhaps the most important being their graceful advancement down the path to maturity. He didn't enjoy his physiology's increasing signs of aging, but he took solace in knowing his hair would soon match the color of the vehicle's distinguished exterior. The sedan had been too useful to be considered pristine, but it was dependable. These were conditions he aspired to…although when honest with himself he had to admit he was only halfway there. The odometer revealed over 200,000 miles, but the engine still purred like a savannah cat when she was properly warmed up. They were partners—the Lone Ranger and Silver. The 300D was the only car he owned; it faithfully took him to work every day.

He had bought the Teutonic machine at an estate sale five years earlier, when he had first arrived in Las Vegas. The acquisition had been a stretch financially, but he understood the power certain status symbols had on his daily feelings of well-being. The leather interior alone was worth the price of admission. Every time he slid behind the wheel he felt like he was rejoining an ancient club, replete with the auras of decorum and gravitas. The experience gave him comfort in a way that was difficult for him to explain. It was as if the car gave him hope that there were still remnants of a Western European tradition in which civilized, educated people (with temperaments like his) could take refuge. A world of restraint and etiquette, where citizens weren't abusing the language—and each other—and where those in positions of power felt a fiduciary responsibility for the welfare of others. Where people and things worked as intended. He wondered if every generation, in their later years, felt like the bulwarks were crumbling around them. He considered the term "conservative" and the root word "conserve." An honest assessment would make clear that he was paddling his way, begrudgingly, towards that end of the pool. How ironic that someone like he, who had so willingly and comfortably upset the societal apple cart, was finding himself yearning for tradition and order.

The adventure had started earlier that morning, before sunrise. It was a time of day he had grown to appreciate in his arthritic years. He had spent an hour assembling the provisions that would allow him to look forward to the drive. Six Cuban cigars, a full thermos of freshly ground, imported coffee, a box full of his favorite cassettes, and a bottle of Stolichnaya. He actually had the foresight to review the car's vitals: oil, water, tire pressure—check, check, check. Proper preparation allowed him to glide into the long drive with few nagging trepidations…and now his life was good. The sun was rising over a mesa to the east, he had a full tank of gas, and he was headed to the coast.

Everything but the music had been acquired from the casino where he was employed as a "whale watcher"—a concierge to high rollers—a sort of modern-day butler. He felt the job was beneath him, although he knew he was lucky to have it and it was his longest stretch with one employer. He served mostly the financially lucky who misidentified their accumulation of wealth as skills-based. These men—and they *were* mostly men—actually thought they could beat the house as a result of a misguided belief in their superior intellect. Despite his modest repugnance when it came to his job's daily requirements, he fulfilled his responsibilities with a mature panache that his clients and employer appreciated.

Aloysius long ago realized that no job really suited him, but there was the unfortunate problem of dignified survival. Although he respected the virtue inherent in any work, he seemed to really struggle with the soul-sucking monotony of it all. He was supposed to have been born wealthy (yet another miscommunication in the cosmic absurdity called his life), so when that burden never materialized he was eventually forced to start scavenging. No matter where he landed, sooner or later things got numbingly routine. He preferred to self-diagnose as having an "active mind": it allowed him to avoid thinking of himself as lazy.

Permitting his mind to drift back to the provisions in the car, he reminded himself that the vodka was a reward to get him through the last hour or so of the drive, when the boredom could become unbearable. He figured he would pick up some fast food and caffeinated drinks along the way, as his urges required. There was a hole-in-the-wall in East LA called El Tepeyec that had the best pork burrito on the planet. His mouth started watering as he thought about the *chili verde* sauce. His long fingers pushed his favorite desert driving tape into the cassette player. He was pretty sure no album had ever nailed the essence of the American West as purely as U2 had with *Joshua Tree*.

I still—

—haven't found—

—what I'm looking for...

He smiled at the words. *Damn, it's like these Irish kids are channeling my thoughts.* How did artists do it—create works that could resonate so deeply with such broad, disparate audiences? He took another pull from the thermos and reached over for his first stogie. It was going to be a hot one, but right now he had the windows down, and he was comfortably pushing the old Mercedes at seventy miles per hour across the magnificent landscape. The air was still cool from the night's reprieve, and he had only passed a handful of cars. The arid, chalky horizon spun off in all directions.... Was anything missing? Maybe (he began to wonder) a woman? No, that would have been too much trouble. Besides, his equipment seemed to be malfunctioning lately. *Ix-nay on the oman-way,* he told himself. *Right now everything is perfect.*

But the next moment a contrary thought seeped in.

Well, "perfect" is a pretty strong definitive. He did, after all, appreciate intelligent female companionship. *A wife could cook and sew for me,* he acknowledged.

He hummed to himself.

*I'm reviewing
the situation…*

Did that make him Fagin? He'd like to think not. *Just my active mind again.*

He was only an hour out of Vegas, but his daily responsibilities seemed a lifetime away. The freedom of the road. He found himself searching for a phrase…a famous quote…maybe Oscar Wilde or Robert Louis Stevenson? Working his way through his cerebral locker room he eventually found the gem:

To travel hopefully is a better thing than to arrive.

CHAPTER 17—

The King of California

It was Thursday morning, and Keenan checked his luggage one more time. He had a full schedule and needed all the right gear. That night a client dinner was scheduled in downtown LA, and the next morning he needed to be out in Santa Monica for a site visit and early breakfast. After hustling to meet an appraiser in mid-Wilshire, he had to get to a late lunch in Orange County. On Friday afternoon he had to fight traffic all the way down to North County San Diego to beat the seven p.m. deadline to check in for the Horny Toad Triathlon. The schedule was doable, but driving in Southern California on the 405 was notorious for destroying the best laid plans. He needed a travel-ready suit, tie, dress shirt, triathlon gear (including bike), and some casual clothes.

Lola stood on the front porch, holding the younger of their two boys on her hip, while giving a gentle stiff-arm to the oldest. At issue was who was receiving the most attention from their mom; Sam aspired to replace his sibling. It was at that moment that Lola lost all doubt that the boys were getting too big for her to pick up.

"Do you have everything, Keno?" she called.

Just then the oldest punched his brother in the thigh.

"Samuel! Enough!"

Keenan was focused on his travel preparations.

"I think so."

The younger brother, Augustus, started simultaneously crying and kicking at his brother.

"Gus, you're gonna be okay."

She struggled to keep the rivalry from turning biblical while helping her husband to escape.

"The presentations for Friday?"

"Oh sh—…jeez! Almost forgot. Thanks, beauty girl."

Sam was circling Lola and Gus like a great white would an injured seal. Like most moms, Lola had been here before.

"Samuel, I'm warning you…don't do it."

She continued to stare reproachfully at her oldest boy.

"Bike, helmet, shorts, Speedo, goggles, dress shoes, suit, tie, shirt, wallet, money, sunglasses, sunscreen, toiletries?"

Her husband was now moving towards the Trooper.

"Check, check, Czech, and mate. Bike's in the car, all the rest is packed. I gotta go, baby, I'm already running late!"

Just before Keno got into the car, Gus started howling. Keno stopped, turned, and walked back to his family. Lola let both boys go, and they ran, with Quinn trailing, to their dad.

"Come here you hellions! Squeeze hug!!"

He picked up both boys simultaneously and hugged them hard. Quinn wagged aggressively. All four arms wrapped around his neck and returned the hug with such gusto that Keenan acted like his head popped off.

"*Pop!* Oh, my head! Put it back on! Quick!"

Then, the boys, in Keenan's arms, started pantomiming the necessary reattachment of their father's head to his neck, using a variety of fasteners.

"Staples, paste, buttons, nails, glue, tacks, Band-Aids, stitches, epoxy…I think you boys got it! Thanks! I almost lost my head!"

Everybody enjoyed the oft-repeated ritual. Keenan put both boys down then squatted to their eye level.

"Listen, Thing 1 and Thing 2. You take care of your mom and Quinnie-boy when I'm gone, got it?"

The two boys nodded obediently.

"I'm sure you'll both be extra-good, and if you are, I'll share my beef jerky and chocolate with you…and Santa Claus will receive an official 'Nice' letter, understood?"

More obedient nodding. They loved the goodies their dad brought home from the road.

"Also, as much as it hurts me, if I hear really bad reports from your mom… no beef jerky, no chocolate, and I will tan your bottoms until you won't be able to sit down for a week."

Now he *really* had their attention. Keenan had found that with Gus and Sam, the carrot worked most of the time, but fear could also be a tremendous short-term motivator. He didn't like to use the stick, but when he was leaving Lola alone with the savages for a few days, he felt justified in doubling the dose for prophylactic measure. In the San Francisco Bay Area the practice of spanking was so socially reviled that Keenan and Lola rarely revealed that they were infrequent practitioners. He didn't think it was yet a criminal offense, but he was pretty sure if outed they would be placed somewhere between smokers and polygamists on the ostracism scale.

After one more squeeze, he turned them back towards their mom, giving them each a little directional pat on their bottoms.

"Good-bye, babies, I love you soooooo much."

As he stood up and headed back to the Trooper, his mind starting drifting from affectionate to analytical. For a variety of reasons the trip south from San Francisco to San Diego was something he had been looking forward to for a while. He had grown to appreciate the early morning and planned on using the alone time to work through some issues that had been floating in his mental periphery. Driving provided just enough low-level stimulus to keep him occupied, but not so much that he couldn't engage in higher-level thinking. His brain worked well in this context, especially with the help of a little caffeine and sugar.

Even though it would mean adding three hours to his trip, he had decided to avoid the flat, dusty, inland route, Interstate 5, which ran through the farms of the Central Valley. He would motor south, closer to the coast, on the 101, all the way to LA. The proximity to the ocean was worth the extra time. The panoramic view of the sparkling Pacific that burst into view just south of Carpinteria was a sight he never grew tired of, and he felt that experience alone could be enough to renew one's faith in The Great Mystery. If he made good time, he would turn west in Oxnard and take Highway 1 along the water. Point Mugu, Zuma Beach, Malibu, Topanga, and Santa Monica….There was a reason so many people lived in California, and it wasn't because the taxes were low and the traffic was zippy.

He had already provisioned the Isuzu with a quart of brewed green tea, a few green apples, and three Snickers bars. He knew a great Mexican place in San Luis Obispo where he could grab a late lunch. Right next door was a butcher shop that sold artisan jerky. He had about ten hours of mixed tapes that would take his consciousness to memorable events in his past. In his younger years he would've picked up a six-pack as sunset approached, but that was no longer an option. He considered his metamorphosis and knew he was lucky. Wonderful wife, kids, house, job; he didn't want to fuck it up. He'd had a front row seat at that shit show. Sometimes he yearned for his previous self…but mostly he abided.

Speaking of "that shit show," he was meeting his dad that weekend in San Diego. Unexpectedly, Aloysius had reached out by phone. Surprising, because they hadn't talked in years. He was living in Vegas now and wanted to drive out and see his son. Keno told him about his weekend plans, and offered him a position as his *domestique*. The dad had agreed to spend the weekend with his son, including dinner on Friday and Saturday nights, and Keenan was a bit unsure of what to expect. It had been over twenty years since his dad's emotional move out of the house in Clearwater, and there had been limited correspondence since. He was worried maybe his dad had cancer…or something.

Mostly he remembered how dissimilar they were.

Lola corralled the boys and interrupted his thoughts by tossing one last question across the front lawn.

"Socks?"

"Yep!" he yelled over his shoulder as he simultaneously opened the door of the old Trooper and remembered the three pack of navy blue GoldToe socks he had thrown in his bag the night before.

God he loved this car. So many great memories. A bit faded around the edges, but still ready to rock and roll! Just like me! he admired to himself.

Quinn wanted to go, but his age precluded him from displaying much ambition. Lola had him by the collar.

"I need you to stay here and be the man of the house, Quinnie-boy."

Lola restrained Things 1 and 2 with a practiced precision as she watched Keenan's back recede with mixed emotions. She wanted to get in a car, any car, and drive south, with no kids and no responsibilities.

How sweet would that be? she postulated silently.

But she knew she would quickly miss her boys…all three of them, counting Keno…or *four*, counting Quinn. They were a team; she did her job and Keenan did his. She had a lot invested in this man, and he was delivering.

How can I possibly consider doing any less?

Plus, now that Keenan was making some real money, she had been able to become a stay-at-home mom. She had met other similarly positioned mothers in her Marin neighborhood and had been able to tuck into a nice social group. She'd even been able to wrangle some childcare and tennis lessons out of Keenan's penny-pinching budget. Raising kids was work, but doing it in Northern California, with some money, was a pretty good gig.

Keno called out as he started the car and rolled down the window.

"Bye Lola, I love you, *Mi Preciosa!*"

Lola and the boys waved as he backed down the driveway…into the street… and out of the gravitational pull of his family.

As she watched the Trooper drive away, Lola remembered back to the turning point in their relationship, twelve years earlier. She had gone back east to her parents' house for a visit that had originally been scheduled for a week. Every night she called home, and every night, whether he answered the phone or not, she became more certain that Keenan was a mess. She had no idea what he was doing, or when (or if?) he got home on the nights the phone went unanswered. In her father's study, she would return the phone quietly to its cradle and go to sleep pissed off, chastising herself for staying with such an inconsiderate bastard.

He wasn't even trying, she'd think.

Now, turning from the driveway and guiding her boys back into the house, she couldn't believe they'd threaded the needle.

CHAPTER 18

Scout

About five miles east of Barstow, while enjoying his second Monte Cristo, Aloysius saw the hitchhiker. Later, he couldn't recall the act of pulling over as being a conscious choice—it just happened. In his younger days, Al picked up hitchhikers every now and then. He found helping others was an easy way to make himself feel good. But he hadn't stopped for anyone in a long time. Obviously, there was something unusual about this wanderer that compelled him.

As Aloysius slowed the Mercedes, Scout began hustling down the shoulder with her bedroll and pack, hoping this wasn't some rich, Republican asshole trying to fuck with her. Noon was still a few hours—and twenty Fahrenheit degrees—higher, but the sun and her first ride had already clocked in as unpleasant. The ride with the pervey trucker had started out nice enough, but the vibe had turned weird when her host learned she was a student. The suddenly aspiring academic started asking her about campus sexual activity "nowadays." He tried so hard to appear nonchalant and knowing that he came across as uncomfortable and disturbing. When it became apparent Scout wasn't looking for a hook-up with a greying, potbellied, server-of-creepiness, he flipped personalities like a coming-of-age raccoon. His somewhat civilized persona switched to that of a mercenary wall-street trader, as evidenced by the bluntly offered, unimaginative trifecta of rhyming barter options not lifted from a college economics text:

"Gas, grass, or ass, girlie. Nobody rides for free."

Scout made her decision without hesitating. Still, she remained cautious, given the lack of transparency on the trucker's part.

"Sorry, not interested…I'll get out anywhere you can pull over."

While he disgustedly downshifted his rig to the shoulder, she gathered her few things and hoped that he had already reached his limit of indecency. She stayed alert and kept her hand near the sheath of the hunting knife she kept inside her bedroll. As the truck lurched to a stop, she quickly opened the cab door and scrambled to the gravel spot she would later run from when the Mercedes pulled over. As the trucker shamelessly departed, he left a rain of gravel and dust.

Aloysius had started running the car's air-conditioning about thirty minutes earlier, when the exterior temperature had first climbed above seventy-seven degrees. *Uncomfortable* was a region he liked to avoid.

As Scout approached the car, Aloysius rolled down the passenger window.

"Where ya headed?"

"Back to school. Pomona College? In Claremont, just east of downtown LA off of Interstate 10?"

It was clear now that she was female. When he had first seen her, he wasn't sure of her defining demographics: gender, age, ethnicity, height. Later, he would reflect on how strange it was that she had made such a strong yet nonspecific initial impression….

I'm happily cruising across the desert at about seventy-five miles per hour and haven't picked up a hitchhiker in years, he'd think. *I see a nondescript road-ghost and immediately decide to stop? Just weird. Especially given how indistinguishable she was. Some sort of strange mojo going on.*

She was wearing indigo jeans and an untucked, loose, dark, long-sleeved cotton T-shirt. A forest-green quilted vest and a camouflage knit cap provided an extra layer as insurance against the early desert chill. Broad shoulders, slim hips, and shoulder-length dirty-blond hair framed her strong, tanned face. Combined, her features had conspired to make her gender utterly indeterminate from a distance. She carried herself like an athlete or a soldier or a dancer, Aloysius was still trying to decide which. It was clear now that she had breasts, but they were far from prominent, mostly by wardrobe design. Her vest was unzipped, and he could see white block letters on the front of her shirt: H8SBAD. It took him a second, but he liked it.

"I'm headed the same way," Aloysius observed. "Put your pack in the back and hop in."

Scout took in the scene. The driver seemed harmless enough: blue Oxford button-down, slacks, receding grey hair kept tidy, tortoise-shell Wayfarers, clean shaven, around sixty.

Deciding to accept his charity, she reached for the door handle. "Thank you."

They drove in silence for about ten minutes. That suited her fine as she had already developed a somewhat calloused veneer around men. Ever since adolescence, attracting male attention hadn't been difficult, and her mom had offered voluminous warnings about the shortcomings of "the testicled ones." Scout was just here for the transport.

Aloysius was curious.

"So, college, huh? Have you decided on a major?"

"English."

"Really? Me too. Although it was a few years ago at this point."

He glanced over at her and smiled. She forced a similar but enfeebled response.

A few minutes of silence passed.

"Do you have a name?"

"I'm Scout."

"Scout…interesting name for a girl."

Struggling to find the right conversational balance, she didn't want to seem unappreciative or rude; she understood the concept of social give and take, but she also didn't want to open the door too wide.

"Thanks a lot for stopping. It was really starting to heat up out there."

"You're welcome, Scout, and pleased to meet you." He again offered the smile. "I'm Joe Gargery."

A long pause.

"Where are you coming from, and how did you end up on that stretch of road? If you don't mind me asking?"

"It's a long story, but I'm coming from the East Coast."

Her mom had taught her to be a sponge not a faucet.

"That's a long, potentially dangerous trip for a single girl. Are you camping alone?"

Here it comes, Scout thought. *The awkward, obligatory overture from the dinosaur who thinks he's a modern-day Humbert and I'm his Lolita. Damn...I was just starting to enjoy the air-conditioning and quiet ride.*

"Mostly. I've stayed with some friends along the way. It's not too bad," she answered guardedly. Maybe she could divert the expected proposition? "You were an English major? What's your favorite book?"

"Hmm...well, Scout, right now I'd have to say *To Kill a Mockingbird.*"

More silence.

"Do you have a favorite?"

"Well Mr. Joe Gargery, right now I'd have to say *Great Expectations.*"

Al looked at the road with a Cheshire Cat smile. It was nice to be understood. He fed the cassette player some Stevie Wonder and let Scout settle in. *Well played, Scout, well played indeed,* he thought, as he turned up the music.

But isn't she lovely?
Made. From. Love.

They rode in quiet for a long while, descending out of the San Gabriel Mountains and dropping into the densely populated flatlands. As they engaged the concentric circles of the Inland Empire, the drive became more of a slog through the congestion and visual drudgery of greater San Bernardino. Aloysius noted the monochromatic setting and wondered how these people survived the tediousness of it all. Having Scout in the car reminded him of his own college days...his mind veered off to *The Divine Comedy*. He thought that if Dante were right, he'd probably end up somewhere in the poet's second or third circle for his carnal sins. With the external temperature approaching one hundred, Al considered the possibility that he might already be there. He ached for the Stoly, but Scout's presence served as a restraint.

Al ejected *Songs in the Key of Life* and inserted Lyle Lovett's newest release, *I Love Everybody*.

"No way?" Scout looked incredulously at Al. "Lyle Lovett? This album is a-maaay-zing."

Al turned to her as she began nodding her head to "Skinny Legs." Raising her hand she pushed her hair behind her ear. Aloysius noticed that her green eyes might even be showing a modicum of respect.

For her part, Scout felt people with good musical tastes couldn't be all bad.

"I love Lyle, too. 'North Dakota,' from his last album? *Joshua Judges Ruth*? Has to be one of my all-time fave songs."

Scout forgot her veneer for a moment. She became a twenty-two-year old girl.

"Oh my god, can you believe Julia Roberts dumped him?"

"How do you know he didn't dump her?"

She looked at him skeptically. Scout was tired of people older than her bringing up what she thought were remote possibilities just to make a point. It was as if her age implied an underdeveloped wisdom that required instruction regarding the probabilities of life. She found it patronizing, and it interrupted the flow of the conversation.

"Why'd you pick me up?"

He carefully considered the question.

"You don't seem like the type," she clarified.

"Hmm…I don't know. I wondered that myself. Maybe there was something familiar about you…I'm not really comfortable trying to explain it."

He paused. She didn't respond.

"Why do you ask?"

"I'm interested in people's motivations."

"English major…with a minor in psychology?"

She let her first sincere smile slip out. He took the smile as an opportunity to probe.

"Why'd you pick a college so far from the East Coast? Avoiding a complicated relationship back home, maybe?"

He nailed it. But she didn't want to admit to being so predictable to a stranger.

"Nope. Just wanted to see what all the fuss was about…California and all."

"Makes sense." He nodded but didn't believe it. "I think California's the real deal. In my experience, some of the most beautiful landscapes emerge from the confluence of mountains, desert, and ocean. Unfortunately, too many other people seem to agree."

"I'm no cartographer, but that makes sense to me."

She was starting to feel just a tad more comfortable.

"How long until you graduate?"

"If all goes well, I'll be done in June."

"Then what? English teacher?"

"Why, is that what you do?"

Aloysius laughed, although she couldn't tell which he found amusing—the thought of the job or the thought of him *doing* the job.

"You already know what I do…I'm a blacksmith."

"Yeah, right."

She rolled her eyes and moved on to the next question to keep control of the conversation.

"Where'd you get your English degree?"

"A small school back in New Jersey."

"Rutgers?"

"Something like that."

They were about to merge onto Interstate 10, which would take them west towards LA. A road sign declared Claremont to be twelve miles away. The air pollution in the San Gabriel Valley was not as suffocating as usual, and they could clearly see Mount Baldy, topping out at around ten thousand feet, on their right.

They continued bathing in the ear candy of the stereo's Texas troubadour.

"In about five miles, you'll want to exit on Indian Hill Boulevard and head north towards the mountains. You can drop me off anywhere around there." Scout looked at her benefactor with a grateful smile.

"Roger that, Scout…and I insist on taking you to your front door. I'm not in a hurry, and I've always wanted to see the Claremont Colleges."

"Thanks, I really appreciate it."

From the speakers, Lyle continued to share his auditory art.

Penguins are so sensitive,
penguins are so sensitive,
penguins are so sen-SI-tive,
to my needs…

"So, Mr. Gargery, you never said, how's the blacksmithing business?"

Aloysius looked at Scout with a sober compassion.

"Please, call me Aloysius."

He had considered a short, clever answer, but his deeper, darker thoughts had been scratching for the surface, and for whatever reason he thought Scout was the right audience. Reaching for the stereo volume knob he diminished Lyle's presence. He had something to share and wanted to be heard. He took a deep breath and started unloading the burden.

"It's hard, Scout…life in the modern world is hard…long boring days, with lots of responsibilities and little in the way of excitement to break the monotony. Your boss is an ass and your customers are insensitive. Your colleagues are lobsters, and you're all stuck in the same tank. After six months you know every nuance of your job, and your mind starts to wander to more invigorating places. Unfortunately your body can't follow because you have a mortgage and five mouths to feed. You try to start an exercise program and practice better nutrition, but you discover there's a difference between 'simple' and 'easy.' Eventually, you can't wake up without caffeine, and you can't go to sleep without alcohol or pills—or both. You start to extrapolate, and you realize your dreams are rapidly becoming unrealistic. With horror, the truth of your situation sinks in: Sartre was right, you're stuck in your own little *Huis Clos* for the next thirty years, until the mortgage is paid, the kids are through college, and you've hopefully saved enough to retire. Your calculations bring to your attention that over those same thirty years you'll have had sex exclusively with the same partner over fifteen hundred times. At the future golden moment of liberation we call retirement, you'll likely be sharing your bed with someone's grandparent, and both of your bodies will be far along their way to an infirm, long-term system failure. As you more fully comprehend your situation, you realize your kids are sentenced to the same fate, and so you double your daily alcohol dosage, or, in some extreme cases, search for the mouthpiece to your handgun. Over time, the alcohol Band-Aid becomes a body cast, and you struggle to maintain a semblance of sanity. The uniform dullness and tedium of your existence continues to grind you down until drowning seems like a pleasant option. And then…you die."

Continuing to look straight ahead, he paused, reflected on his testimony, and realized he might've overdone it. Unfortunately he couldn't help it, the dark thoughts had been welling up, invading—and his usual antidote was hidden in the socially unacceptable bottle under his seat.

Lyle Lovett's tenor voice soothed in the background.

I love everybody—
Especially me.

Aloysius glanced at Scout then offered his last piece of wisdom, trying to tone down the darkness:

"Tread carefully, young Scout Finch. I advise you: Don't follow my path. Find a career that allows you to avoid the gloom that inhabits most of humanity."

Scout was respectful as her driver completed his soliloquy. From the start she could see where he was going; she didn't want to deny him his dramatic pleasure. It wasn't a new thesis for her, and she granted that it might encapsulate a truth for many…ants marching, and all. But she was committed to not falling into the trap. She just wasn't sure how.

A few seconds passed. Al was comfortable that he had provisioned Scout's philosophical pantry with some real-world food for thought. Etiquette required she acknowledge his wisdom. She first considered a multi-millennial, longitudinal, quality-of-life response. A sort of compare-and-contrast compendium of indulgences. She had used this approach before in late-night campus conversations of a similar ilk, though admittedly never while sober. Her *modus operandi* included a reference to the multitude of present-day advantages, including the relative absence of predators, disease, poverty, and starvation. Then she would highlight the more nuanced modern daily indulgences like chocolate, penicillin, tobacco, electricity, birth control, airplanes, vaccines, champagne, indoor plumbing, tampons, books, modern dentistry…and Lucinda Williams. She would usually close with a rhetorical flourish:

Surely, if you are walking the planet today you are one of the luckiest-ever members of our species?

Then she remembered something her mom used to say when Scout complained about being bored. It was her mother's favorite response to the adolescent daughter's rebellion against the routine chores of homework, school, piano lessons, and swim practice. Scout liked the words, but back then she didn't really have the perspective to fully understand the message. If she chose to use the axiom in reply to Al's stance, it would be less belittling than the quality-of-life response she was considering, and it would provide a slightly different perspective on his thesis. Al's sermon had precipitated the resurrection of the small memory while simultaneously giving her a better understanding of the meaning and nuance of her mother's adage. It seemed a good fit given the current context.

She chose Option B.

As Al prepared to exit the freeway, Scout casually looked over at him, shrugged, and with just the slightest tinge of smugness liberated the maternal aphorism from her cranial attic:

"Even Mick Jagger gets tired of singing 'Satisfaction.' "

Scout offered a hesitant smile while Al immediately stiffened up.

That's a strange turn of phrase, he thought.

He'd heard the words before, but he couldn't remember when or where. He felt the syllables had some significance attached to them…something sensual, but not quite satisfying. Searching the files in his mental hard drive, he waded through the years of corrosion and dust mites to find the source. When he finally recovered the experience off of the aging disk the implication hit him like a punch to the solar plexus. He had to force himself to take a breath.

Could it be…?

He felt light-headed and was worried he might pass out. He looked over at Scout for clues.

Not! Possible!

Luckily a traffic light stood at the bottom of the off-ramp. He success-fully made it to the line of stopped cars and was granted a minute to regain his composure.

Scout didn't notice anything was afoot.

"Turn right here and head up about a mile. We're only about three minutes away. You can use the on-ramp over there to get back on the westbound 10."

Al studied her face closely.

"I'm sorry, can you repeat what you just said about Mick Jagger?"

"Even Mick Jagger gets tired of singing 'Satisfaction'?"

She misread the purpose of his request as a need for clarification.

"You know…even the best jobs become routine over time? If you're always happy then happiness loses its meaning? The whole relativity-of-life thing. Peaks and valleys."

She looked in his face for evidence he understood what she was trying to say. Nodding absentmindedly, Aloysius seemed to be a million miles away.

Al had heard that phrase once before. Twenty-two years ago. It was 1974, and he had been out at a Tampa watering hole near his office. He remembered that the bar was named Confetti, and that he had been staying at a hotel one block away, a relatively new Holiday Inn. A week before, his family had asked him to choose between sobriety and them, which he felt to be an unfair, irra-tional request that was based on a false premise. They insisted he had a drinking problem, and he disagreed. He was not an alcoholic, as he could quit whenever he wanted; he just didn't want to. Sure, he had taken some missteps, but he had a job, a home, good teeth, and he habitually changed his underwear. These were *not* the characteristics of an alcoholic. Based on principal he walked out, confi-dent his family would come to their senses and collectively invite him back. He remembered it was the middle of May, because they had just celebrated Clay's birthday. It would be the last moment they all shared together. After three days at the hotel with no familial invitation to return, he was really very lonely. It was apparent his value as a parent was lower than he had estimated. A week later, with no family communication, he found himself considering other options for companionship.

He ended up at Confetti buying Happy Hour drinks for a small group of female Air Force officers who were throwing a bachelorette party for a colleague. After several hours of dancing, drinking, and increasingly suggestive conversation, he was able to convince one of the women to join him back in his room. She was a college-educated, brown-eyed, tall blonde, with a strong jaw and an athletic build. Lilly. She was smart, with a wry sense of humor and a no-nonsense approach to men. She was forthright about her needs sexually and lack of needs romantically. Foreplay lasted considerably longer than was usual for Aloysius: it included room service delivery of champagne and strawberries with whipped cream. At several discrete moments—or as Al recalled fondly now, indiscreet moments—she provided Al with very specific oral instructions. When they were finished with the lovemaking, Lilly hung around long enough to order more room service. While they were engaged in small talk, waiting for the food, and before she had fully sobered up, Lilly mentioned she was stationed at MacDill Air Force Base, but that she traveled a lot and wasn't active military. She also mentioned "the company" and frequent trips to "Langley." Al put two and two together and figured she was a spook. His recollection of her last name was murky, but he was pretty sure about the "Lilly" part, and he remembered wondering if it was code for *Lilith*, given her unusual mating behavior.

While they were eating the steak and lobster the room service attendant had brought, he mentioned that her job sounded very exciting.

She shrugged. Then she sucked the meat out of another lobster claw and tossed the vacant shell down on the plate. Finally she answered his hopeful question with an unenthusiastic observation: "Even Mick Jagger gets tired of singing 'Satisfaction.' "

She left about twenty minutes later. She had refused his offer of a ride home. He never heard from her again.

He hadn't used protection.

His eyes still on the road, he quickly did the math. It was definitely in the ballpark.

"Turn right here…almost there. Just three more blocks."

"Got it. Hey Scout, where were you born?"

"What?…Why?" She realized it was a harmless question. "The Tampa Bay Area?"

"Single mom?"

"Ummmmm…yeah, but that's a little creepy."

She refocused on directing him.

"Here it is. Pull over in front of that white stucco building where it says *Walker Hall*. On the right."

Aloysius Barton pulled the Mercedes into the loading zone out front. He hopped out and hustled around to the curbside to help Scout with her bags. Scout was firm about not letting him help her carry her stuff to her room, as she didn't want a stranger knowing precisely where she slept. More maternal caution.

"Thanks a lot for the ride, Aloysius. I really appreciate your help."

Al Barton was uncharacteristically at a loss. He hadn't a clue what to do. Everything was happening so fast. Did he have some sort of responsibility to share his suspicions? He wasn't even sure he had suspicions. Maybe…premonitions?

What the fuck just happened? he thought. *I mean, what are the odds? My daughter? Who knows how many kids I may have floating around out there?*

"No problem, Scout," he said. "Good luck with your classes."

He did an about-face, closed the curbside doors, and paused for a second before turning back towards the building's entrance. *What was the best thing for this young woman?* Serendipity had brought them together for a reason. He had to know.

"Hey Scout, can I ask one more question?"

Scout slowly turned. She was already over this guy, mentally preparing for her heavy academic load. Plus the last questions felt a little invasive, like he knew her a little too well.

"Sure," she said with a mild tone of resignation.

"Were you born in February of 1975?"

She tensed up with apprehension, as if a stranger had moved uninvited into her personal space.

What the fuck? she thought, eying him closely.

He had a one-in-twelve chance; she figured that wasn't a coincidence. The suspicion rose more quickly than she could manage it. "What did you say?" she asked

She didn't give him a chance to answer. He had spoken clearly. She had started to raise the volume and harshness of her voice. By habit, she reached inside her bedroll for the reassurance of her knife.

"Okay, Mr. Al, Joe Gargery, Kreskin, Carnac, whatever the fuck your name is…who are you?"

Aloysius was afraid this might happen; he had always been uncomfortable with conflict, especially when it came from women. Raising his hands palms down, he pushed them quietly toward the ground: the universal sign to calm down. Several nearby pedestrians had taken note of Scout's irregular tone. They slowed down and turned attentively towards the pair like zombies made aware of fresh meat.

"Please, I'm at somewhat of a loss here as well. Can we just sit down and talk somewhere quiet?"

Scout wasn't one to be easily pacified, especially when her hackles were up. Her mom had warned her to always be vigilant. The world was a dangerous place.

"Not until you tell me what's going on." She paused to think further about her situation. "And even then probably not."Aloysius lowered his hands. His head and shoulders slumped as his breathing started to become restricted. It was all just too hard, the cohabiting with women. The responsibility. The account-ability. The need to filter thoughts, words, and deeds. The emotional swings. The stifling demands for money and structure. The obsession with communi-cation. The bilateral disappointment. The gut-wrenching endings. (*Especially* the gut wrenching endings!) He was in it deep now, but he saw a slight shimmer of hope when he realized it wasn't too late to beat a hasty retreat. That was a comfortable path for him. She didn't even know his name. This could all be in the rearview mirror in two minutes. He turned away from Scout and headed around to the driver's side of the car.

Yes, just leave, he told himself, *before you have no option and end up drowning in the deep end.*

Scout watched defiantly as Aloysius opened the driver's side door and prepared to get in.

"Good…get out of here…creep," she whispered.

Whatever unseen force had made him pull over outside of Barstow reas-serted its control. He stopped and looked at Scout over the roof of the car. The closeted secret was demanding fresh air. He jingled his keys in his hand and felt the contours of the church key as he looked down, studying the leather seat that should be happily carrying him away from this whole mess. He felt nauseous. Not wanting to, he knew he had to. As his heart was still exploding, he slowly reengaged her eyes and filled his lungs.

"Scout…you'll probably think this is crazy…I know I certainly do…but…I think I…I might be your dad."

There, he did it. His heart immediately throttled back.

God it feels good to release that!

He watched Scout, ten feet away, hoping for feedback. He needed some-thing from her.

She couldn't speak. A flood of emotions overwhelmed her.

This guy can't be MY dad…can he?!

He wasn't anything like she had imagined. The fantasies had all been so different.

Not this *guy?*

Simultaneously she felt a sense of attachment and belonging.

He isn't that *bad....*

She wanted to believe, but it was all too much. He held her gaze. She hadn't previously noticed his green eyes.

"Can we at least talk privately?"

"Why should I trust you?"

"If my intentions were nefarious wouldn't I have already acted?"

She thought about this for a minute. It wasn't watertight, but it did make sense. He followed up with an invitation.

"Come to lunch with me. I know this amazing Mexican place about thirty-five minutes away. They serve the best pork burrito in the world."

"El Tepeyac?" she asked.

It was a start.

CHAPTER 19

El Tepeyac

The hostess had directed them to a two-top table in the back, away from the bathrooms.

"Which chair would you like?" asked Al. He was hungry to sit down.

Scout shrugged.

As a self-described gentleman, Aloysius took up station behind one of the chairs at the table. As Scout approached, Al slid the chair two feet from the table in the traditional ritual of etiquette and access. Scout, mistaking her dad's behavior as an indication of selection rather than chivalry, walked around to the other side of the table to sit in the unclaimed chair. Waiting behind the chair, Al wondered if she would recognize the miscommunication. He had hoped to start the meal off with some credit for his manners, given the illegitimate context of his daughter's birth. With no recognition forthcoming, he kept his mouth shut and sat down facing Scout, chalking it up to generational differences.

The waitress brought menus and asked what they wanted to drink.

"*Horchata*, please."

"*Dos Equis, verde. Con limón, por favor.*"

The Latina waitress confirmed their orders in perfect English.

Aloysius started helping Scout with the menu, but she cut him off.

"I know this place."

"Sorry, I forgot."

Chastened, Al retreated into his menu. He always ordered the same thing, but he needed a few moments of refuge from the contentiousness. During the drive he had tried to pry some personal history from Scout, but he would have been more successful peeling the stripes from a tiger. So far, nothing with Scout was occurring as he had hoped.

No tearful reunion. No long, unrestrained, emotional sharing. No search for meaningful connection. She showed little interest in who he was.

She's a chip off the block, observed Al silently. *Just not* my *block.*

It would be a cold day before she relinquished her trust and abandonment issues, he foresaw.

During the drive over they had at least been able to confirm their biological connection. Scout had been born on February 17th, 1975. Her mother had worked for the government for years, in Florida and the D.C. area, although she had never revealed much about her responsibilities. Having been very protective of Scout when she was growing up, Lilly always brushed off questions about Scout's father. Scout's mom's real name was Aurel Stein, but she had always gone by Lilly. She had unusual beliefs when it came to men, and she had never married.

Lilly had been hospitalized with mental health issues about seven years ago. Her problems started when she had insisted on going topless in public environments wherever convention allowed men to do so. Typically this occurred at beaches and swimming pools, but health clubs and spas also had to deal with her peculiar convictions. Even a stroll through a park on a warm day could be interesting if Lilly was your companion. She was making a statement about gender equality, but she didn't identify as a "feminist" even though the label fit tightly. Not wanting the encumbrance of commitment, she didn't join a political group or search for others with similar beliefs. It was much simpler than that, and all seemed so obvious to her: the restrictions were blatantly unfair and illogical. She felt that the Constitution provided her equal protection under the law, and that vestigial indecency legislation would be retired if someone just asked in a noticeably public way.

This wasn't a crusade for her, more like a hobby. She had a child to raise and a full-time job and wasn't looking to complicate things too much. It was just something to do in her spare time when the opportunity presented itself. Low-hanging fruit, so to speak. It didn't hurt that her *décolletage* was world-class.

So far her actions hadn't attracted much attention, aside from some local drama. That all changed on a summer weekend during a business trip to San Francisco. She decided to wander out to Candlestick Park and watch the Giants host the Dodgers. The day before, she had given a lecture at the Monterey Naval War College titled, "The USSR: Understanding the Demographic and Economic Effects of Heroine and Alcohol Addiction." Her presentation had been well received, and overtures had been made about a visiting scholar position. The response had her feeling confident and allowed her to indulge in a fantasy about a potential new life on the West Coast. As she considered the possibilities, she became more excited.

Scout would love it out here, she rationalized.

She was starting to feel very comfortable in Northern California.

They understand me here, she asserted.

Towards the end of the 9–1 rout in favor of the Giants, a *Chronicle* photographer captured a topless Lilly enjoying beer and hot dogs with some similarly exposed right field bleacher bums. The late afternoon fog had started to chill the air, and things were pronounced. The next morning she made the front page of the *Sporting Green*…with her areolae blocked out. She was sitting amidst a cluster of fourteen bare-chested male Giants fans—and none of them had their eyes on the game. The surrounding bleachers were empty. The caption to the photograph read:

Who Cares Who's on First? I'm Headin' to Second!

That morning circulation doubled. It was a slow news day, and the wire services picked up the story. Lilly went viral before people even knew what that meant.

Becoming an overnight sensation didn't please her government employers, who had previously been unaware of Lilly's part-time, amateur rebellion. Being in the intelligence and surveillance businesses, they became quite uncomfortable with the publicity and the potential for intrusion.

Of course, journalists and agents started calling. Everyone wanted a piece of "the San Francisco boob girl." Fourteen-year-old Scout was mortified. Their neighbors already thought they were "weird"…and now there was confirmation. Lilly wasn't so stupid as to believe she should quit her day job, but she did take the opportunity to be heard on the topics of gender inequality, free speech, and women's rights *vis-à-vis* issues pertaining to their anatomy.

Lilly found all the attention somewhat gratifying (even exhilarating) until the religious right got involved. Not wanting to miss an opportunity to highlight the disappearance of morality from modern society, the fundamentalists organized a counter-offensive to beat down the evil intentions of "the Satan boob girl." The stress mounted as 3 x 8-hour shifts of Bible thumpers picketed around her front lawn. Soon the media joined the circus, hoping for some drama…and maybe a quick peak.

It all died down soon enough, but not before Lilly had taken her professionally necessitated level of paranoia to new extremes. Her irrational levels of distrust, when coupled with her analytical convictions, engendered a form of intense cognitive dissonance that pushed her peculiarities to new levels of deviance. She continued to champion her right to wander with breasts unfettered (it was, after all, her signature move), but some of her other behaviors started to become more conspicuous. Her previously gentle bipolar symptoms became debilitating. The obsessive compulsions overwhelmed her attempts to comply with societal norms in simple, daily, public interactions. She would find herself frequently correcting strangers when they spoke in grammatically imperfect ways, or fixing their twisted collars without warning. While waiting for her grocery or restaurant bill, she would mentally calculate the sums to the penny, and many times found people were cheating her. The interior of her house cycled between spotless and unrepentant. Communal bathrooms could be particularly problematic, as she had strong views on the resting positions of toilet seats and the adjacent paper rolls.

She habitually countered the omnipresent *Have a nice day!* with *Don't tell me what to do!*

This usually led to an angry, *All right, **don't** have a nice day!*

To which she would threaten, *I really mean it! Stop bossing me around!*

She thought it was hilarious and became frustrated when people didn't get the joke.

Her disorder quickly reached the point of instability when she began hearing voices and missing work. Her employers threatened to pull her security clearance unless she met with their doctors. After two weeks as an inpatient, she returned home with several new prescriptions that moderated the symptoms and allowed her to put in two more years in a lower security clearance role. She retired at forty-four with full health-care benefits and a decent pension. Scout found living under the same roof with her to be challenging, but not impossible. For college, Scout headed as far west as possible.

The waitress returned with their drinks and took their food orders.

Aloysius suggested they split a Manuel's Special—a five-pound *chile verde* pork burrito of some local renown. It came with a "twofer" feature: a second five-pounder at no charge, as long as the first burrito was completed unassisted.

Scout said she wanted her own.

By the time the waitress returned with two five-pound burritos, Aloysius was beginning to think he had made a mistake by getting involved with Scout.

As he tucked into his burrito and worked on his second *Dos Equis*, he became less concerned about Scout. He would be on his way soon enough.

Naturally, that's when she started talking.

"So what should I call you?"

"What are my options?"

"Dad? Father? Pops? Al? Aloysius? Joe G.?"

Outwardly Al maintained a poker face; but inwardly he smiled. *At least she didn't take the obvious pejorative shot when it was there*, he thought.

"I kinda like Joe G. We could pronounce it as one word, *Jojie*. It can be our inside joke. Remind us that a higher force put us together," he offered optimistically.

"Do you always drink in the middle of the day?" she asked with barely disguised disapproval.

He stopped focusing on his food and took the inquiry as an effort to shame him. While chewing and swallowing his current bite he looked her right in the eye. He had a lot of history here, and she was skating on thin ice.

"Not always."

They looked at each other for a long while, with neither giving an inch but without an ounce of aggression on his part.

Your move, Scout, he thought.

"Why didn't you ever come looking for me?"

He took a deep breath. Now he finally understood. Looking across the table he saw his abandoned daughter.

"Oh, Scout…"

He struggled for composure…swallowing then looking away…and thought about all those years when she needed a father to be there…and he wasn't. He lost the internal fight, and an involuntary tear rolled down his face.

"I'm so sorry…I…I…I didn't know you existed," he stuttered.

She had decreased the intensity in her voice and her posturing; consequently, she was losing some of her hardness.

"How did you meet my mom…?" she whispered.

He could see she needed the truth. No bullshit required to soften the impact. She was tough enough.

"We met at a bar. It was Happy Hour and she was with some friends. I found her attractive…we had some drinks and danced. Several hours later, she accepted my invitation to join me for dinner. I wasn't wearing a wedding ring even though I was married. My ex-wife and I had separated. We ended up getting divorced."

"Did you end up dating?"

"No."

"Just a one-night stand…" Her voice trailed off.

He didn't know what to say. She had a distant look as she picked at her food. A few mutinous tears rushed down her cheek.

"It's what people do, Scout…they search for intimacy…to alleviate the loneliness."

"I suppose."

"You didn't do anything wrong."

"It's hard to feel good about yourself when your whole existence rests on a drunken neglect of birth control."

"You probably just described over half the population."

She tried and failed to suppress a short laugh while wiping at her tears with her sleeve. A small, forced smile escaped her lips as she looked across the table at her dad.

"Well, Jojie…are we gonna eat or what?"

After they both made decent dents in their burritos, Aloysius pushed his plate away and wiped his mouth. He was sated. Scout mimicked her dad and started again with the peppering.

"So, you're driving a Mercedes…are you rich?" she teased.

"Just in experience," he gently bit back.

"What do you do?" She immediately caught herself and narrowed his options. "When you're not at the anvil?"

"I work as a concierge at a Las Vegas hotel and casino."

He paused, calibrating where on the scale between self-aggrandizement and self-deprecation he should position himself. Quickly making up his mind, he took what for him was the less traveled path.

"I'm a glorified gofer."

There was a pause in the conversation as the waitress brought Styrofoam "to go" containers. The interruption gave him a chance to take emotional inventory. He must be enjoying this honesty thing: he felt pretty comfortable.

Of course, he allowed, *maybe it's just the beer?*

"What are your political leanings?"

"I'm against the aggregation of power."

"Nice…an anarchist." She nodded with respect.

"Isn't that the devil?" He thought he was being clever.

At first she was confused by his question but quickly figured it out. She gave him a slight courtesy laugh.

"Umm, you're thinking Antichrist?"

She neglected the implied "asshole" at the end, as she still needed a ride home.

He responded with dramatic enlightenment. "Ahh…that's right."

He drained the remnants of his second beer.

"What about you…Republican?" He guessed sarcastically.

"Progressive Independent," she responded.

"Good for you. Don't let them label you, but make sure you give your college friends enough so they think you're one of them."

She stuck her tongue out at him.

"What about you, Mercedes man? Republican? And enough of this 'aggregation of power' BS."

He usually didn't do this, but given the context he thought he would take a deep breath and give it a few minutes.

"Sounds like you want details?"

She nodded.

"Okay, remember, you asked for it. At the family level I'm a Communist and at the national level I'm a Libertarian…with a heart."

A twenty-second pause as she took a last bite and considered his comments.

"How does that work?"

"Well, on a small scale I believe in 'from each according to their ability, to each according to their need.' But with three hundred million people at the national level, I believe you lose all practical nuance and accountability, and so communism breaks down with rampant fraud and mistrust."

He shoved a huge cube of sautéed pork into his mouth.

God this is heaven.

He chewed while she pondered.

"You've done this before."

He forced the words through the *picante* sauce that smothered the pork.

"Politics or the burrito?"

"Both."

"A few times, yeah."

He swallowed the meat, took a deep breath, and tried to generate some enthusiasm for the topic as he gave it another shot.

"At the family level, the parents can allocate limited resources to whomever needs them most. They have daily interaction with their kids, so they know who's sincerely trying and who needs a swift kick. You have a good shot at achieving good, non-wasteful decision-making at the confiscation and redistribution levels. The parents are the proverbial 'benevolent dictators.' Now size it up from your family or church to three hundred million people distributed over ten million square kilometers. It's really hard for a federal employee who is a thousand miles away to have much conviction about who needs what and why. As a result there's incentive for everyone to always ask for everything. As I said before, we lose all nuance and accountability. Those who are actually honorable, practice restraint, or voluntarily comply fully with the tax code, well, they end up feeling like suckers, because all their neighbors are cheating and never getting caught. Increased rules, policing, and documentation are required. The whole thing just collapses in a bureaucratic mess of corruption."

"Whoa," Scout said, "that's pretty cynical."

"That's a whole 'nother topic. For now, I'll offer Exhibit A—the Soviet Union, and then I'll rest my case for the day."

Growing disillusioned with politics a few years out of Princeton, he'd reached the conclusion that most politicians and their supporters were just competing for a place at the government trough. He had felt the trough was built with tax dollars clipped from those who couldn't adequately defend themselves, or those who were just naively oblivious. Meanwhile, whoever was smart enough to coordinate into voting blocks was rewarded with government favors.

He started shoveling the remaining three-pounds of burrito into the doggy box.

Keenan might like this, he thought.

When finished with the packing he tried to catch their server's attention.

Scout started in again.

"But with a bigger population, you get better economies of scale in terms of managing the collection and redistribution process. It gets pretty redundant for every local jurisdiction to create and administer bureaucracies that are the equivalent of the IRS, Medicare, and Social Security."

"I think that's the essential question *after* you've decided you want governments even doing those things."

"Meaning you need to figure out if the loss of nuance and accountability gets offset by economies of scale?"

"Yep."

"Who else would do these things if not governments?"

"Governments didn't invent compassion, they just want you to believe they did."

"You don't really believe the private sector—'churches and families,' I believe you said—would actually take care of all these needs?"

"They already do. The government just administers it all and takes a cut. Kinda like the Mafia."

This was vexing to her. She didn't like the comparison to organized crime.

"You really think all those rich people would voluntarily give up a chunk of their income if we didn't force the issue by legislating a progressive tax code?"

Aloysius saw Scout winding up for a much longer, passionate conversation. He might've had the energy if he were her age, but instead he tried to defuse.

"Maybe?" He shrugged noncommittally.

It was hard to fight someone who was already lying down.

Scout took out her frustration on the *horchata* straw as she sucked the diluted remnants from among the ice chips at the bottom of her plastic tumbler. The waitress walked by.

"One more round please."

Aloysius tried to wind it down.

"Look Scout, I'm not necessarily one of those people who thinks greed and selfishness are good. I actually think we all have a moral obligation to help others. I just don't believe the federal government is the best mechanism for the implementation of compassion."

The waitress brought the drinks; Aloysius was getting tired. It was late, and Al still had a drive in front of him. Each minute that went by left him exposed to the incoming tide of rush hour traffic.

"We've got to get you back to school—and me to San Diego."

Scout got the message. The political Q and A was over.

He turned back to the waitress and asked for the check.

"*La cuenta, por favor.*"

The waitress sighed. "No problem," she said.

As Aloysius drove Scout back to Walker Hall, he kept Leon Redbone at a conversation-inhibiting level. Scout was uncomfortably full from her burrito and all the sugar from the *horchata*. The combination of the music, the car, and the company made her feel like she had traveled back in time. She had a mild feeling of vertigo, but it didn't make her queasy. More like she was edging close to a precipice and was filled with the fear and anticipation of how she would feel and what she would see. Even though she and Aloysius had only had a few hours together, she begrudgingly admitted to herself that she felt something, maybe a belonging, when Al was around. She wondered how much of this feeling came from a deep place of wanting—and now *projecting*—after she had discovered he was her dad. She felt he was actually a pretty interesting guy, although dated in many of his habits and views. She also wasn't comfortable with his drinking and driving. Neither one of them had a clue what came next. Al knew it was his place to navigate the tree limb they had ventured out on, so he inhaled deeply then took the first step.

"Do you want to do this again?" he asked Scout.

"I would like that."

"Me too."

He paralleled the Mercedes back into the loading zone then took out a pen and paper.

"Here are my numbers at home and at work. Call me whenever you want. I know where to find you."

Scout grabbed the paper and got out of the car. Al was hustling around from his side to help her.

"You don't need to do that."

"I know. I want to."

He put his arms around her. They did an awkward, butt-out hug.

Heaven forbid we allow proximity of our sexual organs, Scout thought.

She hoped they would get better at that with time. Aloysius looked directly into her eyes…and promptly saw his eyes staring back.

"I'm so sorry I missed the first twenty years, I'll try to do better going forward." He smiled and forged on. "I'm so happy we finally connected."

As he heard the words come out he hated himself for their generic nature. *What tripe*, he thought. *Sometimes it's better to say nothing.*

Not taking offense, she chose her own pleasantry.

"How crazy has this day been?"

He took the question rhetorically, smiling, then nodding his head in sympathetic disbelief. He was learning.

They separated and moved in opposite directions. Neither looked back. She headed for the dorm stairs to her room then abruptly stopped. *My brothers and sisters?* The thought hit her out of the blue. *I forgot to ask about them!*

Later, as he pulled onto the freeway heading west, Al again wondered at the highly improbable nature of what he had just experienced. A favorite Tennyson bastardization crept into his consciousness.

Ours is not to reason why, ours is just the long abide.

CHAPTER 20—

Torrey Pines

K eenan was ready to exhale. The trip south had been executed with relaxed precision.

The beauty of planning with a lot of extra time built in, he thought with satisfaction.

Avoiding much of the traffic in Northern and Central California had allowed him to enjoy the stretch from Carpinteria south to Santa Monica on the Pacific Coast Highway. All of his business meetings had gone well, and he even had five pounds of beef jerky packed safely in his gear bag.

With the work week and his professional "to-do" list now completed, he grinned with well-deserved pleasure. *Now let's see what the paterfamilias is up to then get tucked in at a decent hour so I can get some sleep before the early triathlon alarm.*

Lately he had not been sleeping well. His work schedule had effectively precluded him from much training, and he started to question the wisdom of registering for tomorrow's race. Moreover, the course was challenging, especially the bike segment: fifty-six miles, with lots of climbing in the coastal mountains above North County San Diego. He hadn't completed a race since this same Horny Toad event two years ago, and his quads were already complaining in anticipation. Out of habit, he always approached a race with competitive optimism, actually contemplating the possibility that he could win. But the current reality mandated by his (neglected) fitness was starting to set in; it was clear, even to his optimistic self, things were going to be difficult in the morning. It was at this moment of self-doubt that one of his many internal voices decided to start in with the coaching:

Who you kiddin', boy? You ain't been competitive in a race for nearly a decade. For you, participating is the new winning.

Then, after the taunting was completed, a touch of charity:

Just keep your expectations low. You'll do fine.

At thirty-six, with a full-time job and family, he was a totally different athlete than his younger self. It wasn't just the aging process that had slowed him; he could also no longer afford to spend five hours a day training and ten hours a day sleeping. This was the only race he had entered for the last few years, and he didn't come because he thought he could win; he did it because he enjoyed the camaraderie he had established with the group of Southern California attorneys who organized the competition—aka the Horny Toads. They were a fun-loving group of professionals that he had integrated into his business network. The friendships he had developed while racing had turned into a number of lucrative business leads.

Fourteen years earlier, he had been inspired to try a multi-sport endurance race after reading about the Ironman event some US Naval officers had invented in Hawaii. He had some experience in all three sports. As a preadolescent he had been a decent swimmer for his age group; he had been riding bikes recreationally since he was four; and he was a better than mediocre runner for a big guy. It was 1982, he had just graduated from college and was working his first corporate job at a bank in Los Angeles. All of the time indoors, in a suit, with no physical activity, was driving him crazy. That summer, on a whim, he decided his debut race would be the Horny Toad Triathlon. As a twenty-two-year-old with no money, he decided to race as a "bandit," a competitor who didn't register or pay the entry fee. Conforming with the style of the times, and his limited budget, he was going to do the whole race in a pair of snug Dolfin shorts designed with a nod to the Stars and Stripes. He made the early Saturday morning drive down to San Diego from his girlfriend's house, just as the sun was peeking over the eastern horizon. The traffic was unusually light, and he pulled in to the beachside parking lot ahead of schedule. As the seven a.m. start time approached, he kept to himself, away from the milling crowd of about forty competitors as they walked from the parking lot transition area to the beach. Triathlon was a relatively new sport, and the athletes were much more friendly than they would be later, as the prize money and sponsorships in the early days were negligible. He had left his bike leaning against his parked car, away from those of the other racers: he was apprehensive about not belonging and not paying. His goal was to swim, bike, and run the course, but not to use any of the infrastructure—the aid stations and support vehicles—offered by the race organizers. He figured the competition was on public property, and he wasn't doing anything wrong if he was just out training over the same routes at the same time. This justification somewhat assuaged any guilt he had about not paying the entry fee.

The surf was rough that morning, but his adrenaline did a pretty good job of carrying him through the one-mile open water swim. He guessed he was in the top fifteen as he laced up his running shoes and prepared to hop on his bike. His problems started about fifteen minutes into the ride, as he began the first of many climbs. One of the Horny Toads, a wiry, bearded attorney in his early thirties, pulled up beside him and started a friendly chat. Keenan didn't realize how obviously inexperienced he appeared to the trained eye, and his new friend was too polite to overtly say that was the case.

"Schwinn Varsity! Wow, you don't see a lot of those out racing. How long have you owned it?"

The incredulous attorney sported the usual competitive cycling attire— racing cleats, a helmet, and chamois padded bike shorts. His bike weighed half of Keenan's forty-five-pound dinosaur, and his body weighed thirty pounds less than Keno's. The younger man was struggling with the grade but still managed a smile with his response.

"I'm borrowing it from a buddy for the weekend. I'm sure it's been around the block a few times."

Keenan was wearing only his skimpy shorts, sunglasses, and a pair of running shoes. No sunscreen.

"I'm Mark."

"Keenan."

"Have you ever done this ride before?"

Keenan was really beginning to work. The hills were steep, the bike was heavy, and his technique and equipment were abundantly lacking.

"No…" he replied. "I'm from LA…" He gasped for air. "I don't know this area very well…I've never ridden a bike this far…" Again, he gasped. "But I've got…pretty strong legs…."

The day was heating up. After being chilled by the swim, Keno hadn't hydrated properly during the transition to the cycling leg. Now he was starting to get thirsty. The sweat poured out of him.

"Where's your water bottle?"

"My what?"

"See that cage on your down tube?"

Mark pointed to a spot on the metal tube that traveled from his handlebars down to his pedal hub.

"You're supposed to fill a plastic bottle with water and store it there for long rides."

"Oh yeah…that make sense…I think I've seen those before, but…I don't have one."

Mark was beginning to worry that this fast-twitch, unprepared, beast-of-a-manchild would get lost and expire somewhere up in the hills.

"Here, I have two. Take one, you'll need it. This is a long, three-hour ride."

In contrast to Keenan, Mark was pedaling easily and smoothly, tracking a steady, straight line as he handed over one of his water bottles.

Keenan was struggling for more oxygen and barely missed clipping Mark's bike as he reached over and gratefully accepted the plastic container.

"Thanks," he said. "I really appreciate it."

"Good luck, *amigo*"—and with that Mark stood in his pedals and dropped Keno like a power window.

Keenan's competitive instincts compelled him to try and keep up with his new friend, but it became immediately apparent that he wasn't capable. His fatigue rapidly overwhelmed his courage. He had no concept of the torture that lay in wait.

I'm a football player, he told himself. *I've taken hits from guys twice as big as these stick figures. How hard can this be?*

By the time Keno returned to the transition area, he had been on the bike for four hours. Everyone had passed him. So far was the distance between he and the other competitors that "back of the pack" would imply a proximity that didn't exist. He felt like a burnt English muffin, with all of his nooks and crannies filled with hurt. He was sunburned and dehydrated; the chafing between his legs was excruciating. Every contact point between his body and the bike was numb, and he was worried that his *raison d'etre* would never again function due to permanent circulatory damage. The only thing that kept him pedaling for the last hour was the absence of other transportation options. He had long ago decided to forego the run.

As he rode into the transition area, a group of ten or so attractive young women met him with applause and encouragement. These were the Horny Toad wives, girlfriends, and transition area volunteers enjoying the lovely, spring, Southern California morning. They weren't sticklers for detail and hence couldn't tell Keenan was not an official entry; they just saw a sweaty guy on a bike and rooted him on.

"Way to go! Just ten more miles!"

"Great job! You can do it!"

"Lookin' great! Only one leg left! Keep it up!"

Keenan was in a bad, pessimistic place, but he hadn't lost his ear for a sexual pun. He was strongly convinced that the racing bike seat was a derivative of some medieval torture device, or at best a crude form of ancient male contraception, with only slight modifications to subtly conceal its origin and purpose.

Despite Keenan's advanced and prolonged state of pain, for a young male there are certain circumstances under which the maintenance of appearances is required, regardless of one's inner turmoil. For Keenan, at twenty-two years of age, female observation was one of those circumstances, though he wasn't consciously aware of cause and effect. As he prepared to dismount, he rapidly devised a plan that would obviate the embarrassment of quitting in front of these potential mating partners. He would pull it together long enough to make it out of the transition area, as if he intended to run the ten miles required to complete the race; but as soon as he made the turn to the north, under the railroad trestles about fifty yards away, where he would be safely out of sight, he would collapse in a heap in the nearest spot of shade and wait until all the hotties had dispersed. Then he would quietly creep back, tie the bike to his car, and stealthily drive home. There he would soak his sunburned, aching body in an ice bath. Reinvigorated by his plan and its tangible path to relief, he climbed off of his bike, leaned it against his car, and started an awkward, limping run. Unfortunately, as he rounded the first corner, two more women in tight, neon-lime tank tops were manning the initial aid station. He definitely couldn't wimp out in front of them. In fact, they were so enthusiastic about his effort he actually started believing he could make it a few more miles. After drinking as much as he could stomach, he continued, in a stumbling jog, in the direction of the next aid station.

One foot in front of the other, he told himself. *Just keep moving....*

In similar fashion, he closed down each of the five aid stations up the Pacific Coast Highway to Cardiff-by-the-Sea. And back. During the return portion of the course, the temperature approached one hundred degrees on the asphalt. The congested traffic added to the feeling that he was suffocating. His feet were so hot that he was hallucinating about the soles of his shoes melting into the pavement. As the last competitor, he asked the aid station attendants to just dump the whole container of ice water over his head after he had drunken his fill.

At the final station a couple of shapely, ponytailed volunteers wearing T-shirts and cutoffs joined him for the impromptu wet T-shirt event. He could swear he felt a jolt of testosterone surge through him as he headed home for the final mile. Everyone was so sincerely supportive that Keno felt he couldn't let them down. His young narcissism was such that he actually believed his finishing was a big deal to everyone.

He finally made it back to the railroad trestle, turned left, and staggered the final yards to the finish line. Keno was so spent you could have poured him into the heel of a boot. The expected jubilant fanfare was *in absentia*. Most everyone had packed up their gear and left the morning race far behind, reengaging with their days and lives. Only a handful of people mingled in the transition area, sharing a few beers and hastily readjusting Keenan's sense of self-importance. The few remaining finishers looked up at the race anchorman and politely offered a few *"Attaboys!"* No hot girls waiting to celebrate his feat. The course marshal, who was also the president of the Horny Toads, walked over and asked him where his race number was. Keenan was bent over, hands on knees, exhausted. Realizing he didn't look anything like the other super lean, aerobic athletes, he felt as out of place as shoes on a snake. He had basically willed his mesomorphic musculature through the three disciplines and had learned a great deal about his limits in the process. He looked up at his inquisitor, too tired to care about consequences. The easiest path was the unvarnished truth.

"I'm sorry, man, I don't have one."

"What do you mean?"

He decided to throw himself on the mercy of the court.

"This is my first triathlon. I borrowed my shoes and bike...I just graduated from college with a bunch of student loans. I couldn't afford the thirty bucks, but I wanted to try a race, so I drove down this morning and jumped in at the start without a number."

The president so appreciated Keno's situation that instead of lecturing him on the evils of fraud and stealing, he took him under his wing, escorted him over to his friends, and insisted Keno have a beer and a T-shirt. By the time he finished his beer, Keenan had been asked several times to retell the story of his four-hour climb on the Schwinn Varsity, and his charm and perseverance had endeared him to a new group of friends.

Rather than be repelled by the suffering he had endured, Keenan fell hard for the camaraderie of the group and the challenge of the race; he returned to Torrey Pines to race with his friends for ten of the next thirteen years. In the earlier races, he committed to a rigorous training regimen and twice placed in the top ten. But as he aged, things changed, and as he hustled over to make the seven p.m. check-in for his fourteenth year, he started to reflect on his relationship with the Horny Toad event.

It's been a good run. But it's getting harder and harder to carve out the time to train and travel. It's just not high on my priority list anymore, with a growing family and successful business. Plus, the races aren't as much fun when there are over three hundred entries and everyone's passing me.

He hated to admit it, but this might be his last year.

About thirty minutes before the shut off time he found himself picking up his race packet, dropping off his bike, greeting a few of his longtime friends, then heading out to meet his dad at The Spot in La Jolla for dinner. As he was leaving the registration venue, he found himself respectfully acknowledging all of the planning that went into running such a big event; but he simultaneously couldn't help but notice a strong yearning for the uncomplicated nature of his first race. Upon further reflection, he wondered if it was the simplicity of the race that he missed, or rather that brief moment in time when responsibility was limited and spontaneity was the norm. He let the thought drift away as he reengaged his itinerary and climbed into the Trooper for the drive to meet his dad. Not sure what to expect, he picked his way through the North County San Diego traffic, hoping he wouldn't be late.

CHAPTER 21

The Spot

Arriving a few minutes before their seven p.m. dinner reservation, Aloysius asked the hostess to seat him and then promptly ordered a pitcher of Guinness and two frosty mugs. He hoped Keenan would approve, as he was trying to reestablish a relationship with his children, and, given his geographic proximity, Keenan seemed a natural place to start. He also needed something else from his second son, but he wanted to be careful how he asked for it. He had had an auspicious (if unexpected) start with Scout, and he hoped to continue the trend.

When a thirty-six-year-old man in an out-of-place business suit walked in at 7:05 p.m., Aloysius barely recognized him. Elizabeth had maintained contact with her ex, keeping him in the loop regarding the major life events of each of their children, but that was about it. He couldn't remember the last time he had seen Keenan, probably at his graduation ceremony up at Davidson College, but he hadn't had much interaction with any of his family since then. His second son had filled out a bit, had short-cropped hair, and carried himself with a confidence that bordered between appealing and threatening, depending upon your perspective. The last few years had brought Aloysius's sixty-year-old body to the point where his hairline and muscle tone were in retreat while his grey streaks and his paunch were in irrefutable advance; though still relatively thin and tall he worried his son wouldn't recognize him. He nearly always required his wire-rimmed bifocals just to navigate the hurdles of daily living. The casual pizza joint, filled with families and young adults in beachwear, made the elder Barton feel a little out of place. A gentle hum and gurgle of conversation and music filtered throughout the restaurant as Keenan stopped at the hostess station and scanned the room. Aloysius watched him with an anticipatory smile. After Keno's first sweep failed to stop on the elder Barton, disappointment set in for both.

Keno frowned with a mild amount of dejection. *I can't believe he's not here yet. Just like him to be late, or stand me up. Old dogs, new tricks.*

Al shook his head in self-pity. *He doesn't even recognize his old man; apparently I've aged more than I had imagined. Betty Davis was right…old age ain't no place for sissies.*

Aloysius had been invited to participate in Keenan's nuptials, but after a lifetime of indulgence, he came down with a severe gall bladder infection the week of the wedding. The day before the rehearsal dinner, Al had to be raced to the hospital for surgery; hence, he missed his flight—and the event. Being aware that his reputation with the family was one of not being dependable, he didn't even offer his legitimate reason for the absence. He figured no one would believe him anyway and bemoaned the whole episode as another example of his perpetual bad luck. After being released from the hospital he went on a long bender. The family had pretty much written him off since that debacle nearly eleven years ago.

Aloysius stood from the table and began waving his napkin.

"Keenan!"

Keenan stared. From the back of the room an older gentleman was waving at him—and Keenan realized it was his dad. He waved back in acknowledgement and headed over. The smell of pepperoni was overwhelming; Keno was salivating by the time he reached their table. He was glad he had stayed in his suit for dinner, it imparted a degree of gravitas and success he wanted his forebear to feel. Aloysius would always be his father, but in every other way the son had surpassed his biological instigator, and he wanted that to show. After arriving at the table, Keno engaged his dad in a brief hug then crumpled into his chair in an exhausted release. It had been a long day.

An hour passed quickly. It seemed to Keno that dinner was going smoothly. They had split a pepperoni, black olive, and pesto pizza. Al had been pleasant company, keeping the conversation going with questions about Keenan's wife and business, and Al's grandkids. The senior Barton had consumed most of the Guinness, and was aware that Keenan was still sipping his first mug. He made an attempt to find common ground.

"Big race tomorrow. Makes sense to go easy on the beer."

Keenan understood the history and intent underlying his father's remark. He made a modest redirect, without intending to imply judgment.

"There's probably some of that, but I'm just not much of a drinker anymore. I don't really miss it. At some point the downside just started outweighing the upside."

"Good for you," Aloysius affirmed with a smile—and then a topic refocus: "What's the expected duration of tomorrow's Herculean task, and what do you need me to do?"

Keenan smiled at his dad's word choice. He had always admired his extemporaneous abilities. With experience, Keno had gained a different perspective on long aerobic competitions like the Horny Toad race in which he was about to participate.

"Probably more Sisyphean than Herculean," he said, poking fun at himself. "My goal is just to finish without being totally spent. Hopefully I'll be done in a little under five hours. I should mention, watching triathlons is kinda like watching paint dry. Why don't we just meet back at our hotel after I finish? It should be sometime around two p.m."

Al eyed his son across the table with a look of firm commitment.

"No way, partner, I've missed too much already. If my own flesh and blood can go out there and push his limits for five hours, the least I can do is provide moral and verbal support. I'll be up and ready to go at six a.m."

He paused and smiled before continuing.

"Besides, the gradual removal of excess moisture from paint is something from which I derive great comfort."

Keenan smiled at his dad's corny humor. That was probably as close as he would ever get to an apology from the old man. He realized he enjoyed similar wordplays, and the dinner reminded him of the likely source. He pulled his napkin from his lap and wiped pepperoni grease from the corners of his mouth. *My youth wasn't all bad*, he thought. *There were plenty of great times—and a lot of that fun came from Dad.*

He reminded himself of his ongoing pledge to keep a positive mental attitude.

"So Dad, it's great to see you and all, but you've been in Las Vegas for five years…why come out to California now?"

Aloysius had an agenda, but he wanted to appear as if he didn't. Perhaps if he could get Keenan to ask a leading question…?

"Well, with the passing of my mom last month, both of my parents are gone, and it's made me reflect on family and legacy and time."

"That's right…sorry, Dad. Mom told me about Grammy Dot. Was that hard for you? I mean, wasn't she sick for a long time?"

"It wasn't unexpected, and it was her time to go, but I find myself missing her more than I would've guessed."

Keenan picked up another slice of pizza and Al reached for the pitcher, welcoming the restaurant's noisy, enveloping hubbub. The jukebox surfaced through the background noise with "Train in Vain."

Did you stand by me? No, not at all.
Did you stand by me? No way.

Al didn't know the Clash, but he recognized the appropriateness of the lyrics. He filed a silent protest with his Guardian Angel. *Okay*, he acknowledged to himself, *I probably deserve that. But at some point can we put all this "Dad is bad" stuff behind us…?*

Tired of trying to manipulate people and outcomes to meet his needs, he decided to tell Keenan what was going on, and let the chips fall as they may.

"Keenan," he said, "your Grammy always saw something in you, a sort of moral fiber she admired."

Keenan's mind had been wandering to the first time he had heard "Train in Vain." He was partying in a friend's college dorm room—everyone was smoking weed but him—and Billy Simms was mauling his ex-girlfriend, Heather, on a futon in the corner. The whole scene had left him strangely indifferent.

"I'm sorry, I was spacing…what was that, Dad?"

Aloysius repeated himself. He saw that he now had Keenan's attention.

"Your Grammy left each of her kids a lot of money, but there are stipulations that must be fulfilled before the attorneys will release it."

"Stipulations?"

"Yes. She felt that sacrifice was character-building…good for the soul. So in an effort to motivate her children from the grave, she'll pay each of us our inheritance if we fulfill certain requirements. If we fail to fulfill the requirements, the money goes fifty percent to a specified charity and fifty percent to the next generation."

Keenan was gaining interest.

"Are all of the requirements the same for each sibling?"

"No, they are custom-designed for each person."

"What do you have to do?"

Al took a deep breath and laid it out.

"I have to quit drinking alcohol for one year."

"Really?"

"That's not all."

"What else?"

"I have to get physically fit, as defined by very specific parameters."

Keenan couldn't fully stifle a grin.

"Such as—?"

"I have to be able to do one of the following: run a mile in under eight minutes; run ten miles in under two hours; or swim a mile in under thirty minutes. I *also* must do one of these following things: ten chin-ups without letting go of the bar; bench press two hundred pounds; or one hundred push-ups in two minutes."

"Wow." Keenan smiled. But underneath his calm facade, his brain was cheering: *Awesome, Grammy Dot!*

"Yes, my mom was ahead of her time when it came to the benefits of exercise…and creative in incentivizing me to see her point of view, apparently."

"A point of view which you've happily ignored for most of your adult life?"

"Pretty much. But who ever listens to their parents' incessant droning anyway?"

Aloysius raised his eyebrows and looked pointedly at his son. Keenan grinned back.

"Apparently you're listening now. What are you going to do?"

"I don't know, I want the money, but I'm not sure where to start. I've lobbied the attorneys for exceptions due to physical ailments, to no effect."

"How much is 'a lot of money'?"

The senior Barton took a deep breath and looked directly into Keenan's eyes.

"Five million smackers."

"No way."

"Yep."

"Who's the arbiter? The attorneys? Some doctor?"

This is where it gets interesting, my boy, thought Aloysius.

He locked his eyes on his son's for a split second before releasing his surprise.

"You are, Keenan."

Keenan's eyes went wide; he hadn't seen that one coming. Agendas were now more apparent. He wondered what came next.

Aloysius was too sophisticated to outright offer a bribe, but he wasn't averse to massaging the rules for five million dollars.

"Any thoughts you have would be welcome. Of course I'd be willing to consider payment for any great ideas or…assistance."

Keenan considered the word "assistance" and decided to make his position clear.

"I think that someone with moral fiber would have trouble with that one."

His feeler rejected, Aloysius scrambled to get back on the high road.

"No…of course not. I meant that I'd be willing to pay for a personal trainer, or a physician's assistance with oversight or medication."

"Excuse me, Dad, but my back teeth are swimming. I'm gonna hit the head."

A few minutes later, Keno had worked his way back to their table. He had been totally engrossed in the ramifications of his father's predicament and had realized that each year that Al delayed made the fitness challenge more difficult. Grammy Dot had clearly given this a lot of thought. His Dad had been able to choose alcohol over his family once before…would he be able to turn his back on five million bucks? If he were able to quit, did that imply a lower-than-five-million valuation for his family? How much lower? That was a sobering thought. He allowed for inflation adjustments over the past twenty-two years. It stung even more. He started thinking about how long Aloysius had been gone and the many times when he wished he had been available to provide counsel. He looked over at his father boxing up the remaining slices.

"Hey Dad, why didn't you ever remarry?"

Aloysius stopped and looked at his son's brown eyes. This was a change of direction.

"I guess I never really lost hope that we would eventually get back together. I tried several times, but by then your Mom realized she didn't need me and…" He had to think carefully about what came next. "…she was appropriately wary of my shortcomings."

Keenan didn't want to put him on the spot about leaving, so he tried a tangential path.

"Did your experiences over the last twenty-two years change your mind about anything?"

Aloysius knew what his son wanted but wasn't sure he could give it. Acknowledging that he had been a selfish prick was a tall order for him; twice in one day might be impossible.

"I would be a pretty stunted person if I didn't learn a thing or two over the last twenty-two years, don't you think?"

Keenan gave him a *go on, I'm listening* look.

Al reached deep, down to the many thoughts he had mulled over the years. He tried to confess in a way that might be useful to his son.

"Keenan, this may sound sad, but your job right now is to absorb pain. Sure, you want to be there for the laughing and loving, but your family needs you most when they are hurting. Your job is to make that hurt go away. Sometimes it's simple, like a Band-Aid on a scraped knee or taking out the trash. Sometimes it takes money. Oftentimes it's just a shoulder to cry on or being someone to listen. When they're frustrated and say hurtful things, you shouldn't escalate. It's usually not about you. Absorb the poison that kills relationships and develop healthy ways to exorcise it. Like that black inmate, John Coffey, in *The Green Mile*. You remember him? The guy who would absorb others' pain and then exhale it in green bubbles?"

He stopped to make sure his son was listening.

"Awesome movie, awesome character," Keenan acknowledged.

Each gave a nonverbal affirmation to the other. Al read Keno's silence as a signal to continue.

"You have to be there. Often it's a thankless job. You have to be strong. Above all else, do no harm. That's where I seemed to struggle the most. "

Keenan found himself nodding his head appreciatively without really intending to, as he had been feeling particularly overwhelmed lately; sometimes it felt like everything was unraveling. Overworked and under appreciated, he often felt there was no light at the end of the tunnel. He was beginning to wonder about his long-term commitment to Lola. Lately he didn't feel they were giving each other much in the way of love and understanding.

Aloysius continued.

"If you do it right, unlike me, you might actually end up with something of substance, a family that loves and cares about you, even when you're old, smelly, and unattractive."

Keenan hadn't expected much in the way of wisdom from Al. He was glad he had asked the questions.

"This marriage thing is a pretty tough gig."

"So I'm told."

While Al finished boxing up the pie, Keno beat him to the check the waitress delivered.

"I got it, Dad. I can expense it."

Al's eyes were laughing. "So much for moral fiber."

"After you get your five million, I'll let you pay for everything."

"Deal."

As they walked out the door together, Al's mind was working down his checklist: Grammy Dot's will. Scout. The small matter of righting past wrongs with his family *Well,* he thought, *it's a start. I haven't told him about his half sister yet, but that will come in time. At least we've reconnected.*

As they split towards their respective cars, Keno remembered a key, unresolved detail.

"What room are you in?"

"Three-oh-four."

"I'll knock at six a.m., be ready to rock?"

"Roger that, young fella."

"Good night, Dad."

"Good night, Keenan, I love you."

Keenan nodded. "Me too, Dad."

CHAPTER 22

Lilly

L illy was hustling up her front porch steps, her arms filled with two bags of groceries. She liked to take the steps two at a time, just to show Mr. Gravity he wasn't winning. By habit, she counted the steps to herself.

Two, four, six, she powered up briskly…

The phone started ringing inside the house just as she realized it was her "odd" day. Struggling with her affliction, she reached for the front door knob while simultaneously realizing she wouldn't be able to let the numerical discrepancy go. Running back down the stairs she started again.

One, three, five…

On the other end of the line Scout waited patiently, doing her own counting.

Six, seven, eight…C'mon, Mom, pick up the phone.

She was definitely hanging up after ten rings.

Just as Lilly reached the kitchen one of the bags ripped, and her organic apples, which had been roaming free next to the canned goods due to Lilly's desire not to contribute to the Great Pacific Garbage Patch, spilled all over the floor. She glanced at them and immediately realized, with some alarm, that she had only thirteen apples, not her usual fourteen, and would now have to either return to the market that evening or stay up all night obsessing.

Despite her earlier self-established limits, on the other end of the phone Scout persevered.

Sixteen, seventeen, eighteen…I am absolutely hanging up at twenty!

Lilly answered the phone in exasperation.

"This better be good."

"Mom! What's going on? Are you okay? Why didn't you answer the phone?"

Lilly recognized her daughter's voice and struggled with the contradictory forces: the nurturing instinct…and her frustration with illogical questions.

"I didn't answer the phone because I wasn't at home, and then I was, so I did."

She reviewed the previous series of questions and realized her answer had been incomplete. "Yes, as you've probably guessed by now, this is your mother. I'm okay. How are you, Scout?"

Scout was used to the seemingly incongruous way her mom communicated, so she pushed forward with her agenda.

"Mom, listen. I think I have a job for you."

"Thank you, dear, but I'll have a little more faith in your headhunting skills when you position yourself in a paying role that doesn't involve childcare or the quick-serve restaurant industry. Changing topics here, have you read any of the research on intermittent fasting?"

"I have extensive experience with fasting Mom, I'm poor."

"Oh?…you're poor? That can't be a surprise? I assumed that's what you wanted with all those poor choices you insisted on making during your adolescent years."

Knowing from past history that she could take only so much parental direction and implied maternal disappointment, Scout soldiered on, hoping to get to the finish line before she would be forced to hang up in anger.

"Haven't you done enough teacher-training hours to now be a certified yoga instructor?"

Interesting, thought Lilly. *My daughter hasn't been* totally *self-absorbed during the last year*….

"Yes, I am now a certified yoga instructor—so nice of you to remember. I teach several classes a week at The Shavasana Center, right next to the O'Reilly Funeral Home."

Scout knew what was coming next. It would be the story of her junior prom, to which she had gone with one of the O'Reilly boys. Finn. Being a huge *Harold and Maude* fan, Finn deemed it cool when he pulled up in front of her house in a hearse. Lilly saw the hearse as a bad omen and forbade her daughter from riding with the boy. Pushing through her mom's objections, Scout went anyway. After the dance, Finn took her back to the family office, and they ended up making out in a silk-lined, deluxe, walnut-and-brass, XL coffin. Scout had a default "above the waist" rule at the time…and she wasn't making an exception in the cramped, ghoulish quarters. Her date became insistently disrespectful of her rule, she had fought back aggressively, and, during a particularly violent tussle, the coffin lid ended up slamming shut, locking them both inside. Finn's claustrophobia overwhelmed his libido, and he ended up vomiting spiked punch all over her torso…including her two otherwise naked breasts. At some point in the early morning the police were called and a search was effected; but it wasn't until the O'Reilly patriarch opened shop at eight o'clock the next morning that the couple were discovered slowly suffocating in the slimy, sour-smelling stew.

Lilly thought the whole episode was an appropriate punishment for her rebellious daughter. Ever since, she had had trouble letting the event die.

"You remember the O'Reilly family?" she asked rhetorically, "You dated that boy that used to drive around in a hearse and paw at you like you were Morticia Addams?" Lilly snorted at the oft-repeated line.

Scout took a deep breath. She counted to five while gently tapping her fingers on her breastbone. This technique she found to be somewhat effective at relieving anger and frustration.

"Mom, listen," she said. "I met a guy who needs a personal trainer. He has some very specific goals he needs to reach, and you could make some real money if you were to help him reach those goals."

Scout had yet to tell her mom that she had been communicating with her dad. The silence on Lilly's end of the conversation was misconstrued as indifference, when in fact Lilly had been busy counting a line of ants that were crawling along her marble backsplash. The words "real money" refocused Lilly's attention on her daughter's words. Lilly had wanted to open her own health and wellness center in a warmer, less humid climate. She had found the government's retirement benefits to be generous relative to her day-to-day expenses, but niggardly within the context of her entrepreneurial ambitions. The oppressive East Coast weather and caste system had grown tiresome; she found the summer humidity and winter snow to be the worst of everything, and all the men seemed to care about were academic and professional pedigrees and golf handicaps.

"Could you please quantify 'real' for me?"

"I'm not sure…I think it's negotiable…But if you can help this guy reach his goals, then he gets a few *million* dollars."

Aloysius had been afraid of growing old alone and impoverished, and had been depending on his inheritance to help solve both problems. Mild paranoia had also been a long-time companion, and with five million dollars up for grabs its presence was growing. Al had not been specific with Scout about how much money was at stake, but he had said "millions" when they had spoken on the phone. Hoping to use this challenge to potentially pull him closer to his kids, he admittedly also didn't really like or trust his contacts in Las Vegas. His regular thoughtless and irresponsible behavior had pretty much burned all of his bridges. At one point he had considered asking for Keenan's direct help in achieving his goal, but was worried about the embedded conflicts. He also knew Keenan was making plenty of money at a job that required all of his bandwidth—*and* he had a young family. So he probably wouldn't be able to prioritize the father's goals. No one knew where Clay was…and Paul was in a wheelchair. Aloysius needed someone who had legitimate fitness and nutrition credentials but who also could put their life on hold for a year. Someone who could light a fire under him and whom he could trust. He had reached out to Scout, knowing that she was not listed in the estate instructions as part of the "next generation"…so she wouldn't be aware of the potential conflict. In his heart of hearts, he was also hoping she might have a friend or an acquaintance, maybe a nubile youngster who had the right training and personality to motivate him. The clock was ticking.

The ants had now marched out of Lilly's consciousness. She considered a move from her cramped townhouse in Annapolis.

"This all sounds illegal. Where is this person located?"

"Las Vegas. Mom, tell me about your nutritional training?"

Las Vegas was warm. She had a friend who had recently returned from a vacation in the Nevada desert. The woman said that Las Vegas was "like Disneyland for adults," and then winked at Lilly in a very naughty way.

I could use some naughtiness, Lilly permitted herself. *It's been a while…*

"Is this a straight weight-loss gig, because those can be tough…I'm not a psychiatrist, and food issues— "

"No weight loss involved, Mom," Scout replied, cutting her off. "This is more of a holistic mind-set thing. Diet, fitness, meditation."

Scout wanted to sink the hook a little deeper before revealing either the patient or the alcohol angle.

"For the right person I think they would cover all expenses," she continued. "The big payday would come if you helped him achieve his goals. A performance-based fee structure."

Lilly was gaining interest.

"I took an accredited course at the local community college, so I have some training as a nutritionist. But really, most of my experience is from trial and error."

"Do you mind if I share your resume with this guy and see if he's interested? He wants to get started right away, and I think you would be great."

Lilly's mind started to picture a rose-colored adobe building adorned with a tasteful sign: *Desert Lilly's Health and Wellness Center*. Inside would be spa facilities…yoga and pilates studios…a meditation center…a tasteful apparel boutique…perhaps, even, a paleo restaurant…?

1997
Las Vegas

CHAPTER 23—

Rock Bottom

The EMT was monitoring Aloysius's vitals as he drifted in and out of consciousness. The wail of the siren intruded into Al's self-loathing as he realized he might've really overdone it this time. From the belly of the ambulance he considered a justification for his destructive behavior. He comfortably reached for the old parental standby.

If the old bitch hadn't plagued me with this hugely unfair burden of having to perform at an unreasonable level, then I wouldn't be in my current predicament. Unbelievable. She's still judging me from the grave.

He heard a voice from over his shoulder.

"We're losing him!"

Who gives a shit? Aloysius thought. *He's been lost for decades.*

Al woke in a hospital bed with a fleet of IVs and monitors attached to him. A wave of depression swept over him when he realized he was still alive. He knew he didn't have the courage to effect the alternative, despite his recent efforts. The lack of contrition surprised him as he vaguely remembered the three previous days of debauchery. The whole slide had been initiated by him firing his most recent personal trainer in a fit of anger and disappointment. Otto was a large man with a "my way or the highway" approach to training. He had been referred to Al by one of his casino clients, who had raved about the ex-NFL strength and conditioning coach. At first Al bought into Otto's alpha-dog style, absorbing both the punishing workouts and the stories of injecting Joe Namath's knees with painkillers before each Jets football game. The heavy lifting, low rep regimen was effective in allowing him to gain muscle mass; however, it wasn't helping his running or swimming. Otto was also stunningly counterproductive to Al's attempts at sobriety, as he would enthusiastically recount Kenny Stabler drinking stories and often absentmindedly invite Aloysius out for a few beers after their workouts.

As the weeks went by and Al reached a plateau of eight pull-ups and a 185-pound bench press, he realized he could've enlisted in the Army and suffered the criticisms of a drill sergeant for free. In contrast, Otto charged sixty dollars an hour. Despite Otto's general lack of awareness, as Al started to question his trainer's methods more aggressively the dinosaur coach slowly realized he was wearing out his welcome—and his meal ticket. That's when he went out on a limb and convinced Aloysius he was ready for Keenan's scrutiny. Otto had nothing to lose as he was behind on his mortgage, automobile, and child support payments, and was already counting on his performance bonus when Al reached his goals. Keenan had already been out once to witness his father fail spectacularly in the mile run (he pulled a hamstring), but that was six months earlier, and with a different trainer. Otto was sure with a "little extra mojo" Aloysius could get over the top in the bench press, and he told his client he could just "gut it out" in the ten-mile run. Neither Otto nor Aloysius had ever run more than two miles, so their ignorance made it easier for them to dramatically underestimate the difficulty inherent in an untrained, sixty-year-old body trying to run ten miles in under two hours. Fortunately for Aloysius, he never made it to the run.

Keno dutifully flew out to witness his father nearly kill himself on the bench press. Otto had prepared a pregame meal, which included the supplemental, aforementioned "little extra mojo," which turned out to be a beverage of strongly caffeinated coffee, sugar, Ecuadorian dark chocolate, and some coca leaf extract, the recipe for which originated with an Andean kicker whom Otto had roomed with in the sixties. Aloysius was so "naturally" stimulated as he strained to press the two hundred pounds off of his chest that he herniated the tissue that kept his testicles separated from his abdominal wall and nearly decapitated himself with the barbell. Keno couldn't recall his perception of an event changing as quickly as it had that day. In the course of three seconds his father's efforts had struck him at first as earnest, then comical, and finally, potentially fatal. To his credit, Otto was spotting his client carefully, and promptly returned the barbell to a nonthreatening position before Al's agonized visage turned purple.

Aloysius had been trying really hard with Otto. He was comfortable admitting, ex post facto, that his first trainer, Randi, had been more of a masseuse/escort girl than a fitness or nutrition expert. A petite bombshell, Aloysius had coveted her from afar but had never had the discretionary income to sample. He brilliantly negotiated a contingency contract with her, which included a few significantly discounted rub and tugs, but no real training. In exchange, she would receive fifty thousand dollars if he reached his goals. After a few months she realized he wasn't doing the things necessary to get her paid, so she started demanding that he run a few miles before she would service him. She was a heavy cannabis user and not particularly ambitious in the monitoring department. Recognizing this, Aloysius would jog the first few hundred yards around the corner, until he was out of her sight, then grab a midday vodka gimlet at Mickey's Tavern. He would return twenty minutes later and find her, in his living room, smoking a spliff and reading his *People* magazines. After three months of biweekly massages, she grew tired of their arrangement and insisted he try to pass the fitness tests. He had no idea how fast he could run, but he did have an inflated view of himself; so he actually thought he had a sub-eight minute mile in him. Using the same uninformed logic, he figured any dope could do one hundred push-ups.

Keenan was summoned from San Francisco, stopwatch in hand. Randi, in pink, high-heeled sandals, stood next to him. Together they watched Aloysius from the UNLV stadium infield. It was a bluebird spring day, and Al started strong, spurred on by the hooker's enthusiastic support. As he headed down the backstretch on his first lap, he pulled up lame, clutching at the back of his right leg as if he had been shot. At this point Randi unleashed a potty mouth of cursing that Keenan thought qualified as outstanding. The son hustled over to help his hobbled father as Randi headed out to the parking lot to smoke a bowl of infuriation and erase Aloysius Barton's name from her address book.

233

Al had made a much greater commitment with the strength and conditioning coach, including drying out for four months while Otto put him through his paces. With a spring in his step and a whiff of hope in the air, he sincerely felt he had a chance of successfully executing his assignments; to date he had paid Otto six thousand dollars for his guidance. He was embarrassed that Keenan had flown out again to no purpose and was maddeningly disappointed that he was no closer to his five million dollar inheritance after all that suffering. As he crawled out from under the barbell and slid onto his knees, an overwhelming understanding of the Herculean nature of his assigned tasks began to crystallize. A dangerous stew of depression, anger, and pain started invading his grey matter. He decided he badly needed a drink. So he sat up on his haunches, looked at Otto, and fired him on the spot.

"We're done, Otto, I no longer need your services."

The father then asked the son if he could help him to his Mercedes. Which, of course, the younger Barton did. Keno then offered transport assistance to a doctor, but the paterfamilias declined. He then left his boy, without another word, in the gymnasium parking lot, and drove straight to the Mustang Ranch, where he engaged his credit cards in a limit-challenging, intoxicated, sexual journey. On the third day, in a drunken haze, he became frustrated with his inability to perform and solicited one of his favorite girls for some pharmaceutical assistance. The girl prescribed the kitchen sink, which he gladly accepted, snorting a few lines after chasing a Viagra with five shots of tequila.

The convulsions started soon thereafter.

The ambulance shortly followed.

An hour after he woke up in the hospital, Aloysius asked the nurse if he could use a phone. Sober reality was overwhelming him, and he was desperately in need of money. The nurse complied, and he placed a call to Scout. He had burned through nearly all of his savings with Randi, Otto, and the Mustang Ranch, and he was still no closer to his inheritance. He was worried he might get fired after going AWOL for three days, and he was sure his medical bills were going to be significant. As usual, his first attempt at surmounting a challenge was the easy way—devoid of any concern for morality. He needed his inheritance. But the combination of hard work required to meet the trust's stipulations and the uncertainty of outcome left him feeling defeated.

"Scout, I'm at my wit's end. I need your help. Please call Keenan and ask him for an advance on my inheritance. I've had a medical emergency and my insurance doesn't fully cover my affliction."

Al didn't have the guts to call Keno directly—he was hoping Scout would do the dirty work. He correctly assumed his daughter would inspire less diligence from her half sibling, given the newness of their relationship. It was just recently that Al had introduced them, and Keno had made the effort to host Scout for dinner a few times during his trips to LA. By now Scout knew her father well enough to understand his flaws. The fact that he had lost his self-assured confidence and was pleading with her on the phone spoke volumes. She decided to let him down gently.

"Oh my god, Jojie…what happened?"

Aloysius had always been quick on his feet.

"Scout, I'm really in a bad way right now. I strained some tissue in my lower abdominal cavity during the bench press, otherwise I would've put up the two hundred pounds."

Being aware of the estate challenges her deceased grandmother had placed on Aloysius, Scout immediately understood his reference; but she was also pretty confident he wasn't in real physical danger. She wanted to make him say the words and was hoping he wouldn't lie.

"Where are you now?"

"I'm in the hospital."

"For a hernia?"

"There are complications."

Scout considered her options.

"Sure, I'll talk to Keenan. Just have the hospital fax me the bills with a full description of the treatments so I can be prepared."

Her response made it clear that his long shot wasn't going to work. He had already slunk to the low road, so he supposed this next step could be considered subterranean.

"Scout, I've been really trying with these fitness tests, but I think they are just too demanding for a man of my age and…temperament. If you can get Keenan to sign off on the inheritance distribution, then I'll split it three ways with you two."

Scout sighed in resignation. *Well, at least he had the balls to say it. Stay positive,* she reminded herself. *He's already full of self-loathing.*

"Dad, you know I can't do that. Even if I wanted to, you know Keno would never agree. I know how terribly you must be feeling now, but you can do this."

The unsolicited lecturing provoked an immediate angry response—*Easy for you to say in your ignorantly optimistic youth…you know nothing!*—that he was barely able to restrain. He writhed in the hospital bed like the injured and cornered animal he was. Not knowing where else to go, his mind wandered to the end.

To be or not to be, indeed, he thought.

Having just previously rejected the latter, he begrudgingly stumbled across the familiar territory, dragged by natural forces, where, on the other side, he recognized his horse, which patiently awaited the remounting.

God this is difficult, he complained. *And so fucking lonely.*

"I'm really struggling with my reality right now. Do you think your mom would still be willing to help me with these fitness tests?"

Scout wondered what had happened that was so bad to get him to change his mind. When she had first suggested Lilly as an option he had dismissed the idea immediately.

"I can ask her, Jojie, but I think she's already made other commitments."

Scout was positioning her mom for the potential negotiation. Lilly's schedule was pretty much wide open.

"Scout, I'm desperate here. I'll provide her room and board in my condo guest bedroom, and give her five percent of the money—two hundred and fifty thousand dollars—if I complete the trust stipulations under her watch."

Scout couldn't believe the offer and realized he must be quite desperate. Her mind raced as she started bouncing up and down inside, but she played it cool on the phone. She felt uncomfortable about being manipulative with her father, but she also felt that he had brought much of this on himself.

"I'll call Mom and get back to you ASAP. Sound good?"

"Sounds good. Thank you."

As Aloysius hung up the phone, he realized he had just needed someone who could help him shoulder his responsibilities. A person who was more adept at managing his particular set of challenges than Randi or Otto. As he reached over to buzz the nurse, a brief glimpse of optimism started invading his gloom. The irritation previously evoked by the rhythmic chirping of his monitoring devices now registered as soothing. When the nurse arrived he asked for some codeine for his hernia, pulled the covers up to his chin, and closed his eyes.

Third time's the charm, he hoped.

CHAPTER 24

Phoenix

O ne week later, Lilly delivered via courier a simple contract that stated clearly the terms of her engagement. Aloysius signed and sent it back that day. Lilly sublet her furnished Annapolis apartment to a friend, packed a few personal belongings, and moved to Las Vegas ten days after receiving the executed document. Her plan with Aloysius was to build a multi-pronged, collaborative strategy that required his buy-in every step of the way. Scout had already informed Lilly that the client (Aloysius) was her dad. After several emotional phone calls, Lilly reluctantly accepted Scout's belief that the random and unlikely reunion was a good thing. A sign from the gods. What other choice did she have?

Before moving in with Al, Lilly had spent long hours on the phone talking to Scout, asking about Aloysius's current condition. Through Keenan, Scout eventually connected Lilly to Lola, and they discussed different strategies to help Aloysius with his addiction to alcohol. Lilly felt pretty comfortable with her nutrition and yoga knowledge, but didn't have a clue as to how to help with the substance abuse issues. Thoughts poured through her head, but she couldn't find any evidence that any of her ideas were substantive. She decided to try the non-oppositional behavioral therapy that Lola had described in conjunction with her yoga, meditation, and Paleolithic diet. For a shot at two hundred and fifty thousand dollars, Lilly thought she could suck it up for a sixty day Hail Mary. Lola had emphasized her view that unsolicited advice would not be helpful when working with Aloysius.

"Don't preach to him; the Barton men have heard it all. They know what to do, you just have to create an environment where they want to do it—and then hope they can execute. It's their choice. Don't put too much pressure on yourself, you're just the supporting cast."

Lilly had to do some specific research on appropriate training techniques for the fitness tests that Al needed to pass, but all the studies that focused on older men seemed to be pretty straightforward. Basically, the research suggested starting with a low-intensity, shortened approximation of the task, then slowly increasing intensity and duration. Crawl, walk, run. She had been a swimmer in college, and given Al's hernia injury she thought laps in the pool would be a good place to start. Lola had told her she needed to sincerely care about Aloysius if she were to be successful in connecting. Lilly worried that the biggest challenge would be walking the fine line between enthusiastically supporting Al and engaging in a sexual relationship, especially in light of their history…or lack thereof. Given what she had heard about Al's current state, she wasn't interested in a physical relationship, but she guessed he would be. She didn't remember much about him, except that he had been somewhat…accommodating.

When Aloysius arranged to pick Lilly up at the airport, he had told her he would be holding a sign that read H8SBAD. He hoped she would get the reference. As Lilly walked out of the gate area, she saw an older gentleman about fifty feet away holding a stick that was supporting a professionally prepared 1-foot by 2-foot sign with the designated letters. She walked in his direction hoping she could keep it together. *Disappointment* was the word that probably best described both their feelings when they were visually reacquainted. Neither had aged particularly poorly, but the shock that accompanies the collision of past memories with current reality can hit hard regardless of emotional preparation. Happily, they both shared a level of civility and education that provided a comfort zone in which they could operate. If a connection were to happen it would have to come later. As Al drove Lilly home from the airport, he made polite small talk about current events and his sailboat racing experiences on the Chesapeake.

"…then as I hauled in the jib sheet while simultaneously giving the command to tack…"

Lilly tried hard to seem interested, and interesting. She nodded and smiled, focused on presenting a relaxed facade. After she had made the commitment to come to Las Vegas, an ever-so-faint whisper of anxiety started developing at the furthest recesses of her consciousness. With the exception of a handful of brief overnight trips, she hadn't slept in a bed other than her own for nearly ten years, and she had grown quite accustomed to the familiarity of her Annapolis surroundings. She had been able to keep her remote fears under control, but as her plane had headed west, the inklings had grown into a palpable attack of agoraphobia. By the time she landed, gathered her bags, and was escorted to Al's car, she was just inches away from a full-scale breakdown. While Al was embellishing his role in the heroic 1954 Princeton sailing victory over the Midshipman of the US Naval Academy, Lilly's fingers had been rapidly typing the words of their conversation on a theoretical keyboard located in her lap and hidden under her purse. She was also carefully breathing to a six-six-six cadence to try and keep the panic attack from overwhelming her.

Breathe in deeply, 1-2-3-4-5-6. Hold, 1-2-3-4-5-6. Exhale, 1-2-3-4-5-6. Repeat.

Al had moved on from his racing exploits, feeling that he had appropriately established his credentials as a sportsman. He was now ready to share his feminine side. In his experience, there were certain topics that drew universal enthusiasm.

"My oldest grandson, Sam, is in the third grade. He sent me that valentine on the dashboard. He made it in art class."

He looked at Lilly with a big smile, but she didn't seem to be paying attention.

He tried again, "Grandkids are such a gift."

Lilly seemed to be either intensely buried in thought or outright frowning. Al was concerned he had touched a nerve.

"Lilly, are you okay?"

At a recent Georgetown reunion, Lilly had been with a group of longtime girlfriends, and the topic of grandkids and how wonderful they were had also come up. One of the group had been a large donor to Planned Parenthood, and another held a senior position in the Sierra Club. Lilly took the lone contradictory position. Now her mind went back to that moment, and her agoraphobia started to recede as her sense of moral indignation began to build. She knew it was socially problematic, but she couldn't help herself.

"I don't understand the obsession with grandkids."

Aloysius was taken aback; in all the sensitive interactions he had accumulated throughout his years, grandkids were about as bulletproof as you could get. He looked at her with a combination of curiosity and fear.

She continued with a question.

"What's our largest current problem?"

It was apparent that the conversational tone had changed. With clouds on the horizon, Al pulled out his rhetorical sextant and started navigating with trepidation.

"What do you mean by 'our'?"

"Our species, *Homo sapiens*."

"Environmental degradation? Pollution?"

"That's a good start."

"Gainful employment at a living wage?"

"Not bad. What's the number one cause of death globally, for those under sixty-five?"

"Mosquito-born diseases, heart disease, cancer?"

"All decent guesses, but no. Dehydration as a complication from diarrhea resulting from the ingestion of non-potable water."

"No shit?"

He recognized his poor word choice a second too late.

Lilly did too, but refused to acknowledge the unintended pun. She was nodding her head and opening her lungs for a deep inhalation. Then, she let fly the full force of her frustration.

"I don't understand how someone can simultaneously claim to care about our world yet support the unquestioned celebration of the birth of another one of...*us.* I understand the appropriateness of celebrating birth at a time when mortality rates were high, when rulers wanted more soldiers and taxpayers—but today? With seven billion people soiling the planet? All of our biggest problems come from too many of...*us.*"

There, Lilly thought. *I put it out there for him to see, to know that I'm an unfeeling monster. Not too late to return to the airport and send me back from whence I came....*

Aloysius was mesmerized. He had no intention of separating himself from the idiosyncratic creature in his passenger seat.

*Fuckin-eh! This chick has balls! And the stuff that comes out of her mouth is **fun**!*

He foresaw no boring pleasantries on the horizon with the woman sitting beside him.

Thirty seconds later, he broke the silence.

"Okay, then...glad we got that out of the way."

Lilly noticed that she had stopped the phantom typing, and that her breathing had returned to a somewhat stable pace. It seemed she had regained a semblance of normalcy, and, upon reflection, she tried to backpedal a bit.

"I'm sure Samuel is an exemplary child...and...given your position of relative affluence, and, without sounding like a white supremacist, he may be one of the few who...with the right guidance...is positioned to make the planet a better place."

He wasn't even sure how to begin deciphering all the caveats buried in her sentence, so he turned up the Lyle Lovett and let the music take them home.

And they look across the border

To learn the ways of love

Over the course of their first few days together, Lilly spent many hours talking with her client about which approach he thought would provide him the highest probability of success. It was not only informative for her but highly therapeutic for both of them. Before the end of the first week they had a chance to discuss the sequence of events that had led to Scout's conception, and they then loosely used that conversation as a launching point for sharing their experiences over the ensuing twenty-three years. At the end of the first week she put together a twenty-page road map that she shared with Aloysius. Her CIA training had sharpened her preternatural attention to detail to a fine point. The road map was essentially a timeline that spelled out a specific logic sequence in an if/then format. She had every minute of every day plotted out for the next sixty days, including alternative options if they (she insisted Al consider her his teammate) "failed" at different points. The number of permutations alone was impressive.

Aloysius couldn't afford to leave his concierge position, and that made things a little more challenging. The Las Vegas strip was designed to encourage people to indulge, and Al's job was to reinforce that enticement. Luckily, he had been in his role for long enough that he felt a bit like the pastry chef who has grown weary of éclairs. He could still encourage his clients to sin big, but his personal appetites had grown a little muted with time (his actions at the Mustang Ranch excepted). The real risk was just fatigue from a long day of servicing people and being away from the watchful eyes of Lilly. He worried he might be tempted to stray from the plan on a Friday afternoon at the end of a long week. They decided Lilly would drive him to and from work, and stop by daily to join him for his lunch break. What else did she have to do?

Aloysius had agreed with Lilly's idea to first try a swimming and push-up program, given the complementary nature of those activities. Al had done some competitive swimming as a boy, and understood the basics of the freestyle stroke, although the variation he had learned was a bit dated. They decided they would give the swimming/push-ups segment two weeks and then reassess according to the data—which Lilly would assiduously record every day—including how long Aloysius took to swim how many laps in the pool, and how many push-ups he did, and how proficiently he did them. If they weren't making satisfactory progress, they would consider an alternative path specified by her written plan. They would try not to overwork Al, as they both wanted to avoid an injury and the accompanying time loss. Lilly would prepare or arrange for all of his meals, but he would have input regarding the menu. She wanted him on a low-carbohydrate, unprocessed diet that kept cravings to a minimum—no grains, no dairy…basically a Paleolithic diet that had him eating meat, fish, nuts, vegetables, and fruit. They would wean him from his roughly five hundred milligrams of caffeine per day to about fifty. The plan even included an incremental tapering of alcohol consumption that got him to zero by the end of forty-five days. Lilly knew the first two weeks would be the hardest, as he would have to retrain his body to burn protein and healthy fats rather than his current diet of predominantly simple and complex sugars. All of the road map's specifics resulted from detailed collaboration, and Lilly made it clear that this wasn't her plan, but Al's. She was just there as a witness and consultant.

Before the end of the first week, Lilly escorted Al to the office of his general practitioner, and received an assessment of his ability to engage in a fitness regimen. Al's doctor had been pushing his patient to be more active for years, so it wasn't surprising that he green-lighted a modest exercise program. As part of his annual checkup he had received an EKG, which showed his heart was in relatively decent shape for a man of his proclivities. As Aloysius drove Lilly home in the silver Mercedes, they reviewed their plans for the following week. Lilly was impatient to start, but it was a weekday. It was important, she felt, not to translate stress to her client. She also wanted to be careful not to push him the other way by offering unsolicited input that Al might interpret as a threat to his position in their two-person hierarchy.

"Now that we have the doctor's approval, when do you want to start?" She asked the question as noncommittally as possible.

Al was anxious to start too, and he wasn't encumbered by any of Lilly's concerns. In fact, he had been enjoying her company, liked her detailed, quantitative approach, and noted that the structure of the plan was effective in allowing him to build confidence. This reaction of his seemed strange, given his historical resistance to externally imposed discipline. He had also noticed that Lilly had grown quietly more attractive over their first week; now, whenever she donned her yoga attire, even at fifty years old, she easily held his attention.

"Can we start Friday?"

It was late Thursday afternoon. Lilly tried to sound clever by offering a sound bite with an affected rural accent: "It's your rodeo, cowboy. I'm just here to keep the bull from stompin' ya." She ended up sounding like a dork with an affected rural accent who had tried, unsuccessfully, to be clever.

He let her comment fall awkwardly, untouched in the silence that followed; then, he released a small chuckle. Her little quirks delighted him—she obviously left Randi and Otto in her cerebral dust; he only hoped she wouldn't become too predictable. He considered the irony embedded in the rodeo event of bull riding: a crazed bull trying to gore a similarly insane rider, with both participants having something painfully unnatural happening to their testicles. His mental rodeo image included another player.

"I guess that makes you the clown?"

Lilly simultaneously considered her current position and her hard-earned doctorate in International Relations from Georgetown. Scout had let her mom in on the unusual "Joe Gargery" conversation that she and Al had had when he picked Scout up outside of Barstow, and they both thought the Joe G nickname was cute in a soft, nonthreatening way. Lilly had decided she would use the moniker when she felt it was appropriate, and that, if necessary, she would roll the syllables together like Scout did, because she felt *Jojie*, as a term of endearment, would defang Al a bit.

"Maybe, cowboy, but with a PhD…and don't you forget it, Jojie."

It seemed to work. Aloysius redirected the conversation, steering it away from the flirting and back towards the start date for his resurrection.

"Maybe we should wait for Saturday to start. I have a few things to tidy up at work, and my abdominal injury is still a concern."

"Great, we'll start on Saturday morning. Let's go over our schedule on Friday night—plan our work and work our plan."

Al barely stifled a groan. Every once in a while one of her comments came out more trite than treat, and he had never been much of an orthodoxy fan.

By eight a.m. on Saturday morning he was already one hundred yards into his first workout at the local community college pool. Lilly had scheduled five hundred yards for the first day. She sported a summer dress that matched the color of her yellow legal pad. A pair of Wayfarers sat nestled under a white visor that allowed her to enjoy the morning Nevada sun. Watching his stroke turnover was making her inwardly cringe. She walked along the edge of the pool, scratching a pencil across her pad. The students at the community college were still in bed recovering from their Friday night shenanigans. This meant that Al could plod through the water with uninterrupted ineptitude. He would rest in between each twenty-five-yard lap, holding on to the wall as he caught his breath. At least his lower abdominal strain was only slightly discomforting. His new Speedo swimsuit wasn't flattering, but it was quite functional in a least-resistance kind of way, and he was pleasantly surprised at how much more leak-proof modern swim goggles were relative to those of his youth. After each lap he would remove and examine the goggles in disbelief. He would then make minor adjustments and return them to their intended position before pushing off the wall on another seventy-five foot embarkation. This inefficient, obsessive behavior antagonized Lilly to no end. The first day he swam three hundred yards in twenty minutes. He would need to swim 1,760 yards in thirty minutes to pass that part of his inheritance fitness test. Lilly fought hard to disguise her disappointment. Al's technique and conditioning were so awful that Lilly started to worry that she might be in over her head. She reminded herself that at least she was enjoying some desert ambience on someone else's dime. Worst case? Only fifty-seven days to go.

Following the swim, while still in his Speedo, Aloysius wanted to see how many push-ups he could do. Lilly, as an example, flawlessly executed six (hopefully motivating) repetitions. Al noticed with envy—and excitement—that she could lower herself only three-quarters of the way to the floor. Lilly made a note to herself to avoid low-cut tops on push-up days. After Al struggled with his first attempt, they both decided he would start with knee push-ups and work towards incline push-ups against a table or chair. He resigned himself to accepting embarrassment as a regular companion during his first few weeks. Finally, over time, they both hoped he would move his incline angle down to a fully prone position.

On the first day he did eight knee push-ups.

To document their progress, Lilly had brought a camera. She had taken several "before" shots of Al standing in his swim trunks, swimming in the pool, and then trying some push-ups. There was hope that after he won his inheritance they would look back and laugh at the photographs; but after his amazingly lackluster initial performance Lilly was pessimistic about his chances. She wondered how a man who had recently bench pressed one hundred and eighty-five pounds couldn't do one normal push-up. Lilly believed that he might have an embedded anatomical incongruence, the significance of which might interest the people at Ripley's. Her only option was pushing on.

They had an established schedule: Monday, Wednesday, and Saturday were early-morning pool days. Tuesday and Thursday were yoga and push-up days. She let Al rest on Friday and Sunday, during which time the two of them would spend as much time as necessary discussing Al's progress and how they could work together to improve the program. Lilly insisted that Aloysius journal his experiences at least one day a week, and Aloysius usually dragged his feet until Sunday to collect his five-hundred-word minimum thoughts and leak them through the tip of his pen onto the pages of his notebook. At first this chore was challenging, but over time he recognized its value and started feeling more comfortable with the writing. He was willing to give Lilly's ideas at least a sincere four-week try out.

As Lilly had expected, the first two weeks were challenging on all levels. Al didn't yet have the upper-body strength necessary to execute a correct crawl stroke for more than a lap or two. Like many casual swimmers, he didn't understand that most of his forward propulsion originated from his arms, and that his legs were quite inefficient in the water, especially over longer distances. She quickly convinced him to switch from a six- to a two-beat kick, immediately saving him a tremendous amount of energy, while still allowing his legs to trail behind him without effecting too much drag. Despite Lilly verbally preparing him for it, he complained of muscle soreness regularly, as if it were unhealthy; even though she had explained it was actually a good indicator that the effort he was putting in to his workouts was resulting in the growth of muscle tissue. At the end of the first few days, Lilly realized that he was a mess in all four of her fitness categories: strength, cardiovascular, flexibility, and balance. She regularly wondered if "Otto" was a fictitious trainer fabricated by Al for sympathy. The good news was that as long as he didn't die, he could only improve. She hoped his flaccid muscles would grow and strengthen quickly as a result of the stimulus they were receiving daily, as both trainer and trainee needed to establish an early positive trajectory.

The attempt to change Aloysius' consumption patterns was also a significant problem area. He appeared to be addicted to alcohol, caffeine, and sugar; decades of daily infusions had developed strong cerebral tendrils that needed feeding. While planning their strategy, she had offered Al the choice of going cold turkey or not. He had chosen "not," so they followed a path of incrementalism. Lilly's powers of persuasion *vis-à-vis* nutrition were no match for his justifications *vis-à-vis* addiction, but she had a secret weapon. Lilly was brewing her own organic, fermented, green tea. Her plan was to get Aloysius to substitute his coffee and alcohol with this magic elixir, known as *kombucha*. The ancient drink was acidic in flavor and registered about a 4.0 on the ph scale. Lilly knew the concoction was an acquired taste, but she also knew that the delectable tang could be addicting. Slaving over several early batches, she tried to orchestrate a higher sugar and caffeine concentration than she would usually brew, to help ease Al's transition. She also tweaked her fermentation process to bring the ethanol levels to around one percent ABV. The mixture was full of naturally occurring probiotics and flavonoids to help repair Al's digestive and immune systems after years of abuse. She wove this strategy into her overall gradualist nutritional program, serving higher fiber foods like almonds, spinach, and avocados for his main calorie source whenever possible. She would keep his taste buds entertained with large dollops of olive oil, butter, and salt, as he was fortunate in that he showed few symptoms of hypertension. She also integrated spicy peppers into his diet; the capsaicin would help provide an endorphin lift, which in turn would distract his tastebuds from all the sweet they were missing during his migration from less healthy options.

The transition to a holistic menu was the first area where they seemed to gain some traction: Aloysius went through the first week with only limited dietary complaints. In fact his acquiescence was so uneventful that Lilly became suspicious and sat him down for a lecture in which she reminded him of the need for self-compliance in this (i.e., *his*) process. Al's assurances of commitment seemed sincere, and Lilly moved forward with only periodic skepticism. She resisted the urge to search his work space and car, knowing that doing so would set a bad precedent.

At the beginning of the third week, on a shimmering Saturday morning, Lilly allowed herself a glimmer of hope. Not only was Al's form showing promise, his results were improving measurably. He was able to swim three hundred yards, nonstop, in under ten minutes. He swam seven hundred yards total that day in under thirty minutes. No longer fiddling with his goggles, he was bringing a new sense of purpose to his workout. Two days later, on a rare rainy Monday morning, he did three regular push-ups followed by thirty knee push-ups, followed by a forty-five-minute beginner Vinyasa yoga session. His body was changing with the routine. He was noticing a decline in his intense evening cravings for sweets. He was still imbibing, but with Lilly's presence he was down to two or three drinks a night.

As part of an intermittent fasting regimen to which Lilly had introduced him at the beginning of week two, he now limited his post-eight p.m. intake to water or decaf tea. He started the following day with kombucha, and did not eat his first meal until Lilly joined him at his office for an early lunch at around eleven-thirty. This methodology was keeping his insulin spikes (and hence his energy swings) to a minimum, thereby also reducing his sugar cravings. Afterwards, she and Aloysius would take a long walk, away from the casino, during which Al would pick Lilly's brain about nutrition and exercise, and ways he could improve the probability of fulfilling the estate's stipulations.

"How come whenever it's time to work out I'm always reluctant, but after I'm finished I'm enthusiastic?"

"That's your limbic brain initially overruling your cortex. The older, emotional brain doesn't want you to needlessly waste calories, because it evolved during a period of scarcity. Your newer, rational brain knows you have access to plenty of calories, that exercise is good for you, and that you'll feel better after. If you're like most people, it will take a while for you to rewire your neural pathways to accept, without effort, the newer brain's conclusion."

"Is that why I keep eating donuts and bacon, even though a part of my mind is screaming that I should stop?"

Lilly had never thought of it that way, but at a casual glance it seemed a reasonable comparison. She smiled at the quirky way her client's mind worked, recognizing that to some extent he was intentionally playing at being the petulant boy.

"I think that's pretty much the same internal fight."

"Do you have those struggles?"

"Sometimes, but I mostly have the food and exercise issues under control."

"How long did that take you?"

"Years."

She didn't want to leave him feeling like self-control was out of reach. She also didn't want to set herself up as being something she wasn't.

"You know, Aloysius, I'm far from perfect; I have my own set of internal battles."

"Like what?"

In an effort to keep the conversation oriented towards him, Lilly opened the door to a new option and gave him a nudge through the entryway.

"If this is an area you're really interested in, it might make sense to talk a little bit about meditation."

Aloysius had never found the idea of meditation to be even remotely appealing. He wasn't sure why, but sitting quietly still for any amount of time seemed to him to be an unimaginably difficult way to waste time. Lilly could tell from his body language that he was feeling uncomfortable, but she remained silent to see how he would unsquirm himself. Against his baser instincts, he decided to venture ever so slightly out of his comfort zone.

"Do you have an elevator pitch for meditation?"

The pressure was on. Lilly thought some form of intentional thinking practice could very much help most people, but she had never been asked to convince someone of the benefits of meditation. She took about twenty seconds to gather her thoughts; what came out next wasn't poetry, but it would have to do, given the time constraints.

"Sitting quietly reveals how random and uncontrollable one's thoughts can be. Once you become aware of this mental cluster fornication, you may then take steps to better understand, and maybe even defuse, your thoughts and emotions, rather than have them control you. The defusing comes not by suppressing, or resisting, but by observing in a non-judgmental way. Basically it's a technique that teaches us that we are not the sum of our thoughts."

"What are we then?"

"I'm still working on that."

Al was hoping for an insight that would compel him to meditate like donuts and bacon compelled him to eat. Lilly's explanation didn't disabuse him of his suspicion that trying to "do" meditation was going to be a challenge. He didn't have a lot of patience for activities where the payoff lay somewhere in the ethereal future. His job at the hotel—and this new exercise program—were already more than filling his quota in the "delayed gratification" category, and for both of those endeavors a well-defined path to getting paid had previously been established. Meditation seemed to be a somewhat squishy remedy for an affliction he couldn't even define.

"I assume you meditate?"

Lilly nodded. "For about seventeen minutes most every day."

"I don't want to offend, but can we hold off on integrating that into our routine?"

She fought the urge to convince him and offered her brightest, non-judgmental smile. The seed had been planted, no need to trample it before it took root.

"Of course, Aloysius. This isn't my program, it's yours."

After a few more weeks, things started gaining momentum, as if Aloysius were running downhill. The daily workouts started feeling less Sisyphean, more Jamaican bobsled. Lilly spent most of her time steering and counseling rather than pushing and cajoling. Aloysius was changing in front of her eyes, becoming maniacally focused. At the two-month mark, it became apparent to Lilly: there was a reasonable chance they would succeed. Al was consistently swimming five hundred yards in nine minutes, and though he hadn't actually tried swimming a mile nonstop, in one workout he had swum eighteen hundred yards, with a few breaks, in thirty-five minutes. His push-ups were also progressing nicely, as he could regularly perform thirty in rapid succession; at the ten-week mark he performed one hundred in three minutes. They were hoping Keenan would be a little lenient on his judging, as Al's push-up form emphasized speed over perfection. His body seemed to be responding well to the level of stimulus they were loading on him, and Lilly had to restrain him from overdoing it, as Aloysius's enthusiasm grew with his positive trajectory.

Four months into their program, Keenan flew out at Lilly's request to fulfill his role for his grandmother's estate. On a warm, summer, Las Vegas morning, his stopwatch in hand, he watched in amazement as his dad swam a mile in twenty-nine minutes and forty-three seconds. The old man was sixty-two years old. That afternoon, after an early lunch and nap, Al performed one hundred push-ups in one minute and fifty-seven seconds. The last twenty were pretty sloppy, but there was no way Keenan was going to disallow them based on form.

Aloysius's intensity and effort were so apparent to Keenan that the son noticed he was starting to develop a modicum of respect for his father. It made Keenan realize how much he had wanted a father of character, a father whom he could look up to; but at some point the younger man had given up hope, and then, finally, insulated himself from the never-ending disappointment that had accompanied their relationship.

Aloysius had been sober for three months. He had the blood tests to prove it. Keenan documented with the estate attorney that Al had completed two of the three tests…all that remained was to stay sober for nine more months. Lilly was already making her kombucha with much less sugar and caffeine, and the traces of alcohol in the vinegary liquid were too small to register in the blood tests. Her plan had worked; she had successfully swapped several less healthy addictions for one healthy one.

The reformation of Aloysius Barton was astounding to all who knew him. If Keno and Lilly hadn't been present to bear witness to his change no one would have believed it. He claimed to not even crave alcohol or cigars anymore. He hadn't eaten a hot dog or donut in months, but he was still able to enjoy bacon, as Lilly allowed him a regular BLT breakfast burrito with two scrambled eggs wrapped in a warm *maize tortilla*. Lilly seemed to understand just how much she could push Al before he would break; and so, over time, she had personalized his whole wellness approach to decrease the odds of failure.

Nobody seemed to be aware of the real reason that Al had changed. He had fallen in love with Lilly at some point during their first month together. After his usual flirtatious strategy had gained no traction, he had been driven by her presence, and his infatuation, to try an alternative course of wooing her. For the first time in his life, he retreated from his stubborn, selfish positions and allowed that someone else might have a better way. He dropped all of his behavioral rationalizations, which over the decades he had developed to justify his addictions, and went to work trying this new way.

The money had definitely motivated him—his deceased mother had gotten that right—and he had been in a position of deep need and vulnerability when he reached out to Lilly via Scout—but what really pushed him over the finish line was trust. He wasn't sure which had exited his life first, trust or hope, but at some point he had lost both. For some reason, probably a combination of necessity and desire, he had found a dollop of courage somewhere deep inside that allowed him to trust Lilly and her strategy. This ability to trust opened the door for hope…which eventually led to love. He used this kindling to push himself physically; and as his health and fitness improved, his confidence in Lilly grew, and he successfully entered into a self-reinforcing cycle of wellness. The whole process was filling a toxic pit in him that had regularly released malodorous fumes in the form of destructive behavior.

His love for Lilly wasn't just intangible. He often wondered if she was emitting some sort of pheromone to which he was chemically inclined. She seemed to have a noticeable, proximate, physical effect on him, although, like Pavlov's dogs, his brain wasn't particularly adept at disentangling all the sensory inputs that arrived when she did. Her scent and confident posture; her kombucha; the bacon breakfast burritos she allowed him; the intelligent conversation he had with her; and the countless other small, shared intimacies they enjoyed together all seemed to be working their way into his consciousness in a pleasant and captivating way. He didn't give it all that much thought, he just knew she made him feel good.

The morning after Al successfully demonstrated his fitness prerequisites, and only a few minutes after waving their good-byes to Keno at the Las Vegas airport terminal, Lilly floated the idea that she should return to Annapolis.

"Aloysius," she said, "I think my work here is pretty much done. How would you feel about sending me back to Annapolis so I can get out of your hair?"

Her comment hit him like a punch to the stomach. He didn't feel good about her suggestion at all…but it also came as a surprise that her statement had left him with such a strong feeling of vulnerability. Attachment wasn't a feeling he was used to, and his need (and her indifference) left him feeling exposed. He felt a wave of nausea and panic approaching as he considered his daily routine *sans* Lilly. Just as he was pulling away from the airport, he pictured a palette loaded with *his* five million dollars, the inheritance money wrapped tightly into plastic bundles, flying off in the cargo hold of the FedEx 747 that was gaining altitude on the other side of his windshield. His next thought started with a double martini…and his willpower seemed to be diminishing by the second.

He didn't know the origins of what came next, something from deep within his brain—a previously unexcavated partner to the "fight" or "flight" options. Whatever it was, it came devoid of sugar coating, just a simple package without a bow or a card. He didn't give any thought as to how he should deliver or phrase the request, so he just allowed it to arrive full of naïveté, innocence, trust, and hope. He pulled over to the side of the road, closed his eyes, took a deep breath, opened his eyes, then turned to Lilly and released it.

"Lilly," he said, "would you please marry me?"

2004

Tampa Bay

CHAPTER 25

Pablo Picasso

Paul was getting frustrated. Finally, a gallery had found his work compelling, and in two weeks he was scheduled to show several of his pieces in a watercolor exhibit. The gallery was located in Clearwater Beach, and catered mostly to tourists. The exhibit, titled *Easter Awakenings*, had been well publicized in the local media, and Paul knew the other two artists would be showing the usual beach landscapes. He had confidence in four of the paintings he would include in the exhibit, but for the final three he wanted to push his work in a new direction. Paul respected the talent necessary to paint a good sunset, but he had a lot bubbling inside that was finally trying to work its way to the surface, and he was hoping to make a statement with these imagined new pieces. Every time he started working on an interesting idea, he got blocked. To his mind, every brush stroke looked like tripe. The clock was ticking, and he was angsting about descending into a self-loathing pit of depression.

His benefactress, the gallery director, was a thirty-four-year-old woman of Persian descent who went by the single name Roshan. An Art History major from Barnard, she wasn't afraid to take chances. About a year ago, while on vacation from New York City, she had met Paul at a local open artists' studio. Paul would often frequent the same Clearwater studio when he wanted to get away from the stifling two-bedroom bungalow that, for economic reasons, Elizabeth had moved them into years ago. Paul was still in a wheelchair, but soon after the night of the air guitar event and the beating at the hands of the Tampa police, he had regained the use of his arms and torso. The first few years were very difficult for him, but he had finally found a routine and outlet with his painting. Eventually he had settled into his new reality.

After being introduced by a mutual friend at the open studio, Roshan found something compelling in Paul. She invited him to dinner that night. He had dated a few other women since his accident twenty-four years ago, but for a variety of reasons—reasons Paul considered somewhat obvious—nothing took root. Most young, healthy women weren't interested in a relationship with a wheelchair-dependent man who had no money. At forty-one, he was pretty sure he wasn't the right romantic fit for this intriguing girl from the big city; but after two bottles of Merlot, the progressive Manhattan native invited him up to her room. That night Paul surprised a curious Roshan when she discovered that, with few limitations, his sexual capability was as fully developed as his intellectual fortitude. A blossoming romance unfolded, and Roshan decided to hang around for a bit longer to see how this strange coupling would evolve. The gallery she was helping to manage in Tribeca was functioning admirably in her absence; so over the ensuing three weeks she and Paul spent nearly every night together in her room at the Clearwater Beach Hotel. During their days together they would work their way down the boardwalk to the beach, luxuriating in the sand, sun, and bathtub-warm Gulf of Mexico. Roshan was amazed at how well Paul could get around with his overdeveloped upper body, and she soon learned to stop attending to him so overtly. She would manage beach towels and sundries, and Paul would slide himself out of the chair and pull himself seal-like to their anointed resting spot. She also fell in love with the still, relaxed pace of life on the beach and started fantasizing about living in Clearwater full-time.

After postponing her return flight several times, Roshan finally journeyed back to her loft in Soho. Paul missed her tremendously, but was grateful for what he suspected would turn out to be three weeks of isolated charity. She obviously had a vibrant life back in New York, and he was literally immobilized in Florida. Years earlier he had done an intense exploration of Buddhism to try and help him deal with his pronounced mood swings. He gained three primary insights from the delving: first, life was suffering; second, and tangentially, unmet expectations were the source of all misery; and third, change was constant. All of these lessons were reinforced when Roshan returned to Manhattan. She had brought an energy and light into his life that hadn't been there before.

260

Two weeks later, unexpectedly, Roshan called from New York.

"Paul," she said, "is that you?"

Paul was stunned that, first, she was calling, and, second, that an unfettered enthusiasm bolstered her voice.

"Roshan…is that you?"

"Yes, yes, it's me!" Roshan exclaimed. "What are you doing?"

"Pining," he responded with comedic earnestness while trying to restrain his expectations.

"You've missed me…?"

He was afraid to be, or sound, too needy, but her voice was so free of guile that he took the chance and held nothing back.

"Haven't you received my letters? I've missed you desperately."

"You haven't found anyone else yet, have you?"

Paul thought the question strange, but in a promising kind of way.

"No, baby, of course not. I dream about you every night."

There was a pause as Roshan left him twisting for a moment before speaking up. Paul's heart rate accelerated. He was feeling exposed.

"Oh Paul, that's totally the right answer, baby. I'm flying down tomorrow *and* I have a backer who wants to open a gallery on the Sun Coast. I hope to convince him to do it on Clearwater Beach. Can you find some time to help me?"

Despite Paul's self-regulating tendencies, he found himself overwhelmed with joy.

"Of course I'll make time for you! It will be impossible for you to be rid of me."

It wouldn't be until Roshan was more certain of Paul's intentions that she would reveal that her father was a wealthy, well-known, New York real estate developer—and the backer of the proposed gallery. She had found that if men knew she came from a wealthy family the revelation would often change the dynamics of the relationship, and she would then find herself regularly questioning their motives. She loved that Paul cared for her without even knowing her last name. In her opinion he had the most beautiful, intelligent, and kind face. His art spoke to her; she could see past his injury to the whole man beneath. It also helped that he didn't seem to have a selfish bone in his body, which was evidenced by how hard he worked to make her happy, both in and out of bed, and how the smallest of indulgences brought forth in him an immense gratitude.

Roshan flew down, and within a month she had leased and started renovations on a small retail space a block off of the beach. The Euphrates Gallery was open within three months. Without the burden of needing to turn an immediate profit, Roshan was able to take some chances artistically. She developed friendships with the bored, local art community and charmed the newspapers into providing positive coverage of her edgier artists.

Paul fell hard. Every minute he wasn't painting he was with Roshan, and she reveled in his attention. She might have wanted something different as a younger woman, but Paul Barton seemed to press all the right buttons for what she needed now. She had experienced the egocentric hunks that washed ashore in Manhattan; and though she enjoyed the arm candy—and the envy of other women—she was often frustrated by the selfish vacuousness. A recent, painful experience with an unfaithful boyfriend had also made her wary of overly attractive men. The incident had led her to conclude that their options were too many and their willpower too limited. She was able to recognize that Paul's physical limitations likely made him a better companion.

After analyzing her parents', her own, and some friends' failed relationships, Roshan identified stagnation (which often led to infidelity) as one of the main stumbling blocks to maintaining a committed relationship. She was afraid she would lose interest in Paul if he wasn't willing to move beyond his comfort zone and bring something new to their romance. She worried about ruining what they had, but she also wanted to show his art in her gallery. To her, creativity was a catharsis, and she felt advancing one's art in new directions could engender discomfort but also personal growth. They had been together for about eight months when she finally worked up the courage to push him in a way that might be considered non-threatening. He had expressed a desire to explore a new creative direction, but so far he had stayed with the watercolor themes that worked commercially with the tourists. "Pablo, I'm thinking of doing a spring show of watercolorists in a month," she said. "Could I hang some of your pieces?" Maybe with the proper motivation she could persuade Paul to explore his talents?

So far Paul had sold most of his pieces to friends and family, although he would periodically set up shop at low-key street fairs and sidewalk shows that would expose him to new clients. He was still insecure about his talents, even though he had been painting for years.

"I'm not sure I'm ready for that sort of scrutiny, baby."

"No pressure from me, maybe just think about it? We could hang four of my favorites, and then give you *carte blanche* on two or three new pieces? You know, just to keep everyone from falling asleep," she teased.

The offer was generous. Paul knew many artists would sell their souls to be featured in a gallery show; but he had struggled with committing. Ten days later he finally agreed to prepare three new pieces to add to the four Roshan would pick for the exhibit. Now he found himself sitting at his table, challenged by the deadline, and realizing he hadn't been living with much urgency for the last two decades. He had hoped the stress of the exhibit would lead to new creativity, but now he wasn't so sure. A vague notion lay somewhere within him that he wanted something that would stand out and challenge the viewer…perhaps a mixed-media approach. But so far he hadn't been able to translate the inner turmoil of his last twenty-five years to his work.

As the day's creative drought continued, he decided to put aside his brushes. He turned and rolled his wheelchair towards a more accommodating distraction, his desktop Dell. He had taken a computer science course and was teaching himself how to code. Whenever his painting frustrated him, he would turn to the computer, put on his headphones to encourage further introspection, and work on a simple game he was building from scratch. It was similar to Pong, except that one could substitute people's faces for the paddles and the ball. He found a mixed CD he had made that contained his favorite songs from a new group he had been drawn to named Kings of Leon. Their first EP had come out in 2003, and now, a year later, they had followed it up with another killer record. He inserted the disc, turned up the volume, fired up his CPU, and started working on the game's color separation while silently singing along with the Followill Brothers.

Uncover your head and submit to me
we'll make a joyful sound...

The song he was listening to was called "Holy Roller Novocaine." The musicality blended raw sexuality and biblical verse in a way he found compelling. He had read that the band members had grown up in rural areas with a gospel-preaching father, and the imagery came through powerfully in the lyrics.

We'll go up to the mountain top
There I'll show you all the goods I got;
Don't look back keep your eyes ahead
This could be the night that the moon goes red...

Satisfied with his pixels for now, he started polishing up some of the code to make a more efficient interaction between ball and paddle. The Kings of Leon continued.

Lord's gonna get us back,
Lord's gonna get us back,
I know, I know...

Out of the blue it hit him.

He turned from the monitor and rolled back to his painting table, where he grabbed a black pencil and started sketching the images in his head on a sketch pad. The strokes were quick and rough. After an hour he lifted his hand and leaned back to take a look at what he had. All three drawings were variations on the Jesus crucifixion scene he had been taught in Sunday School. He worked some more to get the details of his drafts close to what he saw in his head and then paused for a glass of water. The headphones were still proselytizing with the gospel of the Kings of Leon.

You'll be hearin' me comin'
But I can't come inside…

There was a chronology to his work. In the first image he had drawn three men crucified on three crosses. The Messiah figure, in the center, was flanked on either side by men on slightly shorter crosses. Jesus and the man to his left were both thrusting liberated, black-gloved fists skyward, while their heads were hanging down in shame or disrespect. The central figure had his right arm raised, while the man to his left had his left arm raised. He drew the two protesting men with obvious African features. It was an attempt to meld the Black Power protest movement with the torture and execution that Jesus Christ experienced on Mount Calvary. At the bottom of the page, in non-uniform block letters, Paul wrote, "They Have Risen." In his head he titled that piece *Persecution*.

The second drawing depicted a single Jesus figure, with African features, being crucified. Two Tampa policemen, both with devil tails and horns, were pounding nails—one into his feet, and one into his right hand. The left hand was already impaled. The cop securing the hand was standing in a wheelchair, and both officers had "TPD" on their backs. In uniform block letters at the bottom of this page Paul spelled out, "Gary Donovan" and "Dante DaVito." His title for that piece would be *Purgatory*.

In the third vignette, an uprooted cross leaned on the ground with ropes and nails at the appropriate spots, but no body. In the foreground was a fornicating couple with the woman on top, her back to the viewer. The man was wearing a crown of thorns. The block letters at the bottom read, "Not Forsaken." He wasn't sure what to title that piece—either *Tigres* or *Tigriss*—an amalgamation of his nickname for Roshan and the unnamed river in the name of her gallery.

He looked down at the sketches he had created and was pleased. Knowing what he wanted the final product to look like, he just had to get the images onto a larger medium.

Just as he pulled out three pieces of two-foot by two-foot watercolor paper, there was a knock on his door.

"Mom…?"

He assumed it was his step-mom, Elizabeth.

Elizabeth opened the door and had a portable phone in her hand.

"Hi Honey." She smiled briefly to her son. "Roshan is on the phone."

Elizabeth loved Paul's girlfriend. She had spent hours enjoying her company as they discussed sculpture and architecture. She didn't want to jinx it, but she was hoping that Paul would finally get a break in the romance department.

It was obvious he was in love. *After all,* she thought, *what's not to like about Roshan?*

Beyond Paul's left shoulder she noticed a new creation taking shape and nonchalantly tried to take a peak. She wasn't sure what he was trying to do, but she could tell right away it was different. Years of prickly negotiation had led to Elizabeth not offering unsolicited comments on Paul's art.

Paul wheeled over and took the phone from Elizabeth.

"Thanks, Mom."

He smiled into the receiver. "Hi Roshan! Can I call you back in a bit? I'm working on an idea and it seems promising."

Paul knew to curb his enthusiasm when it came to his work. He had difficulty distinguishing between genius and mania.

Still standing in the doorway, Elizabeth was surprised to see Paul de-prioritize Roshan. It was a behavior she had never observed in her adopted son.

Roshan also registered the rejection as unusual… then curiously sensed her residual irritation morphing into a sympathetic wave of joy for his breakthrough. She shook her head incredulously.

I must really like this man, she thought.

"Baby, I'm so happy for you," she told Paul candidly. "Don't worry about me, just keep working as long as you feel compelled."

Just then Paul glanced at his watch and realized they had dinner plans—for fifteen minutes ago.

"Oh Baby, I'm such a loser, I forgot dinner. I'm so, so sorry!" he told Roshan. "Please forgive me, I'll drive over right now."

Her last vestige of abandonment now extinguished, she repeated her plea that he keep focused on his work. She would come over tomorrow and take him to breakfast, as she was excited to see what he was up to. They expressed their love and bid each other farewell; then Paul handed the phone to his mom and returned to work.

Using colored pencils and charcoal, Paul redrew his three vignettes on a more expansive scale, one on each of the square sheets. He had to be careful, because the paper he was using was unusually large and hence limited in terms of it's availability in the art stores that dotted the Tampa Bay area. He was hoping to nail the images on his first try…and after a few hours he was successful. After he got each drawing to a place he was happy with, he applied a fixing agent to both the front and back of the paper. This would serve to secure the charcoal and colored pencil so they wouldn't turn into a mess when he implemented the rest of his idea. The next step in his vision was to use a selection of pastel watercolors to paint a benign beach scene over each crucifixion image, to make it appear that the disturbing images had been superimposed on the benign painting, or vice versa. He wanted the Easter egg watercolors to be symbolic of the way various segments of society could coexist in close proximity and yet be dramatically unaware of the others' experiences. He had painted the happy, beach landscapes thousands of times; they would be easy.

Five hours later Paul was done. It was one a.m. He had been riding a wave of creative energy that had carried him to this point, but now he was spent. He put down his brushes and went to bed exhausted.

As he fell into a deep sleep, his dreams came to him with vivid clarity but confusing imagery. He found himself back at Bone Daddy's on the fateful night. He was with his prize from the air guitar victory, Kat, and they were making out in the back parking lot of the club. This part of the dream set off a powerful sense of ecstasy in his brain…he wanted to interminably wallow in the youthful sensuality of heaving flesh, fertile smells, and animalistic breathing. With nary a nod to physics or moral reservation, a moment later Kat twisted in his embrace and was bent over the hood of a white Cadillac, naked from the waist down, encouraging him. People wandered nearby, but nobody seemed to regard the couple as anything unusual. A few would call out greetings to Paul as the reigning air guitar king, and he would happily respond back with a cheerful wave while unsuccessfully trying to penetrate. The air was hot and humid, and both he and Kat were sweating—their slippery skin interacting with the intoxicating smells. He looked over Kat's thick head of hair, through the windshield, and could see his brothers partying in the back seat of the Caddy with Michelle, Kim and a cooler of beer. All four of the young people were in various stages of undress, with taut, tan skin in abundance.

Just as Paul began growing frustrated with his inability to perform, a left arm unexpectedly wrapped around his chest from behind, caressing him. He partially turned his head to see Robyn, the pink-haired girl from Dunedin. With her right hand she manually guided him to insertion, then pressed rhythmically against Paul with her hips, establishing his pace. Paul was focused on the back of Kat's head as Robyn gently pressed her warm, moist lips against his ear and whispered:

"Lord's gonna get us back,

Lord's gonna get us back
I know, I know…"

Just as he approached climax, it began to rain. He could feel a tidal wave of malevolence approach, like a moving wall of gnashing teeth and reaching claws…but he couldn't run away. The rain became an oily mixture of salt and blood. The people faded away. He could see his brothers running, naked into a forest. He was left standing, alone, as two large jackals circled him. He tried to run, but his pants were still around his ankles, and he fell. The jackals began to close in…

Roshan shook him awake. Paul opened his eyes to see the sun pouring into his room and the woman he loved smiling down on him.

"Paul…they're amazing. I'm totally gaga over them," she gushed.

At first Paul was confused. Then he remembered his three watercolors. She had obviously already seen them. He sat up and wiped the sleep from his eyes while Roshan gave him a big hug and kiss on the cheek.

"What time is it?"

"Nine."

"You've already seen them, the new pieces?"

Roshan's eyes opened wide. "Yes, yes, and yes."

Smiling broadly, Roshan couldn't help but think she was partly responsible for the new work. From across the room her reflection in a simple wood-framed mirror smiled back at her, and she realized she was just as pleased with the feelings Paul was expressing as she was with the technical aspects of his pieces. The work was edgy—she knew the powerful images would be provocative in the suburbia of central Florida—and she suspected they had therapeutic value for Paul. He had told her about the night he had suffered his cervical damage; she had been amazed he was as normal as he was given the circumstances.

Paul was trying to stay humble, but he was proud that she approved.

"Can you use them in your show? They're not too big?" He was fishing for more compliments.

"No, no, no...I love the scale, they're magnificent. They will be perfect for our *Easter Awakenings* exhibit. Have you given any thought to titles?"

"I was thinking *Persecution*, *Purgatory*, and *Tigriss*."

Roshan pondered the titles for a moment, and, recognizing her pet name, she came up with a plan.

"I think I know which title goes with which piece, and I like."

Paul beamed. The mirror caught her in a thoughtful half smile as she tried to be supportive but not too obviously effusive.

"Oh, Pablo Picasso, I'm so proud of you!" she exclaimed.

Like the morning mist on a warm summer day, the troubling Bone Daddy dream rapidly receded.

One week later, after a particularly intense lovemaking session, Roshan suggested that Paul name the final piece *Heaven*. Occupied by a deep feeling of contentment, Paul considered her idea in conjunction with his work and knew it was good. That night he went to sleep smiling.

Heaven it was.

CHAPTER 26—

Easter

Gary Donovan read the front page of the *Tampa Tribune* "Weekend Arts" section with alarm. A somber phone call from his campaign manager had alerted him to the offending article, and that news, in combination with a rollicking hangover, had the candidate in a foul mood. His schedule had been relentless for months. Last night had required a wee hours schmoozefest with some hard-drinking union officials who wanted to get to know the candidate better before giving their endorsement. They were really just jumping late onto his speeding bandwagon, but he pretended not to notice. He was used to kissing asses and making promises, playing the role of grateful public servant. Exhausted but content, he had fallen asleep dreaming of victory: the polls had him about ten points ahead of his opponent in the Tampa mayoral race. His calendar demanded attendance that morning at a ten a.m. Baptist service, which his advisors insisted would make him a lock with the black community. The campaign was gaining momentum, and the last thing he needed in the home stretch was negative publicity. So the *Tribune's* review of a local beach gallery exhibit had he and his campaign team concerned.

He had spent the previous thirty years climbing the career ladder, first as a cop on the beat, then a detective, and finally in a series of ascending managerial roles that had concluded with him attending law school at night and eventually being appointed deputy district attorney. His ambitions fueled his leap onto the campaign trail, as he successfully ran for the district attorney post from which his boss had retired. After a benign term as DA, his backers asked him to consider running for mayor against a weakening Republican incumbent. Paroled felons had committed several high-profile home invasion murders during the previous three years, and even though the overall number of violent incidents was down in Tampa, Donovan was successfully using local media outlets to push his "tough on crime" legacy to a frightened electorate.

The article that was causing him so much consternation was a pictorial spread of the Euphrates Gallery's *Easter Awakenings* watercolor exhibit. The show had opened two days earlier, on Good Friday. The review focused on the three mixed-media pieces by Paul Prudeaux Barton: *Persecution, Purgatory,* and *Heaven.* Barely mentioning the other two artists, the writer raved in hyperbolic fashion that "Barton's work brought the local art scene into the twenty-first century." The critic was a Safety Harbor-based high school art teacher whom Roshan had cultivated as an ally. As a sometimes journalist, the art teacher wasn't even aware that the election to decide the mayor of Tampa was only thirty days away…or that Gary Donovan was the frontrunner.

Donovan pulled out his reading glasses and looked hard at the middle piece, *Purgatory.* As noted by his campaign manager, there at the bottom of the painting, one could clearly make out the two names. "Gary Donovan" and "Dante DaVito." He cursed out loud at the breakfast table, surprising both his wife and dog.

"What's wrong, Gary?"

Donovan excused himself from the table.

"I'm not sure…probably nothing…" he told his wife as he walked from the kitchen. "I'll be making some calls in my office, then a car will pick me up at nine for the Calvary Baptist thing over on Dale Mabry Boulevard."

"Do you want me to go with?"

Donovan's wife was tall and willowy; she had peculiar eating habits. She also had a nervous condition that gave her sonic hiccups when placed in situations of public scrutiny. After several embarrassments early in Gary's political career, she and Gary decided it was better if she stayed at home during his campaign appearances. During the few times that she did join him, she was so heavily sedated that all she could do was smile and wave.

"No, Mary," her husband said, "this one will be quick. Just be ready to glow on election night when they coronate me," he semi-joked.

Once he was in his office and had closed the door, his first call was to his best friend and campaign manager, Dan DaVito. Gary immediately peppered him with questions.

"I just saw the paper. Who's behind this attack? Who the fuck is Paul Prudeaux Barton? I thought you had connections at the *Tribune*? What's the plan?"

DaVito had been totally blindsided by the publicity, and he resented the tone coming from his longtime partner. He had no memory of Paul Barton, no idea if this incident was a random coincidence or a coordinated effort, and hence he had no plan. Not one to sit idly while unidentified threats circled around him, he had already been able to get ahold of his contact on the editorial board of the paper, who assured DaVito that he had neither input nor interest in the "puff pieces" that were embedded in the Weekend Arts section. Dante tried to reassure his boss.

"Relax, Gary, we're gathering intel as we speak. This isn't coming from the Op-Ed board, I think it's just a random coincidence. I'll find out more about this Barton guy, and then we'll make a plan. In the meantime, just stay cool, and if a question comes up, act surprised and give them the usual 'this is an unfair and inaccurate attack with political motivations.' Are you good with that?"

Donovan's paranoia had a tendency to grow with his fatigue. He was also a man of action and generally grew anxious when he thought he was being attacked. Politics was a dirty game; he was comfortable breaking the rules when he believed the ends justified it.

"Can't we have Chalk break in and vandalize the gallery? Maybe a fire? Blame the white supremacists or religious right?"

DaVito was getting worried that Donovan was overreacting. He tried to talk his man down from the ledge.

"Why draw more attention to something that might be a nonevent? Let's be patient with this one, let things wind down. I bet in two days we'll wonder why we cared."

"How long does this exhibit run?"

"The paper says two weeks. Tomorrow all the tourists fly home; Clearwater Beach is gonna be empty. I think this exhibit will be ancient news in seventy-two hours."

Donovan wouldn't let it go.

"What about slander, can we sue for defamation of character? I want to appear strong, not equivocal. I want a background check on this artist asshole. Drug use, delinquent child support payments, mental health issues…we need to destroy this Barton guy's credibility, whoever he is."

DaVito knew not to be overly patronizing with his friend.

"Maybe…let me do a little work with our counsel and see about our options."

Donovan didn't like being managed. He had a bad feeling about this one, but he decided to follow his campaign manager's advice and give the whole situation a few days. If things developed in a bad way, he would be ready to attack on multiple fronts if need be.

"If this doesn't go away, I want to be proactive. Let's not let this thing get out of hand."

"Roger, that, Mr. Mayor. You need to get ready, the car is coming in fifteen. Remember, the pastor's name is the Reverend Draymond Fraser…and you've met his wife, Allison. Good luck, only our friends from the press should be there."

"Got it, piece of cake. I'm tying my lucky tie as we speak. Let me know about this artist as soon as you learn anything."

"Done," DaVito assured him. "Bye, Gary."

At first, Paul was just happy his work wasn't dismissed as crude or unoriginal, but then the superlatives started coming in, and he allowed himself the luxury of thinking he might have some talent. The drawings meant so much to him on so many different levels, and he was pleased that he was able to express himself in a way that resonated with the public. The usual creative dilemma intruded: he was torn between being silent, and thereby letting others interpret his work through their own filters, or speaking out and clarifying what he was trying to communicate through his art. He finally got the phone call that he hadn't allowed himself to hope for. A *Clearwater Sun* reporter had seen the review of the show in the weekend *Tampa Tribune* and wanted to come to the gallery, see the featured works, and meet with Paul in person. The journalist wanted to better understand the message in his *Purgatory* piece, given the provocative image and the current Tampa mayoral race. They set a date for the next day, Monday, at noon.

On the other end of the line, Tate Chalk smiled to himself as he hung up the phone. The paunchy, balding, private investigator was somewhat charming, ethically bereft, and had a narcissistic streak that sent him to the tanning salon several times a week. He could be quite productive in his various roles, able to effect a friendly, capable façade; but underneath the surface lurked a barely functional frequent drug user. In his small, South Carolina High School he had played football and received average academic marks. But as he tried to forge a path beyond his home state, and the competition in the real world labor pool grew more intense, his cerebral shortcomings and slim work ethic began to hinder his wealth ambitions. At some point he discovered that, when the compensation warranted it, he was able to numb his conscience and do things others found distasteful. People of his ilk were useful to people in power, and, over time, he built a reputation for getting difficult things done quickly while leaving no fingerprints. He was regularly employed by DaVito whenever there was a need for some dirty work; he had a violent streak that he was comfortable accessing when things seemed intractable. Both Donovan and DaVito referred to him in private as *the Scumbag*.

He showed up at the Euphrates Gallery the next day at noon, showed his phony press credentials, which identified him as Timothy Babich, and then proceeded to gather all the information behind the *Purgatory* painting that Paul was so willing to pour out to him. He wrote down details, dates, and names about the night at Bone Daddy's, asked a few lightweight questions about the art…and then disappeared. He immediately took the information back to DaVito, who was doing his own research through the public records. That night DaVito met at Donovan's house and shared his news. DaVito started with what he had unearthed.

"Barton is a colored kid we arrested a bit over twenty years ago. Remember the night some guys jumped us in the Bone Daddy's parking lot and we leaned pretty hard on the one we caught?"

"Vaguely."

"Well, he was the one we roughed up. He ended up in a wheelchair as a result. He plead out to resisting arrest in exchange for no jail time. He rents a small bungalow with his mom over in Greenwood. He sells beach scene watercolors to the tourists, and the mom works as a bookkeeper for a small ball bearings company. Neither has any record of arrest, outside of the one incident—not even a traffic violation. No other dirt that I've found yet. Chalk paid a visit with him disguised as a reporter, Basically the asshole is venting some long-festering suffering via his art."

Donovan considered his options carefully as he looked at DaVito.

"Are you thinkin' what I'm thinkin'?"

DaVito was nodding and smiling.

"Threaten with a big-money defamation suit and then let their side settle, with the artist issuing a public retraction and apology?"

They had seen this strategy used once before, when the former police chief was under fire for some homophobic comments he had purportedly made in a private setting.

"Yep. They have no money, we'll scare the shit out of them with our lawyers."

DaVito considered. "Can we wait a few more days first, and see if this thing dies of natural causes?"

"Agreed, but as soon as I see fire behind this smoke, I'm pulling out my club."

Donovan had no problem mixing metaphors, in fact his constituents found his folksy, uneducated style comforting.

"Agreed. I gotta run," DaVito told his partner. "I promised I'd help Robbie with his homework tonight…as if I know anything about geometry. Talk tomorrow?"

Donovan smiled and patted his friend's shoulder as they both got up and headed to the front door. They had a plan and felt they were back in the driver's seat. As they passed the collection of framed commendations Donovan had hung in the hallway, they took solace in the fact that they had been in these sorts of situations a few times over the years. Fate had always smiled on them.

Paul thought it strange that another reporter, Patti Chambers, also from the *Clearwater Sun,* contacted him on Monday night after his meeting with Tim Babich. This reporter also wanted to meet with him and discuss *Purgatory,* but she claimed to work for the Local/Politics desk. Initially, Paul just figured it was a situation of one department not communicating with another, but at an early dinner that night with Elizabeth and Roshan, the odd coincidence surfaced as they were discussing the crowds at the gallery. His girlfriend immediately became suspicious. She excused herself from the table then grabbed a phone book and called the *Sun.* She first asked for Tim Babich in the Arts department, and, after a brief hold, was told that there was no Tim Babich on the staff in Arts, or anywhere else at the paper. She then asked for Patti Chambers, and was promptly passed through to her voice mail. After leaving a message asking Chambers to return the call, she then came back to the table. Elizabeth and Paul had watched the whole scene with a focused curiosity. They had both been beaten down for so long that they had developed a sort of resignation that events were just going to happen to them, and that their job was to endure passively. Watching Roshan take a proactive approach fascinated them.

When Roshan sat down, she looked distracted, as if her mind was noodling a particular thought. She finally looked over the table at Paul and Elizabeth.

"Something strange is going on. I'm not sure what it is, but I'm a little freaked out."

With a combination of medication and counseling, Elizabeth had learned to better manage her perpetual anxiety, but Roshan's comments grabbed her attention and urged her nervous system to ratchet up the level of concern. The last thing she needed was trouble; money was already tight every month, and Paul's meager proceeds from his art sales barely covered his recurring medical expenses. Her brow furrowed, making her face an unattractive pinched mask, and she started releasing all of the second thoughts she had harbored about Paul's recent explorations outside of his comfort zone.

"What do you mean?" she queried. "I knew this whole *Easter Awakenings* venture was a bad idea! Paul shouldn't be dredging up trouble from the past and making enemies with powerful people."

Roshan curiously observed her brain struggling with all the problems she perceived in Elizabeth's fear-driven statement. Ten years earlier she would've just blurted out her objections, but now she first considered them one at a time from varying perspectives. Grammatically, she wanted to point out that if making enemies was your goal, then one should definitely engage in that endeavor "with" the help of powerful people. She decided to let that one go. Then she wanted to note that generally little was gained without a bit of "venturing," but again, she thought better of what might have been considered a reprimand, given her knowledge of Elizabeth's challenged history and economic position, and a general respect for her elders. After a brief consideration, she decided she would reveal the interesting phone calls and anonymous notes that she had been receiving ever since the *Easter Awakenings* show had opened. In Manhattan, she had been accustomed to hosting controversial art in her galleries. Usually the harassment tapered off after the first day or two: she would ignore the invective, and the haters would move on to something else. She had followed this strategy for the Easter show; but this was not New York. She was feeling vulnerable without her usual support structure. In addition, if anything, after three days the threats were increasing in frequency. The phony reporter had also shaken her, as she felt things were now getting personally invasive. She finally broke the silence with the disclosure of what she knew would be disturbing information.

"I've been getting anonymous hate messages from people who are offended by Paul's work."

Paul and Elizabeth simultaneously blurted out their unsettled protest.

"*What?*" Paul cried.

"Why didn't you tell us? How many?" Elizabeth said.

Roshan wanted to be respectful of her hosts, but she also wanted to try to get them to see her perspective.

"About a dozen or so," she purposefully underestimated. "Mostly people offended by the 'fornicating' couple or the 'niggers where Jesus should be.' "

To reinforce the fact that the offensive language wasn't her own, Roshan held up two fingers from each hand to make "bunny ears" around the quotes.

Paul and Elizabeth both knew that it wasn't that long ago that the Grand Dragon of the KKK was based in Florida. Their moral indignation was easily outweighed by their impoverished fear. They didn't need to poke that bear. Roshan was working from a different place. She chose her words thoughtfully in trying to get her hosts to understand.

"When you manage art galleries and encourage provocative work, this sort of thing isn't unusual. You know, the usual racist or religious nuts offering hate pablum and harmless threats. They're usually just looking for publicity…a larger platform to spew their message of hate. So I ignore them. One could argue that art is meant to provoke a response…to make a point…. And so when there is an elicitation it could be considered a compliment. The worst response for an artist with something to say is a collective yawn."

Paul could relate to her point. For two decades, fear of failure or ridicule had kept him from taking any risks creatively. Elizabeth understood Roshan, but had suffered deeply and repeatedly from risk-taking behavior, so she wasn't as sympathetic.

Roshan continued:

"This most recent invasion…someone committing the resources and guile to send in an agent to gather information under false pretenses…this is different…it isn't something I'm used to."

Roshan was trying hard to present a relaxed visage, but her brain was racing on a variety of fronts. She had the presence of mind to consider her predicament with some objectivity and was simultaneously concerned and intrigued; she recognized this situation may evolve into the fight she had been aching for since college. Here she was, a US citizen of Persian descent, operating an art gallery south of the Mason-Dixon Line, being threatened by racists and religious fundamentalists for exercising her First Amendment rights. She knew if certain people got a whiff of a story like that it could get pushed to national prominence. The fact that she was featuring the work of a black, handicapped artist who was expressing his frustrations with both personal and societal indignations could only add fuel to the fire. As the realization crystallized of how powerful this narrative could be for her, Paul, and the gallery, if managed correctly, she worried that she hadn't the right to expose Paul and his fearful mother to the potential danger. She decided on a strategy that could fan the flames while also offering a degree of protection.

"I think we should consider holding a press conference, and potentially notifying the police."

The following Saturday, Donovan and DaVito met over breakfast at the candidate's house. Three days earlier the local media had converged at the *Easter Awakenings* press conference; the indignant response had been powerful. The demographic vestiges of the rural south had long been overrun by retiring snowbirds who brought with them a greater cultural tolerance. The anonymous threats had alarmed a small percentage of these migrants into action, and the Euphrates Gallery had been packed daily with rubberneckers who felt virtuous for showing their support for free speech. Roshan joked with Paul that the only way they could've grabbed more attention was if someone had spray-painted swastikas on their front windows. Paul didn't laugh. He was at the exhibit every day, in his wheelchair, tirelessly telling his story, including details from the night at Bone Daddy's. All the local news outlets had reported Paul's account of events, and some larger media groups were sniffing at the edges, trying to calibrate the potential magnitude of national interest. Most of the focus was on the hate messages, but Gary Donovan and his campaign for mayor were also getting attention. So far, in response to press inquiries, Donovan had characterized Paul and his *Purgatory* piece as the "fantastical work of a disturbed and disillusioned man who long ago suffered from a sad, drunken, violent, and criminal lapse of judgment."

Donovan and DaVito didn't realize it, but Roshan was already noticing a decline in interest for the exhibit, and it was only one week old. The Saturday crowd, which usually was the largest of the week, was half the size of Friday's, and her phone was no longer ringing off the hook. She had had local interest in buying Paul's pieces, but she wanted to sell them as a set of three, and she was also trying to coordinate pricing with a peak in media attention. Six collectors had found the idea of owning the set attractive, but two had already withdrawn at her suggested pricing, and now she was considering the logistics of an auction before the story got too cold.

While Roshan was trying to pump a few more minutes of fame out of the controversy, Donovan was under pressure from the Calvary Baptist Church and Reverend Fraser. The pastor wanted Donovan to respond to Paul's allegations with more detail and force, as he felt the black community was simmering about what was perceived to be systemic racism in Tampa law enforcement. Donovan and DaVito did not have access to Roshan's data points and hence were not aware that the froth over Paul's work was already receding in terms of media and community attention. They were discussing their options, given the recent decline in Donovan's polling numbers.

"Dan, I've worked too hard for too long to see this crippled asshole destroy my career. I want to bring in the lawyers and pound him now. We have to smear his credibility."

DaVito knew when his boss's mind was made up, and he wouldn't try to dissuade Gary. The campaign manager had already misjudged the magnitude of the fallout from the exhibit. With his credibility on the wane, Donovan, in a fit of machismo, was getting more insistent during the decision-making process.

"I also want Chalk to throw some fucking rocks at *their* glass houses so they can feel some of the pain that I'm feeling."

DaVito recognized with irony that vindictiveness was what had gotten them into their current mess. He hoped that over time his boss's anger would subside. For now he tried to mollify Gary.

"Got it. I'll get the lawyers going on a multimillion-dollar defamation suit, and then work with Tate on some ideas to make their lives difficult."

"I want to be reading about what a malcontent this kid is in tomorrow's paper. I've got Draymond breathing down my neck. Am I understood?"

DaVito got up to leave. He didn't like being treated like the help, but if they won this election his career options would open up significantly; then he could tell Donovan where to shove it when his partner decided he needed someone to kick. DaVito disguised his growing resentment with his usual departing affirmation when things were tense.

"Roger that, boss man."

Early the next morning, a week after Easter, Paul was preparing his first morning cup of coffee when there was a knock on the door. He was home alone, as his mom had spent the weekend down at a girlfriend's beach house on Sanibel Island. Roshan had started feeling a bug coming on the previous day, and so to protect Paul she had stayed at her apartment for the night.

Paul wheeled to the door. When he opened it, he was met by two men who seemed to be there independently. The one on the left, clearly the younger and more sloppily put together, he didn't recognize. The older man was successfully managing to not sweat while wearing impeccably pressed wool and standing in the early morning heat of a Florida spring day; he appeared to be a greying but vibrant version of what he remembered his father to be.

The former man spoke first while placing his hand inside his messenger bag.

"Paul Prudeaux Barton?"

Paul had a mug of hot coffee in one hand and a leftover Krispy Kreme in the other. He was uncomfortable with everyone's body language and wasn't sure what to say, so with mouth full of partially chewed donut, he briefly nodded. The process server pulled an envelope out of his bag and thrust it in Paul's direction.

"You've been served."

The second man, Mr. Vibrantly Impeccable, reached over with his long arm and snatched the envelope from the younger. His onyx cuff links revealed themselves during this action, gracefully unsheathing themselves from the wool foreskin of his blue blazer.

"I'll take that, I'm his attorney."

The process server, who was merely trying to earn some spare change during his first year of law school, was caught unawares but quickly gathered his wits.

"And you are—?"

"Aloysius Barton. Thank you for your time. Please enjoy the remainder of your day."

Aloysius placed the envelope into the breast pocket of his blazer then raised his eyebrows authoritatively, as if to say *Why are you still here?* As the young man stood, uncertainly, staring, Aloysius showed a curt smile and made it pleasantly clear what he was implying.

"Elsewhere."

The youngster began losing his footing under the pressure of the Brooks Brothers' stare. He looked about furtively then capitulated by pivoting on his heels and heading back towards his car. The scenario that had just concluded hadn't been covered during the brief instruction he had received, and he hoped he wasn't somehow being tricked in an effort to keep Paul Barton insulated from the court-mandated communication. He wondered how to spell Aloysius.

The father then turned his attention to his seated and gaping son.

"May I?" he asked rhetorically.

He stepped across the threshold and simultaneously relieved Paul of donut and coffee.

"They're poison, you know."

He then continued his ambulatory tour of the home by skirting around the wheelchair and ducking into the small foyer of the two-bedroom bungalow. He stopped, looked briefly at the framed pictures, and then in two long strides headed down the faded hallway leading towards the kitchen. Just before he turned out of sight, Paul heard his tenor voice resonating back down the hall:

"Have you ever tried kombucha?"

CHAPTER 27—

Geronimo

Aloysius' utensils were focused on the remnants of the two grilled pork chops that had been submitting to his ravenous appetite. The sautéed spinach and corn were receiving occasional affection, but the near cousins to bacon were the obvious stars. He momentarily shifted his gaze across the table and locked on to Roshan's moving mouth. Her teeth were orderly and white, like a picket fence, moving in symphonic harmony with her lips, tongue, and other hidden vocal accessories. Her words tumbled forth in rapid succession. He realized long ago that he often would focus on someone's mouth when they spoke, as opposed to the eyes, and he hadn't yet discerned why. Even at close range the speaker couldn't tell the difference (he had done a test years ago with a college roommate), but he felt it was a personal deficiency. Like many of his generation, he had been raised to believe that real men were supposed to look others in the eye; it was an act of forthrightness and honest intent. He speculated that his perceived flaw might result from his heightened sensitivities, as avoiding eye contact was a way of lessening the intensity of an intimate conversation. Of course it could be that he was just attracted by the more obvious mechanics embedded in the moving oral parts.

Roshan's words were interesting to him, but the surrounding facial architecture was even more so. He guessed she was Iranian, and wondered if her family had fled during the fall of the shah. Wiping his mouth with his napkin after a particularly carnivorous bite, he wanted to ask her if she spoke Farsi, as he had taken an unusual interest in the Persian culture and had picked up a few words here and there. He knew New York had a concentration of well-educated, affluent Iranian immigrants, and he wondered if she was affiliated with that diaspora.

They were seated at a four top in Chief Geronimo's, a long time Clearwater steak house that had aged well. The restaurant was ensconced on the town's main drag, Gulf-to-Bay Boulevard, and was one of its oldest landmarks. It had been built with rough-hewn blue pine, which, unlike the Barton family, had survived the decades with a rustic, comfortable sort of resilience. Elizabeth could recall at least one family birthday celebration where they had dined inside the cowboy-themed eatery.

Aloysius had invited Elizabeth, Paul, and Paul's girlfriend (once Elizabeth had informed Al that they were "serious") to dinner on Tuesday night. Since dropping in on Paul unexpectedly, Aloysius had spent the previous two days catching up with Paul and Elizabeth, and also playing the tourist. He had been swimming daily at the beach, had wandered a few times through the Euphrates Gallery, and had done a little research on Paul's legal situation. Although Keenan had told his mom about Aloysius's changes in broad strokes, she was still surprised by what she saw of his healthy daily habits. And Elizabeth was shocked by how well Al looked. After unsuccessfully searching his face and neck for evidence, she gave up her suspicions of surgical enhancement. She was curious for more detail about the change (specifically if Aloysius had a love interest), but not enough to inquire directly.

Aloysius had called Elizabeth three weeks earlier and asked if he could come out and visit her and Paul for a few days. Elizabeth had said "sure"; but given his past performance she assumed it was unlikely he would show. Therefore she didn't write down the dates, or even ask if he had an agenda. Her ex-husband was basically dead to her, not from ill will (although there was plenty of that) but mostly from fatigue and resignation. From experience, she didn't want to disappoint Paul, and so she didn't tell him about the call.

Roshan was interrupted mid-sentence by a cowboy-hat-wearing, nineteen-year old blonde who brought in-your-face makeup and hair and an agenda that required a large degree of insensitivity. Her name tag read "Pebbles."

"Hi, folks! How are we doing? Can I interest you in any dessert?" Pebbles inquired.

Roshan felt Pebbles had been pushy all night. Her real name was Mabel, but she had taken on her new persona the day she had gotten on the Florida-bound bus and said good-bye to Racine. The waitress had an excuse: Chief Geronimo's was crowded, and the Wisconsin immigrant was starting to feel overwhelmed. Pebbles knew she had to get on top of things early or it could rapidly deteriorate into a bad night. Conversely, she knew that if she could turn her tables at a good pace her tips would increase accordingly. It had taken her a month, but she felt she was starting to get the hang of what she called "this waitressing stuff."

Most at the Barton table were glad for Pebbles's attention, as they were ready to transition to the after-entree portion of the meal. Despite that fact, Roshan's annoyance at the interruption was pronounced; she was holding a grudge. Paul had picked up on her growing irritation and had attributed it partially to her lingering cold. Although not something he felt comfortable expressing, he considered that the competitive presence of another attractive young woman might also be exacerbating the situation. He was aware of Roshan's presumptive dislike of Aloysius (given what she knew about him from Paul and Elizabeth), but he hadn't been previously acquainted with her disdain for the name "Pebbles." The paterfamilias's attentiveness to the Racine native wasn't helping.

"Hi Pebbles!" he beamed. "We would love to order some dessert."

Ten minutes later, the senior Barton was digging in to his sorbet with berries, while the rest of the group shared two chocolate tortes. As he looked around the table, a thought struck Aloysius. He put down his spoon and reached for his mug of chamomile tea. He was feeling grateful for the amazingly fortunate turn of events since Lilly had come back into his life six years ago. He thought his dinner guests's lack of inquisitiveness about his current situation to be somewhat rude, but he had been able to work his way through the disappointment. Soon he would be back at his hotel; he was flying home to Phoenix in the morning. In a display of magnanimity and patriotism he decided on an innocuous toast that he had used to successfully mark the close of many a client dinner. He raised his mug to signify the start of his vocalization.

"The United States of America…Western Civilization…Capitalism… Democracy…what amazing developments that have allowed us all to enjoy each other's company and this indulgent meal…in peace."

He gestured with his raised mug, hoping for an "Amen" (or at least the equivalent) as he looked successively toward each of his companions. Not meeting any sympathetic eyes, he wondered if these people hated him or were just particularly dull. He quickly decided he didn't need to know the answer; instead, he put on his reading glasses to do one more review of the bill.

Paul inwardly cringed while halfheartedly raising his glass of beer. He knew how Roshan felt about Western Civilization in general and Capitalism in particular. She could tolerate Democracy but felt like the United States practiced a version that was so corrupted by money that it was barely recognizable from its forebears. The dining room buzz did nothing to distract his worry that her philosophical leanings in conjunction with her cold symptoms (and her irritation with Pebbles) would boil over into an antagonistic comment.

Roshan couldn't understand why Elizabeth and Paul were sitting so quietly at dinner, not wanting to rock the boat, while the selfish asshole who had neglected them so egregiously sat on his lazy, smug, pressed and pleated woolen trousers, proselytizing to them about the wonders of colonialism. She had had enough of this philandering, privileged, white man's bullshit, and she felt a need to let him know that not everyone at the table could be bribed into silence by an environmentally insensitive piece of grilled cow. Or pig. Only a few seconds had passed after Aloysius's toast, but the lack of consenting voices had been awkward. Roshan broke the silence but not the awkwardness.

"As long as you're comfortable ignoring the forced immigration and subordination of millions of people into slavery and indentured servitude."

Aloysius realized he had misjudged his audience. The burden of carrying the conversation all evening, of inquiring about each of their lives and interests while getting little from them in return, had led him to believe that the three were devoid of manners, intellect—or both. He was happy to discover a conversational pulse after all, as it seemed the Barnard girl was willing to at least defend the liberal viewpoints her professors had pounded into her. Aloysius was as familiar with her argument as she was with his, and he realized details and presentation would dictate who came out ahead. He responded simply and with civility.

"Excuse me?"

Roshan presumed he had heard her correctly and was pushing for a polite clarification. She went the other way.

"Not to mention the theft of whole continents and all of the accompanying resources from the indigenous tribes through fraud, contract violation, or outright violence."

Watching the two combatants, Elizabeth was torn—she had become so conflict adverse in her later years that any early signs of contention made her want to excuse herself; but, she was also human and hence glued to her seat, waiting for the seemingly unstoppable train wreck that was about to unfold at their table. Part of her hoped they would make a scene. The second part of her scolded the first part.

Aloysius felt he had to navigate carefully. There were certain points he wanted to make, but he wasn't sure how to get there.

"I'm confused? Are you blaming Western Civilization for certain well-documented atrocities?"

Roshan didn't realize that Al had traversed this territory before and so had given no thought to playing defense.

"I'll be as clear as I can be. I am saying that white, Christian, males of Western European descent have been raping and pillaging their way across the globe for centuries. Then, after causing suffering on a magnitude previously unimagined, they busied themselves fabricating prevarications to manipulate history and justify their heinous behaviors."

"Surely you don't blame me for these 'heinous behaviors'?"

"Not you specifically, although I'm sure you'd have happily participated. But people like you."

Aloysius considered two paths. One, argue that she was labeling a huge demographic as "heinous," which should qualify as stereotyping at best and racism at worst. Two, plead innocence by way of insanity, with "insanity" being a reference to evolution and the human condition. He chose the latter but kept the former in his back pocket as a reserve.

"I think there's a lot of truth to what you're saying, and I'm not defending what some might call my 'loosely defined' genetic ancestors's behaviors as charitable, but I don't think the behavior you're condemning has been any more 'heinous' than any other group competing for scarce resources in the history of our species."

Aloysius had bunny-eared his fingers to identify certain phrases as quotes. Roshan started rolling her eyes early in his speech.

"Like I said, here come the justifications."

"Label them what you will, the fact is that what you call 'white, Western European men' are just the current winners in a long history of violent struggle between different humans. The many victors before us came from a variety of colors and creeds: the Assyrians, the Scythians, the Hellenes of Alexander, the Huns, the Vikings, the Rajput, the Mongols, the Samurai, the Moors, the Sioux Nation, the Ottoman Empire, the Romans, and"—…" he paused for effect, looking straight at Roshan—"the Persians. It just so happens that 'we' won simultaneous with the invention and broad use of the printing press and other modern technologies, so that our atrocities could be documented and archived for better and more accurate historical review. And, unlike many of our predecessors, we only effected *partial* genocide on those we vanquished, so there were survivors who could serve as witnesses to the unjust suffering. I'll grant you that technology allowed our brutality to be mechanistic and on a previously unheard-of scale, but our ambitions and savagery are not unique. The strategy for all living creatures is one of competition for scarce resources. There are moments of cooperation, but also moments of extreme violence. Intraspecies and interspecies, there's a long history of struggle, with winners and losers. Bacteria, insects, animals, all feeding on each other. Even trees compete with grasses for rain and sunshine—somewhere, at this moment, there is a slow-motion genocide being imposed on the grasses beneath a growing pine forest; it's just not as offensive to our sensibilities."

Aloysius lowered his intensity—and his gaze—as he slumped back in his chair. He felt he had done a reasonable job defending his ancestors, and he wanted to make sure he didn't overdo it. If he smiled right now it could be construed as patronizing, and he was too polite to rub it in. He stifled a fake yawn, allowing the girl to yield without being humiliated as he focused on paying the bill.

Time to move on, he concluded silently.

There was another awkward silence as Paul and Elizabeth held their collective breath. Both wanted to share some of their historical frustrations with Aloysius but did not want to attack the man who was paying for dinner. Precedent had taught them to think of Al as a periodic meal ticket—not because they were cold-hearted, but because of his historic inability to provide anything else. He would infrequently come to town and buy them dinner—and they, in return, would feign interest in his drunken, pompous bombast. There was an implicit agreement that Al would pay if they didn't bring up past grievances, and given previous shouting matches everyone was comfortable with the detente. It was a diplomatic way of keeping the lines of communication open without forcing a resolution.

They didn't realize that Al had changed and was tonight looking for something more. He just didn't know how to bring it up. Roshan, coming in with none of their baggage, felt none of their inhibition. She was far from surrendering her position as untenable.

From the other side of the room, Pebbles had a brief respite. She observed a pause in the Bartons' conversation. She headed over to wrap up the table and keep things moving.

Roshan took a long pull on her Manhattan, stared hard at Aloysius, and gamely picked up the gauntlet he had thrown down.

"So that's your excuse? 'Everyone else was doing it too'? From the people who nicknamed their Messiah the 'Prince of Peace'? Who believe that 'conscience' and 'choice' are a cornerstone of their religion? Does proportion even matter to you? You're comparing thousands of years of chucking spears and slapping mosquitoes to four hundred years of slavery and dropping nuclear bombs on urban centers with huge civilian populations? Shame—"

Just then Roshan was interrupted by an enthusiastically insensitive Pebbles.

"Hi y'all! How was—"

"PEB!-BLES!" Roshan was pissed. Without averting her gaze from Aloysius she raised her voice to a pronounced and indignant stage whisper while open-fistedly pounding the table in time with her syllables. "NOT! NOW!"

The server, alarmed, retreated under the onslaught, making a mental note to not return to the table for at least fifteen minutes.

Roshan reoriented her efforts back at Aloysius:

"SHAME on you for implying your people's behavior was normal. While freeing your own serfs with the inventions of Democracy and Protestantism, you were imposing tyranny via colonialism on the continents of Africa, Asia, and South America…knowingly using biological weapons such as smallpox to murder thousands of people who stood in the way of your selfish grabbing in North America."

Aloysius was feeling a bit overwhelmed. He had underestimated his opponent. He interrupted with humor to try and defuse some of the power of his adversary's argument.

"Are we considering Australia a continent? Because if we are we wouldn't want to forget the plight of the Aborigines."

Roshan glared at him.

"Not funny. Nearly all the economic, political, and environmental messes on our planet can be attributed to the greed and ego of men of Western European descent. Like you."

Everyone at the table was taken aback by the ferociousness and directness of her diatribe. As Roshan brought her indignation and breathing under control, she realized she may have overdone it. A confluence of events seemed to have brought out a level of hostility that she usually kept under wraps. She was okay with the content of her lecture, but the seething hatred that poured forth was not like her. She had a powerful loathing for the senior Barton; on a broader level, men like him triggered in her a strong resentment for their worship of "Capitalism." They spoke as if "free markets" were some sort of all-knowing and virtuous deity. She saw the whole linguistic legerdemain as a rationalization for the continuation of policies that led to dramatic wealth disparity, environmental plundering, and a general corporate greed that she felt plagued the planet.

In a brief moment of terror, she considered also that Aloysius might be a paler version of her father, and she had never had the guts to have this conversation with him, given her economic dependency on him.

Did I just unload years of frustration on the wrong Dad? she thought in horror.

Of course it could just be that her lingering cold and the vapid Pebbles had made her more irritable than usual.

God, I'm so insensitive. She berated herself silently. *I'm an outsider and guest at a family dinner that the nearly seventy-year-old father of my boyfriend is hosting…and I drop payload on him?*

She would never admit it out loud, but she also started wondering about the proximity of her next period.

Time to just sit and observe for a while, she scolded herself.

Al was impressed. Her content had been pretty good; but what he hadn't expected was the vitriol and emotional force embedded in the delivery. For a moment, he was actually feeling sympathetic to her cause. He decided on a strategy that would hopefully deescalate the tension. He wanted to find some common ground, continue with the insanity defense for his ancestors, and then move on to the other topic he was hoping to introduce.

"As I said earlier, I don't disagree with many of your contentions. Indeed, shame on white men for all their current exploitation of the planet. But we differ on one subtle yet important point. Your arguments imply that without white men, the planet would be a much better place. I believe there is no evidence for that conclusion. If black, Muslim, females were the winners, I think the long-term outcomes would be very similar, and we would be having the same conversation, except each arguing the other's position. Whoever is the winner will always be the devil to those who have been vanquished, or to those who feel left out, or to those who want a more just society. The winners throughout time are just the ones who best learn how to use technology to advance their civilizations. They aren't perfect. There will always be room for improvement and hence legitimate criticism. Today's winners happen to look a lot like me, but at some point others will have their turn, just like others did before us. There may be some luck involved, but over the long run the societies who can best foster creativity and intelligence win. Not just the most barbaric. If you think about it on an interspecies level, our oversized brains are why humans are now at the top of the food chain, not because of our fangs or claws."

Al paused to take a sip of his chamomile. He was worried about coming off as too Hank Rearden, but he had more to say.

"I think in an effort to better make your point, you have described the world as very bleak, and then positioned people like me as the culprits. You can't just focus on the bad while ignoring the good; they are different sides of the same technology coin. You have neglected all the amazing breakthroughs that Western Europeans have brought to their colonies and the rest of the world. For example, in Africa, Westerners dramatically reduced the states of squalor, disease, and death by introducing sanitation, potable water, primary health care, and transportation infrastructure. It's only from our relatively comfortable positions of health and safety that we can romanticize about a world where the noble savages hold sway. An imaginary world where justice and compassion are perfectly distributed. I would argue that few Africans would want to return to the days of Native Customary Law, where your life was the property of the Supreme Chief to do with as he pleased, women were treated like livestock, and cannibalism, magical superstition, and killing of the aged were societal norms. The flaws aren't in the economic or political systems, the flaws are in us, the people who administer them. You think Marxism would be kinder to the environment? Check out the toxic nightmares in the former Soviet Union, from the nuclear disasters in Chernobyl and Mayak, to the mining disasters and deforestation in Siberia. White, Christian men aren't exclusively evil, we're just flawed humans like everyone else. We happen to be the current ones in power, and, like all those before us, we have yet to invent the perfect economic and political systems that equitably distribute justice, income, and compassion. It's this ongoing systemic imperfection that requires us all to challenge those in positions of authority…to require that they substantiate their power by explaining how they are improving the lives of their constituents."

Suddenly Aloysius was feeling exhausted. He could tell he was losing his audience. He wondered if anything he was saying resonated with anybody but him. He decided to wrap it up, let others comment if they so desired, and then move on to his last agenda item.

"By the way, Roshan, I know it's not popular to say this as a white male, but narrowly defining a broad group of people by their physical characteristics, religious beliefs, or commonality of ancestors and then using that definition to imply inferiority or superiority is discriminatory, bordering on racism, and I personally don't appreciate being told who I am or what I think based on your stereotypes. Collecting four hundred years of 'economic, political, and environmental messes and placing them in my responsibility box because of my gender and skin color is offensive, and you should know better. You have no idea who I am or where I come from."

Roshan wasn't sure white men could be victims of racism within the current context, but she supposed on strictly definitional terms Aloysius had a point. So she decided to let his last comments slide. Keeping her commitment to take a break, she restrained her desire to fire back at their patron while searching Paul and Elizabeth's faces.

Aloysius reached for his wallet, extracted his credit card, and placed it in the payment tray.

"But *we* do, Paul and I."

It was Elizabeth who had finally decided to speak up. She had decades of suffering that she attributed to this man, and she was tired of his self-inflating soliloquies. Having heard from Keenan about Al's inheritance, she had hoped he would do the right thing by her and Paul, but it was now apparent to her that he hadn't given them a second thought.

"You may not be personally responsible for colonialism, slavery, and Hiroshima, but you certainly made a mess of our lives. Mine and our three boys'."

Finally! thought Roshan. *She actually does have a spine.*

The only non-Barton at the table had been having second thoughts about the intensity of the invectives she had directed at this old man, whom before tonight she had never met. The silence of the mother and son had left her feeling a bit exposed in contrast. However, with Elizabeth now stepping into the ring, she didn't feel so out of line. She was also grateful to stay out of the spotlight and take a breather in a neutral corner. She could always jump back in if Paul or his mom needed a little help.

Aloysius took a deep breath, steadying himself for what he suspected would come next. He had been expecting this arraignment for years; initially with trepidation, but now with relief. He wasn't going to just roll over and play dead, he needed to push back a bit, just to see how solid were their convictions—he needed to actually hear the charges before he could confess. He also needed the vitriol and the accompanying catharsis to play out before they could move on.

"I guess that depends on your perspective, hmmm? I provided you all with shelter, food, and a decent education. I protected you from predators, disease, and starvation. Compared to most humans on the planet, I think you all were rather indulged."

Elizabeth was outraged.

"That's such bullshit, and you know it. Neither your family nor mine set the bar that low for us, and yet you claim parenting *in absentia* was okay for your kids? What sort of selfish, narcissistic jerk are you?"

"I didn't choose to leave, remember? You kicked me out. Besides, Keenan seems to be quite successful despite my 'selfish, narcissistic' parenting skills. Maybe you, Paul, and Clay are just biologically deficient."

Now it was Paul's turn to be outraged.

"Are you blind?! Of course I'm biologically deficient!" His grip tightened noticeably on the arms of his wheelchair and his torso surged forward in a total body snarl that caught everybody at the table by surprise. "But not because I was born this way. I'm deficient because I was raised by my overwhelmed step-mom and my teenage brothers. What I also needed, what arguably every boy needs, is a mature, caring father."

Paul was just starting, but he was already getting to his dad. Aloysius could either break down sobbing or throw up his defenses.

"Don't you dare pin that night on me. That was a freak occurrence."

"I never had a father who I could look to for guidance and protection. And then, after my 'accident,' my supposed dad never even made the time to come around and offer emotional—let alone financial—support."

It didn't feel good, but it felt right. This was the conversation Aloysius needed to have with his family. He had already had it with Keenan and Scout, but he hadn't been able to gather the intestinal fortitude to apologize to Elizabeth and Paul. It took a lot of soul searching, but he was finally able to identify the impediment. He was afraid they wouldn't forgive him. They had perhaps suffered the most. Eventually he had realized that he couldn't control their feelings or actions; he could barely control his own. He could only do what he could and should do.

Now was the moment he had been planning for, and dreading, since he flew out. He had practiced his speech scores of times. Elizabeth and Paul were both ready for a fight; but just as things started ramping up, he looked down at the tablecloth. *Why is this so hard?* he thought. He yielded, hoping for his family's forgiveness. *I'm not certain I have the courage…just go one word at a time….*

The others immediately sensed a change in his demeanor, and stared at what seemed to be an unraveling man. With a regretful and sincere tone, he reversed engines, buried a lifetime of narcissism, and offered what he hoped would be a path to reconciliation.

"You're both right…I…"

He struggled as the words grew bigger, jagged, and the sharp edges got caught in his throat. He finally just pushed them out, several at a time, like a seahorse giving birth, until it was done.

"I was a subpar husband…no…a miserable husband…and father…and I made a mess out of everything…I'm so sorry…I…I can't change the past…all I can do is apologize…and hope someday you'll forgive me."

The words now lay on the table, naked and unexpected. Unlike all the times he had practiced them, this time they were joined by a few tears.

There, it's done, he thought in relief. *Atonement.*

He locked his eyes on his silverware, as he was terrified to look up and see where he stood.

The group remained silent as everyone contemplated the significance of Aloysius's *mea culpa.* Gravity-imposed glances and general fidgeting ruled the following minute. No one was sure what might come next.

Paul was the first to speak up. He was battling through his tears, still angry, wanting to forgive, but not knowing how.

"What took you so long? Why should we trust you now?"

Aloysius shook his head slowly, finally looking up at his son.

"I don't know," he murmured. "I'm so sorry, Paul."

No one was sure where to go next. Pebbles was approaching fast from Al's three o'clock, but when she noticed everyone at her "crazy" table dabbing their eyes with napkins, she did a quick U-turn and added another fifteen minutes.

Under her breath, Elizabeth murmured:

"You ancient, gigantic jerk. Waiting this long…"

She was hoping he could follow through this time; there had been other efforts, but none had come with such an enormous and unequivocal apology. Even Roshan was feeling non-combative as a result of what she had just witnessed.

Al fought through his emotions, trying to stick to his game plan. He wanted to move on to something tangible before the whole table ended up drowning in tears or accusations.

"What can I do to help you today?"

As the simple words unveiled themselves, the mood changed dramatically. The local three quickly realized what might be on offer. The severity of their current legal situation reprioritized itself as they pulled themselves together emotionally. Presently, they were outmanned and outgunned and stuck behind enemy lines. Each looked at the other with raised eyebrows, wondering how much Al was really willing to help. The other two eventually made it clear that they wanted Roshan to speak up. She had taken the leadership role in trying to figure out how to get them all out of the predicament that the *Easter Awakenings* exhibit had catalyzed, but so far she had come up with zero ideas. She started with the basics.

"You've been to my gallery and seen Paul's three pieces?"

"Yes, I think they're genius."

Roshan interrupted her train of thought to entertain a deviant idea. She wondered whether Al's comment was just parental hyperbole or truly credible appreciation. Putting on her most benign smile, she decided to indulge her curiosity.

"Which piece do you like the best?"

Al realized he was again being probed, but he stared directly at Roshan and answered without hesitation.

"*Heaven.*"

"Hmm…" She fought back the rising blush in her cheeks and took the obvious next step. "Why *Heaven?*"

The dinner participants, who all shared a love for *Heaven,* were focused on Aloysius as he offered up his perspective in a tone that landed somewhere between respectful and reverent. He knew he was being examined, and he tried hard to make his mouth deliver a message that approximated what he felt when he looked at the work of art.

"Let me see…I'm not sure I can do justice to the piece with words…I like the complexity of the message…the idea that an intimate, physical relationship with a kindred soul can arouse powerful healing and even redemptive responses in the participants. A resurrection, if you will."

Aloysius was thinking about his own situation with Lilly during his first comments. He paused and assessed whether his companions wanted him to continue, and concluded he had a green light.

"I like how Paul challenges the viewer to overcome their visual biases by juxtaposing a graphic sexual scene with an iconic religious scene. I think he's forcing us to consider how differently separate groups of people may react to the same image….Some will see *Heaven* as pornographic…while others… including Paul and Roshan, I would guess…and myself, by the way…think the painting depicts a moment of beauty, even divinity, a brief shared instant with the Creator…hence the title. Simplistically, I think it shows the power of love to save us…regardless of our circumstances…which I believe is God's gift."

A warm feeling had begun to spread outward from somewhere deep inside Paul as his dad described what he saw in his son's work. Paul had known from experience that *creating* and *recognition* didn't always occupy the same room; and so to have his father understand and respect his art left him with a feeling akin to pride and satisfaction…but not quite either. It was a feeling Paul imagined a castaway would have after years of lonely isolation, upon discovering another sympathetic, marooned soul sharing his island. He almost started crying again, as a large and heavy lump of loneliness partially receded from his consciousness.

Roshan found herself nodding in agreement to Aloysius's comments, even if only subtly.

Well said, she thought, although simultaneously wondering if her admiration was a result of their heretofore unrevealed common ground. She decided to get their conversation back on track by returning to her original thought process.

"Thanks for sharing your thoughts. Sorry for the detour, but I'm interested in how people respond to Paul's work."

Aloysius nodded in understanding. Roshan took that as a sign to proceed.

"Getting back to how you can help…you're aware of the twenty-million-dollar lawsuit that Donovan and DaVito have filed against Paul?"

"Yes, I was there when he was served."

For the next hour the foursome forgot past grievances and laid out a strategy to defend themselves against Donovan. They ordered another round of dessert and two more rounds of drinks before finally wrapping up the bill—with a generous tip for Pebbles. During the planning Aloysius revealed that he had gone to law school and for the last two years had been practicing immigration law in Phoenix at a local not-for-profit. Using his basic skills, he had already done some digging on the Donovan defamation suit. His research quickly revealed a landmark 1964 case, *The New York Times Co. v. Sullivan*, where the Supreme Court ruled in a way that prohibited public officials from being awarded damages from defamatory falsehoods pertaining to their public duties—*unless* the plaintiff could prove that the statement was made with knowledge that it was false or with a reckless disregard as to whether it was false or not. Al pointed out that the suit would probably focus on Paul's long ago plea of guilty to the charge of resisting arrest. Paul highlighted that at the time everyone had urged him to plead guilty to the misdemeanor or risk being convicted of assaulting a police officer, which was a felony and carried the risk of serious jail time. Al offered his view that the defamation suit wasn't an easy case, and fighting a career law enforcement official in his own jurisdiction made the situation even more challenging.

At the end of the meeting it was obvious they needed money for local, legal representation. Roshan had yet to disclose that she came from a wealthy family, and even if they all knew, she was reticent to ask for more parental help, given the incident under discussion was born of her already unprofitable gallery. Paul and Elizabeth could barely cover their monthly expenses, and had no savings. It was at this moment that Al was able to finally unveil his last surprise. He had offered an apology and had hoped for forgiveness, but there was more. He had just been waiting for the right time. From his inside jacket pocket he pulled out an envelope and handed it to Elizabeth, who was seated to his right. He stared into her eyes, not her mouth, and spoke with a quiet earnestness.

"Liz, I added up all the child support and alimony payments I missed, compounded them at ten percent, and then rounded that number up significantly to three hundred thousand dollars. This is my own version of reparations for the past atrocities of this white, Christian, male of Western European descent. I know money can never replace all the years lost, but I hope this can help soften your view of me and my past transgressions. I am formally asking for your forgiveness."

Elizabeth was speechless. It was the second miracle within the hour. Her eyes bulged at the thin, unopened envelope. The tears started flowing again.

"Oh Aloysius," she murmured between sniffles. "You big dufus, I forgave you a long time ago...I didn't like you, but I forgave you."

Roshan was also incredulous as she mulled the sequence of the evening's events:

This means he's gone through the whole evening with the intent of doing the right thing! As defendant, he orchestrated a hearing...and Chief Geronimo's was the courtroom. Even before we heaped all of our disdain and disapproval on him and his ancestors, and even before he fought back ferociously, he always knew that, in the end, he was going to ask for forgiveness and offer reparations. He's right, she begrudgingly concluded, *I did misjudge him.*

Paul thought of something.

"Mom," he said, "don't take it."

Everyone turned with curiosity to Paul.

"Why, honey?" asked Elizabeth.

"Let's wait and see how this lawsuit develops before we start showing up on people's radars as having deep pockets. Right now we have no assets, so no one is really interested in coming after us. They just want to scare us into a retraction. They didn't name Roshan or Euphrates in the suit because they are better protected than me by the First Amendment. When this all settles down, I think we can trust Dad to make good on his promise. We've waited for this long, right, Dad?"

Paul looked to Aloysius for confirmation.

"Of course, Liz. It's yours whenever you want it."

Elizabeth carefully opened the envelope and looked at the check, luxuriously soaking up all the zeroes. She remembered all the boneheaded financial things her ex had done in the past and wondered how she found the courage to do what came next. She said a silent prayer, placed the check back in its sheath, and returned it to Al.

"For safekeeping."

Aloysius slid the envelope back into his breast pocket, got up, and helped Elizabeth out of her chair.

"Thanks for trusting me."

Al realized he had a lot of work to do. He had to get back to his hotel, make some calls, and change his hotel and flight reservations. He turned to Paul's date.

"Roshan, you'll get me the picture of this Tim Babich person from the gallery's security footage?"

"I'm on it in the morning."

"*Listo?*"

The Spanish phrase dusted off an image in Paul's memory: his oldest brother, nearly twenty-five years ago, in the driver's seat of the Chevy wagon, preparing to shotgun a beer.

You fucked up…you trusted us.

He hoped things would turn out differently this time.

CHAPTER 28—

Dirty Deeds

The men were inwardly grinning like two twelve-year-olds who had just lifted a *Playboy* from the corner liquor store. Planning a comeuppance was something they enjoyed. Donovan loved disabusing lowlife scum of the belief that their first amendment rights somehow protected them from retaliation—that the weak could attack the strong and feel insulated from retribution by some omnipresent social contract. It was one thing to use a stick to poke the lion through the bars of a cage; it was another altogether to provoke the big cat in the absence of restraints. The district attorney's job required that he respect due process, but every now and then he would reach his tipping point and feel compelled to dispense justice in a more direct and economical fashion. He could no longer play vigilante personally, like when he was a cop on the streets, but paying Tate Chalk to do so was still gratifying. It was obvious to Donovan that Paul Barton hadn't gotten his mind right the first time, so he felt justified in reinvigorating the education.

Unlike Donovan, Chalk wasn't pondering the nuances of power versus individual rights; he just liked fucking with people. That Donovan and DaVito defined his targets as bothersome and paid him to exercise his sadistic tendencies was just the icing on the cake.

DaVito was tied up that evening, so Donovan was uncharacteristically meeting with Chalk in person. They had to clarify some details for the proposed job, and Donovan required they rendezvous at a busy public place, so if seen together he could claim coincidence. That night they were meeting at a local Publix Super Market, and as Chalk focused on Donovan's muffled instructions, the annoying background noise reminded him that this was where aging Rock music went to be euthanized.

The district attorney had already established the target during a brief conversation in the frozen foods section, but unwarranted paranoia had necessitated they meander separately to the produce section, where Donovan was anxious to define the rules of engagement and then leave. Both were trying to appear independent as they nonchalantly examined the inventory.

"When do you want me to start?" Whispered Chalk out of the corner of his mouth.

Donovan picked up a rather thick cucumber, his fingers wrapping only halfway around the vegetable as he admired its heft. He considered the nubs that frequently interrupted the smooth exterior.

"ASAP. Level two threat intensity," Donovan replied.

An elderly woman thought she recognized one of the two whispering men across the bin from her. As she suspiciously watched the familiar one with the mustache, he simultaneously fondled and talked to a large cucumber. A fake thunderstorm started as an enhancement to the regular produce misting process, interrupting the women's consideration of her lovely gay nephew, whom she was certain never behaved as reprehensibly as the man she was watching now.

Chalk subtly acknowledged Donovan's directive and, mimicking his employer, reached for a long zucchini. He noted that the skin was smoother than that of the cucumber, and more angular at the stem.

"Got it," he mumbled. "Payment?"

The woman noticed that the pudgy, bald one was now also talking to a squash. She was wondering if she had just "seen something" and hence whether she should "say something." She had recently learned that terrorists came in all shapes and sizes.

"The usual," responded Donovan.

Donovan put down the cucumber and turned away from Chalk. Their business was done. He was a somewhat careful man, and he didn't want to be seen with Chalk in any capacity. He made it home that night before his targets had even left Chief Geronimo's.

Chalk continued to hold the zucchini in one hand while reaching for a plastic bag with the other. He noticed the old lady staring, and he considered repeating Otter's *Animal House* scene.

Nah, too obvious, he thought.

He put down the phallus, walked over to the grapes, and appropriated a bunch of red flame seedless. After wrapping the nascent raisins in the plastic bag, he secreted the bunch in the front pocket of his hooded sweatshirt. As he approached the store exit and the intruding warm night, his pores slowly opened and secreted his particularly malodorous form of perspiration and psychopathy. He shamelessly walked out without paying. You see, he couldn't help himself.

Two nights later, at four a.m., Chalk was parked in a vacant lot three blocks away from Elizabeth Barton's house. He wore navy blue workout attire, including a hooded sweatshirt, and a black pair of Nike knockoffs he had bought for twelve bucks at Wal-Mart. The early birds had yet to rise, and the late-night party crowd had either passed out or been ejected from the bars two hours earlier. Greenwood was a working-class neighborhood, leaning towards downtrodden. Several housing projects were scattered throughout, and the usual lower-income challenges were evident. To kill some time, he turned on the radio, making sure to keep the volume down. Snoop Dogg was offering advice:

When the pimp's in the crib ma
Drop it like it's hot
Drop it like it's hot...

What the fuck? Chalk thought. *What is this shit?*

Chalk was of an age—and complexion—that hadn't yet developed an appreciation for Hip-Hop. He punched the station buttons with disgust until he found some AC/DC.

Dirty deeds, done dirt cheap…

Now that's more like it, he thought as he hummed along to Bon Scott's leering vocals.

After slipping on a pair of thin leather gloves, he reached over, picked up the brick in the passenger seat, and placed it in his lap. With his right hand he pulled a piece of paper and a red crayon from the glove compartment; then, using his left hand (he was right-handed) he scrawled with childlike imprecision the words *JESUS HATES NIGGARS.* He then carefully folded the paper, used a pair of rubber bands to secure the folded message to the brick, and placed the heavy object in the front pocket of the hoodie—where the grapes had been earlier. He quietly climbed out of the car, covered his bald head with his hood, and started walking.

The cool night air was a welcome relief from the heat of the April days, and he glanced up to see the few stars that were visible through the urban light pollution. He knew this short, three-block walk was critical, given the suspicious nature of his cargo. Eight minutes later he was gliding past the target house, alert to anything that might imply someone was awake or could serve as a witness. He walked three houses down and stopped beside a thick oleander bush to bend over and tie his shoe. The lack of functioning streetlights was happily noted as an indication that Fortuna was smiling on him. There was a chorus of crickets and frogs, a few porch lights scattered infrequently on the block, but no sign of movement. He took two deep breaths to relax his racing heart. Then he loosened up his throwing shoulder with a few arm rotations and headed back the one hundred yards to the Bartons' small bungalow.

Elizabeth Barton had enjoyed a few glasses of an oaky yet inexpensive Cabernet with dinner. Before turning in she took a Benadryl to help her counter the histamine reaction she often had to the sulfites in red wine. Usually that combination made her dead to the world, but the concussive invasion of a brick shattering her front window was so overpowering that she woke up screaming, covering her head with her arms. She was certain that a gang of hoodlums had sledgehammered their way into her house, with the intent to harm. After screaming for nearly thirty seconds, and terrified by the presumption that a malevolent presence was encroaching on her home, she scrambled for the bedside phone and dialed 911. As her heart raced and she felt the darkness moving all around her, each second ticked by like an hour. She wished she was wearing her flannel pajamas rather than her thin negligee; anything that made her feel less exposed to the creeping evil. Her thoughts longingly flashed to Sam, their old German shepherd–lab mix who had passed a year earlier. She worried about Paul until she recalled through her panic that he was out at the beach with Roshan. The house was silent when the call finally connected on the other end. Elizabeth anxiously counted three rings before the police dispatcher answered.

Aloysius had checked out of his original hotel the day after the dinner at Chief Geronimo's. Immediately after abandoning his first place of lodging, he checked into a Sheraton that happened to be less than a mile away from Dante DaVito's house. He knew the DaVito address by heart and had been exploring the surrounding neighborhood with his sunrise power walks. His change in plans had required that he notify Lilly he might be gone for a few more days. The Desert Lilly's Health and Wellness Center (located in Carefree, Arizona) ran itself with a wonderful staff and loyal clientele; but Aloysius knew Lilly would be curious about his trip.

Every day he drove his rental car over to Clearwater and had lunch near Elizabeth's office in a crowded Cuban place named Jesus's Comida. It was one of his ex-wife's favorite local dives. He dressed casually to fit in with the working-class crowd, and shared a long table with the others taking their lunch break. Amid the noisy throng, he usually ate in silence, infrequently sharing a comment with his fellow diners.

The day after someone hurled the brick into her life, a disheveled Elizabeth showed up at Jesus's and squeezed in next to Al with her pressed pork sandwich. They casually exchanged a few sentences, and then both finished their lunches in silence. Anybody watching them would not have considered them close.

Early the next morning, at around four a.m., a small scrap of paper partially covered with the word *Persecution* found itself attached by rubber band to a brick that crashed through the front window of the DaVito's lovely Mediterranean-style, four-thousand-square foot home.

About twenty-four hours later, a similar projectile found its way into the Donovan family room. A carefully folded piece of paper had been attached to the brick, on which the now familiar word *Persecution* had been scrawled, barely legibly, in crayon.

What had initially been a bottom-of-the-pile vandalism case in Greenwood now had the police's rapt attention. As a crime scene team worked on-site at the district attorney's house, taking statements and gathering evidence, the Donovan landline rang. It was their college-aged daughter, Erika, calling from Tallahassee in tears. Someone had vandalized her car early that morning. They had slashed her tires and spray-painted *Persecution* on the hood. The police had no idea who had done it and were wondering if her parents had any information that might help them? Were they aware of any enemies that might want to do such a thing? Erika also needed money ASAP to be able to get her car fixed so she could make it to her classes. After assuring his daughter he would help, Donovan slammed the phone down in anger. If it weren't for all the witnesses in the house he might've thrown a world-class temper tantrum. As it was he was already applying pressure to his underlings to start kicking some ass and figuring out who was threatening the "very fabric of the Tampa judiciary." In a statement that made no sense to his colleagues, he suggested they start with "that dangerously subversive Barton kid."

CHAPTER 29

The Best of Disinfectants

Patti Chambers was enjoying her first cup of coffee at the *Clearwater Sun* and had not yet heard about the copycat vandalism spree that had been afflicting the Tampa Bay Area. The Barton incident had been buried in the crime log in the back of the previous day's local section, and DaVito wasn't sure how to massage his and Donovan's situation with the media given the proximity of the election. Regardless of DaVito's efforts at manipulation, the attack that morning on Gary Donovan's house wasn't likely to be overlooked. Patti's first incoming call of the morning was from a source who followed the police frequency radio chatter all night.

"This is Patti Chambers," she cooed into the phone.

"Patti, it's Rick." His voice seemed to have an edge. "You should get over to Donovan's house, someone just threw a brick through his front window and there are racial overtones. Maybe something happened to DaVito too, it's unclear."

"What?"

"That's all I know. You have his address?"

She nodded. "Yep, I know where he lives. Thanks, Rick."

As soon as she hung up, the phone rang again.

"Chambers."

"Is this Patti Chambers with the *Clearwater Sun*?"

This time it was a woman's voice, indistinguishable as to age, but with a very thick, possibly effected, Southern drawl.

"Yes…who is this?"

The woman proceeded with languorous patience.

"I saw a crime, and I need to report it."

Chambers had been here before. She immediately pushed two buttons within inches of each other. The first put the caller on speakerphone, and the second started a recording device.

She tried again: "To whom am I speaking?"

The caller had her own agenda, delivered in a languid, mellifluous rhythm.

"It's my conscience, don't you see? I just can't stand by and do nothing while people are being…persecuted."

The caller rolled the syllables slowly, as if enjoying a spoonful of chocolate pudding across her tongue. Then she sped up her cadence.

"It was a colored boy, in a wheelchair…threw the brick through the Barton house front window in Greenwood two nights ago. I saw 'em. That boy was fast. Good arm too. Just vanished into the night."

Patti had to give it another shot, even though her hopes were low.

"And you are—?"

She could practically hear the belle smiling into the phone as the caller delivered her polite farewell.

"Hmm . . . you can think of me as Lady Justice. I hope y'all have a nice day."

Her words were followed by a prompt disconnect.

The reporter hung up her phone with a frown. The plot was thickening. She was certain she was being played, but by whom? This was the first Chambers had heard of the Bartons being involved, either as perpetrators or victims. She knew about the lawsuit, but from her brief time with Paul Barton she didn't feel he or his mom had the resources or inclination to fight Donovan. Right now the information she had was just a jumble, like a disassembled jigsaw puzzle; but given the cast and early plot, it was pretty obvious that something was afoot. If things kept accelerating this could be a huge story, with racial and national significance, and she wanted a piece of it badly. She didn't get a masters in journalism to cover small town politics her whole career.

The *Sun's* editor-in-chief, Pete Smith, resided in the corner office. He was sitting on the ledge of his open first-floor window, smoking his second cigarette of the day. Getting him involved could be very helpful, or fatal, to her ambitions, depending on his whim. She waffled a bit before deciding on a compromise. Getting up from her desk, she grabbed her purse and started heading for her car. Before she left the building she made two stops. The first was at the desk of her friend, Greta, in Obituaries. Greta's job rarely carried a sense of urgency, and she was always up for a dance with the living. Leaning against Greta's desk, Patti asked if Greta might be so kind as to find out whatever she could about a vandalism that had occurred at some point over the last few days to a residence in Greenwood owned by Elizabeth Barton.

"Anything else you can give me?" Greta asked.

Chambers gave the question some thought. She decided to keep a few secrets.

"It may have something to do with the Tampa race for mayor," she said, adding enough sugar to attract Greta's attention without spilling the whole can of beans.

Then, as a courtesy, she poked her head into Smith's office.

"Hey boss, I'm headin' over to the Donovan residence," she said casually. "Someone threw a brick through his front window."

Smith was going through a messy and expensive divorce, and the family that owned the paper was considering selling to a consortium. His wife and kids hated him for being inattentive, and the consortium was bidding seven times sustainable cash flow. The owners had given the editor-in-chief strict instructions to grow the bottom line, by any method, which meant pushing advertising revenue and cutting expenses. He had to simultaneously inflate circulation numbers and cut the quality of their product, which meant more sensationalism and less journalism. He found himself walking a fine line between attracting eyeballs and offending the local business community.

The long hours required by his job had been interpreted as abandonment by his family. Not unusual given the circumstances, they retaliated by behaving in ways that caused the paterfamilias to suffer. As the vise in which he found himself was tightening, he considered the distance to the ground from the window and realized it wouldn't get the job done. Not having the conviction necessary to climb to the fourth floor, he decided to continue with his slow-motion approach: he lit up another Camel. He noticed Chambers' head was still leaning into his office. He vaguely recalled her benign looping, and offered his old standby.

"No shit? Go get 'em, Tiger."

"Thanks, probably just some nutso vandal, but I thought I should check it out."

"Makes sense," Smith mumbled absentmindedly.

Then he had an afterthought.

"Remember…new policy…the paper's not buying your meals anymore."

"Roger that, Chief."

She was happy to get out unscathed.

Over the course of the morning, three more anonymous calls were received by local dailies in Tallahassee and Tampa. All of the callers had strong rural accents, and all claimed to have witnessed a black, Negro, or African-American male in a wheelchair perpetrating acts of vandalism in the early morning hours. The two self-described Tampa witnesses had male voices. They described the suspect as throwing an object through a window in the early morning hours before disappearing into the night. The Tallahassee caller sounded female, similar to the witness who had called the *Clearwater Sun*, and described a vicious attack on the tires and hood of a Mazda Miata on the Florida State campus. The words *conscience*, *persecution*, and *justice* were used in all three calls, and they all described the vandal as having exceptional physical skills, despite his apparent handicap.

By the time the police found Paul at the Euphrates Gallery, Patti had already spent forty-five minutes interviewing both he and Roshan. After the racially charged attack three nights ago, Paul had been too frightened to sleep at his Greenwood home; so, for the last two nights, he and Roshan had camped out on an inflatable mattress they had set up on the floor of the gallery office. They also were hoping to protect the exhibit if the vandals decided to attack there next.

Elizabeth had taken a few days of vacation. She had headed back to Sanibel and the sanctuary of her generous friend's guest bedroom. She and Paul had planned to return to Greenwood on Sunday night, after the glazier had repaired their front window. Roshan would likely join them, or move back to her beach apartment.

The couple decided not to reveal this to Chambers or the police, but Roshan owned a licensed revolver that she had decided to keep at the gallery, given the circumstances. By his mattress, Paul kept an old speargun that he and his brothers had used decades ago. Both Chambers and the police mentioned that witnesses had described Paul, or someone fitting Paul's description, as fleeing certain crime scenes. They didn't mention a witness claimed to have seen a similar person leaving the Greenwood crime scene. At first, Paul was flabbergasted; then he laughing at the impossibility of the implications. Not only was he physically incapable of executing the attacks and being in multiple places at the same time, but security cameras captured any activity at the front and rear exits of the gallery. Chambers was willing to bet the images showed both Roshan and Paul getting two good nights of uninterrupted sleep. Before the end of the day, the police, able to fast-track the process with the DA's insistence, had successfully secured and reviewed the gallery footage. The evidence was clear: Paul Barton's alibi was air tight. He and Roshan had entered the gallery on both nights before ten, and both times didn't leave until the next morning after eight-thirty.

Pete Smith was depressed, but he wasn't dead. He knew a good story when it fell in his lap. His reporter, Patti Chambers, had some misgivings, but she also wanted to be the first to break the news. As a journalist, she knew she was being manipulated and didn't have all she needed to fully understand what was going on, but she felt she had enough. Most importantly, she had a head start on her competition—a lead that would likely vanish when Paul and Roshan started fielding calls from other journalists. They huddled in Smith's office late in the afternoon, after Chambers had met with Paul and Roshan that morning, and worked on the text and layout. They decided all they had to do was present the well-documented facts—complete with substantiation from police reports— throw in a little sensationalist outrage, and see if the kindling caught fire.

They brought in a design artist and notified production they might have to stay late that evening. By the time they were ready to print, it was late Saturday night, and Smith told production he wanted to double the usual run for the following morning. He went "home" to his motel and watched Donald Trump host *Saturday Night Live.* After unwinding with a few scotches, he decided not to consult with the owners of the paper.

The next morning, Edwin Kania, the patriarch of the family that controlled the *Sun,* and a deacon of the local Lutheran church, went out to his Belleair front porch and gathered the Sunday paper. A few minutes later he was settling down to his morning coffee and unfolding the daily. The front page featured an artist's near perfect rendition of the hand-scrawled note that, attached to a brick, had exploded into the Bartons' home three days earlier. There had been no editing of the dreaded "N" word, and Kania was shocked. He also didn't like seeing Jesus soiled by such close affiliation, especially on the Sabbath. The story went into full detail on Paul Barton, his paralysis and claims of police brutality; the *Easter Awakenings* exhibit; the defamation lawsuit that followed; and the ensuing vandalism. The article quoted freely from the anonymous callers, and specifically mentioned the repetitive use of the words "persecution," "conscience," and "justice." There was also a picture of Paul in his wheelchair, and stock photos of Donovan and DaVito. Kania didn't take the time to read the article, the pictures alone made it clear what he must do. Picking up the phone, he dialed Pete Smith's home number. He couldn't imagine what sort of lunacy had invaded his editor's mind.

The Smith household was in a state of confusion. With four teenaged children, two boys and two girls, behavior could be quite volatile. The youngest two were twin thirteen-year-old girls who had been the result of an overachieving fertility doctor. For the last year they had been embracing their inner and outer Goths, while simultaneously stealing as much of their oldest brother's cannabis as they could get away with. Their commitment to the morbid look required they maintain vampire-like hours, given the powerful ultraviolet intensities prevailing throughout the latitudes occupied by Florida. They worshipped the Cure and could quote from memory every lyric recorded by Robert Smith.

The oldest Smith child, a slouching seventeen-year-old, was transitioning from Grunge to Hip-Hop in an effort to increase his chances of getting laid. He had found that doubling his weed intake (or tripling the amount purchased when he included the surreptitious twins) and loosening his belt three notches had gotten him ninety percent of the way there.

The mesomorphic, red-haired, blue-eyed, fifteen-year-old was an outlying, exemplary, scholar-athlete who often contemplated the genetic probability that his endomorphic, black-haired, brown-eyed, klutz of a father had sired him.

In the last three years the whole crew had managed an average GPA of 2.7, and that included the average-raising 3.8 GPA carried by the second flame-haired son. Omitting the fifteen-year-old, no matter how low the parents' expectations had been set, the offspring had disappointed.

The Smith home phone had been ringing nonstop all morning. As teenagers, all four siblings had held firm to their belief that each call was their intended for much longer than was warranted. Finally, after two hours and twenty-three calls, all for their dad, they unplugged the device from the wall so they could engage with the PlayStation uninterrupted. Their mother, Mrs. Francis Krausman Smith, was asleep upstairs with the aids of an eyeshade, earplugs, and a bloodstream full of Valium. It was from this ongoing contraception advertisement that Pete Smith had dismissed himself two weeks earlier and tucked into the Motel 6 nearest his office. Despite Frankie and Pete agreeing on their irreconcilable differences, Mr. Smith was also protected from the encroaching day by ear and eye hindrances and a bloodstream full of Johnnie Walker Red.

When Edwin Kania finally got ahold of Pete Smith it was nearly noon. He first lectured Smith about decency, then demanded his resignation, and finally requested an explanation. The editor-in-chief had just gotten off the phone with his circulation team, and decided to cut to the chase.

"Mr. Kania, we doubled our production run last night and still sold out of every issue before nine this morning. Our web page crashed at ten this morning because our servers were overwhelmed with one hundred times more traffic than our previous high-water level. My people tell me the phones have been ringing nonstop all morning, with ninety percent of the callers providing supportive comments."

It was at that moment that Smith truly understood the meaning of pragmatic. In less than five seconds, Kania subordinated his moral indignation, recalculated seven times a bigger number, and quickly rehired his briefly unemployed editor. They both then exchanged cordial farewells and hung up. Smith hadn't told his boss that their previous daily website high-water mark was only ninety-three visits. Nor did he share that their IT team consisted of a graduate computer science student who was helping them *pro bono* as part of his Master's thesis. He had taken the website down that morning for routine maintenance. The fact that the Sunday answering service had fielded a total of twenty calls and only two of the callers had threatened violence also remained an undisclosed detail. Smith didn't know about the calls his kids had collected and neglected to tell him about. He was comfortable that his truth-stretching would likely stay buried, because Kania was so dismissive of, and hence resistant to, new technology. The editor-in-chief was pretty sure that if his Luddite boss had been around during the invention of the wheel, the conservative elder would've bemoaned the inevitable loss of the character-building skill of carrying heavy objects.

Happy with his gamble to put the Paul Barton story on the front page, he turned off his phone and buried his scotch-occupied head under the 100-thread count, poly-cotton encased pillows. He hoped that when he awoke he would discover that the products of his procreation efforts had all been a bad dream.

CHAPTER 30—

Chocolate Cake

Allison Fraser got up early every Sunday morning and baked a chocolate cake with chocolate butter cream frosting. It was a ritual she had started years ago to entice her two adult children to come home for church and then, hopefully, stay for dinner. Having grown up in rural south Georgia, her mother had done something similar for Ally and her seven siblings. If either of the Fraser children came to church, Ally would slip them a sliver when they came home after the service—an added incentive to encourage them to stick around. The possibility that her behavior might have diabetic consequences was never considered.

While the morning cake was baking, Ally would sit down at the kitchen table with Earl Grey and do the *Clearwater Sun* crossword. In the background her husband would nervously pace the living room floor, engaged in some game-day sermon polishing. Being a Tampa resident, Ally did not usually find her attention grabbed by the front page of the *Sun*…but her attention was definitely grabbed today. After reading the article that accompanied the provocative picture, she decided to interrupt her husband, the Reverend Draymond Fraser.

"Draymond, I think you should see this…"

"Not now, baby," the Reverend replied. "I've gotta solve this alliteration."

The reverend continued pacing and editing his monologue. He was already experiencing what he called "pregame jitters"—and the accompanying irritability. Despite his years of practice, the Reverend struggled with performance anxiety and had often wondered why the Lord had called him to a job that seemed to cause him so much stress.

Ally got up, walked over to her husband, and put the front page under his nose. He glanced at the picture of the scrawled note, did a double take, and then grabbed the paper from his wife.

The racially charged message on the front page of the *Sun* did nothing to alleviate his irascible condition. Multiple thoughts were cascading through his head, and he started a stream-of-consciousness sharing with his wife.

"That's *our* word, they can't use that word without our permission. Who is"—he searched for a byline—"Patti Chambers? Is she a sister? Don't sound like a sister…."

Mrs. Fraser knew her husband well enough to let his indignation run its course before interrupting. He was in preparation mode, and his questions were a dramatic tool he used to effect a call-and-response sort of dialogue with himself.

"Jesus hates black folks, huh?" he asked rhetorically, as he put down the paper and started to pick up steam. "What the Beelzebub is that? Blasphemy, that's what it is."

Then he considered another financially threatening affront.

"Why in the Hades is the *Clearwater Sun* trying to put *me* out of business? Why I'll put *them* out of business so fast it'll make their heads spin."

He still hadn't started the article because the front page image was so galvanizing. Picking up the paper, he looked at the pictures again.

"Wait a minute." He took a closer look at the paper. "Is that Gary Donovan? We just met with him—he's supposed to be the next mayor, isn't he? What the …who's that brother in the wheelchair? Ally?"

Ally Fraser knew her husband's patterns. He would eventually ask for her advice after he had exhausted all other options. The process had just happened more quickly this morning than usual. Mrs. Fraser finally spoke up.

"Draymond, I told you that man was bad news. I have two girlfriends who swear they have relatives who were harassed by him and his partner. They were detained unlawfully and physically threatened…basically because they were young black men."

Reverend Fraser was torn. The accusations weren't new to him, but he hadn't achieved his level of success by ignoring Tampa power dynamics. He couldn't afford to offend the likely next mayor. The local elections were a place where he and his people could make a difference because the turnouts were so low. He could trade his block of dependable voters for some political influence and pork. It was a simple game for him; he would wait until the last sixty days of the campaign and back the candidate who was leading in the polls. Their platforms didn't matter, since the aspirants were always white males who had very little understanding of, let alone sympathy for, the issues in the black community. It was pure horse trading; whether or not he liked the candidate was moot.

He had a pretty good idea where the conversation with his wife was headed, and he was beginning to feel cornered. Sometimes the confluence of his moral compass and personal ambitions required circuitous navigation; his wife always let him know when she felt his deviations and justifications were too pronounced. Rather than rope-a-dope, he decided to come out swinging.

"I know what those folks claim, Ally, but that was hearsay and over twenty years ago. Donovan is now the district attorney…soon to be mayor. The police have been beating our people for centuries…I'm just one man…these things take time."

They both knew where Ally would go next.

"And what about my sister? When he and his partner shoved her chest-first into a wall and reached up under dress? Was that hearsay too?"

Fraser knew he was losing by decision and was trying to avoid a knockout. Years ago his estranged stepsister-in-law, Denise, had suffered through a horrible experience involving the police and a "frisking" incident outside a local Jazz club. Ally had implored her husband to use his public position as newly assigned pastor to "do something." Fraser had felt the combination of extenuating circumstances and his youth added up to a risky investment of his limited career capital.

"Ally, we both know that was a terrible, terrible thing. But Denise was drunk by her own admission, and they caught her doing drugs in an alley outside of the *Blue Note*. She's lucky she wasn't arrested."

"She was smoking a spliff and minding her own business," Ally returned. "And I think she would've preferred being arrested to being sexually assaulted by two police officers."

This was not new territory for the couple. Reverend Fraser resented his wife's implication that there were times when he let his career goals influence his morality. He was already cranky. This perceived attack started his indignation boiling again, only this time it was directed at a different target.

"It's easy for you to sit there, bake your chocolate cakes, and judge me. You don't have to deal with the pressures I face. Shepherding a congregation through a morally confusing world. Taking care of my church *and* my family's financial responsibilities. Being a spokesman for the black community."

Fraser paused and took on a dramatic tone, glaring at his wife:

"Judge not, woman, lest ye be judged."

Ally Fraser took a deep breath. Years ago she might've escalated, but this topic had already gone more than fifteen rounds, with neither fighter willing to concede. Time had taught her the futility of dwelling on old trespasses.

Just then the oven bell went off, signaling the end of the baking cycle. It was time for her to once again selflessly get her family ready for the next challenge.

"Draymond," she told her husband, "you're a good man. Please, read the article about the boy in the wheelchair, Paul Barton, before you come to any conclusions about villains and heroes."

It took Fraser a few moments to stop feeling defensive. After several deep breaths, he put down his metaphorical fists and began to again see the person in front of him as his life partner, not an opponent.

"You'll be there today?"

"Just like always, baby. Front row at nine and eleven."

She smiled, hiding her knowledge that things would be tight this morning with the responsibility of having to put herself together *and* finish the cake.

He was once again reminded of how comforting her presence was to him.

"Thank you, baby, I promise I'll...I'll read the article with an open mind."

Mrs. Fraser stepped closer to her husband, smiled, and patted his chest with both hands. Another bout avoided. Her mind was already heading back to the kitchen and her chocolate responsibilities, but she had one small, final, spousal adjustment to make. She gracefully pressed her body against his, exposed her neck by tilting her head back and to the side, and, by getting up on her tiptoes, was able to move her lips to within inches of his right ear.

"Good boy, big man," she whispered.

Before he had a chance to react, she casually and innocently separated and wandered back to the kitchen. She felt comfortable knowing that his eyes were locked on her apron strings the whole way.

CHAPTER 31—

The Barricades

Byron Gray sat at a busy Greenwood intersection only two blocks from where he lived with his mom and about a half a mile from the Barton house. He was a healthy, intelligent, unemployed, black man slumped in a wheelchair that had been stored for years in the family garage. The conveyance had been a possession of his deceased paternal grandfather, who had bought it after he had lost his lower right leg to amputation. Gray had been on the northeast corner of Martin Luther King Avenue and Seminole Street since nine-thirty that morning, and it was now eleven o'clock. He held a handmade cardboard sign across his stomach that read "PERSECUTION." Every once in a while a car would honk in support; but mostly people ignored him. Suffering from mild dehydration as a result of sun exposure, he wheeled home, disappointed and tired, at about noon. He had about ten bucks in unsolicited change that people had thrown in his lap. The commitment he had made to himself to do the same thing for a week was resting on shaky ground. He wasn't aware that the brother of a *Tampa Tribune* reporter had seen his quiet protest in passing, and had snapped a picture to share with his journalist sibling.

Xavier Gooch and his younger brother, Jeff, both sat in wheelchairs at the front of the Calvary Baptist Church. Irregular attendees of the church, they were both idealistic, thoughtful, young men who played basketball for Tampa Jesuit High School. They were considered leaders by the school faculty.

After reading the Epistle, the Reverend Fraser paused the formal religious ritual to make some housekeeping announcements to the packed sanctuary. After mentioning Wednesday's potluck dinner and that the usual Friday Night Bingo was cancelled this week, he opened the floor to his deacons. A tall, greying man with a barely noticeable hair lip scar reminded the crowd about the parking restrictions on the south side of the building. Another, shorter man, dressed elegantly in a three-piece suit and working as an usher, added that funeral services for a longtime parishioner, Jonas Owen, would be held the next evening, at seven p.m., at the Rippey Funeral Home.

"Anything else?" Fraser asked the congregation.

The two Gooch brothers made eye contact and nodded. They then rose simultaneously, placing their black-gloved right fists in the air while bowing their heads. Not everyone noticed them at first, but the unusual, awkward silence grabbed the crowd's attention; soon the whole congregation, including Fraser, was riveted on the boys and their protest. By interrupting the patterned ritual of the service, the quiet, somewhat passive statement conveyed a drama and meaning more powerful than any loud, specific demand. It avoided the oppositional imposing of unsolicited advice and was sufficiently vague to allow a personal and potentially unique interpretation by each viewer. This non-confrontational openness gained power through the inclusivity and community of all who watched. After what seemed like an eternity—but which, in reality was only ten seconds—the brothers lowered their fists and quietly sat down in their wheelchairs.

Fraser didn't know if the boys were finished. He was uncertain what should come next, and he was struggling with an inner conflict. The Reverend was respectful of the history embedded in the Gooch's statement, yet he felt a nascent sense of irritation…and he wasn't sure why. Subconsciously, his alpha role as head of the church was feeling threatened. Young men encroaching on an older man's territory wasn't new, but the brothers' actions carried much more depth and nuance than a simple intergenerational challenge. He recognized that he had just witnessed something profound occurring on his turf, and he felt a little miffed that he hadn't at least been consulted beforehand. He was close to saying something that would convey that in *his* church he was the messenger; perhaps a verbal directive regarding how his flock should feel about the Gooch's display that would allow him to regain the upper hand. In the front row, next to the Gooch Brothers, Ally held her breath: she hoped her husband wouldn't do it. Reverend Fraser uncharacteristically closed his eyes, took a deep breath, and counted to three as he silently recited a favorite verse:

The Lord is my shepherd;
I shall not want…

He slowly regained his composure while checking his ego (and his sense of territoriality) then decided to continue the service without comment. Despite his composed veneer, the act had registered deeply with him, as well as with a lot of his flock. Most of the attendees didn't know the Paul Barton story, but after a conflagration of whispering among the congregants, by the end of the service nearly everyone did. The pastor had been trying for years to get young people more involved in issues of community and social justice, mostly with disappointingly weak results. Today's activities had impressed a sense of urgency on him; he mentally moved the Paul Barton newspaper article to the top of his "must read" list.

CHAPTER 32—

Combustion

Tate Chalk was on a multi-day, multi-event, strafing run that paid a handsome fee plus expenses. He loved this part of his chosen profession—he had a strong proclivity for action and a limited capacity for empathy. These traits allowed him to enjoy the chaos that the assignments spawned, but the real pleasure came from the ancillary benefits. As far back as he could remember, he had had a nearly insatiable appetite for carnal pleasures. But his inability to shamelessly sate those appetites, due to his Roman Catholic upbringing, had regularly confounded him. He couldn't subvert the desire, but he also couldn't extinguish the religious voice of conscience. With experience he had developed a way to negate his feelings of guilt by building a narrative around his low-life missions. It was the only way he could somewhat sanely exist with the cognitive dissonance embedded in having two opposing voices in his head simultaneously resenting the presence of the other. Rather than regard his jobs as the simple acts of thuggery that they were, he would build elaborate fantasies. He imagined himself a sort of blue-collar, misunderstood James Bond; a highly trained loner whom women found sexy and whom men respected. In this fiction, his assignments required that he occupy the anonymous margins of society, a quiet, mysterious nighthawk who had secrets that people would find very interesting, *if* he ever chose to divulge. A man who every night slept in a different bed, when he slept at all, always on the move, keeping radio silence with the exception of a once daily voice mail check. Usually his prevarications had him working on a very important and specific assignment; perhaps something to help stymie the cross-country, Marxist insurgency that the leftist universities and biased media were fanning. He reveled in the whole fabrication; but if he were to ever succumb to serious introspection, he might realize that what he really enjoyed was neglecting any semblance of responsibility while he snorted, drank, and lap-hosted his way through the local bars and strip clubs on someone else's dime. Essentially, he was indulging his inner adolescent and justifying his behavior with a back-filled narrative that assuaged what little conscience remained after decades of abuse. During these stints he breakfasted every morning on bacon, donuts, and coffee laced with vodka.

Donovan and DaVito had disagreed strongly on their next step. Neither was aware of the spark that was dangerously close to igniting the smoldering black community. DaVito thought it best to wait on initiating any further guerrilla activity until they could see what sort of pressure the lawsuit engendered. He was seriously worried about the multiple copycat vandalisms, as he wasn't sure who was attacking them. Donovan was just angry. He felt his professional position carried the unequivocal support of the Tampa law enforcement community, and he wanted revenge. These people, whoever they were, had threatened his family, his daughter. He suspected strongly it was the Euphrates Gallery crew, he just didn't know how they were doing it. On Sunday afternoon, when it was time to leave the daily "GO" or "STOP" message for Chalk, they disagreed on which option to choose.

"Gary, in three weeks you're going to be the mayor-elect of Tampa." DaVito's faith in the outcome of the election was unshakable. "Why rock the boat?"

"Because, *Dan*," Donovan replied sharply, "some things are just wrong. We can't let these acts of aggression stand. Did you see the fucking hole in my front window?"

"I have one too, but holes can be patched. Why escalate the fight when you don't even know who your opponent is? I want to be on the record as advising strongly against this."

"When did you become such a pussy?" Donovan stared incredulously at his campaign manager. "We know it's that crippled artist and his Muslim girlfriend behind all of this...I bet if they attacked one of your kids you wouldn't be so sanguine!"

Donovan had made up his mind. To show DaVito his degree of conviction, he ended the conversation by picking up his burner mobile phone and sending a clear "GO" text message to Chalk's cell phone. DaVito watched the whole episode with a modest frown, but inside he was fuming. In his mind this whole mess should've ended a week after it started, ten days tops. But now, as a result of his longtime friend's emotional and hubristic behavior, they were on the verge of turning a modest case of indigestion into typhoid fever. DaVita couldn't believe Donovan was willing to gamble the whole election on some ego driven, revenge-based outlashing. Rather than get into a shouting match with his boss, he just shook his head and got up to leave. He was definitely jumping ship after the election, hopefully as a member of the winning team.

"I gotta get home for Sunday dinner. It's my kid's birthday."

Donovan was still worked up.

"At least your kids' cars didn't get vandalized."

"Whatever."

Chalk picked up the "GO" message fifteen minutes after Donovan sent it. He started shopping for the things he needed later that night.

CHAPTER 33

Jaws of the Wolf

L illy and Scout were having a mother-daughter moment while sharing a
room at the Marriott in Clearwater Beach. They were sitting on a king-
sized bed, eating a meal they had ordered from room service; the hotel was about
four hundred yards west of the Euphrates Gallery. It was early Monday morning,
and Lilly had been trying to be nonjudgmental about the music that Scout had
been playing on her laptop. But some of the rap lyrics were so offensive that
she had to speak up periodically; otherwise she would feel parentally remiss.

I push my seed in her bush for life.
It's gonna work because I'm pushin' it right.
If Mary dropped my baby girl tonight—
—I would name her Rock'N'Roll.

"Oh my god, Scout, *what* are we listening to?"

Scout was up and dancing to the song, seemingly indifferent to the crude
lyrics. "These are the Roots! This song was written by Cody Chesnutt— 'The
Seed (2.0).' You like?"

Scout asked the question facetiously. She paused dancing long enough to
turn up the volume and then, with a huge smile on her face, began taunting
her mom with her pepper bacon cheeseburger.

She started singing with Cody as she gyrated her hips.

Fertilize another against my lover's will.

I lick the opposition cause she don't take no pill.
Ooh, ooh, ooh no, dear…
You'll be keeping my legend alive.

"It's so…*distasteful*." Lilly continued searching for the right words. "And downright…*nasty*." It was the best she could come up with as she eyed the cheeseburger with envy and tried not to ruin their moment by expressing too predictable a disapproval.

Scout couldn't help but enjoy the occasion. Their room had a beautiful view of the beach. She was working on a family project that seemed just (although illegal). And she was vibrating with a manic excitement driven by the contents of her coffee cup and adrenal glands. She and her mom had been sharing the same room for most of the last forty-eight hours: ever since Scout had arrived after the four-and-a-half-hour drive from Tallahassee early Saturday morning.

Having stayed up much of Friday night during the drive, they had both been exhausted when they first checked in; but they had caught up on their sleep in shifts and were now wide awake and monitoring Lilly's GPS tracking device. They had ordered late room service for their Sunday night dinner, and Lilly couldn't stomach the vegan stir-fry she had picked. She kept referring to it pejoratively as "vegan stir-boil," claiming that it tasted like they had poured all the raw vegetables and bean curd in with the rice, let the fetid amalgam boil for twenty minutes, and then added a liberal amount of soy sauce to mask the untenable flavors of the culinary abomination.

Earlier, Scout had been informed that the hotel had the best burger and fries on the beach. Despite her guess that the recommendation was exaggerated, she decided to test the credibility of the cute bellboy who was the source. Thus, uncharacteristically, she ordered the pepper bacon cheeseburger…with extra fries. The food was divine. She was now teasing her dubious but starving mom with the sandwich, while writing off the remaining fries as an indefensible position. Lilly quickly polished off the salty fries but stayed on the hunt for more calories. Scout finally relented (given the pitiful look on her mom's face), took a huge bite that consumed half of the remaining burger, and handed the last quarter to a salivating Lilly.

"Oh my goodness." Lilly was in awe. "I haven't had a bacon cheeseburger in forever. This is absolutely heavenly." She patted a napkin quietly against the corners of her mouth. "We have to order another."

Scout turned down the music and rejoined her mom on the bed.

"Whoa, slow down there, Wimpy," Scout told her mom, "I'm sure the kitchen has more. Besides, aren't you a vegetarian?"

"Sorta. Mostly. Pretty much," Lilly mumbled between bites.

"Hey, where's Jojie? I thought he was gonna be here too?"

"That was part of his original plan, but I sent him home early Friday morning, after he paid a visit to the DaVito's lovely residence."

"*You* sent him home? Why'd you do that?"

Lilly stepped into her CIA operative persona. She started to provide her daughter, in precisely worded sentences, with just the information she needed.

"Two reasons. First, I needed to get my arms around the opposition. After discerning their relatively limited local capabilities, with no broad regional, national, or international affiliations, I felt more comfortable we could spark some sort of social unrest with very little risk of detection, without Al's help. He's nearly seventy now, and I just decided it wasn't prudent having him engaged as a covert operator. Second, a normal counter-insurgency move is to round up the opposition. I was worried the enemy may do some basic grunt work and check all the hotel ledgers for any suspicious occupants. Someone named Barton staying at a hotel next to Donovan or DaVito's house would be too much of a coincidence to overlook."

Scout was putting two and two together.

"So this smells more like *your* plan, not the Bartons'? You couldn't resist one more field operation?"

Lilly couldn't help herself, smiling while responding cryptically.

"Maybe, but I don't recall."

Scout continued.

"You laid the early-morning brick on the Donovan place while I was wrecking the car in Tallahassee? And you found out that Tim Babich was really Tate Chalk, and placed the tracking device on his car?"

Lilly came clean to her daughter.

"When you've played for years in the big leagues, tracking a small fry like Tate Chalk isn't much of a challenge." She couldn't help adding a little boastful color, wrapped in self-deprecation. "Some day, when I'm a well-fed, aging *abuelita*, I'll tell you the story of how I first tracked, and then gained the confidence of Raul Cas—"

The ringing phone interrupted Lilly's reminiscing. It was after three in the morning; only Aloysius knew where they were.

"Hello?"

"Hi Lilly."

She was happy to hear his voice.

"Hello, Aloysius."

"I was worried about you. Is everything okay? How's Scout?"

"All good. How's Desert Lilly's?"

"Nearly a full house. Everything running like a well-oiled machine."

Al missed Lilly badly, but he knew better than to expect any verbal reciprocity.

"I can't remember…have I ever told you how much I like the sound of your voice? Probably not…well, I'll hold off on sharing that for now…we'll save it for a time when you're more…receptively located."

Lilly smiled at his goofy humor. She was certain her current operation was morally justified, and she really liked how the Florida humidity was treating her aging skin; but she was ready to be done and go home.

"I'll be home soon, old man. Please greet everyone for me?"

"I will. Hug Scout for me…and be careful."

"Don't tell me what to do."

"All right." He chuckled. "Have a good night."

"Really?"

"Sorry…I *hope* you have a good night."

"Me too."

Lilly hung up. She turned to Scout and gave her an awkward hug.

"From your dad."

Scout didn't fully understand what was going on between her biological parents. She knew they lived together in Carefree at her mom's wellness center, but that was about it. She was curious if any financial or sexual commitments had been made, but the thoughts made her too uncomfortable to ask either of her parents directly. She decided to try a different tack.

"Do you miss him?"

"I suppose so."

"Why don't you get married?"

Lilly thought the question was strange on many levels. She had always embraced her own privacy, but had been frustrated when Scout did the same. Over the years, Scout had had a few boyfriends, but nothing had stuck. At times, Lilly wondered about Scout's sexual predilections, but she had never felt comfortable bringing up the subject. As Scout approached thirty, Lilly knew it would be natural for her to develop a sense of urgency when it came to children. She hoped her daughter would not be as unconventional in her reproductive strategy as Lilly had been. During Scout's early years, her mother had looked closely for any signs of inherited mental peculiarities. As her only child made it through college and ventured into her mid-twenties, Lilly had been relieved that her daughter seemed to be normal.

After considering the marriage question for a moment, Lilly decided to share some of the more interesting details of her time with Aloysius and see where the conversation led.

"He asked me to, you know."

"Really?" Scout looked at her mom eagerly. "When?"

"Six or seven years ago, when he did his mile swim and one hundred push-ups."

"What did you say?"

"I told him I'd think about it, but I didn't see the point."

"Because you didn't love him?"

"Funny, that's exactly what he said."

"And…?"

"I'm not sure what 'love' means, but I had definitely grown fond of him."

"So why didn't you marry him?"

"I don't think people should belong to other people."

Scout blinked. "What?"

"I guess I just don't understand the purpose of the institution in a world where everything is so"—she frowned as she tried to think of the word— "fungible."

Scout didn't think of herself as ignorant, but she still wasn't getting it.

"I'm not sure that I understand your point?"

"I'm not sure I have a point. This is a very complicated topic—male-female relationships and all that. Much more complicated than my 'birds and the bees' talk you dismissed yourself from in the sixth grade."

"Mom, that was *so* embarrassing." Scout laughed but wanted to continue.

"Tell me what you mean by people 'belonging' to other people."

Lilly was pleased that Scout was finally soliciting her views. Most of the mother's efforts at counseling her on issues of romance had been met with a combination of gratuitous eye rolling and an impugning of credentials. Lilly knew it might threaten her positive momentum, but she couldn't help poking her daughter back.

"I'm really not qualified to talk about marriage or relationships."

Scout immediately recognized the sleight and parried with her own.

"That never stopped you before."

Lilly smiled at the acknowledgement, took the small insult in stride, then launched a stream of consciousness.

"My issues are…you know…all the old archetypes. Men are valued for their money or power, and women are valued for their looks. I think in that context, I viewed marriage as an implicit trade of sex for money, or to put it more gently, reproductive capabilities for protection from predators and starvation. Men get a sex slave and a cook, and women got protection in a dangerous world. A sort of legitimized form of monogamous prostitution, or, again more gently, a way for tribes to plan for population growth at a time when the community needed more people. The agreement increased the probability that the children would survive. It was a trade, a lifetime commitment to help the village better manage the extremely messy and violent process of reproduction."

Scout was familiar with her mom's origin theory, but she was more interested in a modern, idealized perspective.

"What about two people loving and caring for each other and wanting to build a life together?"

"How about a draft where the richest man gets first choice on the hottest, most fertile girl?"

"But that wasn't why Jojie asked you."

"You saying I'm not hot?"

"You know what I mean."

Lilly was concerned that the conversation was becoming adversarial. She didn't want to be the heavy, but she also had difficulty relinquishing her role as the overly protective Mama Bear.

"Aloysius was feeling needy when he asked me to marry him. I think healthy relationships come from strength and caring, not weakness and grasping. Besides, I already provide for myself financially. Why do I need to tie myself to a man?"

"Haven't you ever been lonely?"

Lilly quickly recalled a relationship that had ended badly. She also suspected Scout was speaking from experience.

"Sometimes the loneliest place on the planet is being stuck with someone who doesn't understand or respect you."

Scout was becoming disillusioned with her mom's cynicism. She wanted to hold on to some trust. And hope.

"Can't two people grow stronger together, supporting and caring for each other? I think humans need to give and receive affection to be healthy. We crave intimacy. We are social animals after all."

Lilly worried that she might've gone too far. She didn't want to cloud her daughter's optimism by sharing her aborted efforts at intimacy.

"Maybe."

"I can't tell…are you skeptical about the giving part, or are you just feeling the marriage contract is unnecessary—a sort of belt-and-suspenders thing?"

Lilly was torn. She had yet to finished explaining why she hadn't married Aloysius. She was hoping to share some of her well-earned pragmatism while simultaneously trying to avoid polluting Scout's idealism.

"My recent time with your father has convinced me that with the right incentives people can change…grow…quite dramatically. So why would I want to lock myself into an agreement with someone when we live in such a dynamic world?"

"Maybe if you want to have kids?"

"Maybe it makes sense for someone your age, but that ship set sail long ago for me."

Lilly wasn't able to stop. She had already committed the usual parental sin of advice overload; but she had one more pearl she wanted to share. Scout was already feeling over-coached.

"I also think, over time, marriage can make couples lazy. I like the idea that at any point either party can leave if they aren't getting what they need. I think this forces a more frequent and direct form of communication. People should have the regular pressure of potential dissolution to keep them from taking the whole thing for granted."

"Can't married people do that?"

"Sure, but the threat of failure isn't quite as imminent. That's a powerful incentive."

"In some instances, couldn't the marriage contract get a couple through some rough patches that they might not have survived without that stronger commitment?"

The bedspread pattern was cacophonous enough to effectively disguise years of abandoned stains. Lilly was starting to focus on a particularly provocative manifestation, when she realized Scout had posed a question. She decided to try and end on a happy note.

"I suppose for the purposes of family and commitment the institution can be useful. If I were to do it all again, I think I would—"

Just then the tracking device starting beeping, cutting Lilly off mid-sentence. Both women went silent as the tone in the room shifted noticeably to somber. The beeping meant that the tracker on Tate Chalk's car was within a three-mile radius of their hotel room. Lilly had been in this situation many times, and it always reminded her of the scene in *Jaws* when the crew of the *Orca* becomes aware that the great white is in their neighborhood. Lilly opened up her laptop and watched as the flashing red light slowly moved closer to their location. *It's amazing how predictable this guy is*, she thought, noting the time was 3:41 a.m.

The red light stopped about three blocks away. Lilly and Scout watched it rest for about two minutes before closing the laptop and getting up to implement their plan.

Tate Chalk parked his 1987 Jeep two blocks from the Euphrates Gallery. There was no sense of urgency as he pushed the buttons on the stereo in the quiet of the early morning hours. He had already spent several hundred dollars on lap dances at the Candy Pants Lounge; now, he proceeded to do a line off of the knuckle of his first finger. He was trying to chemically shake off the eight-beer, early-morning haze. His judgment was a little shaky as he hadn't been getting much more than five hours of sleep a night since his initial attack on the Barton home several days previous.

Freddie Mercury screamed from the stereo as *Queen* powered through their anthem....

We will,
we will,
rock you!

Not bad, Chalk thought, pausing for a second before deciding to continue pushing the buttons, hoping for something better on another Classic Rock station.

When your day is done,
and you wanna run...
...Cocaine.

Now we're gettin' somewhere. Chalk paused on the current station. *I can always depend on Clapton to hang with me....*

He reached under his seat and found the bottle of Aristocrat rotgut vodka that he had bought that afternoon. Several mosquitoes caught his scent and started hovering inside his car, searching for a place to attack his sweaty epidermis. He broke the seal on the liquor and took a big swig before putting the bottle and an old cotton sock into a small black backpack he had on the front passenger seat. A can of blood red spray paint had already been loaded into the pack, along with two Zippo lighters and a few other tools of the trade.

As the cocaine and vodka started lighting up his cerebral receptors, he reviewed his plan of attack. Taking a deep breath, he put on his thin, black leather gloves. The radio DJ was droning on about something. Chalk reached up to change the station just as a new song was queued up. He paused to listen.

> *Sex and drugs and rock and roll…*
> *…is all my brain and body need.*
> *Sex and drugs and rock and roll…*
> *…are very good indeed.*

Chalk stared at the stereo. *Holy shit!* he thought. *The radio gods are talking to me!* He shook his head incredulously. *Ian Dury, tellin' it like it is!*

> *They will try their tricky device;*
> *trap you with the ordinary.*
> *Get your teeth into a small slice—*
> *the cake of liberty.*

The drugs were quickly elevating his mood…he was nodding in time with the simple beat. He couldn't imagine being in a better place than where he was right now.

Pure FREEDOM! He inhaled. *That's what I'm talking about. Fuck all that other shit!*

He moved his hand away from the radio then took one more toot in honor of the Blockheads. Three mosquitoes were feeding on the back of his neck, just at his hairline, but he didn't even notice. Flying high as the song wound down, he decided it was "go" time.

Damn, I could use some pussy right now…or at least a good blow job. Then he smiled to himself. *Work first, then play.*

He turned his skyrocketing brain back to the task at hand.

He waited for the song to end then turned off the radio. He grabbed his keys and backpack then extracted himself from his car and started walking towards his target. "Sex & Drugs & Rock & Roll" was stuck in his head…along with the still-feeding mosquito proboscises.

Scout carried an empty ice bucket as she left the room first. She sported a long overcoat and high heels. Both looked out of place at the beach. The smell of fresh paint invaded her nostrils as she headed down the stairs and paused on the ground-floor landing, shedding her overcoat and stowing it behind some cleaning equipment in the corner. First making sure her room key was hidden securely in her skimpy white bikini top, she next pushed open the side door and exited her now underdressed body into the outside, early morning air. She quickly turned and bent down, tightly stretching the yellow spandex miniskirt across her bum as she used the ice bucket to keep the door from closing. As she wobbled towards the Euphrates, she decided to move her room key from her top to the small purse she was carrying.

Lilly left the room two minutes after Scout. She was wearing a maroon jogging suit, and she had inserted a pair of earbuds, which remained silent under her headscarf. Nearly tripping over their room service tray on her way out the door, she headed directly to the elevator bank and rode the first car to the lobby. The graveyard shift receptionist at the front desk didn't notice the middle-aged woman with the small backpack slung over her right shoulder as she headed out the automatic sliding front doors and into the moist, pre-dawn air.

Chalk finished the first swastika in under two minutes and stepped back to admire his handiwork. Red paint had started to stain his right hand, but he was so pleased with the tilt and symmetry of the five-foot symbol that the drippings didn't bother him. As he prepared to cover the Euphrates Gallery logo with a second swastika, he quickly glanced left and right, making sure he was still alone.

Not a peep.

He reached in to his backpack for the vodka, gulped down another few ounces, and then started spraying the second swastika.

Gotta go easy on the booze, he thought. *Gonna need that later for the fireworks.*

He quickly finished the second *Hakenkreuz* and again reached into his backpack for the vodka. As he opened the bottle, he also removed a sock from his pack. He stuffed the sock halfway into the nearly full liquor container. He then inverted the bottle until the sock was soaked with alcohol. As he reached into his pocket for a lighter, he noticed a scantily clad young woman stumbling in high heels about a half block away. Thirty years ago he would've assumed she was a hooker, but with the way kids dressed nowadays he wasn't so sure.

Probably just some drunk sorority chick doing the walk of shame back to her hotel.

The image of some fraternity jock riding her hard and putting her away wet started reorienting his priorities. He was still so high from the coke that he felt invincible and wasn't taking the usual precautions. Regularly, the appearance of a potential witness, no matter how impaired the witness was, would require that he immediately close up shop and move away from the crime scene; but tonight he was so influenced that all he did was a cursory check of his hood, making sure it covered his head and face. Already forgetting about the girl, he noticed the ground was a little unsteady: he needed one more gulp to stabilize his vertigo. Crouching down in the darkness of the gallery doorway, he pulled the sock out of the top of the vodka bottle, and took another slug. As he tried to stuff the sodden footwear back into the bottle, he heard a slurred voice about twenty-five feet away.

"Hey, mister, d'yew-no-wher-tha-merryit-is?"

Chalk was irritated at the woman for intruding. But he was also angry with himself for so egregiously violating his protocol. He kept his chin low, trying to keep his face in the shadows while simultaneously managing to get a glimpse of his antagonist. With contempt, he noted her attire barely covered her curves, and she was swaying precariously on her heels.

Gotta be a hooker, he thought. *Either that or a world-class slut.*

He simultaneously wanted to get into her pants and move her as far away as possible from his work. Duty required he choose the latter, hoping to salvage the evening by scaring her away with a full frontal misogynist attack.

"Get the fuck outta here, you cum-dumpster slut, whore, cunt," he snarled, "before I tie you up, throw you in the back of my truck, and make you wish god never gave you those holes." He barely repressing a bile-and-vodka-laced burp at the end.

Scout took two steps back. The words weren't original, but she had never heard them delivered in such a malevolent way, nor when she was in such a vulnerable position. Every fiber of her body told her to run, fast, away from this man, but that wasn't the plan. She was supposed to distract him briefly, and from a distance, so Lilly could work uninterrupted. Already too close, she felt deserted and claustrophobic at the same time as the silence pressed in. She couldn't see his face under the hood, but she could feel him glaring at her like a lion would a gazelle. Trying to get her heart rate under control, she reached into her clutch and felt the reassuring handle of the stun gun that Lilly had given her. She didn't know what to do, so she took two more steps back and tried to stall further.

"I'm not a whore, I'm a college student."

Her words surprised her for their lack of creativity.

From his crouched position in the doorway, Chalk noticed the effect the cool morning air was having on the woman's nipples as they pressed through her thin white bikini top. The fact that she hadn't run away in fear after his verbal barrage he found disrespectful. He didn't like his threats being ignored, especially by sluts who were wandering the streets nearly naked at four a.m. It was at that moment that his irritation grew into anger, his predator brain kicked in, and he decided that she had hung around too long and seen too much. He knew what he had to do, but first he'd play with her.

Why not have a little fun? he thought.

He smiled to himself as the song returned to his head, mingling with his other, less melodious thoughts.

Sex and drugs and rock and roll…Stupid bitch! She couldn't just walk away… I warned her.

He carefully put the Molotov cocktail down and reached into his backpack. When he turned back to Scout he was holding a handgun. He exploded from his crouch, and in two bounds was now just ten feet away. Scout realized with alarm that it would be impossible for him to miss from that distance. It was now clear that she had badly misjudged the situation in general, and Chalk's agility in particular. While frantically trying to move away from his aggression, she tripped over her heels and fell on her backside. The stun gun was still uselessly secreted in her handbag, as she had to use her hands to break her fall. Her legs were akimbo, and Chalk could easily see up her already revealing skirt. His face now clearly visible under the hood, she was chilled by his cadaver-like sneer. She wanted to move, but she was held, transfixed by his stare. His eyes were rimmed red, with dilated pupils, and no hint of compassion. It was apparent she was just his prey. Pointing the gun directly at her chest, he spoke quickly and with authority.

"You mighta been a college student five minutes ago, but now you're my whore. If you don't scream, and don't run, and do *exactly* what I say, like the good little slut that we *know* you are, you may get out of this alive. Do you understand?"

Just two blocks away, thirty yards from Chalk's Jeep, Lilly was on her hands and knees in someone's front yard, violently regurgitating the pepper bacon cheeseburger her vegetarian system was rejecting. The smell of freshly cut St. Augustine grass mingled strongly with the aroma of the food previously decomposing in her stomach. She knew she was way behind schedule, but she was so incapacitated that she couldn't even get to her feet. As the ground rocked beneath her, she hoped the convulsive heaving would end soon, as she was certain she had already evicted all of the partially digested beef and bacon. The isopropyl alcohol, strips of an old cotton T-shirt, books of matches, and Taser remained untouched in the small backpack on the ground by her side.

Scout was terrified, vulnerable. She was looking up into the face of a psychopath. She had mentally worked through this sort of scenario before, but in each hypothetical the man was plodding and she was cat-like. Invariably she would use her wits or speed to maneuver close enough to execute a sharp blow to the eyes, larynx, or groin…at which point the scumbag would start screaming, incapacitated with agony, and usually fall to the ground. In her current situation her opponent was faster, stronger—and had a gun. He stood a few feet away, removing any chance of physical contact. Her mind, murky with fear, raced with thought.

Where the fuck is Mom? She told me to stay far away from him…why didn't I listen? He obviously wants sex…maybe when he gets close I can shock him with the stun gun? Where's my purse? Is he gonna kill me, leaving no witnesses? He definitely seems capable…

The last thought put her into an existential panic, making it difficult for her to think rationally.

Chalk knew he was exposed on the street. The cocaine had him grinding his teeth and the alcohol was fucking with his stomach… he felt a little woozy from the drugs and lack of sleep. But the fear in the girl's eyes excited him in a whole new way. The anticipation of using this half-naked woman, of forcing her to do shameful things against her will, had a whole new round of mood-lifting chemicals cascading into his bloodstream. He hoped to execute two tasks over the next twenty minutes, but first he had to get her out of sight. *This is my time of night!* he reassured himself. But he knew people would soon start showing up—newspaper boys, commercial deliveries, early-morning joggers. He again stared hard at the nipples pushing through the girl's tight cloth.

"Get up, *now,* and move into that doorway!" he whispered intensely, pointing with his free hand towards the entry of the Euphrates.

Scout got to her feet carefully, grabbing her small, pink, beaded bag. She had a glimmer of hope.

"Leave the purse," Chalk growled.

Scout's heart sank. She needed the weapon. Her mind raced—and came up with a possible deterrent. She remembered she was supposed to make him think of her as a person, not as a sexual object.

"I thought we could use condoms? I have herpes and I don't want to get pregnant. I have some rubbers in my purse."

Her antagonist laughed crudely.

"I have herpes too," he said with derision. "And I'm gonna pump so much jizz in you that I'm *sure* you're gonna get pregnant."

He abandoned the cruel smile. His voice turned colder as he pointed the gun threateningly.

"Drop the purse. *Now.*"

Scout let her purse fall to the street, along with any hope. Reluctantly, she walked the fifteen feet over to the dark entryway where Chalk had left his pack. The gallery portico was roughly the shape of a square, about ten feet by ten feet. A large awning pushed out from the alcove onto the sidewalk, rendering the area darker and more protected from the sight of any passing cars or wandering pedestrians. He followed her deep into the shadows and directed her back against one of the side windows, next to the door. She stood, petrified, avoiding eye contact, her arms by her sides.

"Lock your fingers behind your head, and look up."

Scout hesitated, and started pleading.

"Please, mister, don't…"

Chalk interrupted her sobbing with a sharp slap across the face. He was in a hurry. She hadn't expected the blow, and she immediately tasted blood where her teeth had made a small tear in her inner lip.

"I thought I was clear, *whore*. You do *exactly* what I say, *when* I say it, *with* enthusiasm, and *maybe* you live. Do you understand?"

Scout nodded affirmatively, tears rolling down her cheeks.

"Now, let's try this again. Lock your fingers behind your head, and look up."

Scout understood what he wanted. She put both hands behind her head then raised her chin, exposing her neck while simultaneously thrusting out her breasts. Chalk nodded approvingly, releasing a noise that sounded like a soft groan. He then reached out with the pistol, and at the edge of her lower peripheral vision Scout watched in horror as he slowly placed the barrel first on one nipple and then on the other, rotating the cold steel around each areola as the swelling skin pressed through the fabric. He then used the barrel to slowly caress her neck as he moved it back and forth between each breast. Scout shivered uncontrollably in response to the agonizing stimuli before Chalk finally grew tired of the slow alternation. He took a step back to admire his handiwork.

His sense of control over a trembling lovely, coupled with the visual stimulation, had Chalk vibrating with excitement. He had a timetable; all he had to do was work quickly through his checklist and it would be a perfect evening.

"Take off your top," he hissed, the gun still leveled at her torso.

From his perspective Scout was moving too slowly.

"Do it, bitch!" His mannerisms screamed while he kept his voice subdued.

Scout untied the bikini strings and let them drop, along with her arms, to her sides. The two small pieces of thin, triangular fabric that were stretched across her chest didn't move: they were stuck to her perspiring skin. Chalk reached out a black leather hand and grabbed the string between her breasts. He snatched the top and dramatically flung it out of the way. Scout stood naked from the waist up, her arms by her sides, with her tormentor leering at her. As Chalk reached out again with his left hand, she cringed.

So this is what the rabbit feels like in the jaws of the wolf, she thought.

Lilly's latex-gloved hands had removed the gas cap to the Jeep and were slowly feeding half of the four-foot knotted cotton rope into the tank. She had already doused the cloth with alcohol and was hoping there was enough fuel in the rig to make the outcome reasonably pyrotechnic. Chalk's vehicle was the only one parked in the parking lot behind the liquor store. Empty vacation houses bracketed the small retail space, giving Lilly reason to believe no one would be in the vicinity at the moment of ignition. She was still queasy from her gastrointestinal rebellion, but she moved quickly to make up for lost time. With half the makeshift fuse hanging out of the aperture, she took one last look around to make sure the coast was clear. She took a book of matches out of her backpack and lit the bottom of the fuse, giving her between thirty seconds and a minute, in her estimation, before things would get hot. As the fire immediately climbed up the cotton strips, a bug flew into a tuft of her hair that had slipped out from under her scarf. She quickly threw everything into the pack, slapping haphazardly at the bug as she headed back to the hotel to meet up with Scout. No one would suspect a middle-aged woman out doing some pre-dawn speed walking when the Jeep combusted. She and her daughter were booked on a seven a.m. flight to Phoenix that she didn't want to miss.

Forty-two, forty-three, forty-four… Lilly had been silently counting the seconds since she had lit the fuse. She was already one block away. She was walking rapidly down the middle of the empty street towards the Marriott.

KA-BOOM! went the gas tank just before she counted forty-five.

Lilly instinctively flinched then congratulated herself as the mild concussion wave hit her from behind.

Nailed it! she thought. *The old grey mare's still got it.*

Heel-toe, heel-toe. She was swinging her arms aggressively as she smiled to herself.

She decided to make a quick left and head down one short block, buzzing by the Euphrates Gallery to see what sort of damage Chalk had caused.

The explosion was substantial enough that the assailant and his captive both noticed it. It didn't register on Chalk that his car might have been the target, but he did recognize, despite his pronounced state of sexual arousal, that the eruption might bring attention. At that point he usually would have just finished with the girl and thrown the fire bomb through the glass front door, but he was so focused on his frightened prey and expected climax that he couldn't let it go.

He paused for a second after the explosion. After hearing nothing, he turned his attention back to his topless hostage. Needing to move things along, he started unbuckling his pants with his left hand as he stepped closer to Scout.

"Get down on your knees, *whore*, now."

As Lilly approached from a distance, she first noticed the huge red swastikas spray-painted across the gallery's front windows. Her head scarf in place and earbuds in clear sight, she innocently heel-toed her pronounced race-walking waddle down the middle of the street and past the front door without breaking stride. *Just another menopausal woman trying to work through her hot flashes*—she reminded herself to stay in character.

With her arms and elbows swinging in time with her hips, she looked hard to her left, under the awning, as she passed the front door. She thought she saw people but couldn't be sure. Then, two steps later, her peripheral vision picked up a small, out of place object—maybe a small, pink handbag?—lying in the street.

Scout was now focused on survival. The cold pavement pressed into her knees as Chalk pressed the gun barrel against the top of her head. She could feel her rapist quivering with anticipation, as his left fist firmly grasped her hair at the back of her head, pulling her towards his groin. Her main prayer was that he wouldn't accidentally pull the trigger. In an act driven partially by avoidance and partially by guidance, her hand was now partially wrapped around his engorged penis. With repugnance, she was slowly yielding to the pressure as he pushed her lips towards his shaft.

"Do it!" he demanded as he pushed the gun hard behind her ear for emphasis.

As she began to involuntarily moisten her lips to prepare for the next disgusting act, she heard her mother's voice from beyond the man's slouching shoulders.

"Hey, asshole."

Her greeting served its purpose. Chalk immediately spun one hundred and eighty degrees, necessitating the removal of the gun barrel from Scout's head... and his dork from her hand. As he turned, Lilly fired two Taser darts into his torso from fifteen feet away. In a microsecond the darts transferred fifty thousand volts from the Taser gun to his central nervous system, rendering Chalk incapacitated. As he fell, twitching in agony, Scout was too slow to move out of the way. Chalk simultaneously lost control of his bowels and bladder while vomiting all over her chest. Scout clumsily fought her way out from under Chalk's twitching body while her mom moved with a practiced purpose.

Lilly kicked the gun away with her chartreuse New Balance trainers. She grabbed some quick ties from her pack and secured Chalk's hands and feet. Sirens rose up in the distance, and she knew they likely had only a minute or two as she turned her attention to Scout.

"Go find your top and put it on. Now! If anyone stops us, I do the talking. You're drunk. Got it?"

"Yes," said Scout as she ran, shakily, to find her top on the sidewalk. She picked it up and started tying the material together over her vomit-splashed upper body.

Lilly was looking through Chalk's pack. She quickly found what she wanted. She pulled out the can of spray paint and spelled P-E-R-S-E-C-U-T-I-O-N on the sidewalk, next to Chalk and under the swastikas.

"Mom, let's go...they're getting closer."

Lilly rolled a dazed and soiled Chalk onto his back, pulled the darts from his chest, and returned the Taser to her pack.

Eeesshh! she thought. *He smells like a pack of homeless, fermenting winos.*

She focused on shallow breathing through her mouth and not letting the stench of Chalk's excreted body waste nauseate her. Hustling over to pick up Scout's beaded, pink clutch, she shoved that into her pack as well.

Thank god I noticed the purse, she thought. She blocked out the "what if" image of her daughter being abused in the gallery doorway, not rescued.

Lilly started pulling off her gloves as she quickly inspected the scene for clues.

"Mom! *Now!*" Scout pleaded.

Lilly knew the emergency vehicles would head to the burning Jeep first, not the Euphrates Gallery.

"Just one second," she said to Scout.

She pulled off her left glove and was about to pull off the right glove; just then, something inappropriate caught her eye. She grabbed the can of paint, walked over to the supine man, and sloppily sprayed his exposed genitals blood red.

The cold liquid grabbed Chalk's attention. He started to regain his focus. Using his tongue he tried to clear some of the saliva that had foamed around his mouth. He was panting hard as Lilly slowly pressed her knee to his throat, forcing him to turn his head to the side as she applied pressure to his trachea. She leaned over so her face was inches above his ear then growled a spittle-covered observation:

"You seem to like to put things into people's mouths? How do you like it when it's done to you, *SCUMBAG?*"

She then shoved both of her paint-splattered latex gloves into his mouth while continuing her monologue with a specific warning:

"Twenty-three forty-six Saint Charles Drive…ring a fuckin' bell? Next time I'm gonna blow up your whole fucking house…while you're still inside… ASSHOLE."

She removed her knee from his neck then kicked him hard in the ribs. The next moment she shouldered her backpack and started race-walking to catch up with her daughter. Plucking a palmetto bug out of her hair, she followed the scent of regurgitation and was next to a stumbling Scout in ten seconds.

"Are you okay?"

"Yeah, Mom, I'm fine," Scout lied. She was in shock and moving purely on adrenaline.

"Then let's walk faster, I'm in the middle of my workout."

Lilly was focused on avoiding detection and wasn't aware of the long-term damage that had been inflicted on her daughter.

"Whatever," said Scout. She kicked off her high heels and started imitating her mom's waddle to keep up.

As they raced back to the hotel shoulder to shoulder Lilly noted the pieces of vomit sliding down her daughter's belly.

"Do all of your boyfriends puke on your boobs, or just the ones I tell you to stay away from?"

"Funny, Mom. Really."

After landing in Phoenix at nine-thirty a.m. local time, Lilly and Scout were met at the terminal by Aloysius in his silver Mercedes. On the way home, Lilly took out a burner mobile phone and asked the other two to be quiet while she made an important call. She had to make sure she gave enough detail to be credible, while not providing any clues about her identity. This would be her last effort to stoke the metaphorical fires she had been feeding for the last week.

"Hello…may I please speak to Patti Chambers?"

Aloysius and Scout were curious to see (and hear) Lilly at work, doing what she had apparently been trained to do. They both thought the Southern accent was becoming.

"Hello, Ms. Chambers? I'd like to report a crime."

Another pause—and then she grew impatient and interrupted the barely audible voice on the other end. Lilly knew she was probably being recorded.

"Yes, I saw the explosion in Clearwater Beach early this morning around four. It was three Negro boys who did it. First, they impeded a bald, white, Nazi man with bright red genitals who was painting swastikas on the art gallery windows. Next, they went and blew up his Jeep. After that, they ran like the wind, disappearing into the night. Oh, there's one other thing: one of them Negroes was in a wheelchair."

There was a pause. Lilly listened to Patti's questions.

"How do I know and who am I? Well, I told you, I was just out for a stroll and I happened to see the *persecution* all unfold with my own eyes. I'm just another concerned citizen with a *conscience*."

Another pause.

"Well, I don't know about all that, but I hope y'all have a nice day. Good-bye."

And with that Lilly closed the burner and came in from the cold. *Permanently*, she hoped.

In the back seat Scout trembled involuntarily despite the warm Arizona morning.

That was awfully close. Lilly shivered as her brain conjured the image of her daughter exposed and at the mercy of that cold-blooded reptile.

She worried about the potential for a Proustian olfactory response to the odor of vomit, and decided to talk to Scout about the symptoms of post-traumatic stress injury. A phantom waft of bile faintly wound around her amygdala, hippocampus, and olfactory bulb before exiting into the recesses of her mind.

As she considered what could have been, she glanced over at Al with a look of consternation. Sensing her anxiety, Aloysius was unsure of the source. He immediately implemented a preemptive defense.

"It wasn't my fault…and I didn't do anything wrong."

She smiled at her partner's catchall phrase and fulfilled her role by augmenting his comment with her usual caveat.

"Yet."

CHAPTER 34—

Cascade

The media had a field day with the early morning carnage at Clearwater Beach. Swastikas, exploding cars, the *Easter Awakenings* gallery and its female Muslim owner, Molotov Cocktails, hookers in high heels, Tasers, anonymous calls, a team of blacks in wheelchairs dispensing vigilante justice to the persecuting Nazi—the story had something for everyone. In the first week it became apparent the police were struggling, but at least they finally had a suspect in custody. However, Chalk's story about a Caucasian mother-daughter race-walking team was too incredible to be taken seriously.

Over the next two weeks, there was such a surge in the rental, sale, and theft of wheelchairs that local hospitals had to start reconsidering their discharge policies for fully ambulatory patients. At noon on Wednesday, two days after Lilly's choreographed pyrotechnics, fifteen young men, two of them disabled white veterans, sat in wheelchairs with Byron Gray on his Greenwood corner. The next day the number was thirty. Most of them were holding up large pieces of cardboard with the word *PERSECUTION* spray-painted in red.

Across the bay in Tampa, the Gooch brothers started holding a traveling, daily, thirty-second silent protest that was scheduled and broadcast via their hastily put together website. Four days after what was becoming known as the Monday Morning Awakening (aka MMA), nearly fifty people joined the Goochs on the steps of Tampa's City Hall. The crowd was made up of mostly African-Americans and the disabled, but it also included three ambulatory lesbians from the St. Petersburg Art Institute and a dozen Jews from the local synagogue. Apparently the swastikas had touched a communal nerve. The Gooch brothers were ending every protest with the phrase "Remember Paul Barton," which made Paul a little uncomfortable because he thought the "remember" part was traditionally used posthumously.

CNN had picked up the story, and reporters began pouring in from around the world. The letters *MMA* had already begun showing up on tagged walls all over the Tampa Bay Area, usually in conjunction with the profile of an Afro-laden silhouette in a wheelchair. Everyone had a theory, but none of them made sense to the investigating authorities.

One week after the MMA, the local attorney whom Aloysius had hired for his youngest son was sitting in the Bartons' living room, explaining Paul's options to him. Spencer Chung was going through the basics of civil litigation, starting with expense.

"Arguing the law is cheap. There's usually precedent, and access to a judge is available and comes with a set of rules and guidelines as to outcomes. What's expensive is arguing facts—collecting evidence and debating grey areas. Going to trial is the most expensive option, since it takes weeks to prepare, and often-times the trial process is tediously slow."

Chung paused to make sure Paul and his mom were following. Aloysius had agreed to cover his fee, but he had also made it clear to Spencer that he had his limits. They agreed to start with a five-thousand-dollar retainer and keep the communication lines open as they approached that amount.

Elizabeth got down to brass tacks. "How expensive?"

"I think from five- to twenty-five thousand dollars a day is a good estimate if we go to trial."

"So this could easily get to over a hundred thousand dollars if we don't settle?"

"Yes. I'm happy to go to trial, if that's what you want. For me it would be a lucrative assignment. But I feel obligated to remind you that there is no guar-antee as to outcome, and it can be very expensive."

Paul commented under his breath.

"Justice may be blind, but it sure isn't cheap."

Chung heard him.

"That would be correct."

At that moment the Barton phone rang. It had been doing a lot of that lately; Elizabeth was considering delisting their number. She started to get up to answer the call but promptly sat back down with a muffled groan. Her sciatica had been acting up and would periodically limit her movement. Noisily, the springs of the overstuffed sofa greeted her return like an old friend. The silver lining of her ailment was that it allowed Paul to be the more physically capable member of the household.

"Please excuse me, I'll be right back."

Paul wheeled into the kitchen and plucked the mobile receiver from the cradle.

"Hello, this is Paul Barton?" Despite their tumultuous upbringing, his parents had instilled in their boys a sense of proper etiquette.

"Is this the Paul Barton in the wheelchair?" The voice sounded black to Paul.

Ever since all the media coverage, Paul had grown wary of these sorts of inquiries. He was flattered that people were somewhat inspired by his dilemma, but the accompanying static of celebrity was annoying.

"Yes it is," he answered cautiously.

"Brother, they did it to me too."

"What do you mean?"

"The Po-Po, man, the cops. DaVito and Donovan."

"You're in a wheelchair?"

"No, but they busted my head so hard, I can't see right no more. I had a baseball scholarship to Gainesville, man, and they took it away from me."

At first Paul wanted to sympathize briefly and then hang up, but he got another idea.

"Hey brother, what's your name?"

"Henry. Clifford Henry."

"Clifford Henry, can you hold on just a minute? I have someone I want you to talk to."

Paul called out to his attorney and asked him to come to the kitchen.

Lionel Simmons was the byline reporter for the *Tampa Tribune* on the *Easter Awakenings/MMA* story. He had received ten calls over the previous week, all from African-Americans, all of whom claimed to have been the victims of police brutality on the part of Donovan or DaVito. Knowing this story could potentially change the outcome of the mayor's race, his editor was leaning on him hard to make sure all of the allegations were substantiated. They both knew they were walking into a political minefield, and that they had to be particularly even-handed with their approach. But they also suspected that these first alleged victims were just the tip of the iceberg.

Ally Fraser was full of conviction.

"You *have* to get ahead of this, Draymond."

The Reverend responded pointedly. "Ally, I told you I gave the man my *word*."

"Under false pretenses. He never disclosed to you that he was a racist criminal."

"We don't know that to be true."

"We've had four people we know, either directly or through friends, who've all claimed that Donovan used excessive force on them. Plus my sister. I think we know enough to disassociate ourselves from this man. This thing is growing in leaps and bounds. People are taking to the streets. He's a racist symptom of a much bigger problem."

Reverend Fraser hung his head. He knew his wife was right. It was time for him to stop managing his career. He had to start becoming a leader.

CHAPTER 35

A Sea of Troubles

T he swamp was quietly smothering everything in its humid embrace. With the patience of eons, the soporific beast pulsed up through the layer of human edifice with a languid indifference. The stifling heat was easily handled by the native flora, many specimens of which had been domesticated into the manicured trees, bushes, and lawns of the high-end subdivision. Male cicadas were ratcheting up their daily cacophony as the temperatures gradually worked their way towards the extremes of mid-afternoon. In an effort to attract mates, the bugs were flexing an abdominal organ called a *tymbal*, which in turn generated a buzzing and clicking sound that could be heard by receptive female cicadas up to a mile away.

A few small lizards were darting and halting their way through a late lunch. Dining on the superior selection of insects the subdivision offered, the miniature dinosaurs would multi-task during the pauses with neck inflations that served to initiate the reproductive process. With the exception of the insects, reptiles, and a few landscape maintenance trucks, the upscale enclave was devoid of movement.

When the seasonal shift of the earth intensified the asphyxiating characteristics of the swamp, the Donovans would close all of their windows and turn on the air-conditioning. Every year at this time the peninsula started speaking a language that was unsympathetic to the non-indigenous. Most of the human intruders listened and retreated north, but a few remained behind, using technology to overstay their welcome. They would ignore the implicit natural message and continue their daily activities, all the while forgetting the tenuous and artificial nature of their existence.

In one week, the election to decide the next mayor of Tampa would be held, but the former front-runner's thoughts were miles away. As he sat at his desk, considering his options, he couldn't come up with a scenario that seemed palatable. Everywhere he turned his world was crumbling.

Thirty-plus years as a public servant, he thought, *committed to the orderly observation of our laws…and this is how it ends?*

His poll numbers had declined dramatically, as more allegations had come out about his brutal use of excessive and inappropriate force. He had been placed on paid leave, and his supporters were abandoning him like rats off of a sinking ship. Exacerbating his financial stress, he had been named as a defendant, along with the City of Tampa, in a class action litigation led by Spencer Chung. His old friend Dante wasn't returning his calls, and the local bank had cancelled his home equity line of credit. Most worrying was his suspicion that it was just a matter of time before the Tampa police would be carting him away in handcuffs. Tate Chalk had started singing as soon as threatened with charges that included "hate crimes" (given the accompanying, lengthy mandated sentences). Donovan knew that his rivals in the DA's office would soon be pressuring DaVito, and that his former partner would be hugely incentivized to roll over on his longtime colleague. In his role as district attorney he had many times successfully used the same technique of squeezing the small fish to catch the whale. The media couldn't get enough of the story, and the mobs were rushing the gallows to watch the once mighty fall. He had considered fleeing the country, but after working through the logistics, he realized that was only an option for the extremely rich. Donovan had little in the way of liquid savings; all of his wealth was tied up in his house and his retirement benefits.

The severely depressed candidate had taken to drinking heavily throughout the day. With his loyal Rottweiler guarding his study door, he opened his upper desk drawer and pulled out a bottle of Powers John's Lane Irish Whiskey. He wasn't sure he could survive behind bars in the general population—the public humiliation and private degradation would be unbearable.

How had it all unraveled so quickly?

It didn't take him long to start gnawing at the festering wound.

It was that crippled mulatto kid, Paul Barton.

He would get incensed when he thought of his nemesis.

How did that weak, insignificant, insolent, little prick beat me?

The district attorney was too self-absorbed to recognize that he wasn't the target of Paul's work, just the collateral damage. Paul's indifference to the fight made Donovan more focused on the perceived conflict, and he had trouble understanding how a bastard watercolorist, armed with only an idea and his art, could overcome all the bureaucracy, regulations, and guns he had at his disposal. He had overwhelming force on his side, he was supposed to win. His whole career had been successfully built by following that strategy.

As the dog wagged his tail, Donovan pulled the cork out of the bottle and put the opening to his lips. Before drinking directly from the container, he thought better of it and stopped. His mind was struggling with his current predicament and was building self-important narratives and justifications with strange priorities. Placing the bottle down on his desk, he grabbed a carved glass tumbler from the shelf behind his head. He was defensive, suffering through a crisis of conscience. Feeling that the misinformed rabble were imposing a vortex of chaos on him, he decided he needed to remain civilized in thought, word, and deed. Controlling the context of his downfall might be out of his reach, but he could dictate, to some degree, his level of dignity. As his mental state whirled in the unstable zone, he went over his predicament for the hundredth time that day. The conclusion was always the same: he was cornered with no way out. Calling his dog over, he absentmindedly scratched him behind his ears while considering the rationalizations.

Civilization demands a certain trampling of individual rights at the margins, to keep the Vandals from overrunning Rome. I was the one manning the wall, allowing people to sleep safely at night. I am an honorable man. I won't dignify their accusations and slander with my acquiescence.

His daughter, Erika, would do fine, he thought; but he was concerned about Mary. She wasn't strong, and his absence might unhinge her. He stopped attending to the dog, and it returned to his resting spot by the door.

He measured four fingers of the liquor into a small tumbler then drank three-quarters of it for courage. The whiskey burned warmly down his throat and into his stomach. He wondered briefly about his future grandchildren, and what they would think—how Erika would describe him to them....

While considering his religious convictions, he was again reminded that he had no real faith. This revelation left him with an overwhelming feeling of emptiness, like an untethered astronaut floating alone in space. To him, the physical world that surrounded them was all there was. As a heavy sadness pressed at him from all sides, he opened his lower desk drawer, removed his service revolver, and placed the barrel in his mouth.

To be or not to be, that is always the question...

He answered with a succinct pull of the trigger.

The cicadas paused their crescendo to ponder the irregular noise that exploded from the insulated Donovan household. After a moment's silence, they categorized the human tragedy as non-threatening. As if one, they resumed their reproductive chorus.

This ends Book 1. Book 2, *Only the Trying*, is now available at online distributors.